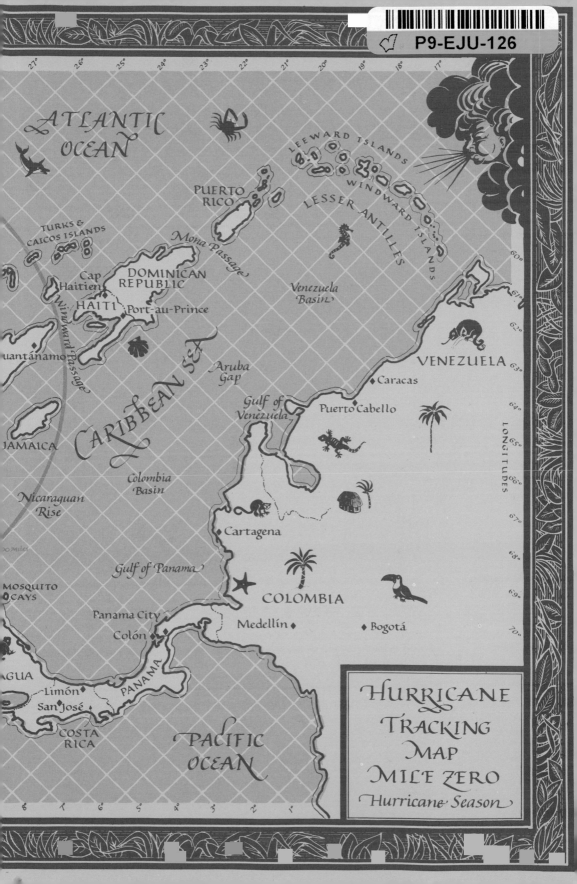

ILE

ERO

THOMAS SANCHEZ

ALFRED A. KNOPF
NEW YORK 1989

THIS IS A BORZOI BOOK
PUBLISHED BY ALFRED A. KNOPF, INC.

Copyright © 1989 by Thomas Sanchez
Endpaper map © 1989 by Claudia Carlson
All rights reserved under International and
Pan-American Copyright Conventions.
Published in the United States by Alfred A. Knopf, Inc.,
New York, and simultaneously in Canada by Random House
of Canada Limited, Toronto.
Distributed by Random House, Inc., New York.

Library of Congress Cataloging-in-Publication Data
Sanchez, Thomas.
Mile zero / Thomas Sanchez. — 1st ed.
p.   cm.
ISBN 0-394-57859-7
I. Title.
PS3569.A469M55   1989   89-2295
813'.54—dc19   CIP

Manufactured in the United States of America
First Edition

SIEMPRE

Stephanie Dante, who
rocked it on
                    water
Jon Lovelace, who
pulled it from
                    fire.

MEMORIES

Robert Kirsch • Dorothea Oppenheimer • Henry Robbins

THANKS TO

The National Endowment for the Arts
The John Simon Guggenheim Memorial Foundation
The Yaddo Corporation

VOUDOUN PRAYER

Mèt Agoué, kòté ou yé
Ou pa oué mwê nâ résif
Agoué, kòté ou yé
Ou pa oué mwé sou lâ mè
M'gê zavirô nâ mê mwê
M'pa sa toune déyè
M'douvâ déja

Master Agwé, where are you?
Can't you see I'm on the reef?
Agwé, where are you?
Can't you see I'm on the sea?
I have an oar in my hand,
I cannot turn back,
I am going forward.

CONTENTS

BOOK ONE

REVELATION

IN REPOSE

1

IT IS about water. It was about water in the beginning, it will be in the end. The ocean mothered us all. Water and darkness awaiting light. Night gives birth. An inkling of life over distant sea swells toward brilliance. Dawn emerges from Africa, strikes light between worlds, over misting mountains of Haiti, beyond the Great Bahama Bank, touching cane fields of Cuba, across the Tropic of Cancer to the sleeping island of Key West, farther to the Gold Coast of Florida, its great wall of condominiums demarcating mainland America.

With coming light come seabirds skimming water, they fathom approaching weather without raising their heads, reading a surface of reflected cloud mountains imprinted over currents roaring through underwater canyons. Seabirds fly into new day, beneath them a watery world of mystery equal to the airy one above, where a man-made bird of steel streaks atop a pillar of flame. Only moments before the steel bird shook off an umbilical maze of flight feeders, its capsule head inhabited by six humans, their combined minds infinitely less than the bird's programmed range of computerized functions. The steel bird pierced infinite space with calculated grace, sending supersonic shock waves earthward, scattering over ocean's surface a new current, entrails of a departing dream hurtling heavenward. Seabirds read this curious current, only their feathered wings stir the air in silent aftermath.

The seabirds do not look up to the man-made future, nor do they stop and circle a boat adrift, its tattered sail limp against a broken mast, the deck crowded with bodies. No sign of life signals the birds to swoop down. They glide on, leaving the boat to whatever current

3

claims it. The seabirds have read the weather of coming day correctly. The solid-rocket blast of the spacecraft shuttling heavenward and the rudderless boat of Haitian refugees do not deter them. The coloration of the ocean portends the day's approaching heat, sustenance must be taken quickly from sheltered mangrove shallows beyond the dark crescent of coral reef on the horizon. The birds do not alter their course. Ahead in the bright is Key West.

"Rise and shine paradise! Radio W . . . K . . . E . . . Y broadcasting from your space-age island in the sun. Another boring day of subtropical splendor from Key Largo to Dry Tortugas. So take the handcuffs off your lover and let him or her enjoy temps of eighty-five and getting higher, humidity seventy-five percent and getting higher. In the Florida Straits swells two to six feet and getting, you guessed it, higher!"

St. Cloud was at sea in a sea of sleep, a dream swimmer born half in air, half out of water, floating toward the same nightmare in Neptune's murky cobalt closet, the submerged vision of a woman on the reef, wealth of seaweed wreathed in her hair, white body pierced by fish, turtles sucking at flowing fingers, her eyes translucent pearls, mirrored souls of ancient oysters. A powerful riptide separates her from St. Cloud, separates the muse from the music. Not easy for a bull to swim beneath the sea.

The radio announcer's voice out of static brought St. Cloud fully awake. He slipped from between Evelyn's thighs where the dream of the night before shipwrecked him.

"If you were knocked out of your bunk this morning by a sound loud as a cannonball, you were part of history. At six fifty-eight in the a.m. from Cape Kennedy, first ever made in the U.S.A. Space Shuttle was launched. Quarter million thrill seekers watched the big bird get it off. Got a couple thousand here waiting for our big launch, minutes away now from the final day of the International Powerboat Championships. Coast Guard's patrolling the twenty-six-mile sea course. Key West harbor's blocked off. If you're not already out there in your own boat to witness the race start, forget it. Coasties say no more boats allowed to cross the race course. Two favorites might break a world record in today's final race. Miami Kid, owned by a Central American consortium, finished yesterday's qualifying heat at an awesome eighty-six mph on the rough-water storm course; the thirty-eight-foot Cougar catamaran, Murdoch's Revenge, piloted

by local Key Wester Karl Dean, was a hull length behind. Contending strong at only thirty-two points off the leaders are the French team from Calais and their boat Bullet Baguette, and the Italians in their Philippine-wood catamaran pushed by fourteen-hundred-horsepowered surface-piercing props. The competition's fierce so stay tuned to your Pirate Island radio station in the wild blue yonder."

St. Cloud's gaze followed the heave of Evelyn's breathing. The green and red bloom of a tattooed rose blossomed at the top of her breast in dawn light stabbing through the salt-streaked glass porthole above the narrow berth. The tide sloshed against the hull, lulling the boat in a sighing rhythm. Bull rocking in a woman's sea. St. Cloud held his breath as Evelyn turned in her sleep. He was where he wanted to be, for the moment. If fate pulled the plug on him he was content to be so close to rock bottom. How much lower can a man sink? Somehow it was making sense to make no sense of it. Evelyn's tanned back was presented to him flawless as an empty movie screen, except for a fading scar beneath a winged shoulderblade, etched into her skin ten years before when they first drifted down to the Keys. America was still at war in Vietnam, and St. Cloud and Evelyn took the core of their love for granted, looking for nothing, running from everything. The first time they swam in vivid waters along the reef they dove again and again into a world pure with color, touched only by their eyes, the splendor robbed their breath, they could not get enough of it, feasted on the sight of brilliant fish scattering along the purple-hued shelf of coral stepping beyond sight into a cobalt deep. Swimming back to the surface their lungs burst with excitement, here was something beyond predictability. St. Cloud noticed blood running from a jagged puncture beneath Evelyn's shoulder. As she dove again a trail of blood lingered, an almost imperceptible ribbon running from her body back up to the bubbling surface. Through clear water St. Cloud could see Evelyn swimming in a new world, oblivious to the wound from a sharp snag on the reef. St. Cloud understood in that moment their lives were going to be transformed, but the very nature of the change was beyond fathoming. The trail of blood going inky and disappearing into the surrounding blue was like an unraveling of their life together, back to the time before they met, when both were separate. Like the jagged scar on Evelyn's back separating her new world from his, the bloom of the tattooed rose foretold a radical blossoming of another change. Before the rose made its indelible impression on Evelyn's flesh, St. Cloud resided deep within the smugness of idealism, accepted the predictability of his wayward youth. St. Cloud not only thought he understood Evelyn, he thought he knew what they both stood for, what America stood for, and how they didn't fit. That was long ago, before their chance landing on Key West, an island made quirky by a dangerous slant of light angling from the tropics. Every time St. Cloud tasted the sweet salt of the rose bloom on Evelyn's skin he awakened to the humor of the situation. More roses were tattooed on breasts of women in Key West than there were real roses in all the fancy Miami flower shops. Whenever St. Cloud removed a woman's brassiere, or she opened her blouse to him, he expected a rose to blossom, or occasionally an octopus to be exposed, its inky-blue tentacles gripping a breast, fixing him with a one-eyed nipple stare. The rose tattoos thrived in a hothouse hum of tropical treachery, a consuming disorientation of desire fertilized by disintegrating ideals, an inescapable rust of the soul. Nothing lasts in the tropics, lovers come and go, ideals bloat and burst, implacable impermanence. Nothing lasts forever, not even eternal love.

St. Cloud had not so much lost Evelyn to the bloom of other roses as he had lost her to himself, betrayed former commitment by allowing cynical corruption to enter his blood. Commitment's distant memory had washed beneath the bridge of time in a torrent of rum. By the time Evelyn's rose was being touched and tried by other roses, St. Cloud was swirling helplessly in a sea of self-pity. He knew Evelyn's passions had long since melded into dark crevices of female flowered gardens, where he committed the crime of bearing witness to the dragon of his jealousy. In the beginning he greeted this inevitability by turning his eyes elsewhere, stared without blinking into endless nights of infidelity. Even though he remained legally married to Evelyn, the divorce not yet finalized, the loss was final, except at times like this, when St. Cloud cajoled Evelyn into deferring to his emptiness, appealed to his own wife for a slick remedy of ecstasy, a mercy bullet to blast him beyond misery. He had lured Evelyn onto her own boat the night before, baited his trap for one last fling with the meat of nostalgia, snaring Evelyn's instinct for female pardon. This was not an exercise in masculine conniving, for the problem was not that women were now the main contenders for his wife's emotions. The reality was St. Cloud no longer contended, could not even contend with himself, except when he attempted to penetrate to the origin of his loss.

The hardening rise of St. Cloud's flesh moved deep into the damp between Evelyn's legs as his lips traveled along the fading scar beneath her shoulderblade. Evelyn turned against the fleshy slide of his body, murmured into the slurring sound of slapping tide, cutting St. Cloud loose, an abandoned bull adrift on a lost ship.

From above the helicopters came. The race was on. St. Cloud reluctantly withdrew from Evelyn, pulled his pants up to his waist over a stubborn stiffness no longer of consequence, and went topside where he was greeted by cheers rising from an anchored flotilla of paint-blistered skiffs, sleek ketches and listing lobster boats crowded with beer-drinking spectators applauding a roaring line of forty-foot-long powerboats led overhead by a flock of helicopters. The spectacle of speed burst from around the far side of the island, an invading force of machinery and technology fueled by glory and risk in a mad pursuit to break former feats of record. In the deafening roar the flotilla seemed under attack, caught in a sudden atmosphere of warlike activity. The waterborne herd thundered by at full throttle into a one-hundred-and-sixty-mile run over a glass-hard surface made dangerous by slippery speed and tentative friction. Boldly painted boat hulls nosed high, sharp bows tilting six feet into the air. Rayed bolts of sunlight reflected off the drivers' and throttlemen's crash helmets deep within cocooned cockpits nearly obscured by white-hot jet exhausts plowing a showering spray to a distant horizon and over its edge.

The superficial veil of sport had been pierced. In the calm left behind the passing disturbance furrowed wakes rose to rock the small flotilla. Evelyn emerged from below, touched St. Cloud's shoulder. An embarrassed silence hung between them as their eardrums re-adjusted to calming water slap against the strain of the bobbing boat's anchor. Seabirds heading in from open ocean cried out overhead. The sudden stillness of the moment was lengthened by the long pull of Haitian rum St. Cloud sucked from a snub-necked bottle. Far above the seabirds a vast cloud was unfolding a design as it sailed by. St. Cloud held the amber bottle up before his eyes, filtering harsh light in order to discern the cloud's quickening shape. It looked like a lofty rose blooming white out of a sun-brilliant vase. Yes, St. Cloud was where he wanted to be. He reached up without looking and placed his hand over Evelyn's on his shoulder. The seabirds darkened into flecks flying across the face of his rose in the sky, fleeting shadows on a soul, migrating in a migrating moment. Evelyn stretched on the bow of the boat, spreading her body to the sun. The shadow from the cloud stole over her, obliterating the rose on her breast. St. Cloud pulled at the last of the rum, watching Evelyn's rose return to prominence as cheers erupted from the surrounding boats, people anxious for the next round of the passing spectacle, bonded in their witness to the true danger of the sport unfolding. Evelyn lay on a beach towel, turning the curve of her back to St. Cloud, then rolling slowly over to face him. Her eyes searched his, not to find something within him, but to show him a way out. The taste of sweet rum was still on his tongue, the bitterness of self-recrimination rattled his thoughts. The spread of female flesh before him was all that was left to him, since his wife had long ago taken flight with the last of her pride and beginnings of her next life. St. Cloud sought refuge in his emptiness, Evelyn was showing him just how endless his emptiness was. He felt a hollow man filling with drunken falsity. The portable radio next to Evelyn's head cast its excited electronic voice over water, releasing St. Cloud from the finality of Evelyn's gaze. The urgent immediacy of the radio voice was undercut by anxious laughter and expectant shouting rising from the small flotilla of boats.

"Have we got a race! Simi-smooth conditions beyond the reef. Hope we don't have a disaster like last year, when defending leader Ron Stinson hulled the starboard sponson of his Cougar cat and catapulted into space with a busted back and both legs fractured. Hadn't been for quick action of the Heli-Vac team Ron would have been so much shark food. It's been confirmed the French boat Bullet Baguette is out with engine trouble. French team was saying at yesterday's press conference their catamaran may be the fastest offshore boat in the world. Well the Frogs will never be able to prove it now, bye bye Baguette! Karl Dean still has a slight lead in Murdoch's Revenge. Looking for a third straight win this season is Miami Kid, hot on Dean's jet exhausts."

Fish gotta swim, birds gotta fly, boats gotta sink, St. Cloud thought, peering at Evelyn through the visual corruption of the empty rum bottle he held up before his face. Nothing is forever. St. Cloud corked the bottle and flung it overboard to begin its splashing journey. The message held in the bobbing amber glass was also in St. Cloud, equally invisible in the moment lengthening into midmorning. The roar of oncoming powerboats chummed the air with anticipation, churned the sea with sudden fury. To St. Cloud the boats' miragelike passing of the small flotilla every twenty-two minutes was the only indication a pursuit to break man-made records while flying over the back of an unyielding sea was indeed under way. For reasons having nothing to do with fame or fortune, St. Cloud began to pay attention.

"Official word on what was rumored earlier. Coast Guard reports a refugee boat has drifted into the race course off the southerly side of Rock Key, seven nautical miles out. What a welcome those folks are getting to the land of the free, twelve powerboats booming across water at them, fourteen choppers swirling overhead, they must think the whole U.S. Navy has pounced!"

Fish gotta swim, birds gotta fly, starving Haitians gotta sail away from plantation island. St. Cloud figured in the grand scheme of things his having become the prince of cuckolded fools had as much to do with the refugee boat as it did with the Space Shuttle, which was nothing. He searched the sky for another cloud, another sign, another hook to hang a different thought on. The sky was empty, no scudding white roses big as battleships, no portentous signs of a hurricane's oncoming boisterous weather for some to die in, some to become heroes in, the majority just to live through, survive without personal fanfare. No seabirds. Nothing. Nothing but blue sky bleeding into blue sea, and somewhere out there a boatload of Haitians. Tide comes in, tide goes out, what goes around comes about. The tide can bring in a boatload of desperate people, or a load of marijuana bales dumped from a cigarette boat the night before by smugglers outrunning a Coast Guard bust. The tide can bring in easy money or hard times. It was an odd time to live in, an odd place to be. St. Cloud had traveled across the first half of his life, and here he was, a self-made prince of cuckolds among desperate refugees and get-rich-quick drug smugglers. It was a world of plenty for the very few. How could some make so much so soon, while others starved so slowly? Everything would come around in the end, right itself right side up, St. Cloud believed that. Meanwhile, it all made him feel cheap and out of the action; it also made him feel like a bleeding liberal anachronism, the last dinosaur to be caught in an ice-age glacier with a mouthful of daisies. The empty bottle of rum bobbed on the current back to Haiti where it came from, its spirits released in a compromised world. St. Cloud felt the message from the bottle was in him. Maybe he had become the message. One thing he knew, he didn't want to know the message's full meaning. He had come too far and run too long to trick himself into believing he could change one damn thing in this world. On that subject St. Cloud was not about to be cheated.

"There's been a terrible accident! The lead boat piloted by home-towner Karl Dean has exploded! Reports from observing helicopters are Dean and his Throttleman were blasted from the cockpit in flames! Remember, boats hurtling at hundred-mile-an-hour speeds across changing waters can snag a bow in a wave and flip! Mother Nature don't get you, then your own machine might! Miami Kid takes the lead, going for a world record, but what a catastrophe!"

2

CAMINA POR LO CHAPEAO. Walk on the smooth side. That is what Justo's father always said, and his father lived long enough to die a happy man in his only wife's arms. They stopped making love stories like that when Carole Lombard and Clark Gable died. It was a good Cuban saying, one Justo's father learned from his father, who also died in his only wife's arms. Now all four were out there in the middle of the cemetery, buried beneath a banyan tree, holding hands through eternity. It was Justo's avowed purpose to join them one day with his only wife, Rosella. *Quien a su mujer no honra, asi mismo se deshonra.* He who does not honor his wife dishonors himself.

Justo was smooth as the gold-plated chicken wishbone hanging from a braided gold chain around his thick neck. The golden bone was rubbed so single-mindedly over the years it fit effortlessly into Justo's palm like the slender hand of his oldest teenage daughter, Isabel. The bone was his good-luck charm, the very bone of faith he wished upon for survival, given him by his African great-aunt Oris fifteen years before when he upped for a second Marine hitch in Vietnam. Great-aunt Oris called on all the Santería saints and African gods to preserve her grand-nephew, and they did. When Justo was born, it was Oris who went out and immediately burned an offering of fifty candles in prayerful thanks to Santa Barbara for there being a pure black boy born into such a light-skinned Cuban family. At last a blessed African black bean amidst all the Spanish yellow rice. The stew of life would surely be spiced up. Oris measured the sum of the good life by its wildly different flavors.

Not only was Justo the only black bean in the stew, he was the last

11

on the island to carry on the Cuban family name from his father's side, Tamarindo. A family named for a tree. The same type of tree under which the Cuban Patriots plotted in 1868 to overthrow their Spanish overlords. The patriots failed and invented the art of cunning exile, patiently waiting until *los Hermanos* of their homeland, the Brothers ninety miles across the Straits of Florida from Key West, were "ready to rise as one man." A tree grows, a family nation takes root. A piece of the patriots' legendary tree was kept in the cemetery where Justo was taken many times by his old grandfather, Abuelo. Young Justo would stand in wonder before a gnarled chunk of bark enshrined behind a scratched glass case set on a pedestal among concrete cracked graves containing the remains of the once far-dreaming Brothers who gave their lives. All the while Abuelo thundered and banged his cane on the cracked concrete, attempting to rouse the sleeping *Hermanos* to fulfill their destiny. If they had lived their plan was to make Key West part of Cuba. A tree would have grown bigger; Key West would still be an island of families, people talking on porch stoops, ice-cream vendors pushing their carts; opera would still be sung inside the ornate Instituto de San Carlos, arias echoing off glittering walls of majolica tiles. There was a reason Cubans once called Key West Stella Maris, Star of the Sea. There was a time when the island's soul was Cuban, when it was prosperous and proud, with thousands of Strippers, Trimmers, Pickers and Packers rolling out one hundred million cigars a year by hand; a time of black beans and yellow rice, of grunts and grits, when a man took his daughter by the hand at age fifteen, led her before all the white picket fences of the cigar workers' cottages barged over from the Bahamas, walking proudly to the San Carlos, where the town waited in all its sunday finery with a thumping band to trumpet the second most important day in a girl's life, *Quince*, to dance her through a joyous celebration of her fifteenth birthday into womanhood, to toast and toast again with sweet *anejo, salud-salud*, toasts all around for the proud parents, salutations to the beaming father who gave rise to a fabulous female flower at the center of the Star of the Sea, center of the universe, and all for the glory of a free Cuba.

Cayo Hueso, Island of Bones, was the name the Spanish first gave the place, long before it had become a glittering star to the Cubans. Island of Bones, because the Spaniards found it littered with the bleached remains of the hounded, deserted and luckless. It wasn't any star of the sea for the Spaniards, it was even less so in Justo's time. Sometimes, to Justo, the island steamed with the same scent of rancid inevitability as Saigon had in the final days before its fall. Justo carried with him a sense of doomed fate, especially now, as he shoved through the shouting and surging crowd along Mallory Dock. Some people on the dock recognized him, stepped respectfully out of his path, others moved grudgingly aside. A lifetime of sun had baked Justo's Afro-Cuban skin to a polished mahogany, imbuing him with a sleek appearance and solid attitude, an attitude the Cubans called *formidal*. People didn't step aside because of Justo's broad chest, made more massive by being twenty pounds overweight, or because years of black belt karate training had articulated itself into a dangerous swagger of thick hips. People stepped aside because Justo was a bull of the streets, a tough cop who had worked his way up from the bottom to the lordly position of detective on a force that by tradition prided itself on being southern and white. Justo wore no badge. The loose blue *guayabera* shirt, always unbuttoned halfway down his chest, its shirt tails flapping at his hips in anticipation of a cool breeze, was his badge. Every day he munched his way through a bag of cold conch fritters, hoping the greasy deep-fried little balls of spicy conch meat would put out the fire of twelve daily *buche* espressos burning a hole big as a fist through his stomach, fixing on his face a sort of beatific grimace, much like the sardonic rapture captured on the faces of certain male saints painted on walls of churches in faraway countries without television.

Nothing escaped Justo's brown eyes, not what happened before, not what happened since, such was his formidability. All gave Justo his due, even those among the crowd on Mallory Dock, some near hysteria, wailing because of the great calamity which had befallen one of the local boys in the race, others cheering the winning powerboat team being sprayed with champagne in front of television cameras surrounding the judges' grandstand. Justo was that rare creature on the island, a man going someplace who knew where he was from. He was an old-fashioned family man, an island of integrity on an island of shifting morality. Long before the town tricked itself out for tourists and rolled over for frigid northerners, Justo had come to this dock for other celebrations. Once a year people crowded onto this cement bulwark at the abrupt Gulf of Mexico edge to cheer the passing parade of shrimp boats, their colorful nets winged out over water on forty-foot steel booms, jaunty as flying medieval pennants, a vast armada with appropriate names: *Black Madonna, Ramona's Prayer, La*

Libertad—each boat passing the dock three times to hand-blown kisses, tossed flowers and the solemn words of the priest praying for "Full nets and a safe journey on future voyages." The priest in his white linen vestments embroidered with a large red cross waved his hand in blessing, called on the miraculous Virgin Mother to fill the nets through all the backbreaking nights ahead with rich, squirming "pink gold" of the lowly but succulent cockroach of the sea, bountiful shrimp.

That was a long ago time when fishing was a poor man's honest gamble in the big casino of the ocean. Every man's net is equal under water. It remained so, but the value of the catch had changed. The shrimp fleet was still blessed, but it was more of a tourist attraction and less a spiritual send-off. The island itself had become a sideshow trick, the native Conchs, the working people, were the freaks. If there was any honesty the priest would bless all the boats used to run marijuana and cocaine. That was the economy people had better pray that the Virgin Mother hold up; without it, the unimaginative, the daring and the weak would all be equally broke. From where Justo stood the island was reduced to nothing more than a marijuana republic, a mere cocaine principality. A man could catch a million-dollar load of marijuana in an afternoon, or his nets yield no more than a ten-dollar bucket of shrimp for a month of nights' work. What the sea gives up to the fisherman is all fair and equal catch, governed by no man-made decree or biblical mandate. Such was the law of the sea, and too, the unspoken law of the island.

The crowd at Mallory Dock had come to celebrate, or grieve over, what the sea had rendered this day. No more than a handful remembered the time when the broad cement dock was a creaky run of bleached board pier studded with cavernous shrimp-packing houses where a boy could venture in a tattered T-shirt and shorts, while away his time talking to seagulls, until the steel boom-wings of shrimp boats approached from the thin blue horizon to spill from holds their briny nocturnal harvest; a boy could stand alongside the men then, a boy like Justo, with strong wrists and fast fingers, could pop off enough shrimp heads to fill a bucket with decapitated bodies of pink sea bugs every five minutes, fill a box every twenty minutes, could earn himself a buck, be his own man, buy his own *buche* and cigars, sit with the best of the town *hermanos* along Duval Street and watch the stream of *niñas bonitas* floating by in dresses bright and vivid as open-mouthed sea urchins sashaying in clear current of a coral tidal pool, but these landbound skirted urchins on Duval Street desired to be fed with praise and promise, a boy had to wait, save his bug money, be industrious, join the Marines, then maybe one of these bright creatures with glistening braided hair coiled atop her head would take notice, turn inky eyes on him in sudden recognition, lower her rope of hair down to him from her lofty perch, then the boy would hear the bright creature's name calling to him. Justo heard one name year after year blowing into him on fresh sea breezes coming ashore unexpectedly when spring winds shifted and swung around from the south, winds succinct with the clear sound of *Rosella,* a name he would one day join with his own to make a family, a name his youth was haunted by as he walked long ago through the packinghouses, the tide of discarded shrimp heads cracking and crunching beneath his white rubber boots, stony shrimp eyes connected to no body, gazing up at wooden ceiling fans whipping moisture from the air, each blade's rotation scattering syllables of the name, flinging them like so many pure drops of sweat across the length of the packinghouse, *Rosella Rosella Rosella.* How could a man not marry a woman with a name like that? How could a man not take all the offered coiled rope in his hands and climb to the stars, roll with Rosella across white-sheeted nights until two beautiful daughters were born, looking just like Rosella and calling him Papa. *Quien se casa por amores, malos días y buenas noches.* He who marries for love will have bad days, but good nights.

Mal día, what a bad day this was. Boat blowing up, refugee boat coming in. Next thing to happen would be for the Space Shuttle shot off this morning to fall out of the sky. Justo figured with his luck the shuttle would fall in the middle of Mallory Dock. He fingered the gold wishbone at his neck, popped another conch fritter and pushed deeper into the crowd, farther away from the judges' grandstand where two new powerboat champions in sleek blue racing suits were being hoisted on shoulders above all. The champions were of no interest to Justo. It was the Coast Guard's job to investigate the cause of the boat explosion. His job was in the opposite direction.

Down at the far end of the dock a rope barricade stretched to hold back the few onlookers trying for a closer look at the boat from Haiti being towed by a Coast Guard cutter. The battered wooden vessel bobbed behind the steel cutter throttling its massive engines to a muffled roar as it swung around to moor the rudderless craft behind it alongside the dock. From the boat's broken mast flapped remnants of gray patched sails. A roar went up from the crowd behind Justo.

He turned to catch the glimpse of a beaming blonde in a brief bikini ascending the judges' grandstand. Cameras clacked and popping bottle corks released a rain of champagne as the blonde triumphantly raised a silver trophy. The blonde wiggled in the champagne rain, exposing exaggerated contours of flesh beneath her soaked bikini before pirouetting on spike heels into the arms of champions eager to claim their silver trophy and the prize of puckered red lips.

"Get away from that rope!" A Coast Guardsman guarding the rope barricade barked his command, one hand snapping to the revolver holstered at his hip, threatening to draw on a long-haired man astride a battered bicycle. The man appeared oblivious to the warning, prodding the front wheel of the bicycle against the rope as if it were the string of a giant bow about to propel him into space.

Mal día, Justo whispered beneath his breath, it was Space Cadet, what was he up to? So many of Space Cadet's brain cells had been burned out on mushrooms, pot and acid that Justo figured just going to the corner store for him must be like trying to cross a continent crisscrossed with raging rivers while all the bridges have been blown.

"I said back off from the rope!" The Guardsman aimed his revolver at the words stitched across Space Cadet's faded baseball cap proclaiming THE NEXT GENERATION.

Justo grabbed the loosely braided swag of gray hair dangling like the rope to a bell from beneath the back of Space Cadet's cap. *"Dios da sombrero a quien no tiene cabeza,"* he mumbled as the muscles in his arm tightened and he yanked the braid. God gives hats to some who have no head.

Space Cadet turned slowly, a queer grin spread over a forty-year-old face remarkable for its unlined quality; the bulging eyes seemed to spin in opposite orbits, washed of all color, too weird to betray weariness. If those eyes ever stopped spinning, Justo often thought, watch out. But the eyes were spinning, taking no notice of Justo. The wail of the electric guitars Space Cadet marched to blared from the depths of a generation long since passed, the psychedelic imprint of those heady, hippie times, now only a blur. Space Cadet himself was one of the last remnants from those times, like the tie-dyed whirl of color T-shirt he wore with its ever shrinking grip on his bony chest.

No hope here. Justo sighed and released his grip from Space Cadet's braid. Let the Guardsman blow this portent of the next generation to kingdom come. If this is the next generation, it's come and gone. What had come was the Haitian boat. Saving Space Cadet's skinny ass from the itchy trigger finger of an overzealous Guardsman was the least of all problems this bad day brought.

Justo looked down into the boat. The horror was worse than he could have imagined, no wonder the young Guardsman was so nervous. Justo stepped over the rope and into the barrel tip of the Guardsman's revolver.

The Guardsman backed off, but he did not lower the gun. "Sir! You'll have to stay on the other side, orders of the Captain!"

"This is city property you Coasties have docked at." Justo flipped his wallet open, flashing the hard metal of his detective's badge. "I'm the Captain here."

The young Guardsman eyed the badge, holstered his revolver and saluted, relieved to surrender authority in an ugly matter he would rather have no part of. "Yes sir! Captain sir! Gangway down there!" The Guardsman shouted over his shoulder, "Captain coming aboard!"

Justo walked to the edge of the concrete bulwark and peered down into the listing craft. Close up, the sight made him sick in his gut, shooting an acid arrow deep into his being, deeper than a thousand cups of *buche* could ever burn their way into. Justo shook his head slowly, rubbing the gold wishbone at his neck, nothing could be done now. *El qué no entra a nadar, no se ahoga en el mar*. He who doesn't enter the sea will never be drowned by the sea.

The only sign of life on the boat was from a *richaud*, a thin wisp of smoke rising like a ghost from the blackened iron brazier. The *richaud* was placed in the middle of the deck, but it couldn't have been used for cooking, for the naked, bone-thin people piled in the boat looked as if they hadn't eaten for weeks. Maybe the *richaud* was being used by the last ones alive, signaling for help, delirious, hallucinating, no longer caring if they risked being taken back to Haiti, burning clothes in the *richaud*, flesh, bones, anything to send a smoke signal of distress from a rudderless leaking vessel. God knows what? No, that wasn't it. Justo knew these people wouldn't be taken back to Haiti alive. Better to swim with the sharks in the sea than be eaten by the dictator on land. Justo did not want to think of the nightmares these people had been exposed to, what final horror overtook them. They were *paysans*, hardscrabble peasants from Haiti's interior, where half the children died by age five. Only the sea separated them from a new life. Better to swim with the sharks in the sea, even if one was a *paysan* and did not know how to swim. Strewn about the deck of the wreck were men, women and children, arms and legs stiffened into grotesque contortions of death, sun-rotted flesh peeling from bones, eyes bubbled white with decay. The boat was less than thirty-five feet long, a glorified raft, its mast a hacked limb from a tree, the sails patched together bed sheets. Justo wouldn't have trusted the boat's splintered hulk to make it across one of the ritzy hotel pools in Miami, let alone six hundred miles of open water, up from the Caribbean Sea through the slice of the Windward Passage, past Cuba into the forceful flow of the Gulf Stream swinging east, then pulled north by the Straits of Florida's fast-running current. Someone had kept the fire going in the *richaud* until the very end. What for? A sign to an African god? Voodoo? Justo fingered the wishbone at his neck and mumbled three Hail Mary's. He would have said more but another roar went up from the judges' grandstand as a voice boomed over loudspeakers announcing prize money to be awarded the race winners. The cheering crowd brought Justo back from his prayerful respite; he tried to focus on the nightmare scene in the boat, hoping his prayers would have made it all a mere passing apparition. The sun had turned the black bodies of the *paysans* blacker. Justo had seen it all before in Vietnam. The team of uniformed Coast Guardsmen in the boat awkwardly loaded the dead into rubber body bags. Memories, uniforms. A buried past rising. Justo thanked the Saints for his belief in Catholicism. He knew what an act of true confession was for, to absolve the living from their guilt of having survived life's hell, to release a man from eternal anguish, to make a man forget. Vietnam was finished for Justo. Over. But this was different, a new devil. How can a man ask forgiveness from a tide of dead refugees? Different bodies, but the same old smell of death swelling a man's nostrils. Justo held his breath, not wanting to inhale the finality of it all. A scream of ambulance sirens snaked in the distance across the island, through palm trees and narrow streets. There had been no ambulances in Vietnam's jungles, only the howl of a jackal in a man's blood, fear bursting in eardrums as medevac choppers roared in overhead. Another roar erupted from the judges' grandstand. Bodies bagged in rubber shrouds were passed up from the refugee boat, along a chain gang of uniformed men up to the dock next to Justo. Half of the unbagged bodies left on the boat were children, black bodies turned blacker, finally gone powdery white in death. Must have been drinking seawater, Justo thought, their bellies bloated, skin parched, an agonizing death for children of dirt farmers adrift in a sea of uncertainty. Justo knew it could be one of his own daughters down there, if he had been born on the wrong island in time. Could be his African grandparents, slumped in each other's arms, only the sea between them and freedom. Three generations after his grandparents came from Africa the tide still brought in the same devil's bounty of misery. Ambulance doors swung open behind Justo, then slammed shut, the vehicles wailing away to the morgue. What was that down in the boat? Something? The last body which had been buried beneath the others. Maybe? Yes. Life had trained Justo for this sort of thing. Four years in an Asian jungle refined his seventh sense, honed his second nature. A boy buried moves. Praise the Saints, the kid was moving.

"He's alive! That boy's alive!"

"Yes sir!" A Guardsman tugging the boy by a bony ankle into a body bag released his grip, as if suddenly aware he had a rabid animal by the tail.

The sound of sirens grew louder in Justo's ears. Behind him the growing crowd pushed with the belligerent force of the savagely curious against the rope barricade. His own men in uniform had arrived, pushing people back. Justo knew that most often people are only curious about other people after they are dead. Another ambulance screeched to a slow roll, dispersing the crowd as it came to a stop before the rope, its blue rooflight whipping a brilliant blur in the sun, back doors flinging open, stretcher-bearers jumping to the ground.

"He's alive!" Justo grabbed the closest ambulance attendant by the lapels of his white frock, shouting above the siren. "I want him! Take him directly to the city jail. Not to the hospital! He's mine! Understand?"

The frightened attendant nodded and jumped down into the boat, helping the stretcher-bearers lift the limp body onto the stretcher.

"Tamarindo!" A tall Coast Guardsman, the metal insignia of a Captain's badge pinned to the starched blue collar of his shirt, bellowed Justo's surname as if it were a command for a dog to heel. "What do you think you're up to? You're not taking anyone, anywhere. This is a Coast Guard matter." The Captain stepped over the rope, flanked by uniformed men with revolvers and handcuffs swaying from jutting hips. "You don't have any authority here."

Blood rushed to Justo's face, bloating it disproportionately in the hot sun, he felt he looked as hideous as the *paysans* pulled from the boat. He turned on the Captain standing between his protectors. "I'll tell you what's going on." Justo struggled to control his voice, slowed it to a low growl. "You don't get your ass off this dock I'm going to bust *you*. Immigration law states any alien seeking political asylum has the right to an attorney. You interdicted this boat in violation of international law. Just because you did it doesn't make it legal. I'm taking the boy."

"What kind of nonsense are you talking? You know our routine. We wanted to get this boat in to the closest shore point in order to save lives."

"You made a mistake. Should have taken the boat around to the Coast Guard dock. I've got jurisdiction here and I'm busting the boy for involuntary manslaughter."

"Tamarindo, you're stepping into a government problem where you don't belong."

"A crime has been committed and the perpetrator is on city property. I think he killed everybody on this boat to survive."

"That's not the issue. You don't know any more than we do about what happened at sea. There will be an inquiry into that. Look at the pathetic kid. He's not even eighteen, so you don't have the right to book him in your jail."

"You got a birth certificate stating his age?"

"Listen, I don't want to argue the point. It's absurd for you to think—"

"Justo!" the ambulance attendant shouted from the boat. "The kid's trying to say something."

Justo jumped into the boat. What there was of the emaciated body was strapped to the stretcher, an IV needle stuck into the faint blue print of a vein in the crook of the boy's arm. Justo knelt next to the stretcher, kneaded the boy's bony hands clenched into feeble fists. The boy's swollen lips cracked open, gasping for meaning.

The ambulance attendant looked questioningly at Justo. "What's he saying?"

"Creole. He's speaking Creole. Got to get somebody who understands it. Might be the last thing the boy ever says. Don't move him." Justo surveyed the crowd pushing against the rope barricade. Mother Mary, there must be someone. Yes, there was someone. An answer to Justo's quick prayer. There he was, standing at the back of the crowd. The guy was a rummy and a bit of a weirdo, but he sometimes interpreted at court trials for Cuban and Haitian refugees. The drunker the guy was, the better interpreter he was, spoke in tongues, leaning so close to the lips of the person he was interpreting for it reminded Justo of Judas about to kiss sweet Jesus.

"St. Cloud! Get down here!"

St. Cloud slipped under the rope barricade, hopped into the boat. He thought the boy was dead. The boy smelled dead.

"Don't be squeamish!" Justo shouted above the wail of more sirens. "Put your ear to his lips so you can hear what he's saying."

St. Cloud fell to his knees, the rasp of the boy's breath coming into his ear.

"What is it? What's he saying?" Justo grabbed St. Cloud by the arm. "Come over here." He pulled St. Cloud to the side of the boat. "I don't want anybody else to hear. Now, what is it?"

"Hard to make out." St. Cloud wiped his forehead, rum made him sweat, kept him cool in the subtropical swelter. "It's some kind of Creole dialect, obscure. Something like, *Hail Papa Agwé who dwells in the sea, loa of ships. The Negro's boat is in danger. Papa Agwé brings it to safety. Hail.*"

"Christ. The poor bastard. There's a lot of African stuff in Santería I learned from my Aunt Oris, but I don't know who Papa Agwé is. Don't recall Aunt Oris talking about Papa Agwé."

"Voudoun, if I remember right. It's been years since I studied it. I think Papa Agwé is a spirit, lord of the sea, symbolized by a boat and—"

"That's enough. Come over here." Justo tightened his grip on St. Cloud's shoulder, pulling him back to the boy. "Okay, men." Justo pointed at the ambulance attendants. "Pick up the stretcher and get this refugee out of here. You know where to take him."

The attendants carefully lifted the stretcher. One of the boy's clenched fists opened in a slight spasm, releasing a small pigskin bag secured with a knot of goat hair. Justo scooped the bag up, hiding it in his shirt pocket. He glanced at the dock to see if anyone noticed what he had done. The Captain was staring directly at him from beneath the stiff brim of his officer's cap.

"Captain." Justo stood up. "We've got to take this political refugee into custody. I'm appointing St. Cloud the refugee's interpreter. He's the only one who can understand him. St. Cloud could save his life."

"This issue won't be settled here, Tamarindo." The Captain turned to go, his men stiffening to attention with hands raised in salute. "You'll be hearing from the Department of Transportation and the

Immigration and Naturalization Service for obstruction of govern-
mental policy. It's your goose." The Captain nodded to his armed
escorts and they quickly opened an exit path for him through the
pushing crowd.

Justo pulled St. Cloud close and whispered, "It's your goose too."

"What do you mean? I just got here, wondered what all the
commotion was."

"You're an accessory to murder after the fact."

"The hell I am." St. Cloud tried to pull away from Justo's hand
digging into his shoulder. "What's going on?"

"I want you to play ball with me, to be a team player. Could change
your life. Look down there." Justo released his grip and pointed to
the splintered planking of the boat's gunwale. Crude letters faded
brown by the sun were painted the length of the boat's upper edge.

St. Cloud squinted at the scrawl, trying to decipher its meaning,
reading the words out loud. "*Re . . . zis . . . to. Li . . . berté . . . ou . . .
lan . . . mo.* Liberation or death."

"It's written in blood." Justo fingered his wishbone, his eyes going
back and forth over the faded letters. "I know the look of dried blood."

While Justo rubbed his gold bone, St. Cloud congratulated himself
for having started off such a strange day by drinking the sun up with
a bottle of Haiti's finest. "Thing is," St. Cloud mumbled, speaking
more to himself than Justo, who turned to hear the slurred words
running together in rum-slickened syllables, "while ago, standing up
there behind the rope watching what was going on, couldn't help
think about something which occurred to me early this morning.
These *paysans* were at sea, probably had no compass, overhead a
Space Shuttle was heaven bound. Can't shake the feeling we're living
in a modern Christopher Columbus age, at the beginning of one
world, end of another."

"That's why this Haitian kid is so important." Justo looked along
the dock, reporters were waving at him, television crews jostling each
other for camera positions. He wished he could go off to the bar with
St. Cloud and drink his way out of such a *mal día*. A cool breeze
flapped the loose ends of his *guayabera* shirt. He turned from the
hectic scene on the dock, his eyes going to the words scrawled in
blood along the gunwale. "I agree with you. Columbus and the *paysans*
on this boat were after the same thing. Both knew they had to keep
the Saints fed to get where they were going. Problem is nobody knows
these days what the Saints are eating."

3

USA 41–HAITI 1. The hand-scrawled message on the chalkboard placed among the bank of colored liquor bottles behind the bar shimmered through misting cigarette smoke. Whirring fan blades overhead tore at the boisterous conversations in the crowded Wreck Room bar, whipping sentences and paragraphs in random patterns, flinging fumbling articulations and drunken declarations onto lips moving with pantomime thickness. It was difficult to tell who at the bar said what and how many drinks back they said it. It no longer mattered. Who cared? Almost no one was watching the television screen aimed at the long bar from a far corner, beaming yesterday's news in the early morning hours, illuminating over and over the image of the hundred-ton Space Shuttle lifting from primordial ooze of swampy Everglades atop six million pounds of orange flaming rocket thrust, performing a quick disappearing act into heaven's blue yawn in less time than the blink of an alligator's eye, leaving behind a five-hour traffic snarl on asphalt arteries spiraling away from the Space Center launch pad, honking cars filled with people headed back to a mundane world, stifling their desire to be orbiting above it all faster than seventeen thousand miles an hour. Such was the news from the television, a comet man-made, followed by the filmed image of a black policeman in a loose *guayabera* shirt standing before a Haitian refugee boat as bloated bodies skinned white by the sun were hefted onto a dock of pressing spectators. *"No,"* the recorded voice from Justo's filmed image made its way from the television up above the roar of the bar into the swirling fan blades. *"There's no proof of cannibalism on this boat. I don't know where that rumor got started.*

23

These people died of exposure, starvation and drinking seawater. There will be an investigation. Yes, one survivor. No, I already told you, no signs of cannibalism have been exhibited on any bodies."

"Whose treasure is it anyway? I'd like to know! I mean, the Indians found it and made other Indians dig for it. Then the Spaniards took it from the Indians. Same thing is going on now four hundred years later in space. I don't see what the difference is if those Space Shuttle guys zipped over to the moon and found themselves some great cache from a crashed Martian flying saucer, a million tons of gleaming platinum scattered around in moon craters. You think those guys are going to let that stuff just lie there for another zillion years? Hell no! They would do just what the Spanish Conquistadores did, load it up and wing it on home. That's what we're doing up there in space. Isn't one bit different from what Ponce de León was up to when he was running around Florida here in the sixteenth century, and it's no different from me diving these Spanish wrecks off the Keys. Finders keepers, losers bleeders. Know what I mean, St. Cloud?"

St. Cloud heard Brogan's words, but he couldn't concentrate on them. Something wasn't right up there on the television screen. St. Cloud had watched the news come around four times so far that night. Something was off. After Justo's image on the television disappeared the screen flickered with the exploding wreckage of Karl Dean's powerboat filmed from a helicopter, shards of brightly colored fiberglass scattered like jewels around the face-down deadweight of Dean's body bobbing in water. The thin line between winning a race and burial at sea had been crossed. But something more had been crossed. Burial at sea for a speeding thrill seeker was one thing, forty-one dead Haitians was another. One man's bait is another man's meal. Everyone races to the same fate, but there was more. St. Cloud felt it wasn't all so simple.

The weight of Brogan's body shifted on the barstool, knocking against St. Cloud. Brogan's heavy insistence was not that of a drunken challenger or an overzealous friend, more like an anxious load seeking universal balance. "Have I ever told you about my brother?" Brogan raised an emptied cocktail glass close to his lips, his words echoing up with urgency. "My brother's a sort of adventurer down in Central America. Yeah, that's what he is, a sort of adventurer."

St. Cloud knew enough to write a book about Brogan's brother and always wanted to hear more, but sliding his attention over to Brogan on the stool next to him was going to be a tricky maneuver.

The blood of St. Cloud's veins hummed with the sugar slush of rum; any coherent thought trying to swim upstream to his brain was almost certain to drown. First things first. St. Cloud struggled to focus his eyes from the television set, down the mirrored wall into the narrow runway behind the bar, where Angelica reigned supreme. He tried to steady the blond vision of Angelica, tears streaming down her cheeks as she poured a Niagara Falls of alcohol into drained glasses held out to her along the bar. Angelica's white shorts were of such insignificant material they could be stuffed into a whiskey shot glass with room left over for two olives. Each time Angelica spun around in a provocative pirouette, bending over to expose fleshy charms as she snagged yet another bottle of West Indies rum, enough silent prayers went up from the men along the bar to have turned the tide of the Crusades. Angelica presented a fast-moving target for St. Cloud, he struggled to keep the target steady as she poured rum to the top of Brogan's empty glass without his asking for it. She wiped tears from her eyes, holding the bottle of rum up expectantly before St. Cloud, her smoky voice delivering the slow curve of a daring confrontation. "Why don't you just take me away from all of this and fuck me?"

Brogan sucked the rum out of his glass in one gulp. "My brother says Central America is where the buck bucks. He says what's going on down there is like a poker game with your mother. You can only play that game one way. To the end. You lose, you are not born. You win and you can't live with your conscience, because you have fucked your mother over. What was that you just said, Angelica?"

"I asked St. Cloud why he just didn't take me away from all of this."

Brogan raised his empty glass to Angelica in an unsteady salute. "I was talking about motherfuckers. I was talking about politics. I was talking about my brother."

"He was my brother and now he's dead." Angelica brushed a new set of tears from her eyes.

"What are you talking about?" Brogan stammered, lowering his glass in disbelief. "MK is not your brother. MK is my brother. Did I ever tell you how MK got his name?"

"Karl Dean is what I'm talking about, you jerk. Karl Dean was my brother and now he's dead."

"He wasn't your brother." Brogan shoved his empty glass across the bar. "He was your lover."

"You're all my brothers." Angelica poured Brogan another drink, her tears splashing on the mahogany gloss of the bar top.

Among Angelica's many charms, which St. Cloud found too numerous at this moment to count, she had one seductive quality that went unrivaled. This quality, which attracted St. Cloud most to Angelica, was that she was wicked and there, immediately available in a way which intended no harm to others. Angelica wasn't a beat me, whip me, bite me, make me write bad checks girl. Angelica was a woman clearly without her own mind and never in need of it; she functioned on a level of selfless emotions. At the point in her life when most other women begin to wear jewelry to enhance their fading youth, Angelica wore less makeup and fewer clothes. Instead of dressing in a manner designed as sensible, Angelica was in headlong pursuit of the irresponsible. She had a reputation, among the town's self-appointed male judges of female virtues, as having at any one given moment the hardest nipples and the softest heart. Angelica was a northern woman who had drifted on a bet and a dare along the high-rise, time-sharing Gulf of Mexico coast, and ended up in the southernmost Redneck Riviera. But Angelica was not a Saturday night tickle to be found seven nights a week in the Wreck Room. She was no hillbilly harlot or card-carrying member of the drug-a-day club, rather, she was the marrying kind who spent her whole life trying to prove she wasn't the marrying kind. Even Angelica's five-year-old daughter knew that. Angelica was the kind of woman who aimed to please, and aimed straight. Right now St. Cloud knew her aim was targeted at him. That didn't stop Brogan from rattling on anyway.

"Yeah, you could call my brother an adventurer I guess. MK's done all the usual stuff. You know, blowing up power stations of little Marijuana Republic islands so his men could load grass onto boats in the harbor and slip away under cover of darkness. MK's been chased by Cuban gunboats in the Bimini Windward Passage. He even had a small nine-hundred-acre garden in Jamaica on the side of a mountain in Rasta Cockpit country. Thick jungle, had to truck the marijuana harvest out on donkeys, MK cut their vocal cords so nobody knew they were mule-training by. Those gentlemen donkeys had their ball bearings whacked off too, so they handled sweet as Bambi. Did I ever tell you how my brother got his name? MK was real decorated in the Nam war. I mean heavy decorated."

St. Cloud wanted to hear the story again. The story always changed a little, but over the years he had heard Brogan talk of MK the central facts remained the same. MK was everything St. Cloud wasn't. MK had been Special Forces in Vietnam during the 1960s when St. Cloud was marching against the war in San Francisco, having people spit on him and hiss *Commie*, that was the usual stuff back then. It seemed to St. Cloud now, after twenty years had passed, some curious circle was bringing him and MK together, fusing them in a bond of unfathomable brotherhood, inexorable and uncomfortable.

Angelica's tears were melting the hardened sugar in St. Cloud's veins. He cocked himself up on the barstool and leaned over the counter, wrapping his arms around Angelica so her face rested against his chest. Angelica's sobbing shook the two of them until St. Cloud almost lost his balance and pitched over backward.

"Karl Dean was a great man!" Angelica sobbed against St. Cloud's chest.

"Yes." St. Cloud held onto Angelica for dear life. He knew if he let go he would take such a fall he would never get up. "Karl was a regular guy." The sugar had not melted so much in St. Cloud's veins that he didn't know Karl Dean was one of the most disagreeable scammers in a town that prided itself in producing one hundred percent disagreeables. Karl was just another homegrown boy who figured out before he left high school that he could pump gas the rest of his life or run a few fast boats around in the dark across shallow water and get paid big money for the least amount of questions asked. Karl had a solid gold watch, but he could barely tell time or count to ten using the fingers of both hands. Karl always had one eye on the next girl in town to turn fifteen, the other eye on himself in the mirror resting on his knee as he snorted up his daily five G's. A real regular guy around the island. Racing boats was not a sport to Karl, but a way of life, same as war games are not games to soldiers. On a small island full of hotshot boys in tight Hawaiian shirts and diamond earrings pierced in their ears, Karl was no different. He bragged about his educational shortcomings, flashed his hundred-dollar rolls of loot, and spent his early mornings in the din of the Wreck Room trying to find some lucky girl to get pretty with him on the mirror.

"Oh God, St. Cloud." Angelica righted herself up and dabbed at her tears with a bar napkin. "I knew you had a good heart."

St. Cloud took the bar napkin from Angelica and touched up the trickle of tears still running down her cheeks. "I don't have such a good heart, it's only that Karl was a regular guy. Me, I'm a man beyond belief."

"Hey! What is this? I'm a professional." Angelica snatched the tear-soaked napkin from St. Cloud and tossed it into the trashcan behind her. "Enough of the wake. Karl Dean was an asshole. Can I offer you boys a mescal nightcap?"

"Delighted." Brogan accepted the offer for the two of them.

St. Cloud knocked back four shots of Mexico's meanest, Angelica's face beaming before him, her cheeks high and dry now, her cheeks ringing red and gorgeous, contrasting against the skin of her slender neck, skin more blond than flesh-colored, almost the same blond as her cropped hair; she was St. Cloud's arctic queen, radiant among the denizens of the tropics. He wondered how she did it. All night in bars, all day in bed. Angelica had the kind of high cheekbones that up north in New York were called money bones, the fashionable bones of a model. She could have made a fortune as a department store rag ramp-runner, instead she ran the gauntlet behind the Wreck Room bar, and gallantly sported St. Cloud to forehead-numbing mescal. He was awed and humbled. Once again he was falling in love with Angelica.

"I'm not going to give it up, St. Cloud." Angelica backhanded new tears. "Why should I? You understand?"

"Why should you. Never. Thanks for the drinks. On the house?"

"The credo of the single woman is romance. I won't give it up."

"Never."

"Why should I?"

"Shouldn't."

"Yes. It's on the house, for you always."

"Always."

"Isn't it just awful about those forty-one Haitians?"

"Always."

The television flickered more ghostly images of the previous day's tragedy. St. Cloud tried to fix his wavering triple vision on the ghosts. Nothing seemed steady. Something still wasn't right up there on the screen where a medevac helicopter pilot was shouting at a television reporter above the roar of the crowd surrounding the race judges' platform: *"Then the two lead boats drew hull to hull, had to swerve to miss the drifting Haitian boat! I don't know how the Haitian boat got on the course so fast, must have been sucked in by a strong current, appeared from nowhere, the pace boat didn't even have time to run a red flag! Suddenly it looked like all three boats were going to eat it! When you're blasting through heavy seas like that you run the risk of hooking the boat if you bank into a tight curve, catching a sponson hull in a wave and flipping! That happens there is a kill cord attached to the Driver which cuts the engine if he is thrown! Today there wasn't time for that! Nobody stuffed under a wave, instead there was just a big explosion! We could actually see Karl Dean and his Throttleman blow right out of the water! Then Miami Kid pulled away, alone in the lead! Things were moving so fast the Haitian boat went drifting through falling debris from Karl's destroyed boat! It was an inferno out there! Before I had a chance to jump from the chopper into the water it was too late. Bloody chaos!"*

St. Cloud felt a stiffening in his neck, a numbing from a viselike grip which sent a persistent ache down his spinal cord. Something wasn't right up there on the ghostly television. Who knows what the Saints are eating these days? Just what did Justo mean by that? Something not right up there but something not right down here. The hoarse laughter in St. Cloud's ear focused him. He hunched his shoulders to shrug off the numbness in his neck. The laughter grew louder, it was not coming from the blurred crowd behind him, but was right in his ear. He tried to turn around but couldn't. He felt his neck was stuck. He realized the numbness was not from the quarts of alcoholic novocaine he had poured into his body since the morning before, but from massive fingers clamping the back of his neck with the improbable iron tenacity of someone whose idea of a handshake was trying to squeeze toothpaste out of a shark. St. Cloud was held in the grip of a man who made his living on the ocean.

"I'm a fishin man! My father was a fishin man before me and his before him!" The words rushed into St. Cloud's ear, the hand clamped on his neck in a shark-killing grip opened.

St. Cloud turned to a fierce red face burning with the fervent desire which can only be instilled in the true believers who imbibe a bottle of cognac before each and every dawn. St. Cloud was too deep in personal disintegration to hail this fellow sailor on a sea of booze. It was all he could manage to create a weak smile of greeting and let the Charter Boat captain belt out his standard line.

"This town is being ruint! Faggots and foreigners tryin to drive us Conchs into trailer camps!"

At last St. Cloud was inspired to summon insightful words to go along with the idiotic drunken smile he felt frozen on his face. "Great to see you again, Bubba-Bob."

"You can see the fruits and nuts skippin all around the island in loafers with no socks!" Bubba-Bob pushed himself back two steps from the bar, spread his feet out and stomped them solidly on the floor. "Lookit this!" Bubba-Bob jerked his fish-gut–stained khaki trousers high off his ankles. "White socks! Real men wear white socks! *Fishin* men wear white socks!"

"High fashion and social sobriety." St. Cloud looked approvingly at the white socks. "That's what you and I represent, sartorial splendor in the turtle grass. The last smart but fashionable holdouts."

"Goddamn right!" Bubba-Bob dropped his trousers and cocked his head defiantly at the unseen sockless hordes about to crash the doors and invade this early morning moment when he was on the verge of hitting someone. "You want a drink?"

St. Cloud crossed his sockless feet beneath the lower rung of the barstool and hoped for the best. "Always a pleasure."

"Angelica! Again for my best bubba!" Bubba-Bob threw an arm around St. Cloud with the fervor of a lifeguard pulling a drowning man to shore. *"Salud!"* He slammed the glass Angelica refilled into St. Cloud's full glass and drank with a hearty gurgle. "Yes sir, you are my bubba. You helped me out once, professor. A bubba never forgets."

"Never?" St. Cloud raised his glass in brief contemplation before emptying it.

"But this town!" Bubba-Bob banged his empty glass down, no amount of alcohol could derail his one-track mind. "This town is finished. I remember this town when wood boats weren't made of fiberglass and pussy was cunt."

"Great memories."

"Hey! You still sniffing around that little girl who works in your wife's parrot store? You want to get women? I'll tell you how to get women. Same way my daddy taught me how to get fish. A good fisherman is not lucky. A good fisherman finds the fish who are *unlucky*. What you've got to find is a woman unlucky enough to end up with an asshole like you."

St. Cloud weighed this logic carefully, smacked his lips in contemplation, then decided to go for it hook, line and sinker, but before he could Brogan leaned around in front of him, staring Bubba-Bob in the face.

The thick gold earring pierced through Brogan's right earlobe throbbed with the shadowed blade reflection from the twirling overhead fan. "My brother says Central America is like a rat without a head." Brogan's words flew from his mouth into the whir of the fan blades. "My brother says everybody down there is running around like rats without heads."

4

IF A MAN wants to get up in the morning he does not drink himself into oblivion the night before. Obviously St. Cloud had not wanted to get up. It was too early in the morning for him to be at the Star of Cuba laundromat, deep into a fifth cup of *buche* as he watched the clothes of strangers crash around behind portholes of scratched glass on dryer doors. At least something was on its way to being dried, if not purified. The machine heat from groaning washers and dryers made the humid day even more unbearable. Why was it the best *buche* shops in town seemed to be in abandoned gas stations turned into laundromats? To get to the source of *buche* in this laundromat St. Cloud had to walk the length of the moldy concrete building, past rows of machines, where a slot had been cut through the wall. A smiling Cuban woman on the other side of the slot cheerfully squeezed from steam-hissing steel nozzles a caffeine nectar to jangle the nerves and propel the timid. Hot liquid in a hot room in a hot town.

Justo nudged St. Cloud, puckered his lips and swigged his seventh *buche* of the morning. "One hour, *una hora*, I want you at the courthouse. The kid's life could depend on it. You're not there it's your hung-over college-educated ass that will be on the line."

"Okay, so I missed the arraignment earlier this morning. You going to have the judge empower you to jail the court-appointed interpreter for contempt?"

"Not a bad idea. You and Voltaire in the same cell. That way I've got the two of you together and I won't have to go searching every bar in town to find you."

"Voltaire's the boy's name?" St. Cloud squinted into heat ascending thick as a tropical mist from clothes being folded at long tables by chattering Cuban housewives, none of the women over twenty-five, each dressed as if ready to run away to Miami, high heels and brightly painted fingernails, tight pants and careful white ankles, a roomful of passion thrilling to the *buches* they sipped to fuel their insouciant chatter. St. Cloud liked their style, among other things. These sultry beauties turned the drudgery of their daily lives into a full-dress operatic rehearsal of jealousy and hate, bartering back and forth a currency of ever changing value, gossip.

"That's the kid's name alright, Voltaire Tincourette. Speaks only that Haitian *paysan* dialect you heard on the boat." Justo pursed his lips at another hot cup of *buche*, looking at St. Cloud across the cup's rim. "Can't understand a thing Voltaire says, except that he's scared as hell."

"Voltaire." St. Cloud spoke the name as if it were a code that would release him from the reality of his own life, allow him to walk through the mist of the laundromat and invite all the lively Latin beauties up to the pink palaces of Miami. He wondered which one of their husbands would have a knife up his heart before he made it past the greyhound dog track at the edge of town. "Those French colonialists really had a sense of humor, naming their slaves after philosophers. Maybe that's what they really thought the philosopher's role was, verbal piecework for the intellectual glory of the race."

"You've got a verbal piece of work cut out for you this afternoon in the courtroom. Don't make me come looking for you again or I'm going to let the husbands of these fine married ladies know what's going on in that diseased mind of yours." Justo laughed and slapped his broad chest, walking into the mist of steaming stacks of clothes. The young women stopped their chattering, glancing at him respectfully with an unconscious slight bow. Justo wagged a finger playfully at them before disappearing through the door. *"Di tu secreto a tu amiga y seras su cautivo."* Tell your secrets to a friend and you will always be her prisoner.

St. Cloud still had some time before he had to present himself hung over and bleary-eyed at the courthouse. He winked at the chattering housewives. They had no reason to show him the respect they showed Justo, they acted as if he were nothing more than an unfolded stack of baby diapers. St. Cloud strolled down the aisle of groaning machines, leaving behind a bevy of slippery tongues and the smoking embarrassment of his shabby fantasy. He opened the door of the laundromat onto the normal high-noon heat, which had blasted all but mad dogs and tourists off the streets. St. Cloud set off sailing down the sidewalk under full *buche* steam. Sweat beaded around the inside rim of his faded salt-stained sailing cap; from behind his black-as-sin sunglasses the world was looking pretty perky, everything clear as a ship's bell. Maybe a line of remembered poetry would come today, had to stay alert in case it slanted at him from around the corner of a freshly lime-color painted Conch house, or came swinging down out of the sun, erupting quick as a Caribbean waterspout in the middle of the rutted street. Just couldn't be too careful when a line of forgotten poetry was out there on the loose, somebody had to stay awake for it. St. Cloud appointed himself the sleeper with a watchful eye, but so many distractions, like a carload of young Cuban housewives, finally unshackled, freed from macho greed of overbearing husbands, a carload of uncorked female Latin sizzle zooming over the Seven Mile Bridge headed to high-rise palaces of pink Miami, brightly painted toenails tapping to a zingy tropical beat, sweat on gold crucifixes swinging between breasts. Why did young Cuban women have such careful white ankles? The cocked concrete finger of the Seven Mile Bridge was such a man-made marvel it could be seen by the Space Shuttle crew two hundred miles overhead, in earthly orbit as St. Cloud shuffled along the cracked sidewalk. All manner of things were balanced in the heavens. A perfect line of poetry could fall to earth like a burning comet or a scuttled Space Shuttle, a mundane-bound metaphoric spin in a topsy-turvy tailwind, ending in so much cosmic dust. St. Cloud had to stand guard for its coming. Why do Cuban women smell like burst pomegranates when they sweat, ruby dark fruit beyond perfume, a very good moment to inhale papaya passion and mango persuasion, take one last breath and die a little bit happy. Perfect ankles in an imperfect world. It could be worse.

ST. CLOUD opened the front door of the bird shop, stepping into air-conditioned air beaten by colorful tropical wings accompanied by squawks and shrills announcing his male intrusion. He stood within a cave of steel cages, trying to adjust to a sudden thirty degree temperature drop and cool overhead fluorescent lights casting an iridescent glow over red-bellied macaws, plum-headed parakeets and suspicious Aztec conures. He wondered where *she* was amongst all this exotic plumage. Got to be somewhere in this fine-feathered sideshow. Talk about a perfect line of poetry, *she* was a singing sonnet, a bluebell on a glacier mountainside, clearly a no-vacancy at the Heartbreak Hotel item, just one look and you could kiss yourself good-bye in the mirror. *She* was a one-way ticket to Lonely Street. Where was *she?* Always have to stand guard, somebody had to stay awake for it, don't know when it's going to show up, what form it will take, what one wouldn't do for just one perfect line of the stuff, search out that fateful potential moment which can offer a lifetime of unrequited love, or a last train to oblivion. All aboard.

"Can I help y'all?"

It was her. Can you save me is more like it, St. Cloud thought. She was here. The perfect line embodied in perfect form. "Yes . . . you . . . ah . . . can," he lied. "I was looking for Evelyn." How can anybody have a voice like hers, every syllable drawn out slowly, writ large with the point of a sharpened stick in her native red Georgian dust. St. Cloud followed her voice down a row of cages filled with the fowl life of preening peach-faced lovebirds and jabbering orange-chinned parakeets. He came face to face with her seated behind a secretary's desk. She looked up at him from a newspaper folded to the want-ads section, a white blouse buttoned at her neck. How seriously she took her job, only a twenty-year-old can be that serious, never again. She shifted ever so slightly, an ill-at-ease, self-conscious breeze. She wasn't used to being in such a position of authority, left on the business side of a desk to deal with the public, responsible. Even with the shield of his sunglasses St. Cloud still had to blink to bring her into focus. So much white. The starched ruffled blouse blurred the air around her, paled the pure green of her eyes.

"Evelyn stepped out but y'all welcome to wait."

The word *y'all* brought her into focus. She sent the word flying, like a yacht in a squall. Probably the closest thing St. Cloud would hear to poetry that day, a sound of southern female antiquity. He was afraid to remove his sunglasses for fear she would see the far from clothed truth in his eyes and call the cops or pull out a gun and plug him dead. Her syllables reverberated in his brain. It wasn't at all what she said, but the source from which she spoke. Syllables with the slow hiss of summer rain hitting red-clay earth on a deserted country road. Thank God Evelyn wasn't here. St. Cloud didn't trust Evelyn with this girl. Who would? He wouldn't trust anyone around such a cool cookie, such a sublime southern vamp. His desire for this young woman made him feel like a fool. It takes a fool to love like a fool.

She spoke again. He stood with a dumb grin on his face listening to a hiss of summer rain. The brief downpour of syllables was followed by a slow breeze pushing between leaves, or was it the air-conditioner flapping her newspaper, a breeze rustling verbs, gentle as wind chimes carrying away leisurely consonants to a whisper, ghost speech of invisible inflections. He wanted to put his lips to hers, capture the ancient ghost of invisible speech, but first he had to disarm this woman who measured the emotions of life with such a different scale. If he understood his southern women correctly he knew the unconscious provocative pout of the red lips before him could swiftly turn into the fatal snake kiss of a swamp cottonmouth.

"Are y'all alright? I said Evelyn's not he'yah."

"Yes . . . ah, I heard you. Just thinking . . . thinking I've been in here four or five times and you always look at me the same way."

"How's that?" Soft rain again, kicking up dust.

"Like you've never seen me before. Right now, you don't seem to be so much looking at me as through me."

"I'm sorry." The green eyes seemed to take him in for the first time, but in an awkward way, the hands of a blind person reaching out to a voice in the darkness. "I really didn't mean to be rude or asleep or anything." Her lips relaxed into a queer smile. "Some people say I'm asleep all the time. But no . . ." The queer smile puckered with embarrassment. "That's not it at all. I'm really right here all the time. Didn't mean to be rude. Y'all are Evelyn's husband, aren't y'all?"

"Sort of."

"What do you mean?" The queer smile returned.

"The divorce isn't final yet."

"Sorry." The smile disappeared. She seemed on a sudden point of sadness. "I didn't mean it to sound that way, that I'm sorry you aren't divorced. I meant I'm sorry, you know, about the whole thing."

No, St. Cloud didn't know. He didn't understand the whole thing well enough to be sorry about it. The fact that Evelyn and her girlfriend managed this bird store together, two sapphic birds in paradise, was she sorry about that, or was she sorry about the fact he still had some unaccountable powerful attraction to his wife and prowled around after her in night gardens like a lurking romeo? Maybe she was sorry he was such a wreck, a nearly twice-her-age man diminished to not much more than a befuddled St. Bernard trying to keep his eyes off of a great feast. It could be she was just plain sorry he was an "older man" radiating a frightening intensity he himself didn't even understand. Who's sorry now?

"I'm sorry too." St. Cloud sat on the edge of the desk, perched with the same unnaturalness as the red-breasted toucan clinging to an aluminum imitation tree trunk planted in the back corner of the store. The toucan fish-eyed him as it scissored sunflower seeds in an immense hooked beak. It takes a fool to love like a fool. If this was going to work, and he was going to defang this southern cottonmouth so she wouldn't strike him, he had to try his entire bag of tricks. Otherwise he would appear to be the one thing that would spook her in the opposite direction, a threatening fool.

"Well . . ." She smiled the queer smile and pulled the folded newspaper close to her body, as if it was a lead apron to protect her from unwanted radiation. "I guess I can't sell you a Moluccan cockatoo today?"

"How about showing me one anyway?" St. Cloud took trick number one from his bag. "I'm very interested in rare birds. You know I named this place ten years ago."

She rose from behind the desk and let the newspaper fall away. There was something brazen about her body, which she held in a very chaste way. All white. She dressed all in white, even the skirt which went straight to her knees. She could be taken anywhere, from some southern cracker capital to a one-gas-station backwater bayou town. She would always be queen of peaches, heart of magnolia. Beyond the cloud of white she dressed in was the sameness of the skin, a flawless disconcerting color. She didn't have a full-bodied tan like those sported so boldly by the island girls lying barebreasted on the beach, rather a hue glowed from within, as if her skin had been anointed with the essence of hickory oil, an amber gleam. She walked between the steel cages, the brown hair cut at her shoulders flew away from her face as she turned back to fix him with the queer smile. "You're the one who gave this store its funny name? People always come in and ask me what it means, 'Kiss My Linda.' They ask me what kind of place this is."

"I think 'Kiss My Linda' is kind of catchy, has a certain spin."

"So?" She slid the door of a high conical cage open and offered the salmon-crested cockatoo inside her slender finger to hop onto from its perch. "What does it mean?"

"Kiss my pretty. But then it could mean kiss my pretty little whatever. That's what it really means. Evelyn asked me once what the whatever was, I told her she had the prettiest little whatever I ever kissed. It's a kind of private joke, because Evelyn never thought the store would make it. I told her if it didn't, well, people could then just kiss her pretty little whatever, the prophecy of the sign would have the last laugh."

The cockatoo swung onto her finger and she withdrew it from the cage. The bird hunched back its feathered shoulders and nibbled at her lips and ears. A low chatter of contentment ebbed from the fluffed creature's arched throat, swelling to a sustained high-pitched twill, exciting the surrounding caged birds to a clattering jungle chorus. "That's a cute story." She spoke her words calmly into the raucous activity around her.

She was from the land of cute. Cute this, cute that, cute love, cute murder, it was all cute, and all so deceiving. St. Cloud wondered why he had such an unaccountable attraction to this woman who had entered his life so recently. She started turning up late at night drifting alone along Duval Street, protected by a serene beauty which scared off the usual needle-boy thugs and hot-rod Navy romeos cruising the bars for someone to write home about. She was after the music, floating from bar to bar where rock-and-roll bands and solo guitar pickers plied their trade to locals and tourists listening for a lyric to hang a bad love affair on. Seldom was she approached, although she was obviously the answer to most men's desire, but packaged in such bright, fleshy reality she prevailed and intimidated. She dressed at night in a loose white cotton dress leaving everything to be desired open to the observing mind's eye. When approached there were always a few words, a slight laugh and tilt of her head, sending the suitor off in an awkward dogtrot, humbled to be allowed the privilege of awaiting his turn at the back of some invisible line that wound out the door, along the neon-lit one-mile length of Duval Street stretching end to end from the Atlantic Ocean on one side to the Gulf of Mexico on the other. Sometimes she was ready to dance, so one of the brave few who approached her was allowed to escort her into the sweating crowd gyrating before the electrical blast of notes from refrigerator-size loudspeakers. She never looked at her partner, the queer smile on her face fixed far away, as if dancing with someone thousands of miles distant. She stayed cool and irresistible, no matter how hot the crowded room or how robustly the randy sideshow suitors hooted their lust. St. Cloud had never seen anything like it, and he thought he had seen things never seen by man before, drunk or drugged. She was one cute player, and if he was going to win he had to play her cute game.

"Thanks for your earlier offer of selling me a bird, but I don't need one." St. Cloud summoned up what he thought was his most beguiling smile. "Maybe I can buy this fellow for you." He pointed at the cockatoo balanced on her finger. "You seem to create quite an effect on him. Seems a pity to keep the two of you separated."

The cockatoo craned its neck, its salmon-crested head feathers stiffening into a brilliant crown. She stroked the cockatoo's outstretched neck. "I'm not so special. This little guy is just a born lover. He's been handled by Evelyn ever since he got out of the egg. Besides, I'm really a dog person. I'm saving up to buy a dog."

St. Cloud pulled another trick from his bag. "That's what you were looking for in the want ads when I came in?"

"How did y'all know that? I found one just today up past Little Torch Key. Someone has a litter and I called and said I'd put down a twenty-five-dollar deposit. They only have one left and want four hundred dollars for him. I don't know if they'll hold him until I can get all the money."

"Evelyn's very good about those things, why don't you ask her to give you an advance?"

"No." She stopped stroking the cockatoo and quickly placed it back in its cage, sliding the door closed with a loud clack. "I'll earn my own money." The queer little smile left her lips. She turned and walked back toward the desk.

St. Cloud now knew what it felt like to be dismissed by her like one of the boys at the bar waiting for a dance, sent to the back of the line. He needed to get another trick out of his bag. She was moving away from him, down the row of cages. Then he understood. The fluid way she moved, as if gravity was an irritant which had to be pushed aside, the sway of hips, the slant of rounded calves, the forward tilt of her shoulders, all of it combined did not add up to the somnolent step of a sleepwalker, but of someone walking underwater. He finally understood what the inexplicable attraction was, why he had to talk to her instead of just tracking her in his nocturnal wanderings. She sat at the desk and looked back at him, the blur of her eyes sea green. Now he knew. She was the woman on the underwater reef in his recurring dream, submerged in Neptune's murky cobalt closet, a wealth of seaweed wreathed in her hair, white body pierced by fish slipping through thighs. He moved toward her between the cages with a newly acquired heaviness in his legs. Not easy for a bull to swim beneath the sea.

St. Cloud made his way to the desk, clung to its edge like it was the side of a life raft. He struggled to get one more trick out of his bag before he drowned. "Can I see you? I must see you. I must talk to you."

"Y'all are seeing me." She straightened in her chair, pushing away from the desperate pleading in his voice.

"I don't mean here. I mean after you get off. I mean tonight. Where do you live?"

"I live on a lane called love." She observed him warily, the fluorescent tubes above cast a cool light over her aloofness. "Do y'all know Love Lane?" She threw the question out unexpectedly, as if sensing the drowning man before her would go under without something to buoy him up. "It does sound corny, but it's true. Love Lane's behind the library. Key West is filled with funny little lanes with cute names."

St. Cloud leaned toward her from the edge of the desk, then pulled back, afraid of getting in over his head. The breeze of the air-conditioner touched up the fall of her brown hair, exposing the sides of her face, slender bones pressed an indentation like inverted quarters of the moon at the top of each cheek. "I live on Catholic Lane." He spoke the words slowly, struggling to put more distance between himself and the green drowning pools. "If we can only get the two lanes end to end we could make one long street of Christian Love."

She wasn't buying his clumsy trickery. "When does a lane become a street? I moved down here from Georgia, up there we have Main Streets and Second Avenues. No matter how small the town, or little the streets get, they never become lanes."

"A lane becomes a street when a pier becomes a bridge."

"What do y'all mean by that?"

"James Joyce, a writer, said a pier is a disappointed bridge."

"I'm not disappointed with my little lane. I'm very happy there. A place of my own where I come and go as I please. I hope my little lane never becomes a street, that would be too busy and complicated. I don't want complications on my lane."

"Even if it becomes a street of brotherly love and kisses?"

"I've got all the love and kisses I need."

"Who are you saving them for?"

"Why . . . my dog, of course." The surface of her green eyes rippled with ridicule at his awkward approach. "I'm saving up forty dollars a week to buy him."

"Maybe your dog will be the adventurous type and want to take a walk on the wild side of Catholic Lane?"

Her eyes went cold. He had gone too far. The green water froze, isolating him in a moment of dead silence, the silence preceding the power of a solid ice surface cracking with a roar of swollen tension. "I'm very pleased with my life . . . my . . . independence. When your divorce is final I'll see y'all."

"It's not that simple. Nothing is final or forever. Not divorce decrees, not eternal love."

"It is simple for me, and that's final."

A sudden electrical surge flickered the fluorescent tubes overhead, pouring cool blue light down upon her. The pools of her eyes widened, the blue light exposing at the depths of each a translucent pearl, mirrored souls of ancient oysters. Madonna on the reef.

St. Cloud tried his last and most obvious trick. "At least you can tell me your name?"

"Lila."

Not easy for a bull to swim beneath the sea.

5

O TE ME TANGUES, St. Cloud. Don't let me down." Justo nervously rubbed the gold wishbone hung from the thick chain around his neck. He peered expectantly down the long dimly lit corridor at the double-glass doors of the courthouse entrance closed against the brilliant afternoon sunlight outside. "C'mon, c'mon, c'mon. Where is Voltaire?" Justo turned back to St. Cloud. "Look, I can't get the kid to say much, what he does say I can barely make out its meaning. You've got to break through to him. Voltaire's scared, doesn't trust any of us. Take him into a side room here and win him over, understand? Then we go in to see the judge. At least we get the kid to answer rudimentary questions. Voltaire doesn't answer any questions the judge can fill in all the blanks. The judge fills in the blanks and Voltaire gets a free ride up to the Everglades detention camp, then is deported straight back to Haiti. *Como te cae eso?* How do you like that?"

"Don't like it. Voltaire's too scared to talk. You can't make a three-legged dog walk straight by cutting off its tail."

"That's exactly right." Justo slapped St. Cloud grandly on the back. "I want you to unscare him. Grow him another leg so he can run away from this whole mess."

"Maybe? Might not be possible. You found out yet what part of Haiti he's from?"

"All he does is point on a map, puts a finger on the lower of those two peninsulas that stick out westerly like crab pinchers from the main body of the island."

"Cibao Mountains?"

"That's it."

"Haiti means high land in Indian. Voltaire's from the highest part of the poorest country in the Hemisphere. Gets to be over six thousand feet up there in those mountains, jungles been burned off, land overplanted a century ago, hardscrabble now. *Paysans* up there have really been isolated, more African than Haitian."

"*Grande* voodoo." Justo whistled softly beneath his breath, rubbing his gold bone.

"*Mucho mucho grande.* Very superstitious people. God only knows what goes on up in those remote mountains, and he's not telling." At this moment St. Cloud wished he had a lucky bone to believe in, anything to believe in.

"They're here!"

The double-glass doors of the entrance flew open, an armed deputy stepping in from harsh sunlight, behind him in handcuffs the slight black shadow of Voltaire, behind the shadow another armed deputy, all three eclipsing the sunlight as they moved down the dimly lit corridor.

St. Cloud wondered how much time he had to work this miracle Justo expected of him. He congratulated himself on having the foresight to bring along a pint of rum, maybe that would stop his body from shaking and shoot him full of confidence. His fingers clutched the neck of the bottle wrapped tightly in a paper bag. He wobbled with the fidgety fervor of an anarchist about to hurl a Molotov cocktail into the jaws of indecency. As Voltaire's thin shadow came into stark relief St. Cloud's fervor was replaced with contempt, contempt for his own meaningless life. Everybody betrays everybody sometime, but St. Cloud knew he had betrayed himself. He was the indecent one, and the handcuffed man-child standing before him, with scabbing wounds healing on a face scourged by starvation and sun, was too pure in his simple act of surviving to contend with.

Justo's voice brought St. Cloud back from the brink of self-loathing. "This is the prisoner. You've got one hour before a Public Defender's attorney gets here to take the prisoner to be arraigned."

"Can you remove his handcuffs?"

"The prisoner is charged with murder on the high seas. He's a very dangerous criminal."

"Maybe he'll be more willing to talk if he doesn't feel like a trapped animal. Besides, where's he going to go?"

"I'm glad you asked me that." Justo grinned. He nodded to one of the unsmiling deputies. "Release the prisoner and stand guard outside the door to this room behind us while the translator and prisoner have their conference. St. Cloud, you know what you have to do?"

"Yes. We've done it before, but it doesn't always work."

"It'll work." Justo rubbed his bone and opened the door behind him into a bare room with a table and two chairs. A boldface black-and-white clock on the wall with a long sweeping second hand served as the only decorative reminder of what the true issue of criminal court is about. *"No te me tangues."*

"Don't worry. I won't let you down."

"I know you won't." Justo slapped St. Cloud on the back with the bravado of a high-school football coach sending in his last bench warmer to save the big game. "By the way, at the end of the hour give the prisoner this." Justo handed St. Cloud an egg carton tightly bound with thick twine. "He'll need it."

St. Cloud watched Justo disappear down the long corridor and through the glare of glass doors at the courthouse entrance. He wanted to follow Justo into the sun, head for the closest bar to stop his body's trembling from fear and alcoholic craving. He reluctantly motioned Voltaire into the empty room, seating him beneath the clock's second hand as it swept past three o'clock. St. Cloud closed the door and punched in the button lock protruding from the knob. He sat quickly and peeled the bag from the neck of the rum bottle, swigging half a pint of amber liquid down in a swift gulp. He offered the bottle to Voltaire. Homesick syrup for the dispossessed. A dumb thing to do. St. Cloud knew the kid wouldn't touch it, would rather bite off the head of a rabid bat and drink its blood than accept anything from this white devil, this corrupt symbol of authority, this pathetic messenger from the land of the free. St. Cloud knew that was not what the boy saw. Voltaire saw power, authority, someone not to be trusted, someone who threatened his security and kept him imprisoned, kept him an indispensable cog in a system he couldn't comprehend. Then again, who could know what the kid really thought? St. Cloud knew he didn't, he just had to trust his instincts, keep his own guilt in the saddle and ride for a touchdown of understanding. Fifteen thousand just like Voltaire had been busted along the shores of Florida in the past year, from seaside Palm Beach mansions to coral beaches of the Keys. Who knew how many got through? Who knew how many drowned or died of exposure on the six-hundred-mile journey of open sea? St. Cloud took another drink. Who knew how those people on Voltaire's boat died? Who had the nightmare script? Who knew what this kid lived through, what horrors he had seen, if he understood his chances of being shipped up to the Everglades detention camp were better than even unless Justo pulled off his miracle? All Voltaire had left was his life, and that was shaved down to pathetic irony, for life to a *paysan* meant land. Land was not only life, but the fountainspring of dignity giving man the strength to rise above being a common animal, walk on two legs with pride. When torrential tropical rains came in small Haitian villages, washing farmed soil loose, eroding it down to rivers and into the sea, the *paysans* would say, "There goes our life." St. Cloud had heard their tales, had translated for hundreds of them. These were a people spun in a cocoon of misery. Like this boy before him, they still had an awesome sense of trust which allowed them to go forward. Courage in their language meant hard work. No matter how unspeakable the adversity, man-made or natural, no matter how inexorably the hardship river of tears washed the soil of life to the sea, as long as there was land there was hope. As long as there was hope there were families. This boy was guarded by all the saints and gods rubbing shoulders in the *hamforts*, the mystery houses, all summoned up to guard the *matelotes*, the shipmates on their final journey.

3:15. Time was running out. St. Cloud removed his sweat-soaked sailing cap and took another drink. He smiled and offered a hello to Voltaire. Nothing. He reached into the inside pocket of his one and only "court coat," a sun-faded blue and white seersucker affair once worn by smart leading men in B-movies of the forties. He fumbled a worn paperback book out of a pocket and placed it on the table. Would it work? It had before. He began hesitantly, reading in Creole learned twenty years before at the university. *"Le Petit Prince. This is the story of the Little Prince."* He didn't have to go too far with this. If it was going to work it would work by the end of chapter six. If not, then never. It was a dumb trick, but there was some magic in it. Magic was what St. Cloud most needed now. He would rather be reading the fierce lyric and metaphoric dazzle of Lorca or Neruda. It was painful to read this naive story. He must make it believable, make the boy believe. Was Voltaire listening? No sign of life on an otherwise smooth face crisscrossed with visible scars of sorrow, stoic. No trust in this room. Let the story work. This was a tale of two lost souls, two

travelers in the void who could teach each other in their similar sense
of loss and longing. This was a world where the distrust of the adult
crossed the trusting path of childhood:

> *I was more isolated than a shipwrecked sailor on a raft in the middle*
> *of the ocean. Thus can you imagine my amazement, at sunrise, when I*
> *was awakened by an odd little voice. It said, "If you please—draw me*
> *a sheep!"*

St. Cloud spoke the words of the book's adult narrator, a crashed
aviator stranded in a desert where his technology was rendered
useless, suddenly meeting a princely boy from a planet called Imagination. Was Voltaire buying it? No sign.

St. Cloud kept reading and thinking. The flashy soldierly uniform
of the small Prince was something Voltaire should be able to conjure,
it was a mockery of the swashbuckling military image modern-day
Haitian dictators so covetously preserved as they scattered clouds of
dollar bills from open-topped limousines to starving true believers; it
mocked as well those who put forth the saber-wielding philosophy of
boule kay, coupe tet, burn the houses, cut off the heads, which prevailed for
ten years of civil war before the 1804 independence of Haiti. Yes,
this Prince was an image of anarchic childhood innocence dressed in
the doom of his aspiration to be adult. Such a French story. How odd
it should take place in the Sahara Desert, another French-colonized
domain. And the story of Haiti, former slaves of the French, barely
surviving the illusion of freedom, ruled for generations by masters
of ceremony dressed in pomp of former French masters. No harsher
master than a former slave. Every master needs a dog, every dog a
bone.

St. Cloud swigged another mouthful of rum. The liquidity of his
thoughts drifted randomly between the lines of Saint-Exupéry's simple
allegory as the sound of his voice floated around the room:

> *As each day passed I would learn, in our talk, something about the*
> *little prince's planet, his departure from it, his journey. The infor-*
> *mation would come very slowly, as it might chance to fall from his*
> *thoughts. It was in this way that I heard, on the third day, about*
> *the catastrophe of the baobabs.*

Of course the baobabs: devils, false messiahs, dictators, Hitlers and Huns, Presidents for Life, totalitarian intolerance and moral intemperance dozing in the *"heart of the earth's darkness, until some one among them is seized with the desire to awaken."* The baobab begins as *"a charming little sprig"* and grows to split a planet in pieces. Where the Little Prince came from, *"the soil of that planet was infested with them."* Where Voltaire came from, the hardship river of tears flowed endlessly to the sea carrying the soil of life. Catastrophe of the baobabs.

3:30. Maybe it wasn't going to work. This time the magic would fail. St. Cloud was running out of rum and running out of time. A red flush rose to his face. He felt raw and hot, a piece of meat flung onto a fire. He felt a fool for wasting his time with this stuff. He should have tried another tack. What happened on Voltaire's boat? St. Cloud was too far into the story to stop and ask. He was drunk and his words slurred. What the hell was he doing here anyway? How did Justo get him into this? He could make all the money he wanted just interpreting for the legions of Latin American drug smugglers and TV-watching, lite beer–drinking wife beaters. He didn't need this, but he had it. The one thing consoling him was the thought that whenever he was all the way up shit creek without a paddle he could always get out and walk to shore. He walked to shore.

St. Cloud continued the story. Their story. The history of the world in a simple children's book. As he read he sensed he was growing dumber by the moment. His clumsy syllables tumbled over each other into the room:

Oh, little prince! Bit by bit I came to understand the secrets of your sad little life.

With belabored breath fueled by fumes of rum St. Cloud staggered on into chapter six. It was now or never. Just a half page to go. If the magic didn't work it was a trip up the Everglades, where the alligators would be the least of Voltaire's problems:

"I am very fond of sunsets. Come, let us go look at sunsets now." "But we must wait," I said. "Wait? For what?" "For the sunset. We must wait until it is time." "I am always thinking that I am at home!"

There it was, a gasp. St. Cloud looked up from the battered book into Voltaire's brown eyes filled with longing and pain, quick breaths heaving his thin shoulders back. Yes, my friend, St. Cloud wanted to say, you may feel for our little Prince here in the book, for he is you, and you are him. So far from home, so far from sunsets, always thinking the nightmare will end and you will awake at home. But your home *is* the nightmare, a planet split by baobab Presidents for Life, or worse:

Just so. Everybody knows that when it is noon in the United States the sun is setting over France. If you could fly to France in one minute, you could go straight into the sunset, right from noon. Unfortunately, France is too far away for that. But on your tiny planet, my little prince, all you need do is move your chair a few steps. You can see the day end and the twilight falling whenever you like . . .

Tears flowed in a silent stream from Voltaire. His lips, scabbed from his ordeal on the boat, quivered. He blinked, trying to dam the tears. He looked at St. Cloud for the answer to stop his quiet sobbing. St. Cloud continued reading, rum ringing in his head, forcing croaking words through a knot in his throat:

"One day," you said to me, "I saw the sunset forty-four times!" And a little later you added: "You know—one loves the sunset, when one is so sad . . ."

"Were you so sad, then?" I asked, "on the day of the forty-four sunsets?" But the little prince made no reply.

It is all magic in the jungle. St. Cloud pulled a kerchief from his seersucker coat and passed it across to Voltaire.

"Merci." The boy wiped roughly at his face, irritating the crisscross of sun-blistered scabs. *"Merci beaucoup."*

St. Cloud wanted to trade places with Voltaire. He clenched his teeth to suppress the emotion welling up through the rum-slowed throbbing in his veins. How much he desired to get this boy off the shark hook. He pushed the egg carton across the table and smiled, continuing to use his college-learned Creole. "Open it."

Voltaire fingered the carton with trembling hands. He pulled at the twine and stopped, looking to St. Cloud for encouragement. St. Cloud smiled. "Go on, don't fear." Voltaire broke the twine bindings, slowly raised the carton lid, tilting his head cautiously to one side to gain an advance glance at unknown contents, which could spring out with the force of a lion onto a lamb's back. He bent the lid all the way over. Eleven of the twelve hollowed indentations intended for eggs were empty. Nestled in one hollow was a small pigskin bag bound by overlays of braided goat hair and knotted to an oil-stained leather necklace. An *ouanga* bag. The same bag St. Cloud noticed Justo pick up when it dropped from Voltaire's fist while he was being lifted onto the paramedics' stretcher at Mallory Dock. Had anyone else seen Justo take the bag? St. Cloud never mentioned that he had seen it. Justo had his way of operating. There were things on the island Justo knew that should never be explained, should always remain hidden, that's why they were hidden. People know better than to disturb an accommodation that has taken generations to establish. Such is the foundation of civilization, an accommodation between opposing forces, good and evil, fear and power. Don't rock the boat. Go your own way. Don't look back, you won't like what you see. This was Justo's philosophy as St. Cloud understood it, so he never mentioned the bag.

Voltaire carefully lifted the *ouanga* bag from the carton, unraveled its leather necklace, looping it over his head so the knotted bag came to rest against bare skin exposed in the V at the top of his unbuttoned shirt. For the first time he smiled. A sense of calm came into him. What was in the bag? St. Cloud wondered. Dove hearts? Bat teeth? Lizard jaws? Crow feathers? Cat's eye? Lucky stones? Snake bones? Anything for some fast luck in the jungle. St. Cloud would probably never know the contents. All he knew was he had to take what he could get. And what he could get from Voltaire was flying fish.

In Voltaire's village people were starving, throughout the mountains people were starving, yet the Tonton Macoutes still came at night searching for the *comoquin*, those suspected of belonging to the club of traitors speaking badly of the government, the spies and cowards who plotted escape to America. The Tontons came with trucks grinding through the night, smashing doors and leading men away in ropes. One night they took Voltaire's father, one night they took Voltaire himself. His hands tied, he stood with head bowed among many men in a truck bumping for miles along a darkened road until stopping, each man pulled out at gunpoint and placed in one of four lines before the stone wall of a prison, waiting to be escorted in and interviewed by the chief Tonton. A few men came back out of the prison and were herded into the truck, most did not return. Before dawn those still left in line began to wail with fear. When Voltaire was taken before the chief he could not stop wailing. "What's wrong with you," the chief demanded. "You have no right to scream like this! I want you to go home and shut your mouth! I never want to hear from you again!" When the truck was ready to go only eight men were in it. The truck swung around behind the prison, rumbled down a cobblestone road, past the stench of the prison dump, scattering surprised dogs that tore at a fresh pile of beaten men with hands bound by ropes. Many on the truck recognized brothers, fathers, uncles, friends. No one made a sound.

Voltaire's mother once journeyed to the prison where her husband was kept, then she was followed by Tontons in a jeep for the five hours it took her to walk back to her village. The Tontons asked questions of her neighbors, people stopped talking to her. What the Tontons did not know was she had no heart to return to the prison, what she saw there was not the man she loved, but a tortured body covered with blood, the face beaten beyond a familiar bone, the mind wandering around with no one to control it, a stream of jibberish flowing from smashed lips. Voltaire's mother later heard the man she loved died breathing blood into his brain. That is when her brother, Romulus, made his decision to escape by boat to America. Romulus did not have the two thousand dollars to pay the smugglers for the trip, but when he got to America the smugglers promised he could earn the money and send it back, he could earn the money to support his seven children too, and send it back. Romulus' boat lost its way. The smugglers had promised there would be someone on board to navigate, but there were only simple *paysans* who understood how to plant by a full moon and harvest beneath a bright sun, they knew nothing of how nocturnal celestial lights could point a boat right. Romulus' boat came into Miami Beach on a cloudless summer day, past speeding yachts and waving water-skiers. Gleaming glass buildings towered in a wall along the sand, cars roared along a palm-fringed boulevard, the loud beat of rhythmic radio music was in the air and a line of police vans was parked, waiting with uniformed policemen watching from behind sunglasses as the Haitian boat drifted aimlessly to shore. There was no turning back, nowhere to run, the policemen had rifles and dogs. The people of Romulus' boat jumped overboard into warm surf, their few belongings bundled and balanced on their heads as they walked among the greased sunbathers of the crowded beach and threw up their hands in surrender.

Romulus was taken to the detention center in the Everglades, held for two months, then deported back to Haiti. The Tontons put him in Fort Dimanche prison outside of Port-au-Prince. Most men do not leave Fort Dimanche; if they are not beaten to death they die of tuberculosis, dysentery, or having the blood sucked from them by scores of vermin. Romulus survived six months and made it back to his family in the village high in the Cibao Mountains, his disfigured body weighing less than eighty-five pounds. Romulus needed all the security he could get to protect him. Romulus needed *le bon Dieu*, Jesus Christ, he needed Maît' Carrefour, the master who stands guard at earthly gates and keeps a protective eye on homes, roads and paths, he needed a thousand *ouangas* to preserve him from the smugglers, whom he still owed two thousand dollars. Because Romulus had taken the sea journey to America and was sent back without money he was made an example of by the smugglers, an example used often, an example no amount of security could protect a man from. Romulus was chopped like a pig, screaming in the night as the goats made milk, axes dismembering his body. You don't pay the price, you pay with your life.

So it was now to Voltaire, the oldest, to support his mother, and his Uncle Romulus' family of seven children. The only way to do this was to leave the village and journey to where the jobs were. Voltaire went to the smugglers and promised to pay for his passage once he got to America. Unlike Romulus' boat, Voltaire's sailed immediately into trouble, horrible trouble. Before Voltaire's journey his mother took him to a mystery house at the crossroads for a *Wete Mo Na Dlo*, a ceremony of fishing a deceased one's soul from the water. But no one Voltaire knew had died in water. He did not understand why his mother had taken him to the ceremony. On Voltaire's first night out the boat caught the Caribbean current toward Cuba, a full moon silvered the sea and fish began to fly, everywhere sparkling wings over water. The people became very quiet and huddled low beneath the gunwale, for they knew that to be struck by a flying fish is to die. A flying fish is the arrow shot from the ghostly bow of a deceased one. The fish flew and flew. No one could hide. Ghost arrows never miss their intended mark.

4:00. Loud knocking at the door brought St. Cloud up from

Voltaire's vision of flying fish. Voltaire stopped talking, looking at the door with apprehension. You don't pay the price, you pay with your life. St. Cloud rose and stretched a trembling hand across the table, not so much to help Voltaire up, but to support him in his ordeal.

"Come, my philosopher friend. Judgment, not justice, awaits you."

6

HANDSOMEMOST Jimmy had one dead greyhound and was about to pop number two. He had to wait for another airplane to take off so nobody could hear his next gunshot. Handsomemost liked the thought that the people in the last airplane, lifting up and off at the end of the runway where the land gave itself back to swampy mangrove marsh, had no idea he was down below taking one more ugly dog out of the race. He could have taken the greyhounds to the city dump to pop them, but that would have meant a long drive with dogs drooling all over the upholstery of his expensive Japanese sports car. The other thing about the dump was the sea gulls, hordes of sea gulls swooping around in thermal gusts over the mountain of garbage that had grown to become the highest man-made point in the Florida Keys. Those sea gulls gave Handsomemost the jitters, ruined his sense of romance and style. Style was what Handsomemost Jimmy prided himself most in, besides, it stank out there at the dump. Handsomemost liked to think he had style in spades. He wasn't just a scammer gambler from the dark side of town. He had worked his way up to a cultivated image. Handsomemost slithered around in tailored black slacks, and no matter what the weather, he made certain their crease never gave out. He sported black silk shirts, kept them open way down the front to display a necklace of two-fist-size doubloons fetched up from one of the Spanish wrecks off the reef. The doubloons were real, not the imitations sold around town to tourist coin collectors, but real gold that glittered like the gold of Handsomemost's heavy bracelet watch. Handsomemost was not to be trifled with. He liked white powder and white women, bought and sold both, used and abused both, it was a man's right. Handsomemost bought and sold racehorses and racing dogs, airplanes and powerboats. He didn't like to be trifled with. He was not one of the local white-boy scammers who figured if he wore a tight Hawaiian shirt, a gold earring, had a visible tattoo and brought a load of marijuana up from Belize, he was a pirate. What that kind of white boy was was just a little less dumb than the dumb narcs who couldn't catch him. The worst thing about white scammers like that was they had bad taste in music, not even bad, terrible. Handsomemost liked to think he was black because he was smart, not the other way around. He liked to romance a dishonest wage from an honest night's work. He prided himself that he was the type of scammer who would shoot a man for a dime and give him change.

Handsomemost was all these things plus impatient. He was growing more impatient by the moment waiting on another plane headed for Miami to lift off with a roar from the end of the short runway. The two greyhounds he held on tight leashes were also impatient, frightened and confused, wanting to run the racetrack, waiting for another shot to be fired from Handsomemost's gun, not knowing the shot would be intended for one of them. Handsomemost kicked the tip of a shiny black alligator-skin loafer at the gravelly limestone which went out under him in all directions between shallow salt ponds into mangrove scrub. Earlier, there had been a kid on a bicycle right when Handsomemost popped the first greyhound. The kid was about twelve and white, he came around a stand of scrub on the gravel path and skidded the bike tires to a quick stop when he saw Handsomemost with his gun pointed at one of the greyhounds tied to the spindled roots of a mangrove. The white kid spun away in a hurry of dust as the groan of a plane lifting off skimmed overhead. What Handsomemost didn't need now was cops, not that cops bothered him. He knew most of the cops had things to trade, things cops liked to know about other people, people whom Handsomemost was not so interested in seeing stay in business. Some of these other people had good-looking wives, even if they were Cuban. Handsomemost was a white-woman man himself. He liked his women snowy as milk, or in a pinch, like coffee, hot and black. When things really heated up he had milk with his coffee. On the subject of women Handsomemost had his particulars, which included no Cubans. But every day could carry an exception to the rule. Handsomemost wasn't so stupid as not to figure a boy goes to school to learn the rules so he can break them. Handsomemost didn't have much use for Cuban men either, thought they were excitable and had bad taste in music, all those jarring happy notes, pee-pee guitars and upbeat skinny voices, uncool. Far as Handsome- most was concerned Cubans could be kept in a deep-freeze for the rest of their lives and still wouldn't come out cool, or know anything about music. The Cubans' toe-tapping sense of rhythm had all the elegance of a kangaroo in heat. Handsomemost considered himself a man of consummate style and innate rhythmic grace, he wouldn't be caught dead eating pig, uncool. The problem with the Cubans was they liked to eat pig more than chicken. How can someone who does that be taken seriously? A pig is a dirty barnyard grunt, a chicken is a clean-feathered pebble pecker with fat thighs and succulent breasts. It wasn't that Handsomemost ate chicken, he hated it, reminded him of his childhood. He was a steak and lobster man at all the finest restaurants in town, he was a big spender and a big tipper. If a bartender gave him seven dollars' change from a ten-dollar bill Handsomemost was insulted, and often as not, even if he was in a fancy restaurant, screamed at the bartender: What am I going to do with this skimpy shit! Can't even make a phone call with it! You keep it! Handsomemost did not like to be insulted, he made big money, measured his life out in one-hundred-dollar bills. He didn't like white bartenders who thought he needed chicken feed change, or smartass scammers in tight Hawaiian shirts like Karl Dean. Karl Dean trifled and now he was history.

Handsomemost could hear one of the prop jets warming up out on the runway. The high-pitched engine whine made the dogs even more skittery. He stroked their sleek arched bony bodies to calm them, then walked them across to the third dog, lying where it fell from a bullet in the head. The two greyhounds sniffed their former running mate, their tails arrowed straight and trembling. Handsome- most tied the dogs to a red-bristling root of mangrove, paced ten steps back and took up his position. Maybe he could pop both burnt- out bunny chasers with two quick shots; one per plane was too slow. Handsomemost didn't have all day for this stuff. It was seven in the morning and he hadn't been to bed. He had been at the dog races the night before, then racing around town doing his usual business till dawn. A man needs a day's rest for a night's work.

Handsomemost raised his gun, steadied it with both hands to take the magnum force of its kickback. The sound of the plane was coming closer faster. He took aim at the greyhound on the right, it stood poised and alert, about to jump from the gate and race the track, eyes expectant and excited as the groan of the overpassing plane was directly above; the sudden force of a bullet smashed into the long pointed face with a shattering impact, kicking the animal off its feet, snapping the body straight out to the end of the leash before it dropped motionless. The other greyhound jumped, confusing the gunshot with the starting bell of a race, figuring its fallen companion had tripped up its post start. The greyhound lunged against its leash. The chained restraint of its neck collar caused it to rear up and flip over. The overhead plane was pulling away. Handsomemost was swearing under his breath. He couldn't get a bead on the last greyhound at the end of the leash as it leapt to its feet, not wanting to be left behind by the invisible racing pack. Goddamn, Handsomemost growled, firing two quick shots which kicked up puffs of white limestone gravel around the bouncing greyhound. Bitch!

"Put the gun down!" The words bellowed above the roaring engine thrust of the departing plane.

Handsomemost did not lower his gun. He turned his body slowly toward the words behind him. He did not like to be told what to do, he did not like to be messed with, especially when he had a loaded gun.

"I'm not going to repeat it! Put the gun down!"

Handsomemost continued to turn his head slowly, until a figure in the bend of the path behind him came clearly into view. Handsomemost stopped turning. The gun held outstretched in both hands before him pointed directly at the figure.

"Target practice is over!"

Handsomemost hated cops, they were bad for business. Especially smart cops who knew the value of accommodation, the cops who would let you run ahead of the pack and not try to trip your pace, figuring sooner or later you would go too fast and throw your stride, trip up. No, Handsomemost didn't like cute cops who liked to mess with minds. He liked cops who either wanted to bust your face wide open or throw a bribe. That was easier and better for business. White cops were predictable, he always knew which card to pull out of his sleeve with them. Cuban cops were unpredictable, like mad dogs. Cuban cops won't let go until they get the bone, especially the one Handsomemost had an unobstructed view of not more than thirty yards away. He could see the bump of the cop's automatic tucked beneath the waistband of his pants, poking the front of his loose *guayabera*. Handsomemost couldn't figure this guy out, half African, half Cuban. He knew this guy all his life and still didn't know if he could trust his African half. Flip a coin, any fool's guess which side this guy was going to come down on. Handsomemost felt his finger on the trigger of the gun he had aimed at this guy he didn't trust. Damn kid on the bike must have called the cops. One thing Handsomemost didn't like was to gamble against the house, he was a short-odds man. Still, there was an undeniable urge to blow the Cuban part of this guy away, splatter his black beans and yellow rice across the mangroves, whatever was left could be trusted. Ah, for the simple life. Handsomemost lowered his gun and shouted, "These here be run-out dogs! Got no gas left to chase the metal bunny round the track! These here old puppies be more better off bein sand-flea butter!"

Justo walked toward Handsomemost, the force of his heavy body digging the soles of his shoes into gravel. "Give me the gun."

Handsomemost did not move. A smile wrinkled his top lip, which had a sprocket of black hairs on it that he kept combed and pasted in a sporty mustache. "Ain't done nothin illegal." He couldn't stop a quick laugh coming through the lips of his smile. He wanted to say: I never did anything legal in my life, you old Tom, but instead he did his arguing dance. "These here be my dogs. Got a right to shoot em. Man don't need no license to shoot his own dogs. Why should I take em to some white vet what's goin to gas em, then charge me enough to buy a new convertible with? Answer me that, huh? Why would a smart black boy like me do a thing like that, huh?"

"Give me the gun."

"Lighten up. You be practicin a mean act for Hollywood or somethin?"

"I won't ask you again."

Handsomemost looked into Justo's brown eyes. Nope, no mercy there. Coptime mentality. Nevertheless he figured he could deal with Justo. Justo knew the accommodation, understood which side his bread was buttered on, knew the Saints had to be fed. Handsomemost relaxed his grip on the gun, let it twirl over his trigger finger, which was studded with diamonds of a fat gold ring. Handsomemost offered the gun with a wink. "Heard any good music lately?"

"No, but you will." Justo took the gun. "I'm booking you."

"Hey! I said lighten up. What it is? We be bubbas. What be wrong with shootin your own dog? These doggies got run out bad and ugly.

Can't win no more races for papa. Best they be put out of their miseries. Their hound-dog days be over. Best you be lucky enough to have somebody be shootin you when your hound-dog days be over and misery time comes callin. Who wants to drag around life losin races all the time? Not me. When my misery time comes goin to be takin this here same gun, send me a telegram through my head from ear to ear. Return to sender. You be understandin, bubba?"

"Let's take a walk out to my car."

"Ain't gettin in no cop's car. You be one crazy Cuban bean, you think that. Sides, ain't been home all night. Needs my beauty rest. You can dig that, bein a family man and all."

There were times Justo enjoyed being a cop, when the heavens opened up and showed him the way, how there was good and evil in the world and one couldn't exist without the other. This was such a time. He wanted to blow the creature before him to kingdom come. Of course Handsomemost hadn't had any sleep, he had done so much cocaine his flared nostrils appeared to be pinned to his earlobes, plus he suffered a bad case of snorter's shoulder, an uncontrollable muscle spasm twitching his right shoulder like a baseball pitcher about to fire off a nervous spitball. Handsomemost didn't have enough moral fiber to make a hatband with. Justo had less than no respect for him. No respect for losers who thought they were the last bastion of romance, hotshot pirates. Justo had more respect for the poor bastard who shovels snow out of his driveway every morning so he can go to work to meet the mortgage. He took perverse delight at being the counterbalance to a corrupt world. To be an honest man was to be the last true outlaw. But Justo knew he couldn't exist without Handsomemost. The pie of life had been divided up between the keepers of the law and the breakers of it, nothing would ever change that, without each other they were out of a job. It's a hot dog–eat–hot dog world. Justo's knee jerked up in a cocked instinctive reaction, straight into Handsomemost's groin. "Don't ever mention my family to me."

Handsomemost rolled over in the white gravel, hugging his knees to his chest, trying to bend the pain at the central junction of his body into nothingness. Handsomemost feared his nuts were cracked. His mouth was dry and he cried his words out. "What's with you! Got your heart in your asshole or somethin!"

Justo pointed the gun at the man in black clothes scraping around in a cloud of white coral dust. One less hot dog in town to supply the street sniffers, sunday snorters, bathroom spoon boppers and back-room needle pumpers. He hated hot dogs, especially the kind cruising around looking for somebody's teenage daughter to needle high, light up some simple girl's life. That was the narrow part where Justo's own teenage daughters came through the door and tainted the entire way he looked at hot dogs. He had recently become intolerant and irrational when it came to hot dogs, forgetting the accommodation. Not more than a week had gone by since he busted a hot dog out in a boulevard motel, smashed through the door on a tip from a dirt bag who had flipped. The hot dog raced into the bathroom, bolted the door and Justo broke it down just as the hot dog swallowed a knotted condom filled with cheap heroin brown. Justo delivered three punches guaranteed to bring up anything in a man's stomach, the hot dog threw up the evidence before losing consciousness, thudding to the tile floor. The hot dog's girl in the bedroom was younger than Justo's youngest daughter, thirteen, pink hair and black fingernails. "You cunt," she screamed, too dumb to have run while Justo had persuaded her boyfriend in the bathroom to cough up his stash. Justo slapped her across the face, knocking her against the bedroom wall. "You lousy nigger cop!" He slapped her again, then did something still following him around in a troublesome way. He grabbed the front of her blouse, tearing it off, her young breasts exposed. She became silent, staring wide-eyed at him. He didn't know what he thought, how long he looked at her, one moment or ten minutes. He ripped a sheet off the bed and threw it at her with a snarl. "Cover yourself up and beat it before I bust you too." No, Justo did not like hot dogs talking about his family.

"Jesus Christ, bubba! I be a respectable businessman. I have rights to shoot my own dogs." Handsomemost wobbled to his feet, hands crisscrossed over his groin in anticipation of another kick. "Ain't gettin ready to blow me away, are you, bubba?"

"I'm busting you for illegal discharge of a firearm within the city limits."

"Oh cooome-ooon, man!" Handsomemost howled. "Don't be givin me the riot act. What it be you want from me?" He hobbled across to the two dead dogs sprawled in a blanket of blood. "How much be two dead puppies worth anyway?" He looked back at Justo. "I know it's not money you be wantin. Out with it. What's the accommodation?"

"Some weird stuff going down in town."

"Always is. George Washington be first president of the United States and there be penguins in Alaska. So what else be new?"

"Don't mean the usual stuff."

"Like dead chickens nailed to doors and goat heads in the cemetery kind of stuff?"

"Yeah. Ever since the last boatload of Haitian refugees came in it's been getting weirder."

"I be hearin that. Yackity here, yackity there, you know how people yack."

"I already talked to my people about it and this is outside my people. I thought your people might know. Might be your people's kind of thing, which is different."

"It be different."

"How different? Suppose you tell me, or do you want me to run a check on this gun of yours to see what kind of exciting life it's had?"

"There be things not to talk about. Don't be a shitkicker. A shitkicker, he sees a big ol pile of shit on the far side of the street, he run over and kick it. Best you pass it on by. The maggots and the flies of this bad world will take care of the shit piles. Ask me bout somethin else. Hey, I got an idea for you. You want a dog?"

"I'm crossing the street to kick the shit."

"This here be a nice dog for you. Don't make a mistake and pass him up." Handsomemost winced from the pain in his groin as he knelt next to the leashed greyhound. He ran a hand along the animal's arched back, down over the thrust of its boned ribcage, underneath to the soft belly, his diamond-ringed fingers stroking the short hairs in time to the rapid thump of a racing heart. "This here dog be a good pal. Keep you out of harm's way because he don't know shit from apple butter. That's why his racin days be over. This fella, he turned into a biter instead of chasin the little metal bunny. Be your pal for life. He don't bite people, just other dogs when he be runnin with em. This biter cost me over eight thousand in handlin and trainin fees. He be yours for the takin."

"Untie him."

"Ah-hah!" Handsomemost chuckled deep in his throat as he pulled at the end of the leash knotted to the mangrove stump. "Knew you be an animal lover."

"I want you to untie him because I don't want him in the way when I blow the apple butter out your ears." Justo aimed the gun at Handsomemost's head. *"Dos aves de rapiña no mantienen compañía."*

"Don't be givin me none of that Cuban mumbo-jumbo. Just what you be talkin, bubba?"

"Two birds of prey do not hunt together."

"No more triflin with me. You be triflin too much. I don't be no triflin man." He jerked the knot of the greyhound's leash free.

Justo kept the gun on Handsomemost as he released the dog. Maybe he wasn't going to get this cagey bird to talk. Maybe Handsomemost didn't know anything about the weirdness and was just playing it up as something he could trade. Justo looked over to the end of the runway where a plane nosed into air, its silver belly passing overhead, the whiny propellers echoing across the mangrove swamp. It seemed to Justo a perfect opportunity to put one more hot dog out of business.

"Don't be a shitkicker!" Handsomemost sensed what Justo was about to do, stumbling backwards into a tangle of mangrove roots with his hands held high. "Remember the chickens and goats! Don't mess with the Saints!"

Justo lowered the gun. "Put the greyhound in the back of my car and beat it before I outthink myself."

"Free doggy bones for everyone." Handsomemost chuckled, stooping to grab the greyhound's leash. "I owe you one."

"Two."

"One. The Saints have to be fed."

7

THE SAINTS have to be fed. Recently it had become more famine than feast. Justo fumbled open the bag of greasy conch fritters on the car seat next to him as he turned off Duval Street, headed toward the cemetery. He ground the chewy conch meat between his teeth and swallowed it in a lump destined to give him a pain before another *mal día* was over. Maybe he should have taken Handsomemost out for the count. Perfect opportunity, armed and dangerous. But then Handsomemost occupied a sort of demilitarized zone of amorality, tap-dancing in alligator loafers between old gods and new devils, owing allegiance to both, offering loyalty to none, enchanted fool. *Aunque la mona se vista de seda, mona se queda.* The monkey in silk is still a monkey.

The greyhound in the backseat tipped its long snoot over Justo's shoulder, sniffing the spicy odor of conch meat, yawning its mouth open and licking Justo's cheek in a nonchalant gesture of familiarity. Ocho, Number Eight, is what I'll call you, Justo decided, fingering another fritter from the greasy bag for the dog. Number Eight because I sense you've spent your entire short life behind the eight ball about to be snookered. Here you go, Ocho, Justo pushed a fritter into the dog's obliging mouth, just don't tell anybody where you got it. Ocho fixed Justo with the caring gaze of a confidant and licked his lips shut. Ocho had the contented look of a dog a man could tell his troubles to. *Mal día*, Ocho, Justo sighed, another bad day begun, how I wish I could have stayed in bed this morning with Rosella. Sometimes I think a man gets up and goes to work just to deny himself the pleasure of his wife. A man walks around all day with that denial trailing him like a tail he doesn't know what to do with, a tail growing right out the back of his pants and dragging behind in the dust. True lust can be a curse. You have to keep turning it down if you want to heat it up. Finally the tail dragging in the dust grows so obvious it trips a man up. That is something you and I understand, Ocho. We are the last of true family men holding the great institution of marriage together while all the other dogs out there are chasing their tails around in circles without understanding why they have tails to begin with. We are the end of the line. After us, nothing. No romance, no self-denial, no one-woman love, just men with tails growing out the seat of their pants and barking dogs. The louder the bark the more frightened the dog. You can understand that, my friend. Justo patted Ocho's head. You know what I'm talking about? Ocho yawned with a pleasant gurgle, tipping his open mouth up in anticipation of an entire bag of conch fritters about to come flying miraculously through the air. A man and a dog do what they have to do. Justo nudged another fritter into Ocho's eager mouth while pondering this latest illumination. A woman does what she doesn't have to do.

At last Justo had somebody he could talk to. Whenever he talked to his Rosella about this, she slammed the door and he felt his tail grow another two feet. The ones he could definitely not talk to about it were his daughters, the oldest, Isabel, almost fifteen and turning every male head at mass each sunday morning. He could feel his power with Isabel ebbing away day by day. With a crumbling sense of the truly helpless he watched her preordained passage, like the tarpon coming up from the deep Cuban waters of spring to sport and spawn in the shallow channels and coral flats along the Keys. What angler would hook Isabel's treasure as she leapt from the dusk of her pubescence into the nocturnal passion of womanhood? Justo wondered. He knew they were out there waiting. Young men. Anglers playing the angles. It troubled him in a way he had never been troubled before. The trouble started in the past year when Isabel would walk into a dimly lit room, approaching him from behind. Justo would think it was Rosella, his mind leaping back twenty years. It was Rosella, the girl he married, appearing in an oblique reverse rush through time. Then the rude realization it was his daughter, Isabel. Certain embarrassment then overtook him, a painful hook of barbed remorse that Rosella had truly not reappeared in a moment of youthful reincarnation. A sense of guilt flowed from the undeniable illumination he couldn't accept this present-day beauty before him as an independent being to be cherished for her own self. Isabel was a ghost stirring distant realities from his attic of memory. Men should not have daughters. A cruel fate for both.

Whenever one of these ghostly encounters would occur Isabel would sit on the edge of Justo's chair and ask what was wrong, and he would ask her about her schoolwork. A jealousy filled his veins. He didn't want to give this girl up. It was like losing his wife's youth twice. Anger overtook his jealousy. Not the anger associated with the knowledge some angling angler would have Isabel for the first time. Anger that he would never have that experience with Rosella again. Why should some faceless boy have it who would not understand its power? Justo was becoming a sorrowful old man before his time. That is what having daughters will do to a man. A cruel fate. Maybe that was why *Quince* was so important to his wife, Rosella. All that fuss and bother about the fifteenth birthday celebration which would surely leave him broke. Two hundred fifty guests, every relative from Key West to Tampa eating roast pig, fried plantain bananas and *yuca*, enough food to fuel a presidential inaugural, plus two bands, six priests, and a chorus of pretty white-gloved waiters to attend the entire circus in the Casa Marina Hotel's high-arched grand salon overlooking the Atlantic. What a feast, fifty pigs giving their lives for his daughter's fifteenth birthday. What a bill. A bill he was willing to pay, a matter of honor and duty, the star of Cuba burns bright with pride. Only now was Justo beginning to understand *Quince's* greater significance, something deeper was going on. In the end *Quince* was not so much a daughter's passing to womanhood, but a wife's having her husband's dreams returned.

Justo traveled the narrowing streets popping conch fritters and ruminating on the mysterious ways of women which eluded all masculine equations. Resting next to him on the front seat of the car was a bouquet of lilies. A prickly sweet aroma exuded from the flared petals, filling the car with the scent of first communions and death. It was the first friday of the month. The first friday of the month Justo always had his lilies and headed for the cemetery to honor the past in order to make sense of the ever-increasing fractured present. This first friday he had been sidetracked by Handsomemost. Justo got the call as he was headed to the cemetery. Shots being fired out by the airport. Probably just the gang of boys who mucked around in the mangroves there playing Yankees and Gooks, replaying a war they were sorry to have missed, and mourned with the misguided fervor only adolescent males seem capable of. The boys built forts in the salt swamps, divided into teams of jungle fatigue–clad Marines and black pajama–cloaked Viet Cong, replaying a video war which had been conjured through twenty-inch holes of television screens a decade before. The boys' play was more real than the distant ghosts of the television war. On especially sporting occasions the boys would load real bullets into their .22 rifles and fire off a round at an outgoing airplane for the glory of the race and erupting hormones. A shot heard round the mangrove swamps, reverberating with the thrilling reality that the thin line between brotherhood and enmity is crossed in a man's own mind long before it is crossed in the politics of killing. But it wasn't the frisky weekday warriors who were getting it off in the mangroves at the end of the airport runway this particular morning. It was Handsomemost blowing away his dreaded canine losers.

Passover Lane and the cemetery were just ahead as Justo aimed his car down the skinny slot of Olivia Street, crowded on both sides with Cuban cigarmakers' shotgun shacks. Most of the shacks had been sandblasted and repainted by northerners to a self-conscious pastel prettiness their original occupants would have been embarrassed by; some of the shacks still retained a stripped-by-the-sun steel gray anonymity. Very few of the quaint little houses sheltered true Conchs, Cubans and Bahamians, who could occasionally be glimpsed on front porches, gazing with a sublime prescient certainty indicating they had seen it all, knew how it was all to end, when Hurricane El Finito would purify the island of outsiders once again.

As Justo slowly made his way down narrow Olivia Street old times called to him from wood-covered porches so close to his car he could reach out and touch them. Justo could not help but recall the spicy scent of Cuban cooking that drifted from these humble houses when he was a boy. Olivia was the street he grew up on. Sizzling garlic and shrimp once permeated the air, drifting on a jasmine-scented breeze. Flaming red bougainvillea grew in haughty arches over kitchen doors then, brilliant yellow allamanda blossoms spilled along the sills of open bedroom windows. Olivia was a street crowded with small houses and big childhood memories. The now vanished Cuban *grocería* on the corner once sold *productos Latinos, buches* to blast your brain back to Guantanamo Bay and curvacious loaves of womanly thin Cuban bread. *Cervezas* kept the men animated in the store's back room crowded with cider barrels, stacked blocks of jellied mango paste, and sacks of black-eyed pea flour. The men argued endlessly about what caused the blight of '39, when the sea went slack, spit up dead lobsters, sponges and conchs, then glittered bright and pristine, as if spread with a veneer of shark oil, the shallow bottom standing out in vibrant relief. Tall glasses of cool *vinos* kept the men betting on *boleta* or sweating through wednesday afternoons around the radio, waiting for the high-pitched voice of an orphan boy in Havana to arrive with a static hum across ninety miles of ocean from Cuba, singsonging the winning numbers of the Lotería Nacional drawing. After the sweltering wait for the numbers a roar or a moan would go up from the men, depending on whether or not Lady Luck had also made the ninety-mile trip across the Florida Straits from Cuba that afternoon. Then the static hum of the radio stretched into a languid Latin rhythm, a distant faraway throb of rhumbas and saltwater breakers striking sandy shores. The music from Cuba filled the back room of the *grocería* with the swish of swaying palm trees. *Bang!* Justo's grandfather's cane would strike the pine-plank floor. *"Niño!"* Justo's *abuelo* called to him. *"Mas marquitas y bollos!"* Off Justo went running with the single-minded intensity of a bird dog about to jump a covey of quail, returning to Abuelo and the men with bags of fried green plantain bananas and boxes of sweet *bollo* penny cakes. Abuelo then poured out shots of *compuesto*. The fiery sugarcane liquor fueled talk of cockfights and revolutions past and future. The urgency of passions stirred the hair on the back of young Justo's neck with reckless excitement, as if the men in the back room were the center of a dangerous universe propelled by big ideals of political gambling. Justo felt he was perched at the edge of this universe, a boy among men, a mouse in a bull pen, unobserved, privileged to be present at the continual rebirth of cultural pride generated by wild talk and selective memories. Nailed high to the back room wall were two fading posters. One bore the fierce-eyed and mustached face of José Martí, the martyred George Washington of Cuba. The colorful poster opposite was the image of the Russian dancer Pavlova. Pavlova once catapulted across the stage of the formidable Instituto de San Carlos, which dominated Duval Street with its towering pillared arches and glittering Cuban tiles. Pavlova pirouetted on the very stage where Martí once preached eagerly to crowds about the seeds of rebellion growing in Cuba to a forest of *Los Pinos Nuevos*, the new pines of independence. Pavlova's thighs swelled from the back room's wall in white dancer's tights hugging a forceful thrust of buttocks, where her daring blade

of black hair came to rest in a moment of tense repose. Pavlova
threatened to explode from the poster in an energetic hurl through
the colossal hoop of implacable male desire surrounding her in the
room, to land squarely on the heart of the matter. Young Justo was
lulled into a deep swim of desire over Pavlova, but so were all the
men, none more than Abuelo. For Abuelo such was not adulterous
desire pricked by lust. Abuelo had all the lust he could fathom in the
cherry-dark crevices of his African bride of forty years. No, this was
desire of another order. Desire for an object to end disorderly
thoughts. Thoughts dwelling on the mystery of that alien race, woman.
Pavlova in her dance of eternal delirium was a desired object to be
understood by men primitive in their intentions and clumsy in their
methods. All were such in the back room, except Abuelo. Abuelo was
a man of *Letters*, looked up to with respect. Abuelo was a man gifted
with the delicious wine of sweet-sounding metaphors and laced with
knowledge spun from books. Abuelo in his youth had ascended to
the altar of respect attained by only a chosen few. At the precocious
age of nineteen Abuelo had become a Lector, a reader in the cigar
factories that once hummed at the heart of the small island's body of
enormous productivity.

Abuelo had arrived in Key West from Havana filled with good
nature, cocky promise, and a generous portion of luck, for he was
born in 1878 at the end of the failed Ten Years' War, when the
Spaniards swung their sword of terrorism with dictatorial precision,
cutting the throats crying "Cuba Libre," releasing a flood of martyrs'
blood to fertilize the seeds of *Pinos Nuevos*. The seeds of *Pinos Nuevos*
lay fallow through a desert of oppression, which would not show
growth until 1895, when Martí called for all men to rise as one, and
final revolt to begin. The revolution began without Abuelo. The
Spaniards tried to conscript him into an army of brothers preparing
to fight brothers. It was then Abuelo's family was smuggled aboard a
schooner to make passage across the Florida Straits to Cayo Hueso,
Star of the Sea shining with bright promise of two hundred cigar
factories producing one hundred million cigars a year, and a powerful
cigarmakers' union, La Liga, organizing among the six-thousand-man
work force. Abuelo's father was a true artist, who had risen rapidly
through the rigid caste system of the cigar factories of Havana, from
a lowly Stripper, who prepared the fan-shaped spread of thin-veined
tobacco leaves for wrappers and filler, to become a Cigarmaker. His
fingers knew the perfect airy weight of the cigar to be born, then

rolled and glued it with natural gum, all in a deft motion of such rapid fluidity only a mere trace of moisture escaped his skin to permeate the impressionable product, taint its natural perfume. The newborn cigar was in and out of his hands in less than a minute. Abuelo's father was one of the few capable of constructing the difficult Cuban Bances Aristocrato. The Aristocrato was filled with the finest Vuelta tobacco, its pliant leaf wrapper tapered the shape of a delicate glass-blown bottle, its svelte end pinched to a flat pucker to meet the flame of a match with the ease of a kiss, releasing a smoky reminiscence of freshly turned humus on a deeply jungled mountainside. The muscles in Abuelo's father's arms grew and his fingers flew as he sat year after year in the center of the two-tiered cigarmaker's table creating the finely balanced rolled contours of everything from cheap Cheroot Pinas to lordly Bances Aristocratos. Finally he was elevated to the position of Picker. Surrounded by the grand sweep of a crescent-shaped table where bundles of finished cigars were delivered to him, Abuelo's father mastered the art of Spanish Picking. From the untied bundles he picked through thirty-two shades of leaf-wrapper colors, carefully matching the correct colorations required to pack four layers of cigars in a proper order demanded by tradition. Cedar box after cedar box he filled. The cedar wood guaranteed no worms or bugs would feast off the aromatic bounty. Only the most appreciative lips would suck on Cuba's finest. All of this Abuelo's father mastered and taught his son before the schooner they escaped on arrived in Key West.

Abuelo, like his father, worked his way up quickly in the cigar factories of his newly adopted country. As a youth he was a Stripper in a *Chinchalito*, a small, independent factory with only ten workers, men from villages around Havana, Spanish mountain towns and West Indies fishing ports, all working together in the confines of a plank-wood shack barged over from the Bahamas. The shacks had been shotgunned closely next to one another by the hundreds, along newly created streets inching across the island to house ever-growing numbers of cigar workers. The intimate working conditions of the *Chinchalito* was soon to give way to grander fortunes for Abuelo. His father had become one of the *Jefes* in La Liga, believing only the union could prevent the Spaniards from once again stealing what was rightfully Cuban. Too many Spaniards were being hired to work against the brotherhood of La Liga, so Abuelo's father took his son from the independent *Chinchalito* and fixed a job for him as Cigarmaker in one of the block-long, three-storied limestone factories off Duval Street. It was there Abuelo's life was given two fortuitous twists to seal the fate of his manhood emerging at age seventeen.

The first twist came in the form of a female body taking every dangerous curve along the course of its supple frame to stop a man's heart dead in its tracks. Her name was Pearl, the jewel in a family of nine brothers and one daughter. Pearl's father was an Ibu, brought to the Bahamas as a boy in chains from West Africa and freed fifteen years later in 1838 by the British. Freed by the very ones who had enslaved him, given a dowry of no money and a new name in a white man's world, John Coe. John Coe worked flat-land crops of Bahamian plantations, but his eyes always went to the vast ocean's reach, where wealth was held beyond the voracious grasp of slave masters. The sea surging between the thousands of islets woven through the great chain of Bahamian islands was a place where a man could fish, and sponge, and turtle. A place where an industrious man could dip his pole beneath the pristine water's surface and stir up an honest meal or a lifetime's fortune.

John Coe became a student of the sea when freed. The sea became John's new master. Turtles attracted him first, their gliding nonchalance, so few flipper strokes needed to navigate through a watery universe, an economy of effort worth emulating, which bespoke ancient liberation from the here and now. John felt kinship with this marine creature's abiding sense of ease, its deep breadth of freedom. John was a simple man who knew not the turtle's source of symbolic power, he understood only the animal's daily inspiration. John learned the ways of thousand-pound leatherback and loggerhead turtles, cruising and blowing water stacks like sporting baby whales. He studied eight-hundred-fifty-pound gentle greens, which fed solely on vegetarian fare, content to snap through carpets of sea grass. He gained respect for the small fifty-pound hawksbill, whose fast bite could gash a man's hand swift as a machete blow and bleed him to death on flat water in hot sun.

John followed the turtles down the length of the Bahamas, around Hispaniola, across the Caribbean Sea, up the Central American coast, riding the warm current of the Gulf Stream. John mastered the harpoon, taking a turtle coming up for a blow with his first thrust, driving the harpoon's sharpened steel peg cleanly into the precious shell. John never lost a turtle as it dove deep after the pegging, its weight strong against the whirring line, pulling for freedom. John went wherever the turtles went. He could con his canoe-shaped longboat by eye through razor-sharp walls of coral, reading the deep-water blue surging with currents of urgency between the yellow-shadowed reefs. John could net turtles, harpoon them or take them by hand. He began to think like a turtle, the taste of ghost crab in his mouth, the brine of shipworms in his nostrils, turtle grass between his toes. In the polar pull of a late winter warming moon John could intuit the male turtle's fervor of romance. It was during this mating season he would capture a she-turtle and heft her aboard his longboat, then wait patiently with his glistening prisoner of passion, until a trailing male thrust suddenly from water, attempting in a heroic leap of faith to hurl his amorous hulk over the edge of the longboat to be forever joined with his mate, not feeling the bite of John's harpoon until it was too late. John knew where turtles roosted at night, deep in sleep beneath a float of soft kelp, wreathed in seaweed. John Coe had their dreams.

John migrated up the Florida Keys with leatherbacks and greens in spring. During nights of moonlight he stalked crescent-shaped trails left in damp sand where females stabbed flippers, heaving hard-shelled bodies beyond the tideline to nest their eggs safely. John turned the she-turtles in the vulnerable moment when their tidal surge of eggs flowed, flipping them over on their backs, where they remained helpless and immobile as he carved his initials, JC, into their soft undershells, the crude brand a warning to other Turtlers that these turtles were his. The flipped females were left stranded on the beach, the fresh cut of JC on their bellies glowed in moonlight as John worked quickly through the lengthening night on other beaches, turning as many females as he could before the moon disappeared from the heavens. In the dawn's early light John returned exhausted and exhilarated to his females on the sandy beaches, laying claim to his prized catch of eggs, meat and shells. This was how John Coe came to Key West, to sell his skiffload of prizes from the sea of plenty, fresh brimming baskets of turtle eggs and live she-turtles, their pierced front and back flippers tied through with palm thatch.

Along the Key West docking wharves of the big turtle canning factory in 1855 talk among the Turtlers was of Sponger money and nurse sharks. Spongers were many in Key West, and many were from the Bahamas, both white and black Conchs, equal in their pursuit to take a livelihood from the sea. John knew their language, the clipped sounds of men given to few words and patient actions as they poled skiffs across shallows. Through glass-bottom buckets dropped over the skiffs' sides the Spongers searched briny depths during the long day's tidal rise and fall for flowering black-skinned sheepswool sponges hiding deep in coral crevices and the wavering underwater flow of grassy flats. More than a thousand men in hundreds of boats left the Key West wharves before dawn each day to harvest the vast sponge beds of the back-country flats. Sharp three-pronged hooks at the tip of eighteen-foot poles brought up tons of yellow sponge, grass sponge, and thick sheepswool. There was plenty of Sponger money for all, but John Coe did not settle in Key West because he became a Sponger. John Coe became a Sharker.

Talk on the docks when John Coe arrived with his she-turtles in Key West was of how a man who knew his way with sharks could make as much or more than a Sponger. On those days when the bottoms of the flats were kicked up by distant stormy weather, sending chops and swells against the Keys for days on end, the Sponge-Hookers couldn't spy their catch in the murk. Mistakenly they would strike at bulging coral heads, dancing sea fans and shadowy jellyfish, anything and everything but the desired object of their deft aim. They could not fill their skiffs. A Sponger who could not fill his skiff could not fill his children's bellies and his glass with rum, so the Sharker became the Sponger's friend fair and true. The Sharker possessed magic to clear storm-befouled waters. The Sharker had oil of the young nurse sharks. A Sponger could swish nurse shark oil a hundred feet across the water on both sides of his skiff, then the murk of the flats would part quick as an underwater stage curtain, the marine heaven shimmer clear beneath the gaze of the Sponge-Hooker standing tall at the bow. A Sponger needed a Sharker on a gray day when promise is dim and the skiff empty. John Coe knew the ways of the shark. To know the ways of the turtle is to know the ways of the shark.

The sea taught John Coe it's a horseshoe conch-eats-shipworm world. John baited his hooks with mackerel heads and feathered chicken wings and searched the shallows of the Keys for the pale brown shadows of nurse sharks nosing across the sandy bottom. John dragged hundreds of six-foot nurses ashore, their mouths hooked, the noose of a rope cinched around their dangerously thrashing tails. Over an open fire John boiled gallons of oil from the freshly cut poundage of shark livers. John sold the skins to leather brokers from Texas, the dried fins to Chinese seamen to make a nourishing soup while on the long clipper-ship passage back to China; where shark fin powder was a fabled aphrodisiac, believed to bestow upon man required properties to prowl through a woman's sea with the stand-up certitude of a bull walrus. John Coe earned his money from sharks, Spongers, Chinese seamen and Texas bootmakers. From the sea of plenty John earned himself enough money to buy a wife.

John Coe was a man of superstitious faith. John believed the natural world exposed signs along the road of life for a man to obey. If the high cirrus clouds deserted the heavens by noon, and a curtain of rolling dark clouds descended on the western horizon, then John did not voyage out to shark on the following morn. When the moon grew full, spilled its silver illumination on a shimmering sea, John felt the shrimp move in his veins and set out on a path of light across the strong current of the Gulf Stream to find a schooling swarm of giant loggerheads. John had faith in the gods of men and animals in the old African world. He believed in the power of those gods to instruct him daily in a godless new world. That is why when the Slaver-schooner *Wildwind* sailed into Key West, its vast open deck crowded by unclothed shadow-dark African bodies thinned to the bone by hunger and fear, John Coe was there to take a wife.

John Coe did not know he was going to take a wife that fateful day. John knew only that the day before the thin wispy cirrus clouds pulled out of the heavens by noon, replaced by brooding thunderheads descending in the west, so instead of sharking he ambled down to the docks where he could hear the Bahamian accent so dear to his ears being bantered back and forth among Turtlers and Spongers. Talk was among the black Bahamians that a Slaver had sailed in from the West Coast of Africa; Mandingo, Ijo and Ibu were aboard. Rich cotton growers from Natchez and New Orleans had come to buy them. Talk was war was going to be fought in America, war over slaves. No one on the docks knew if this meant there were to be more slaves or none. All they knew for certain was sure as good weather follows bad a war was coming. John Coe decided to go among the crowd watching the human cargo from the Slaver being auctioned. This was something unnatural to him. The sea had made John free inside, yet some part of him still felt captured. An indentured piece of John's soul lingered uncomfortably on the meathook of his recent history. John cared not to be around purveyors of human flesh. His eyes could not take the sad old sight, smells of desperation, wide lost look of Africa in the people's eyes. All of this drummed on his heart

with the force of a hammer beating nails into a coffin. John had
turned away from this dark corner of his life, closed the door on his
own origins. Whatever compelled John to be standing among the
crowd at the auction was not something to be questioned, it was
instead a prayer about to be answered. The answer came when John
heard the white auctioneer shout: "Brenda Bee! One Ibu wench age
nineteen!"

Brenda Bee stood perched on a pickle barrel with skinny hands
crossed over the center of her sex, cast off and alone, separated
forever from her former self. Brenda looked not nineteen, but sixteen,
naked and vulnerable atop an up-ended wooden barrel, shivering in
the glare of male eyes crowded around her on the dock. Brenda was
not sound of body. She had narrowly escaped becoming one of the
two hundred who died on board the Slaver as days without food
slipped by on a sea growing wide as a continent. On this new continent
Brenda would have little value in the cotton rows up south. The well-
dressed gentlemen in the crowd from Charleston and Mobile didn't
see anything of value in Brenda worth bidding the hard metal of
dollars for, they weren't even interested in purchasing Brenda for
their breeding sheds.

"Come now, gentlemen!" The auctioneer waved his cane toward
Brenda, as if it were a magic wand which could disperse the white
crawl of lice in the matted braids of her hair. "What is offered the
Company for this good wench?"

"My dog!" A laughing answer came from the crowd.

"My dog's fleas!"

"The blood of my dog's fleas!"

John Coe knew Brenda could not understand any of this, but it
seemed her exposed skin shaded a deeper color of black from a
spreading blush of shame, a black almost obliterating jagged red cuts
and purple bruises spotted over her body. John Coe's hand flew up
of its own will. John was a tall man made taller by pulling the weight
of sharks and turtles from the sea, he was two heads above every man
in the crowd. When John's hand went up a silence fell as if something
evil had tumbled from great height into the midst of civilized society.
The silence was broken by John's voice, thundering deep as a stormy
sound slamming down from a brood of inky clouds roiling in a
summer sky. "Suh, be mah offah! Two hunnah dollah!"

So it was John Coe bought himself a wife in a town where a man
of dark skin was not allowed to walk the streets after the nine-thirty

ringing of the night bell, unless he bore a pass from his owner or employer, or was accompanied by a white person. Nor could a dark-skinned man play the fiddle or beat a drum, unless he desired thirty-nine whiplashes for violating the public peace. John Coe took this woman, called by her captors Brenda Bee, to his one-room shack on Crawfish Alley in the section of town called La Africana. That shack was John Coe's palace, owned and built with hands calloused from pulling turtles and sharks from the sea. Now all the plenty given John by the sea he was about to return. What John and Brenda Bee had in common was an ocean of hardships. As John bathed Brenda's bony body with the humped softness of his favorite sheepswool sponge he vowed to treat this woman with kindness, drive the unspeakable terror from her eyes. John spoke to Brenda in a tongue she could understand, touched her only in a healing way. John brought Brenda red cotton dresses, strolled with her hand in hand on saturday eves down the rutted dirt length of Crawfish Alley, stopping to tip his cap to folks cooling themselves on the front wooden steps of their shacks. John planted a papaya tree behind his shack and a mango in front, for on sundays the preacher man swayed in the stone church before the congregation tall as an eleuthera palm in a high wind, shouting his clear message that the Bible teaches to plant the fruiting tree. A man must sow seeds to harvest. John watched Brenda grow out of her bag of bones into a prideful woman with a strong gaze and firm lips. John measured his prosperity by the image of Brenda's flesh. Tracing the girth of Brenda's strong buttocks and thighs with his fingertips late at night in the shack filled him with contentment. John Coe was man enough to keep his woman solid. When the children came Brenda's hips and breasts swelled and John overflowed with a newfound joy. The ever-increasing size of Brenda's body became a living monument to a niggardly past so narrowly escaped.

Brenda Bee Coe had no envy for the Ship Captain's wife she scrubbed and cooked for in the sooted kitchen shed behind the three-storied house with a widow's walk perched atop its steep tin roof from which tall-masted ships could be spied tacking inside the reef toward the island. Brenda felt gratitude she was living life after death, swept up from the ocean of hardship in the net of John Coe's kindness. Envy did not gnaw at Brenda's soul, only a bitter sense buried deep and hidden from the world that one day the Evil Eye would be upon her, carry her away from the strong arms of John back onto the Slaver into a whale belly of white misery. For this reason Brenda always wore a clove of garlic around her neck on a thinly braided rope, to hold off the Eye of the Evil One lest he come upon her unawares to carry her away from her sea of plenty. Brenda insisted her nine sons each wear a garlic necklace, even though she knew they discarded them when they left the crowded little shack on Crawfish Alley. But Brenda's only daughter, the jewel in her sea of plenty, Pearl, never discarded her garlic necklace. Pearl obeyed her mama. Pearl knew the Evil Eye could snatch her away quick as a pox can worm the life out of a child's heart.

When Pearl turned sixteen and went off to work in the cigar factories, she still wore the garlic necklace. That is what first attracted young Abuelo to Pearl, the creamy colored garlic against a black skin shining brilliant with vibrance of life. Years after they were married Abuelo suspected Pearl had not so much worn the garlic necklace to keep off the Evil Eye, but to beguile him with her voluptuous charms and deeply contented nature. Perhaps, Abuelo thought with a laugh which always sent a bright image of Pearl's lovely face to mind, she tricked him with that jungle religion her mother brought across the seas on the Slaver from Africa.

Pearl became the gem setting which closed the ring of Abuelo's young life. Pearl was the first of two fortuitous twists to seal Abuelo's fate forever. Abuelo believed when his father abruptly took him at the age of seventeen from the *Chinchalito*, it had less to do with his father's desire to have his son become part of the emerging La Liga, more to do with an African plot of love planned by Pearl's mother to put one more ocean between her only daughter and slavery, marry Pearl off to a Cuban man, into the sea of a different society where the Evil One would never find her. Such is what Abuelo thought, that he was ensnared by jungle conspiracy. Like many men who are convinced they have fallen prey to a charmed woman highly coveted by others, Abuelo accepted a preordained fate guiding larger passions which made him victim of an inescapable coup d'état of the heart. Abuelo's love for Pearl came up so big and unexpectedly it overpowered his sense of self, left him trembling with the blind faith of newfound religion. *No te agites qué el corazon no se opera*, that is what Abuelo's father counseled at the turn of the century when his untried son first started with Pearl. *Take it easy, the heart can't be operated on.*

No. In those days the heart could not be operated on, but if it could it would have been to no avail. Abuelo lost his heart the morning he saw Pearl his first day of work in the large cigar factory. He did not yet know she had stolen his heart. Abuelo thought he still had a choice in the matter. Pearl was one of the few women who worked in the cigar factory, the only woman on the third floor where Abuelo began his new job of Cigarmaker. Abuelo was not so much struck by Pearl's beauty, rather by the position she held in the factory. Most women labored in the lowly role of Stripper, who each day untied hundreds of *tercios*, bundled tobacco leaves barged from Havana. The women carefully stripped precious leaves from spiny stems, then pressed them between two boards to be sent on as wrappers to the Selectors. Never had Abuelo seen a female Selector. A Selector was an exalted position held by men with a keen sense of vision to distinguish the air-cured tobacco leaves by true color value. Perhaps Pearl inherited her extraordinary eyesight from her father, who could read the bottom of a storm-tossed sea. To watch Pearl's hands work quickly through stacks of tobacco leaves, eyes searching between colors ranging from golden papaya to ripe mahogany shading called *maduro*, was like witnessing a cat in a dark granary go about its stealthy nocturnal business of separating mice from mountains of wheat. Pearl did not work like a machine, rather as an adroit athlete laughing at a task made simple by exertion of inbred attributes. The creamy clove of garlic on Pearl's braided rope necklace rose and fell where her breasts began their full swell beneath a thin cotton dress. Pearl's skin glistened in the heat, her fingers flew, her eyes did not miss a trick. Blue clouds from the narrow cigars she continuously smoked swirled around her. Pearl appeared to exist in a haloed mist, struck by steady light cascading through lofty north-facing windows blocking fickle sea breezes which could disturb the cigarmakings so carefully laid out on the rowed tables of the great hall. Pearl's body exuded aromas fueling every man's desire high up in the third story of the cigar factory. The perfume of Pearl was a heady mixture of succulent reminiscences, of green dreams and urgent yearnings, of growing tobacco leaves hidden in slippery shade of muddied hillsides, of the pungent burnt scent of garlic rooted from firm earth. In a sea of heat the men of the great hall watched Pearl from afar and on the sly as she selected among tobacco leaves for those of the chosen colors. Perspiration of honest work ran coolly along the back of Pearl's arched neck, then out of sight beneath her white dress, traveling the length of her strong female spine. To the men of the great hall Pearl was a sweeter dish than *boniatello*, the sugary preserve boiled from pulpy flesh of sweet potato. The men of the great hall desired someone they could sniff, lick and eat up, a great gorgeous feast of female. Pearl became the fantasy entrée on the menu of every self-respecting Latin male in the great hall. The problem was Pearl was born with an appetite greater than that of all the sniffing males combined.

Pearl's appetite could be quenched by only one man, the young Abuelo, whose arms had the steel muscles of one born to roll perfect cigars. Pearl's appetite for Abuelo would never be satisfied in a lifetime. She wasted no precious moments letting her desire be known. The job of Selector was to bundle twenty-five carefully chosen leaf wrappers into an earthenware crock, then call for a boy to run the crock to the Cigarmakers' benches. Each time Pearl sent a crock she knew was headed for Abuelo's bench it contained among the perfectly matched leaves a small, star-shaped pink blossom. The flower emitted no scent to distract from the natural aroma of the tobacco, but bore the meaning of not so hidden intentions to be acted upon beneath the eye of future moons. When the future arrived the moon winked time and time again as the hot skin of Pearl and Abuelo's bodies came together crushing the clove of garlic between them in a fateful sea of plenty.

As La Liga grew among cigar workers so too did the family of Pearl and Abuelo grow. By the end of the century Key West was the cigar-producing capital of the world and Pearl and Abuelo had five children. Abuelo's voice had also grown, deep and mellow from free smokers, the imperfect cigars inhaled continuously from dawn till dusk by workers in the great hall. The vowels of Abuelo's voice came strong as notes from a bass cello being played in the depths of a well. It was Abuelo's voice which gave his life its second fortuitous twist, elevated him to unrivaled status among the workers. Abuelo became a Reader. Through the long, tedious days in the great halls of the cigar factories, amidst the flat fall of light from high windows sealed against winds of the outside world, there was one voice above all in the void of passing time. This voice filled ears and minds, becoming familiar as one's own conscience, cajoling like a crony, spiteful as a spurned lover, thunderous as a bull in a spring meadow. The owner of this voice earned more than the lordly cigar Pickers and Packers at the pinnacle of their careers. This man was the Reader, elevated on a platform in the center of the great halls, seated purposefully on a stool, straw hat cocked at advantageous angle. When the Reader spoke, no other talking was allowed, in English, Spanish or Bahamian. The Reader's voice made the day jump with thoughts, translating into

Spanish the island's English newspapers, reading newspapers fresh off the ferry from Havana bearing news of Cuba, Barcelona, Buenos Aires. The Reader read from the classics, becoming every character in *Don Quixote, The Count of Monte Cristo, A Tale of Two Cities.* As he read he educated himself and the others. He became a one-man school for the cigar workers. They paid him a handsome profit from their own pockets, voted upon favorites from his readings, to hear them time and again. Among the glories of literature Abuelo brought to life his personal favorite was the great Góngora, the Spaniard who emerged cloaked in a glowing mantle of lyricism, magically inventing his poetic self from the crusty seventeenth century with a sudden awesome "melancholy yawn of the earth." The great Góngora was a favorite of Abuelo's father. The leather-bound book of Góngora's poems was the only possession his father brought on the smuggled night voyage of the schooner from Havana so long ago. More and more the workers wanted to hear from the great Góngora. Not because Góngora was the favorite of Abuelo's father, who had become the iron-fisted *jefe* of La Liga. Not because Abuelo's father placed his son at center stage of the vast hall to read to the workers. The workers wanted that which could not be faked or bought. The singular fact was, more than at any other time, when Abuelo recited the great Góngora his voice rose from the well of the printed page tinged with mystery of infinity, surged with an inner beat of lyricism on the wing:

> *The bee as queen who shines with wandering gold;*
> *Either the sap she drinks from the pure air,*
> *Or else the exudation of the skies*
> *That sip the spittle from each silent star.*

Years later, as young Justo stood at Abuelo's side in the back room of the Cuban *grocería*, there was still respect for the retired Reader. Ears pricked up at the sound of Abuelo's voice still steady and strong through an ever-present cigar smoke swirling about his craggy face. The cigar factories had long since been boarded up against modern times, when cigars are made by machines in air-conditioned rooms. A generation had passed since La Liga grew so strong among the workers the owners started nonunion factories three hundred miles north of the glitter and culture of Key West. The factories had been transplanted to the swampy palmetto lands around Tampa, where malaria waited, and insects swarmed in rain barrels of precious drinking water drained from roofs of hastily constructed houses. Such was not a place for Abuelo. No. Abuelo's family stayed in Stella Maris, Star of the Sea, where Pavlova once danced at old San Carlos. Even though bright important times had faded to Depression-era gray, the star of cultural pride still burned bright in hearts and memories of men who put the coral-capped island on the map, rolling out one hundred million cigars a year. *Bang!* Justo could still hear Abuelo's tamarind cane striking the floor in the back room of the *grocería*. *Bang!* The metal tip of the cane struck again, all the men coming to attention as Abuelo elevated the cane haughtily as a teacher with a pointer in a classroom of thick-headed boys destined to grow to men forever ignorant of the ways of women, unless they heeded the words of great Góngora. Abuelo raised the cane higher, until the metal tip nudged the white dancer tights banded around the forceful thrust of Pavlova's thighs, her body trapped forever in an eternal leap from the poster nailed to the wall. Never taking his eyes from the curved spirit of Pavlova's leap Abuelo's voice swelled with wisdom of great Góngora, filling every square inch of the small room as if it were the vast hall of a ghostly cigar factory:

> *That fixed armada in the eastern sea*
> *Of islands firm I cannot well describe,*
> *Whose number, though for no lasciviousness*
> *But for their sweetness and variety,*
> *The beautiful confusion emulate*
> *When in the white pools of Europa's rose*
> *The virginal and naked hunting tribe . . .*

Great Góngora's words echoed in Justo's ears as if spoken only moments before by Abuelo in the back room of the *grocería*. Justo last heard Góngora's poetry twenty years ago, in a time of "beautiful confusion." All gone now, gone the way of handmade cigars and natural sponges. The turtles were endangered, and not all sport fishermen let their less than prize catches from the sea off the hook. What would Abuelo think of it all now? This time of rich rock and roll crooners of drug tunes and hot dogs in alligator loafers blowing away slow greyhounds. A time of conspicuous corruption which had less to do with simple survival and more to do with spiritual greed. Stella Maris had lost more than her virginity and glitter. The Góngorian time of "sweetness and variety," which Abuelo once hailed in the now deserted great halls of the cigar factories, gone forever, along with sponges in the sea and arias soaring to the chandeliered ceiling of the San Carlos.

Justo popped another conch fritter into his mouth, let it gather in the sour storm of his stomach. He handed the last fritter over to Ocho in the backseat of the car as he wheeled around the corner onto Passover Lane across from the cemetery. He parked beneath the spread of a Banyan tree shading the high morning sun. Handsome-most's escapade at the airport had not slowed Justo down too much this morning. The iron gates of the cemetery were just being swung open, still early enough so he wouldn't have to deal with mourners he didn't know, or the afternoon scramble of tourists prowling through tombstones gawking at quaint Cuban and Bahamian family names chiseled into granite, or searching among crumbling limestone crosses to discover the locally famous inscription of eternal recrimination cut into a marble slab: I TOLD YOU I WAS SICK. The cemetery was near the highest point on the island, towering a full fifteen feet above sea level. This fact made some laugh with derision, the more timid to look anxiously in the direction of the sea, where twenty-foot tidal surges might appear. The cemetery had been moved to this high ground more than a hundred years before, when the waves driven hard before a hurricane gouged a tumble of bones and buried family secrets from the island's original graveyard, exposing skeletons of slaves rescued from Slavers only to receive a final reward of Christian burial. The town fathers did not want another jumble of bones to bob up in the wake of a hurricane's tidal fury, exposing a nightmare past married to a dream future.

The cemetery possessed an odd calm at the island's crowded heart. It was corralled on all four sides by narrow streets of cigarmakers' cottages and steep-roofed Conch houses, nudging for a better view of this high point on the island, reserved not for the living, but for the dead. An unnatural peace prevailed, as if this were simply a grassy plain overgrown with tombstones, mausoleums and monuments, where island birds found refuge to root undisturbed for grubs and worms, oblivious to grief or curiosity of human passersby. Gaggles of spindly-legged white ibis stalked awkwardly in grassy tufts between tombs, long curved bills held ready. Atop a twenty-foot obelisk erected to memorialize a man of forgotten distinction a swallow-tailed kite hawk perched, alert for an errant fieldmouse to scamper among bouquets of plastic flowers arrayed among weeds crowding hundreds of neglected tombstones. The swallow-tail eyed Justo loftily as he walked along deserted asphalt pathways. Where one pathway bisected another, a short cement monument had been erected, stenciled with avenue designations: FIRST AVENUE, SECOND AVENUE, THIRD AVENUE, avenues not intended for cars, but a grid laid out for ghosts in a city of the dead. Justo's family plot was on THIRD AVENUE, beyond the Jewish section, close to a red-bricked plaza of a fraternal organization bearing the name WOOD CUTTERS OF THE WORLD. Justo did not like being in the cemetery any earlier than he was. Cocks had stopped their shrill crowing in the distance, giving up their demand for longer dawnings and shorter days. The quiet cocks gave Justo comfort, for any Santería ritual carried out in the cemetery during the night had to end before first light. Over the years the cemetery was the scene of many such rituals. At dawn tombstones were discovered with chicken blood smeared across them to drain evil from the graves. Often an entire chicken was found, wings spread, gutted bowels scattered like gaudy rocks to hold down restless spirits. These were normal things, which sometimes appeared as alarming headlines in the local paper. There were other things not so normal, which spooked jittery newcomers, solidified long-held beliefs of old-timers about voodoo spirits prowling from their nocturnal nests. What was to be avoided by all was to arrive at the cemetery before the last cock crowed. To glimpse a nocturnal ritual of private acts and sacred offerings inadvertently was to invite horrifying calamity. Those trying to appease the spirits were not to be exposed, the Saints must be fed, the devils dodged. The innocent onlooker could be overrun in a rush of transcendent deliverance or final evil. Some things are best left undisturbed.

Justo rubbed his gold chicken bone as he made his way quickly through this city of the dead. The swallow-tailed hawk eyeing him from the obelisk's granite point whistled high to the wind and wheeled off into open sky. Ocho crashed about among the tombstones and weeds, not so much on an intuitive hunt, but a tentative exploration. The dog stopped, pointing his long nose at objects not seen, but sensed. Ocho looked back at Justo with a wild-eyed superstitious expression so natural to a dog. Justo took the dog's cue, he stopped beneath the high-arched branches of a leafless woman's-tongue tree. He thought he heard a noise. He held his breath, there was a slight rattle in the distance. Justo's gaze swept across the crowded horizon of gravestones and tombs divided by salt-rusted railings defining family plots decorated with reposing lambs carved in stone, alabaster angels in flight, marble cupids descending and winged cement cherubs rising. Everything was bleached by the sun to an other-worldly sepia. Growing among crumbling mausoleums and cracked stacks of above-ground grave vaults tall trees existed in faded ethereal stateliness. Skimpy palms lined the avenues of the dead back to the cemetery entrance, where it was rumored six hundred men were secretly buried on a dark night in 1909, pieces of their shattered bodies carted in by horse-drawn wagons, intermixed in an anonymous jigsaw puzzle of a common grave. These men, Abuelo had told Justo, had been blown apart in a savage blast while struggling to complete the Overseas Railway, more than a hundred-mile run of bridges across the forty-three Florida Keys, linking Key West to mainland America's way of life. Justo believed the men were buried in the cemetery. When he was a boy he discovered the neatly severed head of a pig resting amidst a tangle of mexican fire-cracker vines covering the rumored location of the mass grave. Some things were best left undisturbed. The sound Justo thought he heard in the distance was now above him. The rustle of a breeze shook the bronze-colored seed pods of the woman's-tongue tree. That was the sound. In high winds the tongue-shaped pods rattled with a pitched racket some likened to the deafening sound of gossiping women. There was only a slight rattle above Justo. He walked on, turning toward Third Avenue to where his parents and grandparents rested in coral rock beneath a life-size marble angel, an eternal offering of spring lilies in her outstretched hand.

Every first friday of the month Justo came at dawn to kneel before the sweet-faced angel guarding his family's plot. He brought fresh lilies to match the angel's stone bouquet, and prayed. He prayed for the souls of his loved ones, dead and living. He prayed for the strength to hold himself steady as a family man in the disturbing winds of change. Someday he and Rosella would rest beneath the angel, forever holding hands throughout eternity. Justo wondered if his daughters would join them. Everything was happening so fast now. Who knows if they would keep the connection. Justo tried to instill in them the connection, the pride. Maybe, if they had been boys, he could have done better. He didn't know. He thought himself a failure with his own women. He knew how to love and protect them, but did he truly know how to guide them? Justo felt his daughters respected far more their own female charms than their family past. Maybe that too was his fault. Lately he doubted his masculine purpose. The women had done that to him. Would they ever understand Abuelo as he had? Could they conjure Abuelo whacking his metal-tipped tamarind cane on the *grocería* floor, raging about the betrayal of General Narciso López's ragtag army training to invade Cuba from America? Would they remember that López's army was ordered disbanded by President Taylor, and when López's ill-trained men landed at Cardenas in the 1850s they were devoured by the Spanish jackals? Abuelo had stormed in the back room of the *grocería* that America would again betray Cuba. Abuelo knew this in his bones. Cubans had to rely on Cubans. That was the history lesson. Justo wondered if his daughters would ever understand their old grandfather, dying of grief and hacking a cancerous cigar cough one week after the Bay of Pigs invasion proved his prophecy of America's betrayal correct. Abuelo's tamarind cane rested now in Justo's living room, next to a statue of the Virgin Mother beneath which Rosella always kept the flame of a novena candle burning. Would his daughters remember they were Tamarindos, carved from the tree of Cuban liberation? Justo always asked himself these questions as he came upon the small family plot with its neatly lined rectangles of aboveground whitewashed graves.

Ocho stopped again, tipping his long nose in the air, sniffing at uncertainty, then moved slowly toward Abuelo's grave at the center of Justo's family plot. A tall stone cross was affixed atop the plain headstone with the chiseled words: MANUELO DIEGO ROSA TAMARINDO ??–1961. Ocho looked back at Justo. Justo grabbed the dog's collar, yanking the surprised animal away from the grave. Two streaks of blood, crossed in the shape of an X, had been slashed across the white rectangle of Abuelo's grave. The blood had come from the slit belly of a South American bufo toad perched dead and drained in the center of the X. The warty five-pound blob's bulged eyes were crudely sewn shut with fishing line, its mouth closed by a nail hammered through the head and out the lower jaw. At the foot of Abuelo's grave a sheet of white paper was weighted down by a rock. Justo turned cautiously, looking back up the long avenue behind him. No one there. Far across the horizon of tombstones, at the entrance to the cemetery, there was only the distant silhouette of a lone bicyclist. Probably someone pedaling a shortcut path through the cemetery on his way to work downtown. Justo turned back to Abuelo's grave. He held Ocho's collar tightly. The milky substance which had foamed from the toad's mouth and coagulated on its fat lips contained a poison which could send a big dog into convulsions, drop a small dog dead. The blood on the grave glistened, still fresh. Someone knew Justo's habits, knew he would be at the cemetery this first friday of the month. Justo slipped the white paper from beneath the rock on the grave. He held it up to read words written in elaborate cursive flair:

OLD FILOR'S SLY AS DE MOUSE
LOCKED DEM NIGGERS IN DE MARKET HOUSE
KEPT DEM DERE TIL HAF PASS NINE
FIVE DOLLAHS WAS DERE FINE

RUN, NIGGER, RUN! FILOR WILL GIT YOU!
WISH I WAS IN FILOR'S PLACE
TO GIVE DEM NIGGERS A LONGER RACE!

The name Zobop was signed at the end with a purple felt-tip pen. Beneath the name was sketched a slinking snake with a man's face, a hissing snake's tongue extended from the human lips. The creature wore a jaunty black top hat.

Ocho lunged at the toad. Justo dragged the dog further back. He looked around among the weeds and plastic flowers for a stick to knock the ugly creature from Abuelo's resting place. There were no sticks, just skink lizards skittering away from the disturbance. Justo made the sign of the cross, then stepped onto Abuelo's grave, kicking the dead weight of the toad with the toe of his shoe. He crushed the sheet of white paper into a tiny ball, hurled it over the right wing of the sweet-faced angel guarding his family. He remembered the words *Casa mala nunca muere.* Abuelo was so fond of saying these words as he leaned on the handle of the tamarind cane looking into Justo's young eyes. *A bad thing never dies.*

Justo turned his back on the bad thing and clutched the gold wishbone at his throat like a man gasping for life-giving air. The veins of his thick neck swelled as he strode down Third Avenue in the city of the dead. In the tumult of his mind two lines of poetry came up

from the past to carry him far and away from this evil, a revelation in repose only now awakening to true meaning.

> *When in the white pools of Europa's rose*
> *The virginal and naked hunting tribe . . .*

Some things are best left undisturbed.

8

THERE is the buzz of heat, scuttle of crabs, creak of deceit, cracking light. There is the steady scurry of decay, the slow hum of tropical time. Thump-thump, it beats a two-step reality in the hurricane dance of my many minds. Soon the furious Eye passes through dead hearts, stirs stormy rebirth. I await. You must pay the band if you want to dance. I above all am the Devil Dancer if nothing else, nothing else except uneasiness, uncertainty honed to edgy anticipation. I am the bee in your ear, the scorpion in your bed, the rat clawing in your belly, scratching in the palm tree outside your window, watching through amber eyes. My mind throbs like the scarlet blow-bubble throat of a chameleon caught on a tin-rusted roof after hiss of rain. Beware your history does not escape me, for I existed here before Ponce de León touched these shores in 1513, that great greedy man himself, all feathered pomp and powdered cheeks, discovering not land, not ocean, but a bastard world of both, from sun to shining sea, a humid hole in the middle of the New World, a martyred universe of twisted knife-sharp coral jutting through tepid brine, a limbo de León named Los Matires, then abruptly left to his nightmares, setting quick sail for luminous youthful vistas, toward visions of waterspouts towering on the distant horizon, filled with the honey of other men's money, and the promised milky rape of eyeless daughters. I existed before other forms of life on these Pleistocene rocks of the swampy Florida Keys. Existed when stone crabs were embryonic ghostly shadows, before their crusted shells turned yellow, before their pinching claw tips turned black to hook unsuspecting prey from briny sleep. I am a Devil Wind born in the Sahara, a destined swirl of dust

rising from Africa, breathing the Atlantic's hot breath as I whirl my course toward you across water. No ancient reef of coral can protect you, nor modern highway bridged across the sea offer you escape. No painted plaster Virgin planted in a man-made grotto of cement will miraculously stand up to protect you against my vicious velocity. The winds of scorn fill my sails. I spit on your castrated creations, your puny world of microchips, the Bible and *Moby Dick*. When I talk to Jesus I call him collect. I am what is least in your world and foremost in mine, a proud beast. I am a lactating drama with breasts bound. I am every generation suckling. I rut with flies and dine with fleas. I allow fish to lament and bats to copulate with hummingbirds. I have seen your Lucy in the Sky with Diamonds, have slept under the thumb of your dissatisfactions. If I throw my hat to the tides it will burn a hole through to China. So when you see me, beware that it is not me, for you see me in yourself. Always after the passion of a passing tropical storm an unearthly air settles over my island, leaden clouds descend to fill this brazen melting pot. The azure sea becomes mute and sighs a blank, unforgiving stare at the exposed heavens above.

Take my hand. I will not hurt you. You should know me well enough by now. We are friends, you and I, less than brother and sister, more than lovers of pig bone and haters of green monkey blood. Take my hand. You need me. You need my comforting wasp tongue. I am the one who stands vigilant at the gate of waters. Without me there is no purity, all would be waste, your soul would be so much mold on rancid breadfruit cake. Take my hand to where it leads you. Follow me to your own history. You don't know your own history, do you? That is why you are doomed without me. You don't know the history of your world, cannot remember from day to day what happened in your own life. You are human, less than animal, for a dog never falls in the same hole twice. You need me now more than ever, take my hand. Does it feel moist? You need my moist hand to guide you. This is the end of the road, this is your way out from the past. Your future begins here, on this mute coral rock, this splayed backbone of calcified dreams. Yes, you will need a guide for this journey through the fractured present. You can't go somewhere from nowhere, so I will light the way. Does my moist hand feel like an unhatched leatherback turtle egg, newly oozed from the sphincteral release of its thirteen-hundred-pound holy mother? Be careful with my hand, it is fragile and uneasy, as are all turtle eggs tucked into sandy nests beyond high tideline, eggs abandoned by a mother in full moonlight, who only departs the sea in the whole of her life to instigate new life. The rocking sea cradles creation, the shore steadies the consequence. Is my hand warm, like the sunbaked membrane of an unhatched leatherback egg? What do you care? You don't. That is why you build condominiums and shopping centers where the turtles are given their first shot at survival, freshly cracked from their eggs, and in their moment of stunned originality they mistake your beams of man-made light for the reflective lure of rocking mother ocean. They head into your false light toward crushing doom of automobile tires, toward domestic cat's claws and rats crazed on eating domestic trash, toward the doom of your modern tundra. The turtles are like *Boteros*, the refugee boat people lured to your shores by bright promises, by beacons of get rich quick schemes, get so rich your children won't have to work schemes. Lured by a brightly lighted universe of falsity, where your sullen young are pampered and exalted. You don't believe me? Listen to your own radiowaves, bearing in the air spores of indolence, crackling with cranky adolescent mewings, an atmosphere of arrogance rife with pimply cravings, lust born of boredom. The insides of your ears have been chewed out by this perpetual rot. You no longer hear the sound of your own ignorance, no longer abide by laws of Nature, deny the wisdom of age. Your mind grows younger as you grow older. You think you are the second coming of Ponce de León, have discovered your personal Milky Way of eternal juicy fruit. Go ahead, take a bite of your perverse produce. You bite down on a big lie, its swallowed pit of decay will grow to a wasp in your gut, bees will bleed from your ears. Hush. Don't cry. My moist hand is in yours, a stillborn turtle growing virtuous. You want to leave me, don't you? You don't like my chat, are fearful of fact. You can hear me but can't see me. You feel only moisture in your palm, sweat on the back of your neck. You don't know who I am, do you? You don't know what thoughts rush through my stillborn brain. My brain is like the Gulf Stream twelve miles offshore, a vast blue river cutting through green ocean, its current pulsing seventy-five million tons of water through it each second, a force greater than the combined sum of all your earthly rivers. I am a torrent of thoughts flowing within society's surrounding sea, a stream of ideas surging with plankton and verbs, a circular countercurrent fury, stalking like a submerged caged beast with no tail or head, like the Gulf Stream stalks, between Africa and the Americas, its great muscular force pacing incessant circles between Old and New Worlds, without beginning, without amens. I have no history because I am stillborn, laden with prescient knowledge. But I refuse to be born into your world, a hapless turtle blinded by condo parking lot glare, my centuries of blood instinct confused, thinking my fins are pushing me toward full moon luminescence. In your world birds and crabs are no longer the sole predators of my turtle's soul, for it is not the lunar pull at all which guides me now, but falsity of light.

Don't go. Come back. I promise to be good. If you stay I will tell you a secret. Do you like secrets? Of course you do, all greedy children love secrets, and you are nothing if not a perpetual adolescent. Isn't that what your society breeds in you? Is not that what is reflected in the rearview mirror of your soul, for is not the soul of your universe the automobile? The automobile is what brought you down here, driving into an ocean larger than Europe on a slot of concrete highway bridged between forty-three islands. Or did you come by aluminum wing, by airplane? You are lucky you have wings to fly with, for you have destroyed the beautiful West Indian doves that once migrated here. Now only the white-crowned pigeon survives, to chart its atavistic course once a year across the Gulf of Mexico from Cuba to Florida. The first scheduled airline flights over water from a foreign country to America followed the course of the defunct West Indian dove, from Havana to Key West. Your pilots did not have sophisticated radio communications then. They had only carrier pigeons, which they took aloft with them in small wooden cages, ready to be released, to fly to Key West with messages of help banded around their fragile legs. You have destroyed nearly all of Nature's winged wonders which once flew over these waters, the rest you have caged and perverted to sustain your murderous existence. Yes, I do mean murderous. You exalt your killers, like that son of a slave-dealing sea captain who headed here in the first half of the last century, your Mr. Audubon, who slaughtered fabulous feathered creatures, wing-shot hundreds of great marbled godwits and great white herons, all for the vanity of painting his version of their image. This son of a dusky Dominican slave mistress likened himself to an Egyptian pharmacopolist embalming the Pharaohs, and counted among his closest friends American firearms dealers and aristocratic European perverts who coveted their egg collections of endangered and extinct birds. Yes, your beloved folk hero trekked a lifetime in search of ornithological splendor with the thumping elephantine desire of killing life to preserve it. This obsessive scribbler, whose very name rings with ecological righteousness, was a wanton destroyer of the very thing he sought to salvage. So you see, I am not the morally bent, stubby creature you make me out to be. I am upright; it is your heroes who are face down in the slime of revisionist history, bubbles of lies exuding from their nostrils. If you do not cling to my truth you too shall unravel. Do you think I tell only things you don't want to hear? Do you think I keep you here only on pretext of letting you in on my little secret? Are you beginning to believe I don't have a secret? Ah, you know me well enough by now, don't you? You know enough to understand I am special, like a queer feeling in your throat, a pain in your heart, a dead bird in your hand.

You have a fascinating problem. Because you don't know your own history you are headed for a downfall. Even though you are repelled by me, you know you need me to catch you when the fall comes. That is why you are pleading with me to tell you something other than unsettling truth, soothe you with something pretty, coo over flight of yellow-crowned night herons, sing of brilliantly hued angelfish, moo about saving the manatees from speedboat propellers, tittle your sense of injustice by flapping about nearly extinct Florida panthers being slaughtered on alligator highways cutting through the last Everglades. You desire I slither like a barracuda, slink like a sand shark, dart like an egret, soar like an osprey over red mangroves. You desire anything except what I am, truthsayer. For generations you have been pumping three to eight million gallons a day of your filth through a two-foot pipe into the ship channel no more than four thousand feet offshore of this island you call home. Your human waste floats and beckons to diving gulls and greedy bottom fish, a dark stain on pure waters, a gaseous floating wreath your children call the Shit Slick. While you chuckle and clink the ice in your cocktail glass beneath a dimming sun-pricked sky, oceans die all around, dolphins weep, flying fish scream. It wasn't enough for you when one man fishing alone could catch a thousand pounds of king mackerel a day, jigging his bright lures to attract excited flash of schooling fish. No, handlining was too slow. Now you chase the excited schools from overhead in spotter planes, sending your diesel-powered prowling posse of big boats out to corral with nets in hours what has taken Nature an infinity to produce. Soon you shall have fished the seas dry. Then you will be reduced to jigging your own Shit Slick. Forced to dine on flesh fed by your own excrement. And you ask me to talk pretty to you. To tell you comfortable lies about progress being your only business. You are disappointed because I won't rhapsodize about Jamaican dogwood in bloom, recount the fifty-two color patterns that recur in the Keys tree snail. Why should I tell you about illusive tree snails which feed on tree-bark lichen, knowing that as I speak you charge their minute domain with bulldozers and poison their insides with insecticides? You have transformed these martyred rocks of the Florida Keys into profane monuments. To guide your maritime commerce of plunder you have built lighthouses one hundred feet above sea level, their beckoning beams penetrating nocturnal ocean wilderness, cutting counterfeit paths across the passage of migrating birds which fly from night, winded creatures, bewildered as they crash into brilliant traps, frail bodies smashing against hot orbs of false light. The spring and fall tides of the Gulf of Mexico are littered with the feathered kill of your insensitivity.

Enough, you shout, you aren't responsible for the earth's ills! So why can't I be generous and entertain you, soothe your trembling hide, coddle you like those alligators you've seen in Everglade tourist traps, where Indian boys wrestle reptilian creatures onto gnarly backs, then rub gator-white bellies with sand until angry snorts turn to snores as the ancient creatures drift off, webbed feet pawing the air as their powerful tails slacken, no longer threatening to break a man in two with a fierce swish. Off to beddy-bye-bye you want to go. When you awaken fresh from dreams I'll still be here, rubbing sand on your belly, rockabying your alibi in an amphibious limbo. I am not a dream. Does your hand feel moist, is your mouth dry? Good, we can get down to business. I'll tell you my secret, now that you have awakened from your stupor of two-bit simps preaching over radiowaves for sympathy from the Devil. The Devil doesn't need your guilt, the Devil doesn't dish sympathy, the Devil desires only souls. I know more about these things than those who are these things. I see the forest without the trees. I see myself in a suit of bones. I have become transparent, invisibly exposed, a vengeful skeleton stalking your island streets. I know by heart your childish songs of rock and roll, mock and muck, incessant patter, mind stagnation, year after year after. Will you never grow up? *I am the Walrus. I am him and you are me and we are them together, whowh whowh!* I am not part of your interminable childish present. I am not the Walrus. I am not you. We are not together, ever. You didn't know that? You don't know anything. But maybe this once you think you do. Maybe you think you don't really need me. It would be the end of you to think that, finality. I must go now because I must put on my suit of skeletal lights, dance into the night, a naked snake in a top hat. Are you coming? I thought so. You have been squeezing the rubbery shell of my hand so intently. Come then, we are off. What? You'll have to speak up. I can't hear you above the water roaring through my head. My secret? You want to come with me to learn my secret? Of course. When I discover the wrongdoers their evil will bleed in the streets. Since you forget your present as well as your past you need me to remind you of this fact. If there is one thing Zobop does, Zobop reminds with remembrance, avenges memory. Hold tight. Listen hard. You've got one last chance to escape before becoming like the hordes of pretenders who drifted to this island south of the south, burning every bridge of hope behind, flying from home without ever leaving the ground, tumbling down to land's end. Nowhere to go from here except to start swimming with sharks and barracuda. Southernmost point it is called, mile zero. Last hope for star-crossed creatures dreaming in tropical pastures at the end of the American road. Last hope.

BOOK TWO

FALSE LIGHT

9

OTHING is forever, not even eternal love. If the rats don't get you the scorpions will. Still, St. Cloud hoped. Lost in his own shadow he trailed the moist impressions of barefoot prints left by Evelyn and her companion along the heat-cracked sidewalk. The full moon hung at the street's deserted end, its orange lantern eye an unblinking target for the barbed lunacy of cats in shadows confessing consummate pain of vented lust. Behind the moon lightning stabbed a distant sky, a tumble of stars fell south across the Tropic of Cancer toward Cuba, thunder boomed beyond the Great Bahama Bank. The streets St. Cloud walked all became dead-end alligator alleys on a coral-capped island shaped by shipwrecked dreams and hurricane reality. An anxious atmosphere presided over the island suspended within the confluence of the moody Gulf of Mexico and the torrent of the Atlantic Gulf Stream. Here luck is determined by the roll of the waves. No matter how complex or simple one's life is rigged all bait becomes equal beneath such vast ocean bodies obeying solar gravitational spin and lunar countercurrent force. Through the centuries this reality exacted from all a fearful belief in the great currents of chance. The island's mansions and shacks of Bahamian freemen, Cuban cigarmakers, renegade sea captains, turtle hunters, shrimpers, sponge gatherers and rumrunners were built with backs to the sea, the direction from which hurricanes and pirates roared ashore. Tide turning winds of unpredictability created an inward architecture. Houses were constructed cheek by jowl, close enough to block boisterous weather and allow the call of alarm to pass from one high-perched porch to another. The island city reeked with an implacable sense of impermanence, was made incestuous by communal fear of the world beyond its protective reef.

Skeletal house shadows stole across deserted streets in moonlight, their fragile outlines leapt over St. Cloud onto opposite rooftops, darkening windows and doors. Dreams of fear and lust clawed through rooftops and beneath subconscious sheets. Intimate shapes slipped into obscure crevices, coupling sleepers, producing progeny of an unspoken conspiracy. The sanest sleepers succumbed to this incestuous scheme. Upon awakening all could abandon responsibility for personal actions, assume a collective cloak of dementia imposed the night before by the genuinely mad, for there were only two types of people on the island, scorpions and rats. That is what many islanders believed. St. Cloud believed it too, and he was not descended from runaway British slaves or clipper-ship wreckers. If rats scurried on the gingerbread spindles of a white veranda, then scorpions were not to be found sunning themselves on the high widow's walk. If scorpions slithered down yellow-pine bedroom walls, no rats were gnawing in the attic. Houses are inhabited by scorpions or rats. That is what the old Conchs say. If the two dwell together there will be the devil who dwells beneath the rock of the island to pay. Certain as calm weather will one day become a howling squall and boisterous weather become hurricane El Finito, rats and scorpions are destined to intertwine in the island's nocturnal wanderings, the sleepers awaken to a reality not yet dreamed.

Nothing is forever, not even eternal love. Still, St. Cloud followed Evelyn beneath brightening streetlights haloed by sultry salt air flowing fresh from the Florida Bay. How does a man track a woman? There seemed only bare skin between Evelyn and the world. St. Cloud used her familiar scent as guide. Her body glowed with cool sweat, thin red material was banded over breasts and clasped in the juncture of a taut back, whiteness of abbreviated shorts flashed at the top of tanned legs. She wore less of something and more of nothing. St. Cloud felt the urging toward her he was never able to control, which over years Evelyn had been able to manipulate, operate the passion of her purpose just beyond his reach. Still he reached, even when he knew Evelyn was beyond touching, was with someone else, as she was now. St. Cloud followed and lurked, no better than the phantom cats screeching in the backyard of the island's imagination. What difference did it make if he and Evelyn were getting a divorce? They were still

married, and the town's screeching cats still had to screw standing up
because the streets were so narrow, while dogs stood on their heads
just to wag their tails. Phantom rapist, why couldn't he let Evelyn go?
This is an island, no matter how far you go you always have to turn
around and come back. What goes around comes around. Maybe that
was it. Evelyn was his history, represented his memories. Without
Evelyn his youth disappeared, his essence evaporated. Maybe he was
simply skulking around his past, a vicarious seducer of distant
memories, raping his own dreams. Could he let her go?

St. Cloud had become a man of limited means and narrow streets,
a lurking back-alley lizard, a three-minute love affair in a two-minute
town. What was the poetic line of that other drunken poetic scammer
he was fond of? That other ranting romantic of song searching for
the muse in the hollow worm at the bottom of every mescal bottle,
the worm which crawls through wood-heart soul of every man destined
to die a boy. St. Cloud had to stop drinking. He was losing it. Come
back, little memory. Now it was coming closer, on its knees, a worm
of an idea crawling. It was about the eye. Yes. *The eye is jealous.* It was
coming back. That's it. Jealousy. *The eye is jealous of whatever moves and
the heart*—always the heart—*is too far buried in the sand to tell.*

Evelyn and the slender woman who held her hand turned the
corner at the end of the street. *Whatever moves.* The heart moves in
sand despite its blind eye. Did St. Cloud want to smash Evelyn's
present reality to keep forever her muse trapped in the perfect bottle
of their shared past? Stars in his eyes, brains in his shoes, another
whiskey waltz. He was not thinking straight. Worms don't move
straight in mud, a sideways slither is often the quickest route home.
St. Cloud was walking underwater again, pushing toward the jeweled
surface. So much history between the two of them. All that water
under the bridge, over his head. He passed beneath the outstretched
arms of a night-blooming cactus tree, its star-shaped flowers winking
back at a starry sky. Stars in his eyes, brains in his shoes, another
whiskey waltz. Evelyn was halfway up the next block, a smooth flash
of flesh. Frogs clamored, restless bull-throated insect suckers baying
at a foreign moon. They could smell rain coming.

Lightning flared closer in the south, storm off the coast of Cuba.
It was late. Radio Havana was finally off the air. Into its static void
rushed powerful stations from Miami, invading the airwaves of the
tropical workers' paradise with promise of faster cars, clearer skin

and prune-slick regularity. American Rock and Roll was coming on strong. Little Richard sí! Marx no, viva Elvis! Rock and Roll the Revolutionary soul. While out beyond the Dry Tortugas Hurricane El Finito lurked, big boisterous blow biding his time before roaring through waning dog days to fix problems for rockers and despots. St. Cloud understood it was all about water, to go out on it, to be part of it, surrounded. The island was an elaborate dock of dreams lost in its own sea of time, kept afloat by the lust and lure of the ultimate siren song.

A motorcycle pierced through dreams, screamed down a steamy side street far across the island, reverberating between houses, entangling in St. Cloud's mind. It was the identical whine of a marijuana-loaded cigarette boat running three skips and a heartbeat ahead of a Coast Guard cutter, losing itself in a mangrove maze of shallow water back country, zeroing in on the promise of a million-dollar profit or a cute seven-year stretch in an upstate panhandle prison. Dreams and schemes tangled as St. Cloud stumbled around to the back of Evelyn's house. He leaned against the smoothed trunk of a banyan, deep in shadow. Through the open shutters of Evelyn's bedroom a ladder of light was cast into the garden, its last bright step falling at St. Cloud's feet. Slouched beneath the banyan he had a cockeyed perspective into the bedroom. Images of two women inside flickered insistent as a silent movie through slatted shutters, movements broken into isolated moments, the full motive of female gestures incomplete. Oriental robes loosened on bodies, silk flash. St. Cloud moaned. This had to stop. The only thing worse than drunken deception is illuminating self-pity. Thank God for the crutch of a banyan tree with its roots anchored in ancient coral rock to hold a man up, to steady the aim of his desire, support his sideways progress.

The Conchs say the devil is under the rock of the island. St. Cloud tried to get a hold of himself. The devil was in him. That's why he was here, on the outside looking in the window of the present, rubbing his loss against the smoky glass of memory. He still couldn't get in. There was no clear glass here, only cocked shutters sheltering silken moments, robes slipping from shoulders, flare of match, damp scent of marijuana floating from within, blending with airborne secretion of jasmine. This garden was sucking St. Cloud into its green hole. Used to be his garden, his bedroom, his wife with a fallen silk robe gathered around ankles, his muse, his Madonna. Why do this, why persist? What snake did he expect to find in this Eden? What music slipping the strange skin of its song did he expect to hear?

Lightning illuminated the garden, exposing at St. Cloud's feet a swirl of ants disassembling an upturned Cuban Death's Head palmetto bug, its many legs already devoured. Thunder bellowed closer. The rain from New Spain was almost here. Not much time. The ants chewed hurriedly, a circular, purposive flurry, spiriting away neat carcass hunks into a secret recess to make an honest feast in a disquieting world. The garden fell back into its dark moments. Warm rain from New Spain arrived, spattering broad leaves. Lizards leapt in the grass, frogs crooned. What was embroidered on those silk robes sliding off bodies? Dragons, fiery tongues entwined? The shutters flew open in the rainy breeze, scorpions slithered up bedroom walls. Evelyn rose from the swell of a female sea. Intruding rain mixed with the sweat of exposed skin. She leaned forward to claim the banging shutters, arms outstretched from the swing of her breasts. She paused. Her words cast into rain hissing across the garden before the shutters enclosed her. "Good night, St. Cloud."

Rain beat on the shuttered world of women. St. Cloud could see nothing within now. Evelyn's words caught him off guard, froze him beneath the banyan in a tropical still life, a mute male statue steaming in the rain. The frogs hushed as beaked turtles went about their stealthy business in deep grass. The island opened to the fleeting rain from New Spain. Out across the Caribbean, over the edge of the world where Christopher Columbus hit his home run, the Madonna on the reef moaned her music underwater. St. Cloud was afraid to move, to lose the strange sound winging on a seaborne wind. The blurred image of Lila swam before him, calling the siren song of a muse emerging anew. If only there were words to capture her illusion. The Madonna on the reef was an illusion, like the Spanish galleons loaded with gold booty from the jungles and towering peaks of New Spain. All illusion. The gold in the ground had no more worth than chalk, until man invested value in it, was willing to die for it, commit a mother lode of sins on two continents for it. One of those ancient galleons had the Virgin Mary carved on its bow, halo of gold around her head, cutting through wind and waves, Mother Protector, Christian Conqueror, Saint of Saints, Virgin Conquistador. Out there on the sea the Virgin struck a reef, the galleon smashed to valueless timber, cut into a thousand pieces by the power of an impervious tide. Sailor flesh becomes fish flesh. Conquistadores are conquered. Gold takes on the currency of sand, a glittering handful of legend. Still, there are those who follow that Madonna to the reef, go down with her, embrace the stormy illusion, all for the transitory chance to touch the glittering legend of their own lives.

10

RUM RHUMBA. St. Cloud felt he was right in step with the scorpions and rats. A tricky whiskey waltz to navigate the risk of cracked sidewalks and woeful fat-bodied Cuban Death's Head bugs plodding to primordial beat, beating a path from his drunken path. He didn't care to crush the creatures. St. Cloud thought them somehow charmed, if not sacred. Others saw them as overblown cockroaches on a filthy-bellied prowl to be stomped from existence. To step on one was to defy the gods, or worse. As Isaac said, it would be like pissing in the eye of the Sphinx. It was Isaac St. Cloud was after now. Only Isaac could put out the fire in his brain, flood his heart with some common sense after a night finally ending near dawn with Brogan in the Wreck Room and more MK talk. Brogan seemed to know so many intimate details about his brother's life St. Cloud suspected Brogan didn't have a brother. Maybe Brogan was talking about himself in a former life before drifting to Key West and dedicating himself to snatching sunken treasure from the jaws of time. Maybe Brogan was MK. St. Cloud didn't know. Everyone this far south of the south seemed to have left behind a shadow life. Perhaps Brogan simply embellished the singular tune of his existence into the full-blown mystery opera of MK. Perhaps, but not probable. There was a strange kinship of spirit St. Cloud felt from what he'd heard about MK. He did not feel such kinship with Brogan. St. Cloud suspected the reality of MK did not originate in Brogan's mind, but sprang from a deeper source. It all had to do with MK and St. Cloud being on opposite sides during the Vietnam war: one, the renegade protester; the other, a trained assassin. It had something to do with that, an odd circle closing after a generation passed. The one who fought the war, the one who fought against it, ironically, the last two who cared. It had to do with that, but that was not everything. Everything was larger, confused and beyond reach. St. Cloud doubted Brogan's drunken meanderings about MK would illuminate final truth. MK was a ghost in more ways than one. St. Cloud had never met the man. MK had come to the island and put his people into place years before St. Cloud and Evelyn arrived. MK was forever on the lips of many, a man seldom seen but whose presence was always felt. St. Cloud listened closely to Brogan's rantings about his brother because it seemed Brogan was talking about what St. Cloud himself could easily have become. If fate had stopped the wheel of chance on an opposite number, St. Cloud would be MK; they were the reverse of one another, queerly nailed together on the cross of time. What St. Cloud had been trying all these years to wash away in a sea of alcohol was a war he couldn't forget, a war nobody else remembered except those who fought in it or against it, the two now like reluctant partners from a bad marriage who, decades after the divorce, are doomed to remember their communal pain, condemned to relive moment to moment the crucial matter of the past, until the past becomes ever present. Enemies of the past now had become survivor warriors of the present. Such grand irony, the few left from the Vietnam generation whose consciences had been burned out were now fated to dance a duet of despair. Brash innocence had been slaughtered a generation before, the heroes of darkness were condemned to the light at the end of the tunnel. St. Cloud understood both he and MK were true POW's of the skeletal memories of a nearly forgotten war, both left with leftover lives to flesh out. Conscience had not been taken prisoner, conscience had long since been lost to both.

The more Brogan talked of MK in the Wreck Room last night, the more St. Cloud felt the busy teeth of a rat gnawing through his rum-soaked soul. The rat finally nested in the unresolved guilt of St. Cloud's failed past. It had been many years since St. Cloud collapsed in pursuit of his youthful purpose, incapable of transcending the entrails of Vietnam, unable to use his knowledge and experience to make himself over into the shape of an anonymous man, like many of the pacifists did after the Second World War. St. Cloud felt the saddle of fear chafing on his shoulders. It was no longer enough to make a career of running from an old life, not enough to work the high wire of self-pity without a net. Those who struggled to stop the war in Vietnam a generation ago knew they had been defeated. Vietnam was not a war that ended in peace, it was a peace made into a war, war with oneself. St. Cloud's fascination with MK was a belief MK had tunneled his way to illuminating light by never accepting personal failure or national defeat. MK's means of escape was to stay at war, keep moving, never come home, become ultimately what all civilized society is at war against. Brogan told St. Cloud MK made the same pact with himself as St. Cloud had, both understood that to come to peace with oneself is certain death.

St. Cloud had searched in his rummy haze for illumination, the bright hope of a burning hoop of completion. As Brogan talked St. Cloud saw the hoop coming toward him, a flaming circle of fire spreading in the green jungle from the dropped bomb of an overhead B-52. The only thing left for St. Cloud was to jump through the flaming hoop. He now understood. Vietnam had opened a world of pain and guilt for both himself and MK, was an aphrodisiac of moral mourning which had become a narcotic. At this point of damning light near dawn in the Wreck Room St. Cloud had another rum and lost control. He tumbled through space, a charred soul. He stumbled out the door of the Wreck Room, drifting like a dog with a cut tail, staggering into early morning. Everything seemed distant to him, far away as his lost youth, even Evelyn's world behind shutters in the garden was a forbidden planet, at best an unreachable moon. There was greater safety behind closed bedroom shutters, where fiery-tongued dragons ruled the lunar roost, than where St. Cloud was headed, up the last one-way alligator alley into the swamp of delusion. His blood hummed with blind idiot intention. He felt suddenly compelled to confess his passion for the barely legal-aged Dixie Peach who resided cool and unruffled amidst the squawks and screeches of Evelyn's bird shop. Isaac would understand how such a southern drawling creature's sensuality could perk up an aging man's downed radar, explode what was left of his common sense. Though St. Cloud was still in love with his lost self in Evelyn, such was puppy love compared to the song of fools aching in his throat for Lila. He cocked his cap and set sail in a desperate stupor toward Isaac. Only Isaac could smooth St. Cloud's ruffled soul, help him snatch sunken treasure from the unforgiving jaws of time. It was Isaac St. Cloud desperately needed now.

The uneven roll of the cracked sidewalk glimmered in morning

mist before St. Cloud, vivid as a silver flashing serpentine wave on a
rough sea. The roots of towering Spanish laurel trees heaved the
sidewalk up in ever-increasing treacherous waves. St. Cloud pushed
on, a high-blown yachtsman in a storm-tossed moment. He was nearing
the end of Whitehead Street. The pavement dead ahead stopped.
The high Atlantic tide lapped against the SOUTHERNMOST POINT
OF THE CONTINENTAL U.S.A., a landmark proclaimed in bright
letters painted on a torpedo-shaped concrete monument, which
informed as an afterthought in smaller letters around the torpedo's
nose: 90 MILES TO CUBA. If Whitehead Street continued another ninety
miles, instead of ending abruptly at the sharp edge of the Atlantic
Ocean, St. Cloud could keep right on going until he walked down
the palm-lined avenues of Havana and into the Floridita Bar, where
he'd pull up a stool, wink at the white-gloved waiters balancing silver
trays, order a round of drinks to toast tropical Marxism in the land
of papaya girls with perfect ankles and pure smiles of mango persuasion. He resisted the temptation of walking on water and turned at
the end of Whitehead up the next block, where the sidewalk had not
only been cracked and lifted by another Spanish laurel, but shattered
by a massive trunk pushing toward the sky in a mighty heave, throwing
thick limbs out to block the sun. From towering overhead branches
tendrils of airborne roots trailed fifty feet back to earth, forming a
roped curtain, obliterating from view Isaac's Bahamian mansion
beyond.

Over the years a wandering path had been hacked through the
dense jungle beneath the tree, leading to the twenty broad stairs rising
steeply to the wraparound porch. It seemed the tree was the house,
of primary permanence, all else was simple landscape, feckless man-
made ornament. Only beneath a tree of majesty could Isaac's mansion
appear dwarfed. The structure was honored as one of the town's
grandest and eccentric; most of all, like the island Conch people
themselves, it was hailed as a survivor. The house originally stood on
a distant Bahamian island, where a hurricane had swept through with
such fury it tossed houses, people and trees into the ocean, right
down to the last coconut, everything except the multistoried Victorian
gingerbread-style mansion of the island's plantation overlord, a deserted monument left in the calm. The painstakingly built society
which gave rise to such grandeur was gone, demolished in the quick
breath of a greater master's plan. The mansion's owner was evicted
on a howling night, tossed out with his slaves into the common grave

of the sea. The elaborate structure lingered in forlorn splendor on an island passed by for a generation by those blessed with memory of how swiftly the well-laid plans of man could be swept aside. The mansion was battered by new storms. Its mahogany shutters slammed and cracked in high winds. The elaborately carved spindles of the balustrade circling the second-story exterior balcony shrunk in the sun and snapped, imprinting an impression of a wide toothsome smile with the teeth missing. The tin-stamped roofs of the cupolas rising above the second story on all four corners, which once stood proudly as castle turrets on guard against the impervious tide of time, had surrendered. The cupolas buckled and collapsed, one after the other, each with a deeper sigh of disrepair as it caved into the silence of neglect. It took a man who thought big to salvage the gingerbread shambles. Even in an age when men thought nothing of floating houses from island to island, moving them lock, stock and dormers, mansards and gables across the seas, it required a grand schemer to restore glory to the mansion. James Fredrick Isaac was such a man. A Wrecker by trade, a gambler by nature, and a humble servant of God who roared brimstone and fire on the sabbath, James Fredrick, some said, understood the truth of false lights, made his fortune betting on the truth of that illusion. There were many men like James Fredrick who arrived in Key West penniless as the eighteenth century came into the nineteenth, loaded with opportunity for fortune. The gilded fate of many was mere miles away, off the westward hook of Key West where magnificent merchant Clipper ships of the day rode high down the Florida Straits, hugged the narrow channel along the reef's jagged wall, into deep safety of the Gulf of Mexico. Not all vessels sailed into safe harbor. When weather turned squally even the most astute shipmaster was hard put to keep his vessel off the miles of shoals waiting on one side of Key West, and the reef on the other. Along the entire length of the Bahama Channel and the Florida Straits only a few weak lights glimmered to warn wary sailors off razor rocks capable of undoing the stoutest hull. So many ships sunk with silk and gold, lace and pewter, and all the bounty of the Seven Seas in between, that by 1850 Key West became the wealthiest town in America. The men who made that wealth were the Wreckers and the speculators who backed them. These men bid their time against inevitable inclement weather and human folly. The Wrecker put his ship and life on the line. The speculator bet his cash to back the Wrecker. It seemed the shipborne riches of the world, no matter what their original destination, were preordained to end up in the mammoth salvage warehouses of Key West. When a ship was torn open on the reef a cry of *WRRREEEEEECK AHHHH-SHHHHORE* went up through the town. Church bells rang from steeples and men came running to crew fast boats to the wreck. The first to arrive at the disaster became the Wreck Master, who laid claim by law to the salvage. But the race to the wreck was normally in savage weather, or on moonless nights across a course laid with craggy underwater traps. Many Wreckers lost their lives on the rocks in their rush to riches. Others died trying to right ships listing on the reef, or raising those sunk to the bottom. Even more were crushed beneath tonnage of a shifting sea and flood tides as they worked to empty a submerged cargo hold. Such was how James Fredrick lost the lower half of his left leg. In James Fredrick's early days, before he captained his own boat, he crewed on a Wrecking Ship with a reputation of sending its divers over the rail before the foundered position of the wrecked vessel alongside had steadied. One blustery night James Fredrick was the first over the rail, leaping across a storming sea with a securing rope. He landed safely on the listing ship as a dark wave swept over its bow with a roar which tore the rope through James Fredrick's hands, slammed him across the breadth of the splintering main deck in a choke of salt water, leaving him buried beneath the crushing fall of barrels filled with Spanish olives.

By the time James Fredrick spied the deserted Bahamian mansion he was a graying man, his stoutness supported by one leg of muscular flesh, the other of solid gold. He clattered forth and fro on his gold peg leg across the deck of his own Baltimore Clipper. The Baltimore Clipper was not a true clipper, but a jaunty topsail schooner with a nine-foot draft needing only a handful of trustworthy men to crew. It could outsail the devil in a basket across the roughest seas. The Baltimore Clipper was the perfect wrecking vessel, except the hectic wrecking days of Key West were over. Two hundred miles of once night-dark waterway, which had given James Fredrick his fortune, were now aglow with lightships and lighthouses. Courts of law and underwriters had changed the rules of wrecking, implemented the gentleman's notion of salvage. None of this bothered James Fredrick. He had made his fortune, surely as Commander Porter had years before run the pirates from these very same waters with his famous Mosquito Fleet, unwittingly making the Straits safe for Wreckers. Some said the only difference between a pirate and a Wrecker was a legal piece of paper. James Fredrick didn't say that, but he said something close to it. Every sabbath he let his congregation in for some front pew brow-beating. James Fredrick had become a reformed sinner. He was no longer the man who dispatched a hardy few in longboats, their smoking oil lanterns winking in darkness to beckon with false lights a confused shipmaster, luring with glaring lies the hold of another maritime treasure into the jaws of a shoal. James Fredrick had filled his purse from Wrecking and cleansed his conscience with Christianity. He became an ordained minister who stood each sabbath sturdy as a stork balanced on one leg, pounding the pulpit with his gold peg, speaking with personal conviction of St. Elmo's fire and how the Lord saved him one stormy night from an avalanche of Spanish olive barrels.

James Fredrick never felt closer to God than when the plank decking of his jaunty schooner supported his peg leg on the high seas. Even though the Wrecking days had passed he still liked to troll for misadventure during the calm Christian working week. He sailed back and forth along the reef, on the off chance he might spy a ship that had its plug pulled on knife-sharp rock. To avoid the underwriters and their true bosses, the courts, James Fredrick sailed farther and farther from Key West, far away as the Bahamas and Abacos, in search of treasures from tragedy. On one of these journeys the old Wrecking Master, who even at sea dutifully wore the white Roman collar of a spiritual cleric, spied the gingerbread mansion. The mansion stood surrounded by eerie glare of salt ponds spotted across a desert of white sand. The fury of the long ago hurricane rendered the island inhospitable even to the tenacious mangrove. James Fredrick set his crew the task of dismantling the mansion and loading it aboard the ship. Sailing home the schooner passed during the night Alligator Reef, Fowey Rocks and Rebecca Shoal, strategically aglow with new lights warning of submerged hazards. The lights also signaled the end of the Wrecking days, but James Fredrick had rescued the greatest wreck of his career.

James Fredrick sited his Bahamian mansion at the southern edge of Key West facing the Atlantic Ocean, a defiant monument to natural disasters past and future, a tongue-in-cheek Christian testimonial to human folly, its intricate gingerbread structure painstakingly reassembled, clapboard by clapboard, wood-peg treenail by treenail. Climbing its broad front staircase St. Cloud was reminded of how over the years the mansion had escaped the fate of the island's other grand houses built by Wrecking tycoons, marine mercantile millionaires, and eccentric cigar factory moguls. The gingerbread mansion had not been chopped up room by room, floor by floor, into apartments and fashionable guesthouses, inhabited by those who did not know a chamfer from a dormer, a mansard from a dowel. The one thing the mansion had not escaped was the onrushing hurricane of time, falling once again into grave disorder and disrepair. It had become, in two generations since the death of James Fredrick Isaac, a dangerously leaning accumulation of exotically cut and fit timbers, threatening to tumble at the slightest human sigh, much less a full blown charge from El Finito bearing hard from Cuba.

The front door was ajar, as it always was. The stained-glass fanlight window above the door was spider-webbed with cracks, threatening to crash down from the creaking of St. Cloud's footsteps. He entered the cavernous foyer, the musty space so grand that after the final cannons of the Civil War sounded it had been pressed into service as a ballroom to celebrate Key West's military crowning as the fortified Gibraltar of America. The deep shadows of the foyer still offered ghostly promise of uniformed officers and hoop-gowned beauties to come spinning in a waltz trance through the forest of white paint-chipped Greek Revival columns. Overstuffed chairs and sofas were shrouded in white, their true shapes hidden beneath draped sheets. From the center of the foyer a circular flyaway staircase ascended, its once lustrous pecanwood steps buffed by time to a dusty dung color. Each step cracked loudly beneath St. Cloud's weight, the sound reverberating into the darkening cavern of the foyer. At the top of the staircase landing the salty scent of the Atlantic fingered airily along a twenty-foot-high hallway. St. Cloud walked toward the end of the hallway where tall arched windows were thrown open to the sea. Bright light from blue water beyond bounced off the yellow-pine interior of hall walls. St. Cloud softened his step in expectation, nearing the door at the hall's end leading into the master bedroom. The door was open. Holding his breath he leaned quietly against the doorjamb, waiting for his courage to rise. He peered in.

The fleshy backside of a standing woman in the center of the bedroom was exposed to St. Cloud. Reflected light from the sea cascaded through looming French windows, catching the woman's blond hair in golden fire. Her fingers traced bare skin, over a curve of breasts, rested slightly on thickening nipples, then continued to her slender neck, rising higher, fingers entangling in the fire of hair.

"That's right. That's how I would do it." The words rose up in a wheeze around the woman, then turned to coughing. St. Cloud could not see where the words came from, his vision blocked by the vision before him. The coughing grew faint, as if emanating deep from a well. Suddenly more words rushed forth, propelled by rasping breath. "Don't take your fingers out of your hair! Ummmm, perfect. Exactly how I would do it. But then I'm a romantic son of a bitch."

St. Cloud pressed his body sideways against the doorjamb, trying to bring the source of the voice into view, cocking an eye along the glittering hulk of a brass bed before which the woman stood. Atop the bed's mountain of pillows was a frail body covered by a sheet up to an astonishingly large hairless head.

"I like the feel of that hair. Could run my fingers through it forever. Could even brush it for you. Long strokes in the afternoon. You and me by the seashore. Languid in the sand. I desire sunlight on your hair just so. Turn a little to the right. That's it, more, perfect. Later I will brush the hair between your legs with my fingers. That's the most difficult light to get. But that's later. I wouldn't sell you the moon so fast. Slowly. Slowly now. Raise your arms higher as you stroke . . . stroke your hair. Arms higher so I can pry underneath. I love it under the arms. Hollow of the sweet pit, secret wet. Damp place for my lips as we roll in the sand."

The voice rose and fell in a tumble of syllables shifting quickly between growls and whines, forming words that rushed up to the edge of the next idea, then peered down over half-formed thoughts, geared up again, went two octaves higher than a dog with its tail caught in a barn door.

"Haaaaaaaaah! You know what it is I like most about you? The glint of sweat caught in the cleft of your fleshy apple. You haven't shown it to me yet. It's the prude that gets the worm. The light hasn't been quite right. Nobody painted apples like the real Renoir. But that's not painting. More like a fruit vendor shining his wares. A French monkey peeling his banana. Know what painting is? Big pictures I'm talking about now, very big pictures which fit the puzzle of life-size space. It's those dark scoundrel dogs barking in the night of Goya's black Pharaohs, hanging mysterious as shanks of illuminated meat in the Prado. Goya's the king dog, not Velázquez, not El Greco, not any of your modern Spaniards with waxy mustaches and quail eggs for eyes. No. Woof-*woof!* Right up your soul. Raise your arms higher. Thought I said never shave under your arms. Don't do that, appears false, camouflage of the flesh, nude not naked. Must trust in life's tiny epiphanies, then there can be painterly exposition. No no, do not cut off your God-given mysteries. That's a spectacle, like a nun swallowing each bead of her sainted rosary after saying it." The voice slowed, the enormous head on the shrunken body turning to address with an expression of playful contempt on its face an elegantly dressed man seated across the room. "Renoir . . . my Renoir, my little practical joke on the gods, fix those window curtains. Wind's blowing them too much, shifting the light. I want her entire fruit plate displayed to best advantage. But what would you know about that?"

Renoir rose from a high-back wicker chair into St. Cloud's view, his dark hair closely cropped, a narrow slice of mustache tracing his upper lip, imbuing him with the theatrical air of a vigorous but old-fashioned movie matinee idol. In the heat of the room Renoir seemed cool. He went to all the windows, fussed the curtains until the light stopped its brilliant bounce and settled evenly through gauzy material, cloaking the woman's body with an even golden glow.

"That's better, Renoir. Sit, you'll interrupt the light. Don't want any shadows falling across such a splendid piece of female business. Can't afford distractions at my age. There's no more muscle between my legs to rise and point with anticipation. But my mind doesn't know that, thinks there is a muscle hardening in pursuit of carnal action. A lifetime of habit has tricked my mind into believing I am still the man I used to be. Sit sit sit. You're blocking the light."

Renoir looked at the woman and shook his handsome head with an air of disbelief. He ran a finger across the close cut of his mustache and sniffed the air distractedly, as if dismissing a waiter who uncorked a bottle of bad wine.

"Renoir! Sit down! You'll ruin the light on her ass!"

"Light is a precious commodity." Renoir spoke with a sigh as he slithered down into the wicker chair. "There's more light at night if you know how to look. Goya's dogs knew that."

"What do you know about Goya that I haven't taught you? What do you know about black dogs? The truth of female flesh is something which utterly escapes you. You have no palette to paint their light."

"I know you can't see a thing without your glasses. Not only is the muscle between your legs soft, you can't even make out what stands before you. Instead you're rhapsodizing about shapes and distant memories, barking dogs in the Prado, and a nineteenth century

Impressionist with green grocer sensibilities. Let the poor woman put her clothes back on."

"Haaaaaaraaaaph! Twelve things you know absolutely nothing about. The first two are art and women."

"What are your first two? Compassion and tolerance?"

"When you drift to the bottom of art history books and become a significant footnote as I've become, the world develops compassion for you, tolerates your every whim."

"What is your whim?"

"To have her pull her shorts down and spank her lovely apple to a real Renoir red. To expose true female color. To show you why Renoir got it wrong and how I got it right. The world will know I got it right. I won't be an art history footnote forever. When least expected I'll float to the top of every chapter on twentieth century art. So much then for the fruit vendors of the world and your schoolboy interpretations of what is real and what is not."

"Just like me, I suppose? Is that what you're trying to say? You did it right, but it came out wrong. That why you named me after Renoir?"

"You aren't as foolish as that mustache makes you out to be. But then how did I know how it was going to turn out? A man sends his sperm up a woman's womb like an ambassador making some kind of a deal. Never know what's going to walk out nine months later. A president or a jackass."

"Get on with it. Pull her shorts down and spank her apple bottom. That's what you keep insisting I come up here to see, isn't it?"

"You're being cruel, taking advantage of a strong man in a weak hour. You know . . . I . . . can't."

"What? Can't get an erection? Can't get out of bed? Can't shine the apple?"

"Angelica! Take the rest off!" The large head rolled toward the woman, the glazed eyes pleading.

"Even my high heels? You told me never to take these off."

"No. No. Leave those on. Everything else goes. Turn your back to me. I want the surprise of light on you. I love that shadow traveling across your shoulderblade. The play of false light. Mystery makes the woman, illusion seduces the man."

Angelica moved her body in a single fluid motion, unassuming as a woman stepping from a bath, an improbable Aphrodite rising from a quivering sea of light in high heels. The octopus tattoo on her right breast spread its tentacles as she exhaled a slight breath. She had a clear view of St. Cloud's face peering from behind the door.

"Is the light where you want it now?" Angelica spoke the words straight to St. Cloud.

"Yes yes. Perfect." The words wheezed from the bed behind her. "Straight light. Pure illusion. Bring on the barking dogs." The voice slowed, rasping final encouragement. "Now take those shorts off."

There was not the slightest possibility even the most worn coin could be slipped between Angelica's tight white shorts and the smooth skin of her thighs. Yet she managed to cock her hips in a provocative angle which loosened the material until it slipped from her body to the floor, simply as a snake discards its skin. She stepped out of the shorts, her only adornment the black spike-heeled shoes which threw her glistening calves into a taut tilt. Angelica's hands glided up, fingers locking behind her neck as she spread her folded arms to form fleshy wings. Sunlight shafting along the tops of her arms struck the short blondish hairs, creating an unmistakable stir between St. Cloud's legs. As Angelica's eyes met his St. Cloud slid through an alcoholic haze, back to a time that seemed close but was at least two years ago, when he was still a happily married cheating husband. St. Cloud slid through the troubled waters of his memory to the day he had taken Angelica out in his small skiff to check for customers in his stone crab traps. Angelica liked to watch him pull the wood slatted boxes up on seaweed-encrusted ropes from the sandy flats. He was fascinated by her fascination that the crabs chased into his traps after cans of cat food punched with holes. Crabcats, Angelica called them, horrified when St. Cloud severed their powerful snapping claws at the upper joint with steel cutters. With a toss overboard, and a final splash, St. Cloud bid the crabs adios until next season. He cracked his catch of bright orange claws. They feasted on sweet meat and cool wine, floating aimlessly in the harbor among the wakes of charter fishing boats, sunday yachtsmen, and cigarette-boat speed demons affecting superior airs of drug smugglers as they roared past with defiant raised beercan salutes at pedestrian boats in their way. Angelica wanted to see the submarine pens. They were easy enough to show her. St. Cloud guided the skiff past Mallory Dock, in among the long fingers of concrete piers at the edge of the Navy base, where submarines once nested while being refitted during the First World War. P-T boats replaced the submarines during the Second World War, and now an improbable new fleet was anchored. Hundreds of abandoned boats bobbed in the wake of St. Cloud's skiff chugging by, crafts of every size and description, from single engine thirty-foot pleasure cruisers to sixty-foot Hatteras convertibles crowned with once gleaming stainless steel tuna towers. Two years before all had made the 180-mile passage to Mariel Bay in Cuba and returned loaded with the crowded catch Castro flushed from his jails and insane asylums. Mixed among these thousands were true political refugees, relatives and friends of those on American shores who had paid boat owners high dollar in a desperate time to ferry loved ones to the land of the free and the brave. The boat owners were repaid by the U.S. government's impounding their vessels, leaving freedom's flotilla to idle, list and rot, while their final consequence was unraveled through the courts. The government could not decide if the boat owners were heroic patriots or greedy opportunists. St. Cloud idled his skiff down to a slow drift. Ahead was a massive concrete bulkhead lined with an even more impressive array of captured craft. NO TRESPASSING ORDER OF THE UNITED STATES GOVERNMENT was stenciled in red paint across hulls of an armada of marijuana tonnage and vast cocaine cargoes. Some vessels had the girth of small battleships, their steel hulks streaking rust into still water as St. Cloud's skiff glided by impounded dreams of enterprise and the great American hustle. Angelica was beside him, sweet crab and wine on her breath. She laughingly pulled her thin T-shirt over her head, exposing shoulders and breasts to a sun piercing the calm of a deserted afternoon. St. Cloud sensed they were drifting from their time into a modern-day pirate ghost town. He was startled by a voice from one of the impounded boats. A husky male voice, its sound detached from any discernible source. Its unmistakable intent rolling steadily across still water. St. Cloud tried to determine if the originator of the words was hidden on the hulking ship with *Matto Grasso Trader* proclaimed on its bow. He saw no one. The voice came again. Its unmistakable target was Angelica. She boldly stepped to the bow of the skiff, a bare-breasted masthead. Her gaze cast across water, hunting the voice. She sought the source of the floating disembodied sounds. The echoed intentions of the words were challenged by an expression of recognition in Angelica's widening eyes. Her naked back arched. Her gaze across water intensified its pursuit, primal hunter alert to sense of prey. The guttural male words became a challenging scent. Angelica's eyes ferreted the source of the voice's lustful intentions, determined to extinguish it, take its flaming wick and snuff it between quick press of thumb and forefinger, drive the male desire back upon itself in a fury of female reciprocity.

In the glittering bedroom light Angelica's breasts held the naked thrust of challenge St. Cloud witnessed years before in the submarine pen. It was an unsettling recognition of sexual origins, when civilizations were controlled by women. Watching Angelica turn slowly in the room, totally exposed within a circle of men, St. Cloud groped for meaning through the alcoholic swamp of his steaming brain. Maybe it was man's desire never to let woman rise again. Keep her under heel and thumb. Never allow Pandora to release the awesome power from the box. Keep a tight leash around her neck. Jerk her whenever she strays. There was so much about being a man St. Cloud mistrusted. Angelica would sell her body to buy shoes for her small daughter, or for a gram of coke. Hers was a world of honest barter in a dishonest world. She knew the value of her goods and wasn't about to sell short. But that was too simple. St. Cloud knew it went beyond that, to the detached voice Angelica hunted years before with wild eyes across water. To the primal strength of her sexuality. The voice of naked male intent, coming across water as a penetrating threat that distant day, had been reduced by Angelica to the cry of a helpless boy, drowning, begging salvation. The hunter's glint in Angelica's eyes was the same now as on that day, as she watched in her imagination the frail white body of the helpless boy go under for the third time before she reached out, ensnaring the hair, pulling the victim from watery fate with forthright passion, kissing cold lips, breathing life into another misguided soul. Angelica was a different kind of woman, demanding a different kind of man. St. Cloud hadn't added up the differences yet, nor did he know if he understood them all, but he had utmost respect for the strength of their source. For this reason he had every intention of surviving the future.

"Have you had your fill of apples?" Renoir slipped from the wicker chair and walked to the open windows, turning his back to the sea beyond, and focused his attention on Angelica. "And you, honey, why don't you get dressed and call it a day?"

"Don't dare tell Angelica what to do!" The voice wheezed from the bed. "I haven't finished with her!"

"You never started." Renoir turned with an air of disdainful resignation, his gaze going far from the room, through the windows to the thin blue horizon beyond.

"There's a lot to be learned here, Renoir. Not only about art, but about life, sex. Look at this beauty. Don't turn your back on her. What are you afraid of? Afraid you'll get your precious weeny between her buns and never be able to get out? She doesn't want your weeny. What good is a man without a weeny? No good to her, you foolish boy. No good at all. You don't understand the first thing about a woman like this. Angelica wants to be equal with you, exchange a kiss, a bow, a handshake, a fuck. It's all in the exchange. That's what women are about. That's what they think when you're fucking them. No great mystery. They don't think of stealing your weeny. They think of the exchange, and that has no face, no photo finish. It is a rush of reality. Gives birth to us all. Women understand that, they—"

"Why don't you ask Angelica what she feels?"

"I don't have to ask her anything. I know what women think about me. They teach me in history of women's art. College after college they hold me up as the enemy. Because I know their secret they stalk me through seminars, eviscerate my virility, study the fetid male entrails. They want to nail my old coonskin hide to the wall, a trophy of the vanquished. The silly witches want to paint themselves. Think they can do it better. It's a great lie. Women will never understand themselves the way men can. I know their game. They want the public to remember me as crazy, because if you remember the artist as crazy, rather than the art as inspired, then it's bad art. My paintings still sell, but not because I have the conviction of raw vision. Forget that. It's because I'm a cultural artifact. A fossil to be studied under a microscope for his anachronistic way of dealing with the gloriously mundane texture of female flesh, its less than transcendent contours, its fettered truths. I've become infamous for a carnality of the intellect. But you want to know the truth, my unfettered confession? I just wanted to fuck them all. I succeeded at that, and in doing so fucked myself. Here's my dark secret, spoken before I go to the grave. Even though I'm considered the most renowned painter of this century whose subject was the female, at heart I thought myself a fraud. Should have become a homophile and painted women from the inside out. Look at Michelangelo's *Libyan Soul* on the ceiling of the Vatican. That silkpants did it better than anyone in the last two thousand years and the next five thousand to come and all he did was put tits on men."

Renoir stepped back from the window and turned to face the room, blocking the full force of the light. "Are you finished? You've given every interviewer the past twenty years this 'I'm really the better painter because the others are gay' speech. Why don't you get back to what we were really talking about? Go ahead and ask Angelica. What are you afraid of?"

"I'll ask Angelica . . ." The wheezing voice whistled to a nervous stop, then coughed. "Ask her anything I want."

"Ask her."

"What?"

"What she feels."

"Angelica . . ." The voice regained its wheezing whistle. "What do you fe . . . fee . . . feeeel?"

"Bored."

"Haaaraaaaaph!" The voice sputtered with delight. "Angelica, you're a beauty!"

"These high heels are killing me."

Renoir slunk back into the wicker chair. "Go ahead, Angelica, tell him what you think. This is your chance, take it."

Angelica raised one leg behind her, reached around to knead a knotted calf muscle. Perched on one leg she resembled a magnificent heron puzzling the surface of shallow water for a fish of truth. "I'm the kind of girl who won't take yes for an answer."

"That's my kind of girl!" The voice chortled with so much pleasure it lost control to a fit of coughing.

"What about you, St. Cloud? Am I your kind of girl?" Angelica lowered a finely tapered leg at a provocative tilt.

"St. Cloud!" The voice stopped its fit of coughing. "Where is he? Now, there's a man who knows it takes a fool to love like a fool." The voice took an accusative poke at Renoir. "Not like you. Not like you at all. Where is my friend?"

Renoir pulled himself up in the wicker chair with a derisive snort. "He's right behind the door watching your tawdry little peep show. He's been there the whole time. I told you you couldn't see a thing without your glasses. Why must you keep this charade up?"

"Bring St. Cloud in! I must talk to him about Goya's barking dogs, about false light, about the art of misunderstanding women, about the lies we lead. This man knows. Knows the pain of it. No one else does. No one else is romantic fool enough to care. People don't even feel anymore, so how can they care? St. Cloud? You there?"

St. Cloud pushed the bedroom door completely open, stepping

into a sultry closeness perfumed with female perspiration. The whooze of booze coursing through his blood put a slight totter in his step. He liked to think he had the gait of an off-duty tap dancer walking uphill, or at least the uneven wobble of a barstool romeo forced to prowl the flat-top world of sobriety. He hobbled to the head of the bed and took the old man's hand between his. The hand was frail, its skin traveled by thickened black veins threatening to burst. St. Cloud caressed the hand. He admired the indomitable spirit of this man, his vitality of desire, the flame of lust refusing to be extinguished by a degenerating body. Long before St. Cloud met the man he had experienced the lustful spirit of his paintings. Even those paintings reproduced in the garish colors of popular magazines possessed the luminescent presence of virile visitation, as if a veil had been swiftly withdrawn from the commonplace, not merely to illuminate or to trick, simply to stab at the heart of unrequited love. The trembling hands that St. Cloud now soothed once wielded paintbrushes and voluptuous bodies with bold confident strokes. But this man began life as the least probable candidate to finesse a vision from the gods, to ascend beyond his living peers into a realm measured by the yardstick of immortality. He was from Key West, his maternal forefather the Wrecker James Fredrick Isaac, whose last name was given him as a first. Isaac's forebear's penchant for moving houses across seas and ships from the ocean floor pointed the way for him to do the impossible, create a painted universe on twelve-foot by twelve-foot squares of canvas. This Isaac was not born with the noble bearing of his swashbuckling ancestor, nor did he possess a profile to be stamped on coins of the realm. No. This Isaac existed as if God were truly a giant up in the heavens, making men and women in his reflected image, busily banging out a race of all things handsome and beautiful. Then one day, out of boredom with such production-line perfection, God lifted his massive hand, formed a fist, banged it down smartly on one of the handsome heads, slamming the man's six-foot frame down to five feet, broadening shoulders to exaggerated proportions, pushing the face in on itself, creating folds of flesh resembling a bulldog, thick lips condemned to a perpetual pout, heavy jowls swinging off the broad triple chin, almost obscuring an abbreviated neck no higher than a tin can flattened by a speeding car. This new man's entire appearance was so devoid of classical balance it signified a defiant aesthetic, a perfection of imperfection. The brown eyes of this creation peered from beneath lidded folds of flesh, cried out for affection with the eager-to-please expression of a dog expecting the gift of a juicy bone to fall from heaven's dining-room tabletop. Having outfitted this new man with an alert and inquisitive animal nature, God in heaven was pleased, sent him to walk head and shoulders beneath lesser mortals of more common abnormalities. It was in his art that Isaac transcended all others. Those who saw Isaac's art knew he had been touched by God. Only Isaac had a good-humored inkling of just how hard God had touched him. Isaac exuded the irrepressible spirit of a creature happy to be alive. Isaac counted himself lucky he had not been crushed to something less than an ant in the moment of his creation.

"You haven't answered Angelica's question, St. Cloud." Renoir stretched his legs before him in the wicker chair, folded his hands across his stomach, a pencil-thin Buddha contemplating the ironic answer to all life. "Is she your kind of girl?"

St. Cloud never noticed Angelica had a small blue squid tattooed on the inside of her left ankle, or maybe he had forgotten, it all seemed so long ago, urgent voices across tranquil sea of alcohol. He spoke softly so as not to sink in the tranquil sea. "Angelica's not the kind of girl you can take home to your wife."

"You did!" Angelica's words rode in on sudden uncontrollable laughter. "Sometimes I took *you* home to your wife."

"That was the beginning of the end." St. Cloud felt himself starting to sink.

Angelica stopped laughing. "For her the end of the beginning."

St. Cloud was definitely submerged, he heard his words glub to the surface, weak with exasperation, a plea for a secure handhold to save him from this mess. "Nothing's forever, not even eternal love."

A defiant grin crossed Angelica's face. "Listen, after you've had an orgasm it's time to get off the stage. Every ham knows that."

"He isn't afraid of these things." Isaac wheezed. "St. Cloud knows how to make a sandwich with what God gave him. The issue here is that some men mate in captivity, some don't. In a moment of weakness I mated in captivity once. Look at the result." Isaac rolled his watery eyes toward Renoir, then thought better of it. "You can only hit a donkey between the eyes with a board so many times before it stops seeing stars in its eyes. Wake up, St. Cloud. I've tried to tell you so many times. Fall in love with a town, not a woman. When you get tired of a town you can always leave it. A town doesn't expect you to call and ask when you are coming back, it doesn't expect flowers, and it doesn't shed a tear for your self-pity."

"Check the bulge in his pants." Renoir folded one long leg casually over the other. "St. Cloud is capable of falling in love with Main Street, he's lucky he can walk down any street without tripping over his third leg. If you put a skirt on every telephone pole in town he would have them pregnant by sundown. Fall in love with a town? What kind of advice is that?"

"Advice you wouldn't understand." Isaac tried to push his shrunken body higher on the throne of oversized pillows. "St. Cloud thinks with his pecker, he's always corkscrewing his life around in a cockeyed direction, that's why he's never out of trouble. By the time he knows where he is his pecker has come and gone two days before. St. Cloud is more of an endangered species than the precious Florida panther."

"Pity the poor panther." Renoir winked at Angelica.

"I think I'm in love." The words squeezed out of St. Cloud's alcoholic swamp. He could not believe he was making a public confession of passion. "Really in love. Only way out is a bullet or a fast train."

"No trains through here since the hurricane of 'thirty-five blew out Flagler's Overseas Railroad. The bullet is your only choice, at least it will save the panthers." Renoir leaned back in the wicker chair and fixed St. Cloud with a salacious wink. "Who's the lucky boy you're in love with?"

"What was that?" Isaac pushed higher on the pillows. "My hearing is going faster than my eyesight. What did St. Cloud say?"

"He said," Renoir shoved out of the wicker chair, "he thinks he's in love. He's excited from watching Angelica's modeling act."

"Honey . . ." Angelica shifted her weight from one high heel to another. "You're just jealous. Remember, getting the candy out of the wrapper doesn't always mean you can eat it."

"It's not Angelica." St. Cloud wanted to set the record straight, though there was no denying Angelica was gorgeous, in or out of the right light. She would be gorgeous in a black room with all the exits sealed. "It's not you, Angelica. It's the girl who works in Evelyn's bird shop."

"Oh brother!" Renoir collapsed back into the wicker chair. "It isn't bad enough you're raping the environment. Now it's *hey little high-school girl where you goin'*."

"She's twenty years old."

"Some difference." Renoir uncrossed his legs. "So it's Heartbreak Hotel time."

"Cut it out, Renoir." Angelica tapped the toe of her right high heel impatiently, a naked schoolmarm about to lecture. "This could be serious. This could be a major league mistake. We've got to make sure he makes it. He's obviously in pain and wants to share. He's very generous. He's fuck struck. Tell us about it, honey."

"Hold on." Isaac sputtered and coughed. "St. Cloud, hand me my breatholator. Steady it for me." Isaac clutched St. Cloud's guiding hand, placed trembling lips to the plastic mouthpiece. He inhaled with a fervent rasping as his dim eyes roved over the shape of Angelica standing at the foot of the bed. He slipped wet lips from the breatholator, revitalized. "Look at this girl!" Isaac rubbed the thick black veins of his frail hands in glee, smiling with uninhibited pleasure. "St. Cloud, this is the girl for you! The softer they are the harder they come. She's the truest Christian on this godforsaken rock, all she has to do is walk down the street to have every man in her wake bumping into the wall as he follows along like a starved hound in search of a butcher shop. Even now she can make me rise. Not really, since they took those big arteries out of my legs, which I made Renoir promise not to let them do before I went in for the operation. I said I'd rather be dead than no longer be able to rise to the occasion. Since the operation I really can't get it to move let alone rise. But I'm at my best with it every morning, because my brain remembers the blood swelling to attention between my legs for seventy-two years. My brain wakes up with a hard-on. The mornings I have Angelica here I'm like a man with an amputated leg who can feel his toes twitch. I'm telling you, Angelica is solid gold right down to her soul. You've been mooning over this girl in the bird shop for two months now. That's going to end badly. No matter how pretty they are, the boredom of a young woman finally catches up with you. You have to train them. Then what do you do with them? It's like training a seal. Endearing at first, but who wants to walk around with a pocketful of sardines for the rest of his life? Forget the Georgia peach. You're better off with Angelica. She's the kind of woman who won't take yes for an answer. Angelica is truth in packaging. Christ, what a package. Look at it! A whore in tart's clothing. You can pay her or marry her. What difference does it make? If all it cost you is money you are coming out ahead of the game. Angelica is like a once-in-a-lifetime bright diamond thrown into a ring of ignorant thieves. Pick it up, boy! Pick it up! Don't disappoint an old man." Isaac's liquid gaze drifted from St. Cloud to Angelica, then poked around at shadows in the room, finally lighting on Renoir, who was turned to the window feigning interest in a large freighter rounding toward the Gulf on the thin blue horizon. "I keep hoping, you know, even at this late date, maybe watching Angelica, Renoir will feel what I can't. I named him Renoir after the monumental painter of female flesh of all time until I came along. The real Renoir was an appreciator, a man with an eye for the knowing. I name my kid after him and what do I get? Look at him, would you? Dressed in that crisp white tropical suit you'd think he was going to run downstairs and set the table for Easter dinner. He looks like a maître d' at the Last Supper."

Renoir turned from his maritime interests on the horizon. "Why don't you give yourself a rest, Dad, at least on your sickbed? Cut the locker-room catechism of heterosexuality and let Angelica go home to her little girl. St. Cloud is going to go out and make a fool of himself, always does." Renoir arched a bemused eyebrow. "He's obviously never met a cock more interesting than a cunt."

"Funny, I've never met a cock more interesting than a cunt." Angelica shifted her body weight forward, anticipating a strong reaction to challenge such obvious profundity. "And let me tell you, I've met some dillies."

"St. Cloud, come, get in bed with me. Bring Angelica." Isaac patted the fluffy mattress next to him with a flutter of his frail hand. "Enough talking." His words sank to a whisper. "Bring the true Christian into bed, the two of you, lie with me."

"Going to cost you extra, Isaac." Angelica bent a foot back and reached around to undo the thin strap of a high-heeled shoe. "Then again," she dropped the shoe to the floor and raised the other foot, "might not cost you a thing."

Renoir slumped into the wicker chair. "You two are going to kill him. Don't you know when to stop feeding his illusions?"

"Don't worry about me." Isaac raised a frail hand. "Always wanted to die in the saddle."

"The saddle?" Renoir shook his head in disbelief. "You can't even get the horse out of the barn."

"Did I ever tell you?" Isaac touched the soft skin of Angelica's shoulder as she slipped in next to him, his voice dropping to the barest whisper. "Why I started to paint, before the women? It was the clouds. Those ever-changing colors and shapes. So obvious. Always preening to natural advantage of the golden heavens. Hiding from false light. Same way the human form does. Space and calculus on the run from reality. Shape and color haven't a thing to do with landscape. Beauty is a bluff, it's false light. You must cut the bodies off from space, eliminate the fraud behind the gimmick so only spinning mass is left. Energy is all. Indelible impression of the vital. Sunrise moment between worlds. Between monsters and humans, netherworlds and upperworlds, darkness and light. Like the green flash out on that big ocean so few people ever see after a lifetime of looking. It's that separating color one struggles to capture. Birthing color turning to no color in false light between cobalt sea and sky blue sky. All my life I tried to get that false light into my art." Isaac's whisper halted, his frail hand slipped from Angelica's shoulder, eyes widening with anticipation. "There haven't been clouds over the ocean for two months. Flat, dead doldrums. Maybe I'll have to leave you all soon. So soon?"

11

BEAUTY is a bluff. Love is a blind man's game. St. Cloud sensed he had a one-way ticket up a self-made Alligator Alley into the jaws of fate. How could a man come so far and not outgrow his stupidity? St. Cloud could no longer outdistance his common sense by flooding a sea of booze over every mindful prick of reality. If beauty is a bluff then Isaac was right about Lila, that after a man reaches a certain age it is difficult to distinguish whether he has fallen in love with a young woman of true beauty, or she appears beautiful simply because she is young. St. Cloud did not know if his heart was being tricked by the fatal attraction of false romantic lights, leading him in desperate pursuit of his own lost youth. Maybe the only thing left he was capable of outrunning at his age was reason. Not much of a victory there, no triumph over the lies he led. St. Cloud was definitely headed up a personal Alligator Alley. There was a fickle feel to it all, a slippery sense he had lost his way. He sensed he had to hang onto his life for dear life. Fate was setting him up, kicking the options out beneath him. He felt the noose of inevitable circumstance as tightly as had an illegal Cuban refugee he had interpreted for several years back. The Cuban was in and out of jail in Miami, then like a piece of steel feeling the inevitable pull of the magnet, was drawn south toward Cuba, finally wandering into a liquor store on Sombrero Key where he found some quick trouble, then was popped in the can for it. The Judge at the Cuban's trial was a good old boy who stood on the solid pork barrel of redneck justice, fed up with seeing riffraff refugees ripping off America's abundance, delighted to have an opportunity to get his hands on one of the foreigners before the Feds could whisk the deadbeat away north to one of the country club prisons, which were nothing more than summer camps for perverts and freeloaders. "Why did you go into that liquor store and shoot the owner?" the Judge demanded in a voice which rattled the skeletal bones of the invisible gallery of ghostly Confederate peers he appeared to be addressing, instead of five people in an otherwise barren room. The Cuban shrugged incomprehensibly; he had the gangly body of a man brought up sucking the meat out of chicken necks and eating hard times for dessert. The Cuban asked St. Cloud to have the Judge repeat the question, then grinned with frankness, the answer so simple. "Because el proprietor had *dinero* in the drawers of the cash register." "Did you know you were going to rob the store when you went in," the Judge thundered. "No!" "Then why were you carrying the gun?" This was it, the Cuban had to have St. Cloud reinterpret the question three times, for he couldn't believe this formidable man in a black robe could ask such a stupid question. The Cuban's grin opened to a full smile. "Why? Because I never go anyplace without my gun." So it was that a dog never left home without his fleas, that the only thing history books get right are the numbers of pages they contain, that a man who falls in love with a younger woman is only trying to bluff the inevitable.

What is the speed limit on Alligator Alley before the obvious crash? Maybe Isaac and Angelica were right, what St. Cloud suffered from was nothing more than a lurid fixation with transitory beauty. If so, he was on the verge of discovering less about himself and more about Lila, time was running out on his bluff. He had long ago reduced his once lofty beliefs into a simplistic profundity, that there are only two types of people in the world, those who want to fuck you, and those who want to fuck you over. He knew Lila was one of those types as he lay listening to her soft breathing next to him in bed. He would not know until he reached the end of Alligator Alley if she was also the other type. A pug puppy, curled against Lila's back, whined and kicked its small legs, drifting along in its dream, pushing closer to Lila's moist skin as it grunted its animal pleasure. Staggered lines of moonlight fell through shutters from the far side of the bedroom, tracing the length of Lila's body, flickering across her skin, creating the illusion she was a shapely heroine in a black-and-white movie. The silhouette of her body fulfilled an unnerving classic vision, appearing to be from another age, possessed of flow and form glimpsed only on certain Greek statues, a timeless suppleness balanced with female fullness, promising perfection beyond the touchable, beyond reach of a mere mortal male attempting to grasp its inner essence. Something glowed from within Lila, surrounded her with a disconcerting aura of antiquity, made more startling because of her youth. St. Cloud wanted to touch her again, simply place his hands on the aura which seemed so palpable and powerful. But he did not wish to awaken her. Did not wish to dispel a moment charged with such vision. Instead he gently moved his fingertips to the exposed pink underbelly of the pug. The dog grunted its pleasure, diminutive feet pawing air in a somnolent attempt of trying to snuggle closer to a dream tit. Such an odd little creature with its shoved-in face flattened to a fleshy pancake, its fat stub of a body ending at a tail cropped unnaturally short. Whatever attracted Lila to this breed was beyond St. Cloud. Perhaps it was the animal's absurd physiology, the fact that it was so much the opposite of Lila's own perfection. The queer little package had definitely been delivered at the furthest end of beauty's eternal measuring stick. Whatever compelled Lila to seek out this breed was now complicated by the fact that the dog had come to play the role of an improbable Cupid. St. Cloud visualized the silly creature flying through clouds, clutching a bow of love with the sharp arrow of romance strung back, set to release quick as a heat-seeking missile searching hapless target. He had offered to accompany Lila on the day she finally saved enough money to buy the puppy, until then the newspaper want ads were growing ever more hysterical: PUGS! THREE BUNDLES OF JOY LEFT! Then, TWO ONLY PURE-BRED PUGS! Finally, LAST CHANCE FOR LAST PUG! After the last ad Lila insisted on making her move. They drove up the Keys in her convertible, top down, wind curling the dress above her knees, hair flying as she roared across bridges from one swampy mangrove mass to the next, the sea going off in inky distance on both sides of the highway as the sun slipped toward the horizon. Afterglow of departing day illuminated an urgency in her face. She possessed a passion which could turn away fatal intentions, or invite fleshy blows, her body orchestrated by an arcane dance, which at this moment had nothing to do with her foot pressed flat on the convertible's gas pedal. Chopped notes of rock and roll flew from the radio as she sped ahead, ever closer to LAST CHANCE FOR LAST PUG!

The male voice on the telephone that afternoon, when St. Cloud called the newspaper's advertised number, mapped out its location in a loud voice: "After you pass Mile Marker Thirty headed up to Miami, look for Tropical Mama's Bar-B-Q-Pit, gonna be over to your left. Turn there, then go five blocks over two canals. Make quick right on the gravel road. Twelfth trailer on left under the concrete power pole with sea grape growing up its side is us. I'll leave the light on case you can't make it before sundown. Don't worry about the Doberman pinscher, eats only bill collectors. Not Cuban, are you? Because Dobbie eats Cubans, even if they aren't bill collectors."

St. Cloud glimpsed in failing light the paint-peeling TROPICAL MAMA'S sign perched atop the tin roof of a ramshackle roadside diner. "You've just passed it," he shouted into the radio's blaring rock and roll.

Lila hit the brakes, skidding off the highway onto the gravel shoulder, hooking the convertible around in a steaming cloud of dust to face oncoming traffic. "Sorry." She smiled into the wind. "Weren't frightened, were y'all?"

"No, I was—"

St. Cloud's words were cut off by the horn blast from a car that had been following closely behind them. A man, old enough to join the army but too young to buy an alcoholic drink legally, preened the upper half of his body out the passenger window as the car sped past, his right hand raised in a familiar salute with the middle finger extended as he screamed a passing verdict on Lila's driving prowess. "Assssssssshooooooole!"

Lila paid no attention to the word curling off into wind-sucking whoosh of more cars speeding by. She shifted into jerky first, the back tires etching through forty feet of gravel before stopping again. Her lower lip trembled, she sensed the dog was close. "Tropical Mama's is our turn, right?"

"Right."

She cranked the steering wheel, plunged her foot on the accelerator, the convertible leapt across the highway through a momentary slot in the sixty-mile-an-hour rush of honking cars.

"Where'd you learn to drive like that?" St. Cloud tried to control the quiver of fear in his voice.

"Georgia." Lila laughed, the convertible racing past Tropical Mama's, the wind again scooping rock and roll from backseat speakers, scattering lyrics and guitar wails across blackened shapes of mangroves. "In the South we learn to drive before we learn to walk." Lila's right hand drifted from the steering wheel, touching St. Cloud's knee. "Aren't frightened, are y'all?"

This was the first time St. Cloud had felt any part of Lila's body. If he didn't answer, maybe she wouldn't remove her hand. He had to stall. He pulled the rum bottle wrapped in a paper bag from between his legs, tilted his head back, sipping long and slow before mumbling into radio guitar wails. "Remember, go right after we cross the second canal bridge."

"Y'all really afraid?" Lila's fingers tightened on his knee.

St. Cloud felt she was connected to him, no matter how tentatively, flesh on flesh after so many long months of carefully holding his distance, couldn't afford to lose her, had to stretch the connection, ride it like the Milky Way crashing overhead. "Remember when you were a kid?" He sucked another mouthful of rum, rolled it around his tongue, then swallowed with a laugh at the heavens, sidetracked by stars of Orion's Belt, a glittery swirl wrapping around the waist of night. Next to him, without looking, he knew the wind flicked a cotton dress above the shapeliest knees south of the Mason-Dixon line.

"When I was a kid, what?" Lila's fingers loosened on his knee. "Where y'all drifting off to? I asked if y'all are afraid."

"Remember when you were a kid, you wondered where the stars went in the morning?"

"Sure, everyone wonders that. So?"

"So I know where they go."

"Y'all been drinking too much." Lila's fingers detached completely from St. Cloud's knee, releasing whatever intimacy the gesture held. Both hands firmly on the steering wheel again. "Y'all are making no sense."

Her words came not as a condemnation, but coolly as a weather report about oncoming hot weather, for she was far too Southern a female to get between a man and his liquor. She would no more think of asking a man to give up boozing than ask someone from China to stop using chopsticks. Lila was born on the losing side of the American tracks, expected her men to behave badly and boorishly. When they hid beneath the sea depths of alcohol she wasn't about to go looking for them, or throw them a life-saving line. Lila was secure with the knowledge she knew right where her men could be found. All she had to do was whistle and they would come swimming up from their ocean of self-imposed exile and flop over into the safety of her boat with a congratulatory grin of well-earned self-pity. Southern men played a predictable game with their women. Lila grew up with the game, accepted it. She recognized it in men who were not even true

Southerners, like the one squirming in her net now, carrying around
more guilt than Lee's Army slinking off from Appomattox, for what
reason she did not know. Sometimes, when this one got on his rum
and pushed himself over the hill of his charming self, out spilled this
stuff about Vietnam, how it destroyed a generation. He had not fought
in Vietnam, she couldn't figure what his problem was, what chip of
heavy loss he thought he had earned the right to carry around on his
shoulder. Being from the deep South she had cousins and uncles who
had died in Vietnam, but none of the family went around talking
about it. For the life of her, Lila did not see what the personal failure
of this Northern man next to her was, other than his being one of
those people too clever for the everyday world, but not clever enough
for the real world. He did have a strangeness which she was a sucker
for. He had the wounded eyes of an underdog in a devil-be-damned
world. She was a simple Southern woman attracted to contrary
Northern lights. The fact this Northerner was older meant only that
they were on more equal footing, gave him more chance of running
an even race with her. Only one other man had given her an even
race, he too was twice her age, but that man had foxed her out of
her hole. She still awaited a sign from him. She found waiting had its
sideshow attractions. This Northern man next to her was a brief
amusement for a young woman who had a mind only for herself, one
blessed with gumption of inexperience, possessed of the power to
pluck common sense from all men, married or otherwise. At this
point in Lila's life she did not care so much where the stars went, as
where they came from. She played her emotions squarely, unaware
there would be no second act to her youthful actions, when emotions
once felt so strongly would be inevitably squandered, played broadly
to an empty house.

"Y'all know what?" Lila's languid drawl drifted around the bend
of some lazy Southern river. "Y'all really are strange. Y'all know that?"

St. Cloud did not know what he knew, except that Lila had better
keep her eyes on the road. "This is your right turn, after the canal
bridge, then up the gravel road."

"Did the man you talked to say whether the last puppy was male
or female?"

"Did he say whether the last puppy was a doctor or a lawyer?"

"Yes!" Lila laughed, swerving the convertible right onto a gravel
road so suddenly St. Cloud was slammed against the door. She was
willing to play with him now. The dog was close. The closer she got

to the dog, the closer she seemed to get to St. Cloud, was willing to venture off on his little excursions of merriment, join him in toppling over the expected and sane. "Doctors and lawyers? Why not!" She liked the way he batted words around as if he owned their true meanings, that was one thing different about him, one of his distracting amusements. She had never been with a man who cared for words, had never really given it any thought. Words to her were so many eggs in a carton, only took them out when needed, and she was a good cook, a great cook really, one who never wasted an egg. With this man words flew as if different colored doves from a magician's hat, to land who knows where.

"What would you say?" St. Cloud pushed himself away from the door handle jammed uncomfortably into his back, his lips thickening into a drunken pout as he fumbled for the rest of his thought before finding it. "If I told you some of those famous disappeared stars were right here in my pocket, what would you say to that?"

"I'd still say y'all are strange." Lila smiled as her hand went back to his knee with a playful squeeze. "Very strange."

St. Cloud felt the stars slip from his pockets, fall with heart-beating thuds into his shoes. He had contact with her again. He marveled at how cavalierly she drew the short syllables out of the word strange, as if absentmindedly peeling an orange. In the radiant glow of the radio's dial lit up along the dashboard Lila's face seemed flushed a soft lavender. The ethereal color she was captured by reminded St. Cloud of a song he heard crooned many times from car radios when he was a teenager. The sensuous thread of the song's central lyric leapt from his memory with alarming velocity, even though the lyric originally sung moved slow as molten lava: *Laaaaveeeendeeer bluuuuue . . . dilly dilly*. Lavender blue, dilly dilly, what in hell was a *dilly dilly?* St. Cloud slipped the rum bottle from the paper bag, drained the remaining liquor with a deep sigh. So long ago those unanswered lyrics, filling the night music of his youth. He realized now, only too late in the game, he would never know the meaning of *dilly dilly*. "God pity the sailors on a night like this." He heaved the empty bottle back over his shoulder to set it on a misguided journey as Lila hit the brakes, stopping the convertible before a house-trailer dwarfed by the towering concrete leg of a power pole supporting high lines of humming conduits. They stared at each other in the sudden humming electrical moment punctuated by the sound of the thrown bottle crashing against the rusting silver wall of the domed trailer. Lila's eyes brightened into a smile. St. Cloud had her where he wanted her. She was willing to see the humor in the ridiculous. Her lips parted to laugh as the fierce roar of an animal broke from inside the trailer. The roar turned to a vicious howling, rocking the trailer on axles sunk into sandy soil. A large beast was clawing from inside the trailer. The door sprang open. A black Doberman leapt out at the convertible before its head snapped back, a thick metal chain trailing from the dog's collar pulling taut, holding the animal at bay with a strangling grunt.

"Thought you said you wasn't Cuban!"

"I'm French and something else!" St. Cloud shouted in self-defense, stepping clumsily from the convertible, trying to adjust his eyes to the glare stabbing from a spotlight above the trailer door. "Third-generation French! Could be what he smells is my Latin blood."

The man holding the dog said nothing. Maybe St. Cloud was pushing his bravado too far. Maybe the rum was pushing him into a well-lit corner with nowhere to run. What a stupid position he put himself in by unthinkingly swinging out of the car like Captain Blood-Shot Eyes. He pushed the bill of his faded sailor's cap lower on his forehead to block the glare he faced, not taking his eyes off the Doberman, relieved when the man finally spoke.

"Alice don't like Cubans, specially Cubans that come over on that boatlift while back." The man controlling the straining dog seemed uncertain, tugged on the taut leash to keep the growling Doberman on its toes. "What you got in that bag? A gun?"

"Rum. Used to be rum. Got another bottle in the car. Want some?" St. Cloud held out the empty bag in a gesture of friendliness.

The Doberman lunged at the sudden movement, jerking the man two steps forward before he overpowered the animal's pulling might. "That what you threw against my mobile home? Empty bottle of rum?"

"Sorry I threw the bottle, tossed it over my shoulder without looking, just careless." St. Cloud attempted to squeeze the shaky mirth out of his voice. This guy had every right to be outraged. With a little probing in the wrong direction he would probably let Alice go to work. Wouldn't be so bad St. Cloud figured, rather have the Doberman tear him apart than face Lila's disappointment at not being allowed in the trailer to see the pug. "Really, it wasn't intended, just that the car stopped so quickly it goofed my aim."

"What about your wife? She Cuban?"

Lila walked around the convertible into bright light. She looked innocent as a schoolgirl off on a picnic, even in harsh light, her skin glowed. The Doberman's growl slowed to a groan of discomfort. "I'm from Georgia, we don't have Cubans in Georgia. Migh name is Ly'lah." She raised her open hand to the man in an offer of greeting. The Doberman growled, opening its wide jaws, its bulging eyes taking in the skin of Lila's legs inches from its exposed teeth.

"Behave, Alice!" The man jerked the chain leash, forcing the Doberman into a sitting position. He stroked the disgruntled animal's bobbing head. "This little lady means no harm, Alice. Come to see the babies, that's all. Hello, ma'am." The man shook Lila's offered hand. "Sorry about this kind of welcome, but like I told your husband on the phone, everything would be okay long as you weren't Cuban types. We had lot of break-ins round here from boatlift people. Some even broke into our mobile home and took the TV, knocked Alice out with a ball bat, she's been pretty jumpy ever since. Like ice tea or something? C'mon inside, got the babies inside. Actually my wife's babies, she works night shift at the hospital so she ain't here now, she would have loved to meet you. C'mon in."

The trailer interior was done up in imitation suburban, the cluttered contents arranged to emulate a solid midwestern tract house which had been swirled around in a massive duster and banged down intact on the less than certain foundation of the Florida Keys. Garish orange Naugahyde recliner chairs offered the only wild moment of colorful tropical abandon, all else seemed dipped in sepia and grays, muted the most synthetic of hues. Ed was very proud of his mobile castle perched precariously at the edge of the Gulf Stream. He said his name was Ed, and he was going to make everybody ice tea whether they wanted it or not, because he knew what a long drive it was out from Key West just to see the babies. Ed appreciated that, appreciated that very much, because his wife took the babies seriously. Ed took his wife seriously. They both took their boys very seriously. Those were photographs of the boys over on top of the organ, grinning away at invisible flashing bulbs in their best public performances to date. The boys were displayed as fussy-haired toddlers, gap-toothed first graders, and now somewhat older, gangly, distracted, a hint of desperation creeping into frozen schoolbook smiles. The boys' faces sprawled over the entire organ top, a forest of photographic memories which would be crowded even if allowed to prowl the grand space of a piano top rather than a tiny lay-away-plan organ wedged into a corner, surrounded by many of the necessities appropriate to suburban living, including a large new television set, tuned to a giveaway game show with the sound turned low, and stacks of well-thumbed television guides. Hung dangerously low from the ceiling by plastic rope were plant holders outfitted with stiff arrangements of artificial foliage defying any identifiable natural origin. Squandering all available space against the back wall was a dirt-colored sofa encased in clear plastic to protect it from the brutalizing bouncing boys might inflict upon it. Alice sat alert before one corner of the sofa, her hulk jammed uneasily against a tall glass case filled with ceramic knickknacks of disparate shapes and sizes, each depicting the likeness of a pug, some sporting painted fur, others short, gauzy fuzz, colored everything from grass-hopper green to spray-painted pink, a few fawned with glassy marble eyes at an unseen master, or were inflicted with opaque saucer-size red eyes glued on flat faces with black button noses; all appeared to be prosaic prizes dished up at county fairs for lucky winners at two-bit games of chance. Laced among this stiff menagerie were fancy red, blue, yellow and green ribbons emblazoned with BEST OF SHOW, RUNNER-UP, THIRD PLACE, and various other declarations of merit garnered at dog shows in towns with names St. Cloud never heard of.

Alice eyed St. Cloud with fierce intensity as he studied the strange case. She too looked unreal in this setting, her bulged eyes a little too glassy, the undersized ax-shaped head bobbing maniacally, threatening to fly off the black-muscled body and do unspeakable damage to humans. St. Cloud noticed there was also something off about Ed. As he scanned the walls, laden with plaques and mounted certificates attesting to PEE-WEE LEAGUE FATHER OF THE YEAR, TO THE BEST CUB SCOUT MASTER EVER, MISTER POPULAR FROM HIS FANS, DAD OF THE YEAR, St. Cloud sensed a serious off-centeredness about Ed's entire family enterprise. He tried to suppress a feeling that great evil was lurking in this cloistered trailer tricked out with all the comforts of a suburban home. Ed's wife probably was not working at the hospital, but had escaped long ago, fled with the boys, leaving only photographic memories on the organ. Ed seemed the kind of monster who beat and bullied his family; thank God they had long since caught the midnight special on a one-way freedom ticket. Where was the pug? St. Cloud simply wanted to get the puppy and get out of this midget suburban nightmare guarded by a slobbering Doberman whose brain had been loosened by a burglar breaking a ball bat over its thick skull. St. Cloud felt cramped and trapped, he desired at minimum an escape to the convertible for another nip of Haiti's finest. "If you don't mind I'll just slip out and wait in the car."

Lila turned from the glass case, where she was bent studying the bizarre menagerie, the green of her eyes dazzling in the subdued tones of the room, they held one unmistakable message: *Don't you dare go anywhere.* Before she had a chance to voice her displeasure Ed appeared with three ice-clanking glasses of tea.

"No no no. Can't go yet." Ed handed St. Cloud a glass, his smile hinting at boyishness, the true age of his face betrayed by gray stubble of a five-day-old beard. "You haven't seen the babies yet." Ed did not wait for a yes or no before dashing in an artful weave between crowded pieces of furniture to present Lila her glass of tea. Alice eyed Ed with an intense look of proprietorship, her tongue darting anxiously between ice-pick straight canines as Lila raised the cold glass.

Lila did not notice she had become the object of the Doberman's uncertain intentions. Her attention was fixed on the organ and its forest of frozen photographic memories. "What cute boys." She spoke the words in a voice mixed with slight condescension and a genuine respect for something that should be of importance to her as a female. "They really are so *cute.*" She ran slender fingers tentatively over the frame tops. There was more than enough of the polite Southern girl in Lila to obey the protocol of family manners. "How many boys do y'all have?"

Lila asked Ed the question with such sincere maternal interest it confused St. Cloud. He wondered if she was serious, or simply playing with this guy just to see his pug, or had she too fallen prey to the cute thought of babies? St. Cloud decided Lila was simply scratching the soft spot on many female Southern souls which itched from guilt if a girl hadn't become a mama before she became a woman.

"Two or five boys, I guess." Ed laughed nervously, gulping his ice tea so quickly he sucked out several ice cubes, which came coughing back into his glass with a choking gurgle. "Care to see my babies?" he spluttered.

"Such a nice big family." Lila ran her fingers down from the photographs onto the polished imitation wood of the organ top. "We used to have an organ at home." She traced the black and white outline of the keys. "My stepdaddy used to play, taught me a little."

"It's my wife's. Care for a refill on the tea?" Ed rattled the melting ice in his empty glass and beamed his graying boyish smile.

"No." St. Cloud interrupted, setting his still full glass down on a stack of television guides. "I mean . . ." Lila's eyes were suddenly all over him with disapproval, as if suspecting he was about to douse the cluttered room with gasoline and toss a match to it. "I mean . . . we would love to have more tea, great stuff, but we have to get back to Key West. May we see the pug?" St. Cloud wasn't drunk enough not to feel like a total fool for being intimidated by this young woman, and allowing Ed the wife beater to get away with putting on the royal dog of hospitality. He had not driven all this way to have tea with a transplanted suburban loony.

"See the pug? Course you can see the pug. What you come for, what I'm here for, isn't it? How many pug puppies are in all the Florida Keys as we speak? Tell you how many, zero, except what I got. Let's get the little cuties to audition for you, Mister . . . Mister . . . what did you say your name was?"

"St. Cloud."

"Mister St. Cloud, funny handle. And what's your young wife's name?" Ed turned his graying boyish beam appreciatively onto Lila.

"She already told you, Lila."

"Ain't heard that one before either. Okay though, Alice loves you both. Don't you, Alice?" The Doberman jumped with a fierce bark, rattling ceramic pugs in the glass case.

"Your last newspaper advertisement said only *one* pug left." St. Cloud finally caught the wife beater in a lie. Lila was certain to commend him later.

"That's because two were sold but haven't been called for yet. Lucky you have pick of the litter."

"Funny the people who bought the first two didn't take them." No matter how quickly this guy dodged the bullet, St. Cloud knew he was all lies. He picked up the glass and swigged the bitterness of a nonalcoholic drink. "Why don't you bring them out? We've got a long drive."

"Yes, bring them out. Yes!" Ed exited the room quickly through a swinging door leading down a narrow passageway.

"Is it true about your stepfather?" St. Cloud set the ice tea down, he wasn't that desperate for something to drink. "Did he really have an organ?"

"Why, yaaas." Lila drawled the affirmative answer with a distracted air, turning to the organ keys and tapping them lightly with her long fingernail tips. She seemed far away, drifting in some unreachable place, like the first time St. Cloud had seen her in the air-conditioned cool of the bird shop, a treacherous wall of ice separating them, threatening to splinter into a thousand dangerous shards. One of Lila's long nails stabbed an organ key, introducing a shrill note into the silence. The Doberman leapt with a snarl, sharp canines exposed, ready to tear off Lila's kneecaps.

"Alice! Shut up and sit!" Ed banged through the swinging door, three squealing puppies held against his chest.

The Doberman backed into the corner with a whine, its body alert to the puppies.

"It's okay, Alice." Ed let the puppies loose on the oatmeal-colored carpet. "The babies are okay. That's a good mama." The puppies bumped into each other, into the furniture, making their way across the carpet to the whining Doberman. "Sorry about the commotion." Ed beamed. "But Alice takes a real interest in these babies. Never been a mama herself, thinks these cuties are hers."

"Where's the mother?" This time St. Cloud was not going to let Ed get away with his juggling act. He was going to insist Ed produce. "You said on the phone you had both parents and we could see them."

"The mother? The father? Oh . . . yes . . . uh. They're at the vet's, had to be left overnight there for worming. Normal thing, you know, pinworms."

"What's the name of the vet?" St. Cloud finally had Ed where he wanted him.

"The name of the . . . ?"

Lila dropped to her knees before the puppies, disregarding Alice's suspect expression. "I don't care about the parents, I just want a puppy." She lifted one of the squealing dogs into the air and pressed its nose to her lips. "I don't have to see any pedigrees."

Once again Ed dodged the bullet, but St. Cloud figured he had one round left in the chamber to blast the liar between the eyes. "How much did you say the puppies are?"

"Four fifty. Fair price. Don't like my prices you'll have to keep on driving up to Miami and buy from those backyard breeders at near twice that."

Bull's-eye. "You said on the phone *four hundred*. We get out here and you raise the price."

"That was four hundred till there was only one left. Supply and demand." Ed beamed his gray smile. "Simple as that."

It wasn't simple as that, St. Cloud finally had the wife beater dead to rights.

"I love this one." Lila was paying no attention to the conversation, busy weighing her choices, coming to a decision after poking and petting her three best new friends. "This one will be fine." She hefted a stubby creature, rubbing its grunting body against her cheek. "Do you think it's a boy?"

"Looks like a little boy to me." Ed nodded encouragingly. "Has the most black in its face, the father had that. I've got pedigrees to prove the father."

"What do you think?" Lila presented the puppy to St. Cloud at the end of her outstretched arms. The creature's tiny paws churned the air, powered by nonstop chortles and whines.

"Looks good, would have been my choice." St. Cloud lied, he was the sort who never made his mind up about anything in short order. Choosing one of these dogs was like choosing a shirt, an enterprise he had had a lifetime of opportunity to execute, but to this day he remained incapable of walking into a store and choosing a shirt in less than twenty minutes, debating its color or collar shape as if the nuclear balance of power depended upon it, feeling embarrassed before a shop clerk impatiently awaiting a decision on such an insignificant purchase. St. Cloud always wore his clothes to a threadbare condition before contemplating a change. "Great choice, Lila. Really the best."

"I thought so too." Lila brought the dog back to her cheek for a reassuring nuzzle. "Knew this was the one right off, intuition."

"Absolutely a perfect match." Ed tossed in the echoed opinion as if it originated from him, his gray smile curved across his face, giving him the beaming air of a cartoon-drawn man in the moon. "You make an excellent pair."

Moon over Miami, sun over Cairo, stars in his eyes, St. Cloud no longer cared. His brains drained into his shoes, blood drumming in his toes, he wanted to walk out of the trailer and drive away to Key West while sipping the secreted sweetness of Haiti's finest cane. He wanted out of this wife beater's midget suburban ghetto, he wanted to wander like the wind in mangrove swamps, where lizards eyed busy fire ants and pelicans gulped baby bonita fish. He eyed the door in desperation. He wanted aboard the freedom train with the wife beater's wife and kids. He wanted the Haitian face of Voltaire to stop floating up in his dreams like a helium-filled balloon pumped to a grotesque explosion of death. He wanted out once and for all. What could he do about it anyway? His idealistic days of chasing righteous answers were over, the ship of his soul was sunk. No more showboat we shall overcome the injustices of mankind for him. Right now he was looking for sunlight shining beneath the rum tide to swim toward. Had to get Lila on the midnight freedom train before the wife beater had his way with her, sporting and grunting atop her, rolling across the carpet while the ceramic circus of dead-eyed pugs in the glass-case gallery howled obscene approval. He moved toward her with steady deliberation, then stopped, not wanting to break the transparent shell engulfing her, not wanting to step into final illumination. He hoped the wife beater didn't see what he saw, what he trained himself a lifetime to look for. Lila kneeling was in a perfect curve of grace, Narcissus at the reflecting pond, body arched, skirt working high to thighs. There was a sense of the unlearned about her, an intuitive nurturing which shined in the feckless act of allowing the misshapen dog to suck at her fingers. She was suspended in an elusive female state of being, defensible and alone. This elusive constant was what fascinated him from the beginning, why he had followed her along Duval Street all those nights, through redneck bars, in and out of biker dives and fancy tourist hotels. What she sought did not exist in the music played in those places. She was the music, the name of the tune was everyone wanted her. Through St. Cloud's rum-thickened blood an insistent message registered, he would die unless he captured her elusiveness.

"Hi, Dad."

The shrill voice was a blatant intrusion into St. Cloud's reverie. Was it a real voice, or that of a ghost?

"You should be in bed, son, school tomorrow." Ed beamed his gray smile beyond St. Cloud, to the swinging saloon-style doors leading off into the narrow passageway. "Alice will watch out for the babies, don't worry."

"Okay, Daddy."

St. Cloud turned slowly to the voice behind, bracing for the worst. Instead of a ghost he was greeted by a grinning seven-year-old in pajamas with a ratty blanket clutched securely at his shoulder. The boy gave a quick conspiratorial wave before disappearing back through swinging doors.

"What a darling." Lila stood, fondling her own new baby. "What's your son's name?"

"Matt." Ed beamed. "Matthew Robert O'Grady." He turned his gray beam triumphantly onto St. Cloud for full effect. "My youngest."

Worse than it first appeared, St. Cloud thought. Ed beat the wife *and* the kids, things got so bad the wife had to abandon the little tykes and run for her life. What a sordid scenario. He didn't like Ed at all before, he liked him even less now. Thank God they could at least save the funny-looking dog from this miniature suburban torture chamber.

"Your son's such a doll. Y'all must be proud." Lila squeezed the puppy until its pink tongue popped out to lick her cheek. "Your boy's so . . ."

"Cute." St. Cloud sprang the word from its trap, not to interrupt Lila, but to show her he too could be from the land of cute, cute love, cute boys, cute wife beaters. Cute transformed everything into the comfortable and reassuring. Cute was nonthreatening, a smooth thing with no spikes, no nasty history. Cute was a bloody mess without a face.

Lila gave St. Cloud a puzzled look, not certain what he was up to, usurping the most used word in her lexicon. Maybe he was trying to belittle her? The concerned look on his face didn't indicate that. Why was it when he spoke the word *cute* it sounded foreign, even dangerous? The pint of rum he drank driving up from Key West must be taking its toll. She decided he wasn't trying to insult her, he was just stewed.

"Why don't we give you your cute money, Ed?" St. Cloud slurred his words. "Then we'll be off to cutie-pie land, give you a cute nighty-nite and the cute four hundred smacks and that'll be our last cute act."

That was it, Lila knew for certain, St. Cloud was drunk and his rum-loosened tongue was getting ready to use those fancy words of his on anybody who got in his way. She had to head him off. "I have the money right here in my purse." She hurriedly struggled to get the purse open, not wanting to let go of the pug for fear she would be separated from it forever. "It's all here." She held out the wad of bills. "You can count it, four hundred."

"Four hundred *fifty*, if you please." Ed beamed.

St. Cloud was pleased, but for a different reason from Ed's. Finally Ed tripped himself up, stepped into the bear trap.

"I thought you said four hundred?" Lila squeezed the puppy even tighter, a look of terror in her eyes at the thought the animal might be yanked from her arms. "I called several times and you said you would hold the dog for four hundred."

"True enough." Ed turned his gray beam down a few notches. "But like I told your husband when you was playing with the babies, last of the litter is four fifty."

"He's not my husband." Lila gave Ed a confused look which went quickly past him to the front door. She was ready to bolt into the night with her bundle of love.

"That's cute." St. Cloud decided it was time the steel jaws of justice slammed onto this wife-beating phony suburbanite. "Real cute, Ed, almost broke the girl's heart. Here." He pulled his wallet out and counted five tens. "That'll make up the extra. Now, where's the pedigree?"

"The pedigree? Yes . . . well . . . it's not that simple. Have to send to the Kennel Club and then . . ."

"Cute. How long?"

"Six, twelve weeks. I'll send it."

"Better yet, I'll personally come back and get it in twelve weeks."

Ed opened the front door. "Come back then, I'll have even more pugs."

"How's that? It's too short a time for your bitch to . . . oh, forget it." He watched Lila hand over four hundred dollars. He thought of the hours cleaning bird cages it took to earn this money.

"Dad, when's Mom comin home?"

The little pajama ghost popped back through the swinging doors, St. Cloud had him in full sight. Alice ambled over to the boy with a heartsick whine and licked his small hands.

"Soon, son. Go back to bed. Take Alice, she's sleepy too."

The boy waved to St. Cloud like they were old war buddies and was gone.

St. Cloud pondered the evil of what he now knew. There really was a wife and she really was working at the hospital. He moved outside and stood beneath the spotlight above the trailer door burning a hole in the night. It was all worse than he could have ever dreamed. Ed was not only a wife and kid beater, his family was so terrified of him that fear for their very lives rooted them here forever. St. Cloud tried not to dwell on the horror. He took solace in the fact he knew where the stars went in the morning. He tipped his head back to see their familiar patterns in the night sky, but all starlight was blinded by the spotlight. The things that happen in the suburbs, St. Cloud shook his head sadly. Lila came through the door behind him, escaping Ed the neighborhood terrorist, unaware Ed so brutalized his family that the hapless victims prayed nightly for his tarnished soul. St. Cloud knew where the stars went in the morning, he knew things that happen in the suburbs are sometimes too evil to contemplate. He stumbled over to the convertible, it was as old as Lila, still sleek, nothing cute about its chrome fins ready to chew off the white line of any asphalt highway. Lila slipped in behind the steering wheel. He couldn't believe how sincere and lovely she looked with the dog licking the flesh of her neck. Desire was eating a hole through his resolve, he yearned to kiss her.

"Ed's a wife beater. Man's a maniac, should be locked up." St. Cloud spoke the words matter of factly, with no malice. "At least we saved the dog."

Lila set the puppy loose on the car seat, it sidled to St. Cloud, nosing between his legs, pawing with the determination of a bear smelling honey. Lila flicked the key in the ignition. The convertible shuddered to a start, sending a burst of black exhaust behind. She plunged her foot down on the gas pedal, a scatter of loose gravel shooting from beneath the tires as she wheeled into the night. She deftly scooped the puppy up with one hand, the other hand fixed on the steering wheel, guiding the convertible between shadowed mangrove shapes edging along the narrow road. The dog grunted contentedly, nibbling at Lila's ear exposed by wind smoothing the hair from her face. "You know, y'all really are strange." Her words were encased in their usual sugar-coated Southern drawl, rolling over St. Cloud with an intimate familiarity, until the last of her thought was fully unwrapped. "I don't know if I like that."

12

URRICANE be comin. Least ways that was the way Bonefish figured it to be. Mean weather casting out lightning spikes from the sun was a sure sign. Nother sign was when the sea grape trees flourished with such fruit their fat-leaved branches nearly bent to the ground. Bonefish seen that happen before the '35 Blow, and he seen it now, kept his eyes open, ever on the lookout for ol Mister Finito ready to come long and make the bad ol world smoothed out again. You wanted to know from hurricane, all you got to do is look for yourself neath the skirts of Ma Nature, don't have to be no scientist nor TV weatherman to figure that, needed no satellite photographs neither, needed a head on your shoulders, eyes to see lightnin and ears to hear thunder. Flamboyant trees would talk to you, you smart enough to listen. Those big ol gnarly ghost gray–trunked trees were up an down each to every street on the island, come over to Jamaica from the Madagascar in Africa, come over to Key West by smart Conchs wantin a fannin shade tree to cool them over in the sweat of summer. Royal poinciana tree was what some called it. Whenever one of the big ol ones forty feet high, its branches throwin a brilliant umbrella of flamin orchid flowers a hundred feet around, was chopped down, newspapers reported nother granddaddy royal poinciana had been killed to beautify the way of progress. Forget poinciana, that was a wrong name. Bonefish grew up with the right name, flamboyant. When thousands of flamboyant flowers blossomed such rich red a Christian person could barely afford to look at them, Bonefish knew then and there Ma Nature be takin a smart man by the shoulders an warnin him bout the truth of the bad ol world. That the rains was comin, the steamy season of flat water an fat clouds was headed this way. Out there in the inky deep the Caribbean cauldron was swirlin, a tropical Atlantic stew was brewin, storms were in the makin. You lucky enough maybe it all wouldn't come your way one more time, maybe it would move off west to blow a hole right through Louisiana. Maybe you'd still be round to see the end of the flamboyant tree's natural cycle, after the flowers dropped, runnin rooster-wattle red in the gutters as hissing rains pummeled the hot an sticky of long afternoons, when lacy leaves would dry up and die, leavin the bloomin tree barren, except for leathery seed pods long as a woman's arm, hooked sharp as a sickle blade. Then those seed pods would rattle their contents in the wind, rattle a new beginnin, wind chimes of birth. You be lucky an thankful you lived to see that, to know you been let off the hook of boisterous weather yet one more time, to have survived the summer in all of one piece to enjoy nother Day of the Dead in the far October, for that day marked the end of hurricane season. A man smart enough to hear thunder knew how to read the message of the flamboyant, knew that tree didn't like Mister Finito at all, knew in its roots that it was a fragile-limbed tree in high wind, its brittle branches would creak an snap, its trunk pitch an groan, an maybe it would rattle a final death gasp in a last whip from a furious gust an topple to an early grave. That tree knew all that stuff an more. It knew to throw the most brilliant canopy of scarlet flowers ever witnessed before or since in its last late spring season before the Big Blow, to show off to the world how glorious it was to be alive, how sad it was going to be missed at the end of summer when El Finito put an end to the show. A smart man knew how to read that tree. Bonefish had never seen such a mess of flowers bloomin on the flamboyant as was blazin right now. No question bout it, the tree was talkin, sayin the Devil's tradewind was windin up to punch the lights out of civilization.

Bonefish didn't consider himself part of civilization. Bonefish considered himself smart. He didn't only run over to the rock grotto, harboring the life-size linen cloaked statue of Mary Immaculate in the shadows of the Catholic church's two towering metal-roofed steeples, to pray for his survival from the Devil's trades when the weather was fixin to be boisterous. No. Bonefish prayed *every* day of the year at the grotto. Bonefish was a man of simple faith. The hare could outrun the hound if the hare didn't stop to shit in the woods. Each day Bonefish got down on his knees, clapped his hands together in prayerful salute and raised them high to the Immaculate Virgin. Bonefish was a thankful man. Bonefish had more than his own day-to-day survival to be thankful for, he had friends and family. What a family. Bonefish considered the island his family, his special domain, his rock of everyday hope upon which he banked his faith for humanity. Bonefish was an old saltwater Conch, born and bred to the island long before the time of the lethal yellow blight killing off the coconut palms, before the walls of condominiums threatened to block a man's rightful view of the broad blue sea beyond, and the ships upon it, passing with one-quarter of all the world's mercantile freight, from Florida oranges to Arab oil to Latin American tin and cocaine. Bonefish was a saltwater Conch, and as such an optimist who cashed the check of his trust in people everyday. Which meant he carried on a tradition of dropping round to chat with folks in order to move along the important concerns of human commerce, such as whose cat just had kittens, whose dog had died, whose grown grandchildren no longer called on them, and this after near raisin those kids one's self. Bonefish was always to be seen walking along the shaded side of the street, stopping to call out a greeting, or lean against a white picket fence, peering over at someone who happened to be outside fetchin the newspaper or waterin the bougainvillea, and droppin the just for your information news that Y's wife was meetin a sailor stationed across the Cow Key Channel bridge at Boca Chica Naval Station every afternoon at the Overseas Fruit Market, or R's son, the one who never graduated high school, but drove a fast shiny car with Miami plates and had three Cuban girlfriends that he loaded up with diamond watches and gold chains, was busted the night before south of Torch Ramrod Channel runnin a two-million-dollar boatload of marijuana onto a coral jut instead of into safe harbor. At sixty-two years of age Bonefish had his common senses, his knack for listenin an tellin, and his bony straight body, which earned him in a town of nicknames a very early and obvious one. What Bonefish didn't know wasn't worth knowing, what was worth knowing he was bound to find out. One thing he did know was last night someone bound a goat by its hind legs, slashed its throat and hung its lifeless body from a rope tied to a high rafter inside that crazy ol bat tower out on Sugarloaf Key. What Bonefish didn't know was why.

Sacrificial goats and mosquito-eating bats were the least concerns churning round in Bonefish's brain. Hurricane coming was much closer and realer, right round the corner of the Gulf, lurking and looming, not leaving Bonefish much time. Bonefish had lots of stuff to get rid of, didn't want to get caught with it, let someone else tote it off this ol rock, not his job. His job was to figure the future and tell its truth, its truth was disaster over the thin blue horizon. Bonefish had to get himself flashlights and batteries, canned goods and bottled water, get rid of all the other stuff that could go flying round to bop him over the head in two-hundred-mile-per-hour winds. Bonefish was staying put when the Big One blew, wasn't going to get caught on the Seven Mile Bridge with lots of panicked rats in cars loaded with dumb stuff like television sets, toasters and family photos. Bonefish saw clear the true fact of life, the Florida Keys are the most likeliest part of America to get knocked by a hurricane from each and every side. The truth looming even larger was in the Keys there was no high ground, there was no ground at all to speak of, nothing that would peak above a storm surge of seawater once Finito delivered his knockout punch.

Bonefish was in one big hurry, almost running down the street, going through the churning in his head looking for something he might have left out or forgotten altogether. Spam. Got to get lots of cans of Spam. Air-condishner, there was one item he forgot to unload. Got to get that ice-breathing monster out of the bedroom window and out of the house. He turned the corner in front of the Shrimp Docks and headed directly into Diver Dave's Diner with his urgent message.

"Anybody need an air-condishner? Got a brand-new one! Just bout year old!"

Everyone was always glad to see Bonefish. Their faces lit up like bright beams of the flashlights Bonefish intended to buy to light up the dark world after El Finito roared through. When Bonefish entered the diner door it was open season to talk about anyone one knew. It wasn't like talking behind people's backs, it was like talking in front of them, because Bonefish himself was a social institution needing tending and respect. Bonefish wasn't simply a pillar of the society, he was the torch of grapevine gossip, which in its time-honored way was to be passed from *buche* shop to *buche* shop, café to diner to restaurant, stoop to porch to veranda. In the old days the moment a person turned the corner onto one of the island's crowded streets word reached folks at the opposite end who it was that was headed their way.

"How much you want for it?" Marilyn at the end of the counter on the last stool let her spoon drop into a bowl of conch chowder and spun around on the vinyl swivel seat. "My trailer's real hot. Could use a breeze." Every day Marilyn was at the counter right at noontime eating with the workingmen. Sometimes the diner was crowded with Shrimpers fresh from the boat in their mucky white rubber boots. Other times the diner was filled with Charter Boat captains moaning in their beer that the wind was up, making the sea too busy for weak stomached tourists to venture out on. Very often there were also a few of Marilyn's old Cuban friends playing dominoes at the corner table beneath the big window facing high-hulled shrimp boats docked in deep water on the far side of a weed-covered field. A rusting radio relay tower from World War I rose in the center of the field, its crisscrossed steel platform legs capped at the top by a man-size cage. Tense young soldiers once guarded for saboteurs from the lofty aerie, now empty as an abandoned eagle's nest. Marilyn's first husband once manned this tower, or one like it, she couldn't remember, since many towers still stood on the island, decades beyond meaningful use, dilapidated monuments to past paranoia and a dubious future. The towers loomed as talismans from a not so primitive, but confused society. Island people are by tradition the most superstitious. Marilyn was an island woman. "Could use me a cool breeze, a cold beer and a hot sailor. Could use me that, brother."

"Don't have the hot sailor. Got the cool breeze." Bonefish squeezed onto the stool next to Marilyn. He was in a big hurry, hurricane was comin, but now there was some important business to unfold, new things to be learned and passed. Hurricane could wait a few minutes.

"Here's couple a beers for you two." Diver Dave popped the tops of two cans and banged them on the counter, their contents rushing with a foaming spurt at the fresh openings. Diver Dave popped a can for himself, worked his big lips over the entire top and sucked the can empty easily as a thimble full of tea. He tipped back on his heels to announce his pleasure with a loud barrel-burst burp of approval.

"Asshole!" the Amazon parrot perched on Dave's right shoulder scolded.

"Up yours, Amigo!" Dave shouted back.

"Up yours," echoed the parrot.

Dave loved his parrot. Some people said Amigo was never off Dave's shoulder, day or night, certainly the powdery dry white river of parrot poop permanently trailing off the sleeve of Dave's beer-stained T-shirt made that idea one of fact more than rumor. Some people even claimed Amigo was on Dave's shoulder whenever Dave had the pleasure of female company in his bed. Certainly Amigo's cocky attitude on Dave's shoulder, his cavalier eye and unerring raucous two-toned whistle aimed at all good-looking women, made this seem more believable than not. Amigo never whistled at Marilyn, although she was not without her own peculiar attractiveness. A sturdily constructed woman in her late fifties, Marilyn kept her hair dyed a girlish light brown, styled in a dated but carefree hint of a bob. She was a woman who loved the sort of outdoor activities mostly reserved for men. Marilyn had spent a large part of her youth toiling in a Key West pineapple cannery. She worked not as a canner, but as a dockhand, unloading ripe tonnage of spiny-hulled fruit barged over from Cuba. Marilyn worked through the middle section of her life on shrimp boats, normally the exclusive domain of men. She did not spend that time slaving over kerosene stoves in hot galleys, or frolicking beneath sheets of narrow berths, while far below pink crustaceans had their migratory underwater path from the Dry Tortugas intercepted by miles of dragging nets. She toiled topside in the dreck and dross of slippery decks alongside the men as a net hauler. Marilyn displayed the fleshy tanned muscles of a healthy laborer, attractive in a handsome sort of way for her time, handsome still. Except Amigo didn't think so, never whistled at her. Sometimes, when Marilyn thought she looked particularly attractive, and even wore a pair of new jeans, she would wait for Amigo's whistle of approval. Marilyn never got it. She never hesitated to let Amigo know what she thought about his insulting lack of taste. "Fuck you," Marilyn would shout her disapproval at the parrot. "Fuck you," Amigo would mock, then roll his green head and whistle mightily, as if Marilyn had a ravishing sister in the back room of the diner no one else could conjure except him with his jungle-piercing eyes.

"Now don't go and start a fight with Marilyn, Amigo," Dave cooed to the ever-vigilant bird as he popped another can of beer open. Amigo ignored the advice, craning his neck and screwing up one beady eye as he surveyed Marilyn, a fowl judge at a beauty pageant whose studied opinion was not to be summarily dismissed.

"That bird don't deserve no attention. He ain't no movie star." Marilyn sullenly slurped her soup while keeping a defiant gaze fixed on the parrot. She knew exactly how to get at the short hairs of Dave. Her slurping grew more pronounced as her defiant gaze melted into a smug grin of triumph.

Bonefish could see what was coming and tried to turn the tide of conversation, banging his empty beer can down as if it was the metal period at the close of a chapter, and he was turning the page. "Okay, Marilyn, you get the condishner. Got to help me get it out the window though. Too heavy for me alone."

"Is it same size as the one you gave me last year?"

"No. This one's top of the line. Could freeze carrots in front of it."

"Bullshit!" The word bellowed out of Dave's barrel belly, his big body puffing up red. "Bullshit Amigo ain't no movie star!"

"Ain't," Marilyn slurped.

"Then what in hell you think those are? Polaroids of Lassie?" Dave jabbed his finger at a gallery of faded black and white photo glossies tacked to the side wall beneath the phony fiberglass glory of a mounted leaping blue marlin Dave caught off the coast of Cuba the day of the Bay of Pigs invasion. Dave had nearly been bombed out of the water by his own countrymen that day, scariest day of his life. "Just you look at those photos, why don't you? Amigo's a fame-ass world-renowned bird!"

Marilyn refused to turn to peruse the wall covered with photos, she had seen it all before. In the 1950s a Hollywood film crew came to Key West to shoot a movie about the fierce battle during the 1920s between the local Conchs and Greek immigrants, bloodying one another over who had proprietary rights to the sponge beds of the Florida Keys. The Conchs won out, forcing the Greeks three hundred miles north, above Tampa Bay to Tarpon Springs. Key West was an island the Conchs were not about to be pushed from, having been over the generations pushed from almost every other island, but in the end Mother Nature's irony prevailed. The mysterious blight of '34 killed off the sponge beds in the Lower Keys.

Diver Dave was a dashing man in the 1950s, with oil black hair slicked back from his sun-darkened face. The Hollywood types thought Dave looked Greek, so they put him in their movie. Dave's job was to wear tight blue jeans, a striped blue-and-white Greek fisherman's sweater, and shout the line: "*Start your boat-engines boys, the Conchs are comin back!*" It took three days of shooting for the Hollywood types to get that scene right. All during the camera takes of Dave rising from his swinging hammock, looking to the sea and shouting his line, Amigo was perched overhead on the arc of a palm frond, playing the part of a pet parrot kept by the Greek Spongers. Amigo's only line in the movie was to discharge a licentious whistle whenever he spied the blond starlet of the film in her pretty ruffled blouse dipped daringly low off one shoulder. During those long hours of shooting Dave's big scene Amigo excreted his powdery white pearls of wisdom onto Dave in the hammock below. Dave couldn't change his position from one take to the next. After a while he learned to judge just how long it would be between the time Amigo snapped a sunflower seed in his beak and an inevitable plop of parrot poop would descend like featherweight hail to rest upon his cheek. The photos on the diner wall showed Amigo with the cast and crew of the film, everybody smiling and waving. There were many photos of the blond starlet laughing hysterically as Amigo buried his green head into the fleshy valley of exposed cleavage between her breasts. Dave got very close to that bird during the shooting, bought him and brought him back to the diner. The two were inseparable ever since. Dave loved that bird with all his might.

"This bird's a phony!" Marilyn jabbed her soup spoon at Amigo. "He's not the same as the bird in those photos. He's a pet-store fake, a scrawny chicken dyed pukey green!"

Dave's big hands clenched into fists, he placed them both on the counter in front of Marilyn's bowl of chowder and leaned over on stiffened arms. "Up yours," Dave hissed. "Up yours," the parrot squawked.

"The conch in this chowder is past its prime." Marilyn batted her short gray lashes at the beefy man bearing down on her. "I think you're using three-day-old amberjack in it again."

Everybody knew Marilyn loved Dave, always had. Marilyn figured the only thing that kept her unhappy all these years, after her fourth husband died working on the new Seven Mile Bridge, was the parrot never gave Dave the whistle of approval to go to bed with her. Dave never went to bed with a woman Amigo didn't call out his craving for. The only thing different about this particular afternoon was Marilyn normally didn't insult Dave's lack of culinary expertise, and his best friend, until after she finished her second piece of Key lime pie. Something was nagging at her.

Bonefish figured whatever nagged Marilyn, at her age it couldn't be her female time of month. No, Bonefish deduced the prompter of the problem was El Finito headed this way, made people jumpy. "Got to go. Can't wait." Bonefish spun on his stool. He saw the eye of El Finito wink offshore, a monster of destruction pushing a fifty-foot-high storm surge before it.

Marilyn knew how to get Bonefish to stay. She tossed him some bait. "I heard some stuff about that goat found hanging upside down in the bat tower."

Bonefish let the stool's swivel seat carry him completely around and stop before Marilyn's grinning face. "What you hear I don't hear?" Bonefish couldn't believe his ears, he was the one who always had the first and last word on any subject, he was the bee of gossip, no pollen was spread Bonefish didn't spread himself. Marilyn was poaching on his territory. Maybe the hurricane comin had distracted him. Sometimes a man gets distracted by other work.

"Santería is what I heard. And I'll have a piece of Key lime pie, if you please," Marilyn smiled coquettishly at Dave.

"Bullshit." Dave turned to get the pie. "That goat's got nothing to do with Santería. Just some weirdo, or frisky kids fooling as usual."

"Kids and weirdos wouldn't go to such trouble to kill a goat." Marilyn's words followed Dave as he turned to get the pie. "That tower's higher than a windmill, who's going to scramble way up thirty feet inside it, tie a goat's hind legs, slit its throat and hang it by a rope? Tell me, huh, what kind of weirdo would do that?"

"Any weirdo." Dave clanked the plate of yellow-green pie belligerently on the counter before Marilyn and snarled, "That's why they're weird."

Bonefish hated to ask the question he was about to ask Marilyn, he liked information to flow to him because of his inevitable attraction, easy as nails to a magnet. "How do you know somebody didn't kill the goat first, slit its throat on the ground, then take it up to the top of the tower?"

"Why should I tell you?" Marilyn cut a dainty piece of pie for herself. "You'll just blab it to everybody."

"Because I'm supposed to know! That's why!" Bonefish's face lost its thin shape and sagged with sadness. He couldn't believe Marilyn's slight. To think he was going to give this woman his new air-condishner. How many condishners can a woman use in a small trailer anyway? Bonefish had been giving Marilyn condishners for the past twenty years. He decided he wasn't going to give Marilyn his TV set either. He decided it was over for Marilyn, she deserved whatever El Finito had up his windy sleeve for her.

"How *do* you know the goat wasn't killed on the ground, Marilyn?" Justo interrupted with Bonefish's original question, leaning forward on his stool at the opposite end of the crowded counter, peering down the long row of Dave's satisfied customers munching on tough shark sandwiches and overcooked squid rings.

"Well . . ." Marilyn straightened, assuming a formal pose, this was official business now that Justo cut in, police business, no longer idle chitchat batted between friends. This could add up to something reported in the local newspaper, a photograph to go with it maybe, maybe on the sportfishing page where the biggest catch of the day was always shown; there Marilyn would be, grinning away right next to the four-hundred-pound blue marlin or the two-hundred-fifty-pound sailfish. "My third husband told me. Andy saw it last night, long before that school-bus load of third graders were taken out to the tower for a picnic and got the scare of their little lives. You know," Marilyn suspended the thought, her face aglow, the attention of the entire diner fixed on her every word. She finally had the audience she had waited some time for. Marilyn wasn't about to miss the opportunity to chum the waters of chance. Maybe her photo would make front page. "I don't know what Andy is going to do for a living. He was thirty-nine when I divorced him ten years ago. Andy couldn't figure out what to do then, he still can't tie his own shoes without help." Marilyn scanned her captive audience for the answer to her question she knew would not be forthcoming, and she knew why. Marilyn considered herself a hardworking woman, she didn't take easy shortcuts like Andy, but this was a town chock full of shortcut men who still seemed to take longer to get someplace than anyone else, not like the rum-running boys she grew up with, those Pelicans had a work ethic, or so it seemed.

"What was Andy doing out at the tower last night?" Justo's question traveled the length of the counter with such inquisitive forcefulness the satisfied customers stopped their chewing and slurping.

"What is Andy usually doing anywhere?" Marilyn shrugged and tossed her bobbed hair.

"I didn't say anywhere. I said *there*." Justo's inquisitive tone changed to impatience.

"Really don't know and really don't care." Marilyn's fingers ran into her short hair and fluffed it. She wasn't going to be intimidated by any man, especially one she wasn't married to, didn't have to put up with that, but she liked Justo, he wasn't a shortcut man, better yet, he had risen to take her bait. Marilyn inadvertently tossed Justo what he didn't realize he was looking for. "All I know is Andy found some writings out there."

Justo swerved off his stool and walked straight to Marilyn. "Now tell me, what kind of writings did Andy find?"

Justo's voice always had a deep roughness, but his eyes had a sensitive brown gloss Marilyn found disturbingly attractive. She had had more than one dream about this dark man with the powerful chest. Back in the days before her second husband there were so few people on the island, sooner or later, everybody dreamed about everybody else, one way or the other. Marilyn definitely dreamed about Justo the other way. She wondered, with Justo standing so close she felt the heat of his body, if he remembered the wild times they had in her dreams, those swollen moments of slick escape. Marilyn was fairly certain Justo did remember, and decided to offer him another little reward since he was popping for all her bait. It didn't seem she could go wrong this afternoon. "Mumbo jumbo stuff. Poetry stuff. That's all I know."

"What kind of poetry stuff?"

"Andy thinks it's Santería."

The two Cubans beneath the big window stopped their game of dominoes, quickly scooping up the black and white playing pieces as if it were just announced a time-bomb had been placed in one of Diver Dave's famous Key lime pies.

Dave was too astute a businessman to lose customers over any dead goat poems, which had nothing to do with his opening the diner bright and early every morning at six to fire up his steamer for the hundreds of cups of *buche* needed to launch the early morning fishermen and all night boozers. "Asshole." Dave laughed. "Asshole," Amigo echoed. "Shutup, Amigo, I'm talking. Andy's an asshole. What does Andy know about Santería? Andy doesn't know the difference between his thumb and a rectal thermometer."

Marilyn didn't like anyone talking about her husbands in a derogatory way, even if they were no longer her husbands, were nothing but worthless louts to be booted out of a straight woman's bunk. "I suppose your educated asshole does know the difference between a thumb and a thermometer? Your educated asshole could tell the difference even if you were blindfolded, you've certainly sat on enough thumbs." Marilyn tossed her sharp barb at Dave and it struck the target.

The satisfied customers grinned and started chewing and slurping again. The snickering Cubans spread dominoes across the table to take up where they had left off. *La mujer vieja* went *mano y mano* with

Dave and bested him at his own game. The Cubans always liked Marilyn better than Dave's parrot. They didn't believe Amigo was a Hollywood parrot. Big-time Hollywood parrots don't end their days shitting on Diver Dave's shoulder in a fishermen's cafe across from the shrimp docks in Key West. The Cubans agreed to themselves with a chuckle, that pukey green bird was a foul-mouth impostor, probably a phony from Miami.

Bonefish jumped off his stool, he finally had what he wanted, pollen for the streets, a dead goat that writes poetry. No time to lose, Bonefish had to spread the word before the hurricane hit. Bonefish brushed past Justo in a hurry to get to the door. Bonefish respected Justo, an honest man in a world rigged for hurricanes. Bugs was Justo's nickname as a kid. Bugs, because when Justo was a boy he could twist heads off netloads of shrimp faster than any man, twisted off so many millions of sea bugs' heads he got their nickname of Bugs. Everybody had a nickname on the island. Hurricanes all had nicknames too. Bonefish didn't know what the nickname of the big hurricane brewing out in the steamy ocean was. Bonefish knew it had a nickname and people would learn to respect it, he already did. Every year at the beginning of hurricane season he gave away all his earthly possessions, because in the end he was going to get them all back. Bonefish didn't know why the Big Blow blew, he just knew it did.

13

HERE WERE no bats in the bat tower on Sugarloaf Key. The tower stood more than a half century since its construction, forlorn and deserted, a south Florida folly rising above swampy patches of mangroves. The tower was stronger than the dream that spawned it, its superstructure of hard pine, its sides shingled with thick cuts of cedar, the thrust of its significant bulk perched on staunch twelve-foot-high stilts. The tower loomed large as an abandoned windmill stripped of its giant wind-turning paddles, but this was no construction of such obvious purpose. The tower had been erected to accept legions of bats winging in through its louvered openings. The blind winged creatures were to be passionately attracted to a secret stench of love bait within the tower's bowels, there to mate and multiply, then swarm in screeching black clouds across the Keys, feasting upon the dread marsh mosquitoes, which forced even the fearless indoors during their bloodsucking season. No stairs led to the top of the tower; its long-since deceased builder did not want his precious pets distracted from their purpose of making his twenty-five-thousand-acre half-water, half-land investment safe from the bite of marsh mosquitoes, and ready for the sting of real estate commerce. The bats didn't buy it. No bat ever took the aphrodisiac bait. The Keys were not yet to be delivered from the pesky bloodsucking scourge of antiquity; the second largest landowner of Florida was defeated by the lowly mosquito. Now, generations later, the tower was part of someone else's vision, or nightmare; mosquitoes were the least of the problem.

Whoever managed to get high inside the deserted bat tower and hang the goat must have been part goat himself, for it was a slippery and risky undertaking to hazard at night—if it had been done at night; that was one of the things Justo still wasn't certain of. Justo was certain the person had *uñas de gato*, claws of a cat. Something more goat and cat, and less than human, was leading Justo on, he felt it in his bones. The teacher of the elementary school children, who came upon the goat that morning, had the hapless apparition removed before Justo could get there, disposed of among the tonnage of debris at the city dump. The goat had definitely been alive when it was carried up to the top of the tower, the animal's hind legs bound with rope, its body left hanging down the thirty-foot narrow drop of the interior shaft. Enough struggling life remained in the creature to spray the dark bat palace walls vibrant crimson from its slit throat. This wasn't Santería. Justo knew Santería. Could be some score-settling cocaine Colombian cowboys from Miami, but if it was that kind of trouble Justo would have heard. The Saints talk, especially if they have Spanish accents. There were no secrets among them.

¿Quien le poner el escabel al gato? Who shall hang the bell on the cat's neck? He didn't think it had anything to do with the children, children were brought on school outings to the tower all the time. There was an evil going around, Justo could smell it. Lately he started praying to Saint Jude, first thing in the morning, kneeling next to his bed as Rosella neared the end of her dreams. Justo envisioned how foolish he would look to the outside world, a big naked cop on his knees beseeching protection from the heavens before strapping on his ankle gun. The Saints were his guiding comfort. In the tropics people came and went, things quickly born went quickly dead, rot always filled the air, a fresh rot bearing ironic breath of a new beginning. Justo's faith was constant, founded in Catholic and Santería Saints, taught to him as a boy by the Church and Aunt Oris. He fed those Saints who guarded him a diet of special prayers and sacred offerings, knew he could call upon them to bail him out of troubled waters. Except when it came to teenage daughters, the Saints didn't know much about them; if they did they weren't talking. The Church had an age-old theory about its young women, marry them off early for their own protection. Had he protected Rosella? Justo never thought of it that way. He didn't think of himself as a protector, nor public guardian nor defender of the peace. Now there was something loose in the streets which didn't fit the accommodation, it moved and surged like

fear filling a shadow, Justo could feel it in the bottom of his African soul to the center of his Catholic heart. There was one clear message coming from that tower on Sugarloaf Key, and it had nothing to do with *guayabitos en la azotea*, bats in the belfry.

What could Marilyn's Andy know about *guayabitos* in the belfry? Maybe Andy had found the recipe for the secret love potion intended to draw bats to the tower. Justo's Aunt Oris always insisted the elixir was nothing more than bat *guano* spiced with ground bat ovaries, and that's why it never took. Oris said everybody knows you've got to throw in some owl liver and hawks' claws to give any potion its inevitable kick, prayers to Santa Barbara wouldn't hurt either. There were sixty-seven species of mosquitoes in Florida and no one had yet figured a way to eradicate just one of the species. You could spray pesticide on them but you couldn't kill them off. Public authorities met the same defeat against mosquitoes as they did in their battle with drug smugglers. You could throw the book at smugglers, but you couldn't put them out of business. That was something Justo thought he had a pretty good handle on, being as how he had an island boy's philosophy and was also in a position of authority. It was all a natural law of commerce, as long as mosquitoes kept breeding in swamps and swimming pools, and the Government kept inventing what was legal and what was not, mosquito-sprayers and guys like Justo were going to be kept in business. Mosquitoes and smugglers were a fact of life, swat one and five more pop up. The only way to make smugglers obsolete was to legalize drugs. The Government perfected that line of thinking when it put the Bootleggers of the twenties out of business by legalizing alcohol. Mosquitoes are more tenacious than smugglers, they won't disappear simply by legalizing their bites. Mosquitoes were in Florida to stay. Given their choice people would rather live with smugglers than mosquitoes. People will always choose to live with an itch on their conscience rather than a bite on their ass.

Andy was one of the irregularly employed and frequently married men about town. Women were a job to him. Andy married women and sponged off their softness until they went hard and pried his leeching little-boy-lost act from their lives. Then Andy was off to the next woman, scamming his way on a magic carpet of endless endearments and pathetic platitudes through the door of another desperate heart. Andy was a middle-aged street boy always up for a drink and down in the gutter where the rat piss flowed. To Justo, Andy was good as a blank check, a gentleman of the accommodation, a true *chivato*, an informer of the lowest rank with the highest yield of information. What could be trusted about Andy was his willingness to scratch his itchy conscience until it bled in order to avoid a bite on his precious ass.

"Tamarindo, you've got to do something about the fucking muggers. Town's crawling with them. Not safe to walk the streets." Andy speared another shifty glob of oyster flesh from its half shell and let it ride around in his mouth. "Mo fukin mucsters ruinin dis fukin I-land." Andy sucked down the slippery creature his tongue was batting around, then ceremoniously backhanded a clear trickle of oyster juice from thick lips. "Why don't you jump on your motorcycle, Tamarindo, ride out and bust chops on those bastards? They're all from out of town anyway. Don't contribute shit to the gross local economy."

"Don't have a motorcycle."

"Ought to have us a raffle, get you one."

"Good idea. We'll have the raffle between your ex-wives."

"You're jealous." Andy speared another oyster on the prong of his fork and winked at Justo. "You been married to the same woman so long your cock doesn't know when it's in or out of the honey."

"Knows enough to know it's not covered with little red polka dots."

"They go away."

"Only to come back again."

"Figure the more women I'm with, more of the little red suckers I give away, sooner or later I won't have any left, Andy's law of averages."

"Great law, if you're Andy."

"Polka dot proof." Andy let his face relax into a smirk. "Want any more of this shit?" He shoved the platter of empty half shells away from him. "Got more inside I can shuck. Two dozen or so. No problem."

"Think I lost my appetite."

"Weak stomach from all those conch fritters you shovel down all day long. Little fuckers are going to be the death of you. Key West's finest won't die of a bullet hole shot through his heart, but a grease hole eaten clear through his gut. Those nasty little conchs are tough as sin, going to outlive us all. After the nuclear bomb conchs will still be coming up out of the ocean and crawling out of their shells. Want to know something about conchs you've never known before?" Andy leaned close to Justo across the table, his breath perfumed with an oyster burp.

"You going to tell me why they're called hurricane ham?"

"Hell no, every school kid knows that. Going to tell you something better. Know what a *verge* is?" Andy tipped back on his chair and let his gaze wander across the tabletop, through weeds and mounds of empty oyster shells decorating the small space between his tiny shotgun cottage and the honeysuckle climbing over his neighbor's backyard fence. His watery blue eyes came back to Justo. "Give up? Don't know what it is, do you?"

"I know what it is to be on the verge of something." Justo didn't like the corner Andy was trying to back him into. Justo knew he was the better word man of the two. Andy was a spit and slide man who memorized five or nine facts, then pulled them out like card tricks at a boring party. He wasn't like those in town who were real word men, like St. Cloud, who had so many words up his sleeve he kept them mostly to himself. "Give up. What does verge mean?"

"Cock." Andy tossed the empty platter of oyster shells into the weeds. "It's the cock of the conch."

"So what?"

"So something you don't know, if the conch gets his member nipped by a curious crab or a hungry eel the conch grows himself a new one."

"Astounding."

"Life in the Florida Keys, eel bites conch cock, end and beginning of story."

Justo felt uneasy, he was being worked firmly into a corner with nowhere to go. "Why are you telling me this?"

"I've only got one cock, with or without polka dots. I'm not about to risk getting it shot off by talking to you about Karl Dean."

"Well, I wouldn't want you to tell me anything I didn't already know." Justo lied, not knowing what it was about Karl Dean he should be asking.

"Good, because you're not going to get it. Why don't you ask me something I don't care about."

"What about Karl Dean?"

"Karl Dean is dead."

"So is James Dean. What's the news flash?"

"Fast boats. Fast cars. Fast life. Vietnam. Florida. Latin America. Same shit."

"Same song, different band?"

"Something like that."

"Colombian band?"

"Said I'm not talking."

"Bubba band?"

"Ditto."

"Let's talk about something you don't mind talking about."

"Let's do that."

Justo lowered his voice to indicate he thought someone might be crouching on the other side of the neighbor's fence in the honeysuckle. "Dead goats."

"Yah, so?"

"Bufo toads with their mouths nailed shut."

"Huh?"

"Cemetery weirdness."

"Know nothing about it."

"Dead goats that write poetry?"

"Yah, like I said, so?"

"So what were you doing up on Sugarloaf Key at night?"

"Waiting for the bats to come home."

"Did they?" Justo knew the answer to his own question. A large shrimp boatload of marijuana had been moved up the Keys that night. As a spit and slide man and small-time scammer, one of Andy's brief jobs between women included little odds and ends as a spotter for smugglers, making certain the Coast Guard was not where it was supposed to be when something big and chancy was going down. Andy's job on the Gulf side of Sugarloaf that night was simply to flash a light or give a radio code-call if things were not as they appeared. Andy was one of many small-time conspirators picking up small change from a major enterprise. In the vast ocean of illegal chance Andy was nothing more than a squid among sharks.

"I think your dog's eating oyster shells." Andy nodded toward Ocho nosing through one of the shell mounds, searching for something more edibly rewarding than pearls. "You get that dog out at the track? He one of those losers?"

"Did the bats come home?"

"They say bats have never been in that tower, that the crazy old coot who built it to rid his mangrove real estate of mosquitoes so he could sell it off to midwestern suckers went broke and crazy." Andy's smirk returned, he loved being pursued, kept him in shape for the women he fooled into chasing him.

"I hear dead goats write poetry."

"Something strange. Can't figure it. Maybe you can. You know a bunch about that Santería sort of thing." Andy always thought Justo knew too much about that sort of thing. Andy nurtured a derisive contempt for Justo, felt his head was stuffed with so many dead Saints and poets it lent him an air of superiority beyond that normally assumed by people who worked behind a badge. Andy considered this unbecoming in a man of such obvious color. Justo spoke in riddles, blabbed words of poets hundred years gone, conversing sometimes in a language an honest workingman couldn't understand. Andy didn't trust himself with this stuff, it was over his head and he wanted rid of it.

"You remember any of the dead goat poetry?"

"Better." Andy stood. "It was on a sheet of paper nailed to one of those big stilts. I saw it with my flashlight, because when I first come on that goat hanging there in the dark I thought maybe someone had gone and committed suicide out there, or at least someone had helped them with the job. So I shined the light on the paper to see if it was a suicide note. Maybe they was going to leave all their money to whoever found the body. But it wasn't that. I tore the paper off because, who knows, might be the key to a lost treasure or something."

"Still got it?"

"In the house. Be right back."

Ocho wandered over to Justo while Andy was gone. The greyhound rested its head heavily on Justo's knee, beseeching him with bewildered eyes, not realizing its source of canine discomfort emanated from a gut full of half-chewed oyster shells.

"Here it is." Andy handed the paper to Justo. "Read up." He sat down with a heaping platter of oysters, deftly splitting the coarse shells open with the thick blade of a rusty knife.

Justo smoothed the rumpled paper on the tabletop. The letters were writ large and purposefully clumsy, executed with various colored thick-tipped pens in the same style as the note left in the cemetery on Abuelo's grave.

A GREEN SAILOR LOOKS NORTH
TO CUBAN MARTYRS
WHERE THE TREE OF LIFE
GROWS FROM THEIR HEADS.
THE ANGEL OF DEATH
SMILES UPON ALL.

ZOBOP

A Green Sailor looks north? Justo had no idea what that meant, what martyrs and angels, goats and toads meant. The shadow was rapidly filling with fear. Maybe Andy was an unwitting player in Zobop's scheme. "You get any of this?"

"Not a thing." Andy popped an oyster shell open and slurped its contents. "Beats shit out of me total."

"Mind if I keep it? Want to compare it with some other writings."

"Be my guest." Andy tossed an empty oyster shell over his shoulder into the weeds. "All mumbo jumbo anyway, your people's kinda stuff. But if there's treasure to be found, we're partners, right?"

"Got my word on it." Justo stood and joined Ocho waiting anxiously before a high wooden gate, the greyhound's narrow face twisted in pain from a shell-stuffed belly.

"Hey, Tamarindo!" Andy called, raising high the rusty shucking knife in his hand before bringing the blade down with a deep stab into the scarred tabletop.

"Yeah. I forgot." Justo stopped at the gate. "Thanks for the oysters."

"Naw, that's not it. You can keep your word about the treasure thing, I don't want it. Cop's word can cause me to lose my conch cock, and I don't have a spare." Andy forced the rusty knife blade free from the tabletop and wiped the wood splinters off on his pants. The smirk was back on his face.

Justo opened the gate, letting Ocho wobble out before turning back. "Don't worry, my friend, you have nothing to fear when it comes to your verge."

"Why?"

"Because, *el rabo del puerco nunca estara como una fleca.*"

"Speak American."

"A pig's tail will never make a good arrow."

Andy's smirk faded in the sun setting over the top of the honeysuckle of his neighbor's backyard fence.

14

'D TAKE my last dollar and spend it to stay warm."

"Well, you in the right place, bubba. So hot out there on Duval Street tonight it's a hundred-ten under the neon. Too hot to wear your own sweat."

"Can't be too hot for me." Brogan rubbed the slick edge of a beer can to his forehead, waiting for the can's welcome cold prick to numb the skin between his eyes. "Did I ever tell you how my brother used to stay cool in Nam on those leech-sucking nights before the monsoon broke the heat belt?"

"Don't give a shit about MK. Good time to go fishing for sharks now, solid amberjacks out around the bridges, eighty, hundred pounders, sharks chasing after them, gobbling them up like candy. Good time to kill sharks. Want to go out tomorrow? I don't have any charters, so hot no tourists going out, slow time on the flat blue. Best way to kill time is to kill sharks."

"Most boring thing I ever heard." Brogan set his beer down and turned his eyes on Bubba-Bob. "Killing sharks interests me about as much as shooting sea gulls or fucking coke whores." Brogan's eyes set into a hard stare, the hard stare of a man who deals in precious metals, other people's precious metals. Brogan was pissed tonight in more ways than one. For one thing he didn't think he was getting any closer to the treasure he had been hunting for seven years. Lately he was going out further and further and deeper and deeper, toward the Tortugas, to where it was too deep to make any sense. Any galleon that cut on a reef would not have sunk that low, all the big-time treasure hunters with their high-tech gear and bottom-sucking rigs had long since packed their scientific underwater sniffing act to a different part of the ocean. Brogan was looking where common sense indicated a galleon would have been blown right off the map. He prided himself on playing hunches, not common sense. Common sense was for sunday preachers and monday sinners. On this hot night Brogan was exhausted from being out on the water for five weeks, coming up from the deep again and again, empty. When a man is that deep and something goes wrong and he loses oxygen, it is only four to six minutes before he's wearing diapers for the rest of his life, if he's lucky enough to be hauled up in time. Brogan's eyes burned from staring through the scratchy glass plate of a face mask for gold coins and cannons encrusted into improbable shapes, searching for aged phantoms of wealth on the sandy floor of an ever-changing sea. Brogan's eyes burned ruby red. When Brogan's eyes burned red enough his thoughts swung away from immediate problems to the brilliant and bad gentleman of trouble's bottom line who was his brother. When Brogan got into this mood his thoughts swung right past the common sense he so despised, he even risked raising the anger of Bubba-Bob, a man famous, at this tip-top hour of the morning after a long night in the Wreck Room, for taking offense at the slightest slight. It required five men to stop Bubba-Bob when he started swinging his shark-killing fists. Brogan had more than once personally been one of the five, having to knock Bubba-Bob over the head with a chair. But nothing worked, no matter how much violence was tap-danced on Bubba-Bob's head he came back for more, delighting in the rhythm of destruction. The type of man who killed sharks for relaxation would tear another man's eyes out for sport.

Bubba-Bob acted like he hadn't heard Brogan's rash declaration of not wanting to slash shark throats from gill to gill. Maybe Bubba-Bob had not heard it, or thought he heard something different in the Wreck Room filled with the whir of overhead fans and conversations shouted in a storm of drunken syllables. Bubba-Bob was more concerned with sharks and women, especially Angelica behind the bar in the shot-glass short shorts. "One time Angelica and me got it on." Bubba-Bob laid a heavy hand on Brogan's shoulder, trying to keep his unsteady gaze pinned to the center of Angelica's thin halter top. "I get Angelica home, chop some lines of toot, woof up and say, Baby, I'm a great lover but I want it to be good for you, fishermen are patient, tell me the truth, what is the best amount of time for you to have an orgasm? Angelica answers, one tape side. I says I don't get it. Angelica says one tape side of music, she likes to put on a music tape and come before it reaches the end of the first side, says if she doesn't come by then it isn't worth it. So I slip on a tape, stuff from the sixties, the Doors' 'Light My Fire,' you know, *Light my fire light my fire light my fire*, romantic, and we strike up the band, but halfway into the tape my cock's going coke-soft on me, squirrelly as an eel on a hook, and I'm thinking we're counting down to a music orgasm and I'm not going to make it and I didn't. The tape ended. I says to Angelica, Now what? Angelica doesn't miss a beat, says there's one whole side left on the tape, so why don't I get down on all fours and lick her." Bubba-Bob raised his glass of rum quizzically to pursed lips. "What does she think I am, a fucking St. Bernard?"

"No, a blowfish."

"A blowfish!" Bubba-Bob tightened his grip on Brogan's shoulder, his powerful fingers digging in with the determination of a first mate hefting a four-hundred-pound marlin aboard boat barehanded, or at least preparing to heft Brogan off his stool and throw him through the smoky plate-glass window behind the bar into the fierce heat of neon lit Duval Street. Bubba-Bob pushed his face close to Brogan's, his thick lips darkened and split by the sun, the big teeth white and sharp, his breath sputtering in a hot blast. "Fa . . . fa . . . fa . . . fucking ba . . . ba . . . blowfish! That's great!" Bubba-Bob slammed the empty rum glass on the counter and howled. "Angelica! Bring your favorite blowfish another round."

"Let's have a little less quiet down here." Angelica laughed, pouring Bubba-Bob another rum. "What's Brogan baiting you with anyway?"

"A blowfish! A goddamn blowfish!" Bubba-Bob couldn't put a cap on his mirth, sputtering a spit of delight. "That's a story I've got to tell next time I get a charter of Texans."

Brogan didn't think what he said was funny. Brogan was still pissed in more ways than one and nodded at Angelica for another drink. Angelica was one of his favorite women, not like St. Cloud's wife Evelyn, whom he considered a witch with balls. Brogan tried to remember if he was sleeping with Angelica during the time he was sleeping with Evelyn. That was a strange time, right before Evelyn stopped sleeping with men, he thought he had something to do with that. Something Evelyn said to him then seemed odd. She said she didn't want to hear about MK and his exploits in Nam, was fed up with Nam, fed up with war, fed up with all the assholes who weren't fed up. Angelica was never fed up, nor for that matter ever filled up,

she was a drinking man's bartender. Brogan was like most serious
drinkers on the island, his allegiance was to bartenders, not bars. If
he didn't like one of the bartenders in a bar he boycotted the whole
business. What he especially did not like were aging college-boy types
who had half of a degree in something and took to bartending as a
way to support the antics of their college dormitory–inspired drug
and alcohol habits. These were the boys who ruin a good drink with
the attitude they could be doing something better than serving it.
These boys preyed on the professional hard luck dropouts, parading
puffy airs from their cloistered days in the idea supermarkets of
higher education. The hard lucks mistakenly thought the aging college
boys were doubly courageous in their choice of a mildly corrupt
existence, since the college boys could obviously be elsewhere. Reality
was they could not, the college boys were simply fast fool artists
masquerading as bonafide deadbeats. Such notions jumped in Brogan's brain, until he found his train of thought again, hopped aboard
before the train pulled out of the station without him. "Yes, I guess
you could call my brother a sort of adventurer. My brother is doing
spooky things down in Latin America, spookier things than he did in
Nam."

"What's up with you, bubba?" Bubba-Bob quickly released his grip
on Brogan's shoulder. "Who in hell is spookin what?"

"MK." Angelica whispered the initials as if expecting to be arrested
for simply uttering them. "Brogan's in one of those MK moods again,
off about his brother."

"Well I'm not St. Cloud." Bubba-Bob sucked sullenly at his rum,
disturbed the current of conversation had moved off comic blowfish.
"I don't want to sit around till dawn like St. Cloud listening to this
crap. I know MK. I've worked for MK. Half the guys in the Keys
have worked for MK. What the hell is MK to me? Doesn't scare me.
I'm not Karl Dean." Bubba-Bob finished off his rum and smacked his
lips. "Blowfish. Now that's funny."

"How about one on the house?" Angelica had the rum flowing into
Bubba-Bob's glass before he could answer. She wanted to change the
subject, the whole thing made her nervous, it wasn't her business. She
sympathized with the boys whose business it was, but she wanted no
part of it. Karl Dean was dead and that was that. Hard to figure who
was right and who was wrong in these matters, really made no
difference in the end. Something got done or it didn't. Someone lived
or died, seemed to make no difference since things continued on as

before. Things unlearned were as good as untaught. "Why don't you tell me what's so funny about blowfish?" Angelica dabbed her bar rag at a trickle of rum left in the corner of Bubba-Bob's mouth after he belted down her latest offering.

Brogan ignored Angelica's attempt to spring him from his complex circles of thought. "MK says there are only two things in life you need to learn. First, how to get along with people. Second, how to get around them. Did I ever tell you how MK got his name?"

"Thousand fucking times you've told me!" Bubba-Bob shouted in Brogan's face. "I hear it one more time I'm going to bash—"

"Good. I'll tell you again." Brogan assumed the air of a man pursuing a meandering trail with no guideposts to offer a way out. "In the jungle there are trails where the hunter has not been, traps are waiting to be sprung. No matter what politics a man carries in his heart, the reality of all revolutions advertises one true message: *This bullet is for you.* In the jungle of Vietnam MK forgot what he looked like, forgot where he came from, from a youth filled to the horizon with broad fields far as the eye could see, a straightforward youth, uncomplicated, unlike the jungle that transformed him, a jungle screaming green with intrigue of life's highest inevitability, death. MK was balanced in the Vietnam jungle at first because he came from the flat, cold land of Minnesota. In the beginning he weighed events with the clear eye of an idealist. This blinded him to the jungle's natural conspiracy, discarded him in the cleavage of evil and good as his comrades' bodies were bagged in rubber sacks, sent away home to be counted, then covered up with dirt. MK waited in the green hell with the living. The living would say to each other every day: You gonna get outta this jungle, man, freedom bird's a'comin, freedom bird's gonna fly you way home. When the freedom bird came it most often was not a great bellied troop transport plane like MK was brought to the jungle in, but a commercial flight routed through Thailand or Singapore to pick up tourists and businessmen. MK was ordered to dress in his civvies for his freedom bird flight home through Singapore, he was not supposed to look like what he was. Even in civvies MK reeked of jungle rot, he could not scrub it from his skin. He would get up and scrub himself with soap every fifteen minutes on the plane. He knew he stank to the other passengers. When MK's freedom bird left Vietnam the United States was a country still counting its daily toll from the jungle. When MK landed in Hawaii, they were still counting. When he landed in San Francisco, they were still counting.

He kept heading east, through numbers adding up bodies, two hundred of them killed today, twenty of us, numb numbers adding up to spiritual novocaine. When he reached Minneapolis MK knew it was impossible to return to the beginning of the flat fields far as the eye could see. He no longer knew what the fields held, who might be waiting for him there, what traps. He knew only where the jungle was, it had become his true center. *MK*, the initials marked the end to his life. He flew across the United States to get as far from the flat fields as he could, but when he got off the plane they were still counting, and he was questioned immediately about the initials at the airport. The smell of the jungle was on him in the airport, he could not scrub it off, everyone knew, so he stood by himself, far from the plane's passengers crowded around a spinning baggage carousel. Finally, the jostling was finished, the crowd gone, only his leather luggage was left on the stopped carousel, each of his bags identified with tags stamped *MK*. A woman approached. She was the age MK was then, twenty-two. MK was light-years from the woman, he was stuck between jungles, he was ancient and stank. She was encased in a crisp uniform, airport personnel, a smile of forgiving authority softened her lips. This was someone MK would have married had he stayed on after high school in the far flat land where roads and lives were straight as arrows. She would have been the wife who birthed twins if he had not gone to the jungle, her crisp body in his arms would have cried out with longing on her lips, unaware he had been nowhere and did not stink, whispering she could not live without him, their souls flying swift as arrows toward a ripe old age across the flat fields. 'Sir, is that your luggage?' The words of the woman in uniform interrupted MK's thoughts of what might have been, her words filled the void where whisperings of eternal love might have been, had she greeted him as her long-lost hero husband who did not stink. 'Yes,' MK answered. 'It's mine.' 'I'm afraid you'll have to claim it then.' Her smile became more forgiving. MK moved toward the carousel to claim what was his. The leather luggage was still supple and new, still animal pungent. He had bought it on his way through Singapore, chose it specially, the harder you are, the softer your luggage. He pulled the bags carefully from the carousel and handed over his claim tickets. 'I was in Vietnam.' The words came from him of their own accord, flinging from the tip of his tongue in a bursting existence of their own, like clouds of smoke lifting from burning bodies he left behind in the jungle, bodies quickly dead from automatic

rifle fire, strewn in mud between thatched huts, the acrid reek of an
exploded phosphorus grenade he tossed on them stinging his nostrils,
orange flames becoming white clouds, changing shapes until escaping
into thin air, but not before imprinting an indelible mark on the
earthbound. MK expected the woman to turn away from his stench.
She gave him a brief smile, unaware his telling her he was in Vietnam
was not a confession but a declaration, unaware she could have been
the mother of his children, unaware there was something dangerous
and unseen in him, unaware he was offering her his exploding heart
on a platter. She raised her fingers absentmindedly to the DEBBIE
stamped into an enameled nameplate pinned above her right breast.
Her eyes went to the luggage, not in search of explanation, but
friendly diversion. 'That's beautiful leather. What does the *MK* on
the tags stand for?' MK had wanted the initials to travel with him
back from the jungle, marked on everything he owned, so those who
paid to make him what he was by disowning his actions would see his
brand everywhere, yet not know the assassin was among them. When
he first came to the jungle from the flat land his body was so cool
and collected his finger held remarkably true on a rifle trigger, so
they put him across the border from where the war officially was,
masked with a tar-black face and black canvas pajamas, dressed to kill
smooth shaven-headed men in saffron-colored robes, and he did. He
did not officially exist, there was to be no killing in the part of the
jungle he preyed in, for no one there had declared war on him or
his country. He was an invisible man regarded with fear and suspicion
by regular soldiers who fought the irregular war, soldiers who knew
not to ask him the number of enemy killed, for he employed his skills
where there was no declared enemy. The regular soldiers noticed
ribbons and medals of battle stretched across the chest of his uniform
when he was on leave in Saigon, so inquired, 'How many monkeys
did you bag over there?' His team of surreptitious travelers was known
as Monkey Killers. The euphemism accumulated in time an eerie
reality, the team thought of themselves as killers of animals, not
village leaders and religious elders. Each man of the team sang a
private song silently as his rifle stock butted into his shoulder, spraying
a metallic clap of bullets to dance and riddle through saffron robes.
MK could not get his song out of his mind, its chorus chanted over
and over as he saw men fall before him: *Hellooo I looove yooou, woon't
yooou tell me yooour name?* Orange robes going red. MK did not know
the past of the men he aimed true at, simply that their names were

cleared from command above to be eradicated, names indicated on aerial topo maps as targets located in villages and towns. Fewer monkeys for the jungle to feed. A monkey doesn't need a weapon to become a guerrilla, intentions precede weapons. A Monkey Killer forgets which side of the border he is on, Vietnam, Cambodia, Laos, makes no difference, no longer matters, the borders of countries, patriotism and demonism erased. The Monkey Killers were good soldiers, skilled hunters. A good soldier did not think beyond the thick leeches sucking at his neck, explosive trip wires at his booted feet, flash of sniper fire in the leaves. To the skilled hunter, the man marching directly before and after him marked his orbit, defined his final purpose. MK heard Debbie's words coming through the tangled jungle of his mind: 'You boys from Nam sure got a strange sense of humor.' Debbie was standing before him with the smile of forgiveness on her lips, but MK was still in the steaming jungle, he didn't understand, he looked for a way out, he asked her guidance. 'What? What strange sense of humor?' Debbie's lips kept up their smile. 'I asked what's the *MK* stand for and you said Monkey Killer. You guys pick up strange nicknames over there.' MK was no longer in the jungle, but he could not declare to those who made him the assassin what his purpose was as he moved among them. Intentions precede actions, invisibility needs no name, a simple initial is more than enough. At the far end of the airport's subterranean carpeted tunnel a neon sign pointed the way: ALL TRANSPORTATION TO DOWNTOWN MIAMI. MK heard himself saying to Debbie, 'No no, you misunderstood. I didn't say Monkey Killer, I said Miami. Yes, the initials stand for Miami Kid.' Debbie handed back the claim tickets to MK's bags, her lips offering all the sympathy of a war widow. 'Welcome home, Kid.' "

The moment Brogan stopped talking Angelica jumped in, hoping to head Bubba-Bob off before he said something stupid. "That's still about the saddest story I ever heard. How about a drink on the house for your brother?"

"Sad!" Bubba-Bob bawled. "You call that shit sad. MK was a goddamn assassin. Whatever he's got coming he's got coming."

"It all happened a million years ago," Brogan continued, oblivious to the conversation around him. "Now MK's down in Central America with all the rats running around without heads."

"MK's one of the rats!" Bubba-Bob shouted at Brogan, trying to break through. "MK's been running without a head since Nam."

"I think it was that perfect girl MK found in Bangkok while on R and R the first time, she changed him."

"Oh, her again." Angelica had overheard Brogan telling St. Cloud about a perfect girl in Bangkok. Months would go by while Brogan slipped around in drunken vexation over MK, fragments of information about the perfect girl would appear solid as iceberg tips in his scattered conversations, then melt in the random flow of disconnected thoughts. Angelica knew Brogan received detailed letters from his brother which arrived infrequently, bound by thick twine over brown wrappers with Central American postmarks. Angelica had never read these letters kept locked in a metal chest at the foot of Brogan's bed. Brogan opened the chest frequently to withdraw substantial rocks of cocaine, exposing the stacked letters, hundreds of well-worn pages which seemed to add up to a book. Angelica thought Brogan trusted her because she never asked about the letters. Sometimes she had the strange idea Brogan wrote the letters and mailed them to himself, for Brogan in other matters was open with her about where he had been and what he was. Brogan had been all over Central and South America, what he was was a little bit of everything. From what Angelica knew Brogan was mostly a gung-ho spun-out Spook who wearied of working for bullets and beans and finally dumped the racket. What Angelica responded to was Brogan's vision of the world as a sublime heaven or horrific hell. Angelica loved men who interpreted life in black and white. Brogan always seemed visibly agitated by the two choices, on the verge of choosing one, afraid if he didn't the other would disappear. Brogan told her MK taught him a genius has no moral or monetary debts. Brogan said he had debts because he liked gold, hard currency was his mistress. Cocaine was powder disappearing up the nose of time, paper money could blow away in any political storm, but hard treasure sunk to sea bottom rewarded the man with stamina to find it. Brogan told her he had seen the hurricane of the future in Latin America, it was blowing across the Caribbean to the United States, touching Key West, soon to reach the mainland. Cocaine was the future's first cloud portending cataclysmic change. Brogan had read the barometer of change, considered himself a dedicated cynic on an island of disbelievers. He had paid his dues in his own share of assassination plots in Marijuana Republics and Cocaine Dictatorships, offered his all-American assets to countries at war with themselves, raising a crop of misery where terror reigned supreme, it turned a hard man harder. Brogan's history was not a political parable, only a shortcut to discovery that a smart man bypasses the business of making paper money for the business of finding hard currency other men have lost. This knowledge had its own cost, its consequence placed Brogan in debt, unlike his brother MK, who was a genius.

"Maybe MK went to Bangkok that first time to reproduce himself." Brogan seemed to be finding answers to his own questions. "Maybe MK sought to regenerate his spirit, he was still young then, but growing ancient by the hour. He had been in the jungle only nine months before he emerged into a delirium of opium and flesh along the back canals of Bangkok. MK desired to penetrate the distant part of himself he held back from death, if he could reach this essence there still might be hope to escape the jungle. MK was taken by cab across many canals floating with flowers and garbage to a special house where women were not for sale by the hour or day, but their very lives were for sale, they were surplus daughters and sisters, sold off in an ancient tradition, justifiable only to seller and buyer. MK had heard rumors of such a house while in the jungle. He saved his money to search it out on his first R and R. If he survived the jungle he was going to find the perfect girl and buy her, the two of them would disappear from all the tears and trials of this earth." Brogan stopped, momentarily losing his way on such a meandering trail. His eyes focused through the smoky window behind the bar, where a nearly naked woman in wavering heat put the tip of her cigarette to a flaming match offered by a young man astride a motorcycle. Brogan seemed reminded of something, a hidden sign. "When MK bribed his way into the special house he saw thirty, fifty girls. The old man running the place stroked his whiskers between nicotine-stained fingers before unveiling a young girl, spinning her out from silken bondage, revealing an object of perfection, a melding of grace and desire to bend the beholder's eye with covetous shame. MK did not avert his gaze. *Hello I love you won't you tell me your name?* This vision could be his salvation. MK tenderly wound the long swaths of silk about the girl's exposed body, preventing other eyes from feasting upon flesh so pure. He ordered a great banquet, and in this country, where women squatted outside the door as man the master ate in privacy and solace, MK fed the girl from his fingertips. In a room alone, with servants forbidden, small plates of delicacies surrounded the two of them as the girl sucked from MK's fingers and lips tiny sweet fish from rivers, dark succulents from the sea, raisined meats and coconut milk. Stretching her full across cushions aglow in candlelight MK oiled and kneaded the length of her supple body. Before dawn he was going to free her forever, from whatever rough hands would defile and demean her. MK had come to save himself and her, a final escape, exit from the jungle. Now that they had each other he slipped the white phosphorus grenade from its hiding place in his knapsack, balancing the familiar weight in his palm. The perfect girl eyed the rough metal egg with curiosity, she was a poor country girl who had never seen deathly weapons. Her fingers reached to the egg, fondling its harshness, tracing the tip of the pin. Before dawn broke MK was going to leave the jungle forever with the girl he could never have in the far flat fields of Minnesota. *Hello I love you won't you tell me your name.* MK was going to blow the house of slavery holding his perfect girl captive to kingdom come. Nothing would be left except a bright flash of orange flame, then a towering funnel of white clouds bearing him and the object of his perfection straight to the mother's milk of stars stretched across the heavens above."

"This is bullshit!" Bubba-Bob roared into Brogan's face. "MK never blew his fucking self up!"

"When dawn came"—Brogan didn't miss a beat—"MK awoke. The perfect girl was gone, but the grenade was still in his hand, she had left that, not knowing what it was, not understanding its explosive value. His wallet was gone, his knapsack was gone. MK thought of popping the pin, bomb Hanoi, bomb Saigon, bomb Bangkok, bomb America, bomb yourself. But he didn't. MK laughed, the first time he laughed in nine months. MK laughed alone in the alone room. MK never laughed again, until years later, watching the fall of Saigon on television in a bar in Belize. MK laughed, he knew he was better off to take his chances in the jungle."

"Too bad the bitch didn't have the sense to pull the pin on the bastard." Bubba-Bob gave Angelica his rascal wink. "Would have saved guys in twelve countries from trying to do it since." Bubba-Bob was in the mood for rock hard fun or a rock hard fight, not parables.

"MK says after his failed encounter with perfection he only sought imperfect girls, very imperfect."

"I say bees balls, bubba! Bees balls to your brother and his turd world exploits!" Bubba-Bob had had enough. He considered himself a patient man, a fishing man, a man who waited for others to run out of luck. Bubba-Bob didn't consider himself a typical Charter Boat captain, because too many guys nowadays had backed into the business sniffing the ass-end of a freshwater salmon, considered themselves sportsmen who gamed for fish, rather than fishermen who fished for meat. Bubba-Bob considered himself a saltwater professional, it made him sick to set tarpon free after they had put up a good fight. Such was the world Bubba-Bob now had to put up with, letting tarpon free and asking coke whores how long it took them to come. It had become a guppy-eat-guppy world, and it stuck a jewfish bone in the throat of a shark-killing saltwater professional just to think about it. "MK's just another Vet who got lucky, was in the right place at the right time and made himself a killing. None of that impresses me. Sure as hell doesn't stand the hair up at the bottom of my dick. I'll tell you what I really think of MK." Bubba-Bob swigged another glass of rum, which Angelica had quickly poured, thinking it might fire him off in a direction of less lethal consequence. "The bottom line is not the dollar, but our Government. We've got a free country that makes room for us to smuggle and deal, legitimizes our petty ripoffs by making them illegal, which makes them profitable. MK's screwing all that up. MK hasn't sold out down there in Latin America just for a buck, but for the sake of selling out to find out what's on the other side of that. MK deals in guns, drugs, high-tech stuff, sells to any side. It'd be one thing if MK was even a Commie, but MK doesn't even have that excuse, he's not even a fucking liberal. MK's sold out his country and he knows it. So I say bees balls, bubba, bees balls to your brother. He ain't no fishin man, that's for sure. MK's going to get unlucky, very unlucky, and when he does he's going to find himself at the wrong end of the food chain."

Bubba-Bob's words hissed in Brogan's face, they were a clear sign for Angelica to beat an acceptable retreat. It was too late to put Bubba-Bob back in his cage, even if five lion tamers were standing by to do the job. Angelica filled glasses and rang the cash register, keeping her eyes on Brogan and Bubba-Bob at the far end of the bar where a silence had descended, dividing the two like an invisible blade. Maybe Bubba-Bob was getting ready to break every bone in Brogan's body, maybe he felt he already had. Maybe Brogan was too drunkenly self-absorbed to have heard a word Bubba-Bob uttered. Whatever it was, it was too good a show for Angelica to pass on, so she slid back down to the deathly quiet end of the bar with a perky smile pressed on her lips, arriving in time to hear Brogan's words, groggy but deliberate, brushing aside the silence.

"MK started tying up his imperfect girls, he became a tie-up guy.

He tied imperfect girls up for more than one reason, but the real reason he found by accident after Bangkok. He had this girlfriend in Saigon, Joy-Joy, a Vietnamese Catholic, not a hooker, but not a saint either. Joy-Joy had parents to feed, couple of younger brothers, she was a great cook and younger than MK. MK set Joy-Joy up in a little apartment, when he came out of the jungle he wanted her there. At first MK tied Joy-Joy up just to look at her, tied her to the bed. Later, he tied her to the doorknob of the only door in the one-room apartment. He tied her carefully, with soft but secure rope. Sometimes Joy-Joy wore nothing, just a gold chain with a crucifix hanging from her neck. Sometimes what Joy-Joy did wear MK took off so he could watch the changes of color on her flesh as hot light streamed through the dusty window. MK just sat there, watching her, listening to all the sounds coming up from the street, hissing motorbikes, shouting foreign voices, he smelled the stink of fish oil from foods frying in other apartments. One day, about a month after Tet, MK had come back from up around Hue, he knelt Joy-Joy down with her bare knees scraping the floor, tied her hands to the doorknob, bound her feet. He took off his pants and came at her from behind. Joy-Joy did not move, not a muscle flinched. MK felt the skin of her buttocks cold as slick steel pressed against his upper thighs. He moved inside her, but nothing happened for him. All MK heard was his own hard breathing. It was as if Joy-Joy wasn't there. An hour, maybe two, he was caught to her like that, nothing coming from him but an aching hardness refusing to go away. Then Joy-Joy slowly arched her back, a great cat preening with determination, her head turned back toward him. MK reached to kiss her lips, aching in the very center of his being. His face came close to Joy-Joy's and she spat. A white projectile of spit exploded in MK's face, he shuddered, falling away from her, his ache gone."

Angelica prided herself in slipping with equanimity between the steamy sheets of perverse moments, but in this instance she glimpsed a shadow far darker than that on the dark side of the moon and wanted to travel back to earth quickly as possible. She offered Brogan another drink. There was no expression on his face, only the curious red in his eyes. She tried to get through to him again, she was beginning to think he might not come back this time, just orbit out there in darkness with his thoughts of MK. "Why don't you and Bubba-Bob come over to my house after I close for a little blowfish?" She watched Brogan's expression to determine if she registered on his Richter scale of existence. She didn't. Brogan's slurred words continued.

"After that MK couldn't come unless a woman spat in his face. There's only one woman he doesn't need to do that with anymore."

"Lucky girl," Bubba-Bob blustered. "What's MK do to her, stick a grenade up her ass?"

Angelica interceded, still hoping for a lighthearted conclusion. "Sometimes, you know, a girl can use a good tie-up job to get the juices flowing."

Brogan didn't take the bait, but Bubba-Bob did. "Yah! Once I tied up this old girlfriend of mine, she started screaming rape. How could I be raping her? That was the third goddamn time we were doing it that night."

Angelica saw her chance to lead Bubba-Bob further away from a dangerous situation. "It all depends on who is the tie-er, and who's the tie-ee. Maybe your girlfriend was just on the wrong end of the rope."

"You like that stuff, don't you?" Bubba-Bob asked the question as if he were about to stumble onto one of life's elusive truths. A simple vision was visited in the part of Bubba-Bob's brain linked directly to the numb region below his belt. In the wink of an eye Bubba-Bob glimpsed Angelica tied in a maze of knots, the tattooed squid surrounding the nipple of her left breast swelling to life, crawling off her body in quick escape. Bubba-Bob winked again to get the image back, but it had fled. Bubba-Bob considered himself lucky to have caught it the first time. A smug expression of sexual martyrdom spread from the corners of his thick lips and puffed his cheeks.

"Now here comes a man whose bed any woman would like to find herself handcuffed to." Angelica nodded toward the door, then quickly turned to fish a special bottle of gold rum from the hundreds of choices rowed behind the bar. She poured a glass of the rum and offered it to Justo as he slid heavily onto a stool. She poured another glass for herself and held it up. "*Anejo* time."

"*Anejo* time." Justo raised the glass to his lips and savored the sweet liquid, trying not to focus on the near nakedness revealed by Angelica's behind-the-bar attire. Justo could arrest her for contributing to the delinquency of adults for wearing those shorts, or whatever that strip of cloth was called. If he wasn't a married man he could . . . well, if he wasn't a married man. "To *la cucaracha.*"

"*Salud*, to the roach." Angelica rubbed her newly filled glass against

Justo's, joining him in a pledge of allegiance to the Cuban Death's Head bug, who will, local legend had it, spin on its hard-shelled body, then stop, its gnarly antennae pointing the direction from which El Finito will roar ashore. It was bad luck to crush these hurricane-predicting insects scurrying by the thousands across the island's cracked sidewalks and shiny tiled kitchen floors. The myth the insect would one day stop dead in a furious spin, indicating the direction from which the end of the world would occur, could be taken seriously or not. Some thought it less of a myth and more of a joke played by local Cubans on the unsuspecting. Others believed the tale, that to squash a bulky Death's Head bug invited one's death by hurricane. Angelica never knew, when Justo offered his undying pledge of fellowship to the roach before downing a shot of *anejo*, if he was serious or not. She had the suspicion he was. After several shots of *anejo* Angelica became convinced he was.

"My brother," Brogan emerged from the original starting point of the meandering trail he had been wandering for the past hour, "says the buck bucks in Central America."

"The buck bucks for anyone who tries to ride it, bubba!" Bubba-Bob slammed his empty glass on the bar. "Nobody's ever ridden that one to the grave."

Angelica was thinking how slender her ankles looked with the straps of her high heels around them. She gazed into Justo's brown eyes, thinking them dreamy and easy for a solid cop whose body bulged with such intentional strength. Her desire was to tie Justo's thick leather belt close about her waist, cinch the cold holstered gun against her hips. "When are you going to carry me away from all this?" Angelica pushed the intention of her solicitation deep into Justo's eyes.

"I'm a married man."

"Honey . . ." Angelica poured them both very tall *anejos*. "Just because you're on a diet doesn't mean you can't eat."

A good thought. Justo chewed on it for all it was worth while eyeing the more delectable parts of Angelica's fleshy exposure. There were times Justo ached to the marrow of his bones to be an unmarried man, matter of fact, twenty or thirty times a day; then, when day went into night and back into early day, like this one had, and he was worn to raw emotion, that was when he ached most, and the bed that contained his sleeping Rosella across the narrow streets of the town might as well be clear over to the Abacos for all the difference it might make. Who knows? Only Justo and his conscience. Mister Conscience was a *formidal* opponent Justo preferred not to go up against, especially since he needed all the Saints' help to rid the island of the evil he sensed swelling the heart valve of public decency. All through this night, and now into the early morning, Justo was a man on a mission; his persuasive call of ideals was more of a lure than Angelica. "Better not to stir the rice, although it sticks."

"Always got some great saying, Justo. But you know your problem? You think too much. Cops should act before they think, it's what gives them their edge. Some day you're not sharp it'll be too late, opportunity will have flown." Angelica pressed her lips to the rim of the shot glass of rum to indicate the true meaning of her intentions. "Have you ever whipped anyone with that thick belt of yours?"

"Don't stir the rice."

"I might be a lousy cook, but I never let my rice stick to the pan."

Justo could not keep a smile from his lips, first time he had smiled in twenty-four hours. The marrow in his bones started to melt.

"Where'd you get that don't stir the rice stuff?"

"Cervantes."

"If Don Quixote were to come back today he'd be a Colombian cocaine cowboy."

"Or a cop in the Florida Keys."

"No, he'd be a drug runner, I'm sure."

"Tilting at windmills in fast cigarette boats?"

"Something like that." Angelica laughed, then she went very serious. "Come home with me. I'm not like your wife. I'll let you read in the bathtub. What time do you get off?"

"Never off."

"Perfect couple, I'm always on." Angelica poured herself another *anejo*. She hated the stuff, liquid honey to stiffen the arteries and pickle the brain. Couldn't tell a Cuban that though, the older ones drank nothing but *anejo*, recalling the days when *anejo* was Cuban-made. Now it was distilled in Florida, had become the all–Cuban-American drink. From Angelica's side of the bar it appeared that, for the most fervent members of the jingoistic Cuban-American tribe, drinking *anejo* was a passionate mixture of confused national prides, a declaration of twisted allegiances. To kick back shots of *anejo*, until the tongue swelled and the lips forgot how to pronounce words the brain no longer remembered, had become a near patriotic act of contrition. Angelica drank *anejo* only with Justo. Justo drank nothing else, but not, Angelica suspected, simply to run his conflicting flags of national faith up the flagpole. No, Angelica sensed Justo was a hard man who liked soft things, a tough spirit who suckled life's sugars. Angelica assumed there were times Justo simply wanted no fanfare, longed to get sweetly drunk. Times like these Angelica harbored the fantasy of slipping clothes from Justo's muscled body, handcuffing his dark feet by the ankles so he couldn't run screaming for his Rosella when the cock crowed at dawn. Times like these Angelica was not above slipping Justo a mickey in order to slip him in. One woman's game is another's pain. Angelica was not about to give up so easily or gladly as in the past. This early morning she would drive the hook of her red fingernails right through this latent Latin lover's heart. She was going to have Justo so deeply within her there would in the end be for them both no way out.

"*Anejo!*" Bubba-Bob raised his glass of rum in mocking salute to Justo. "Rhymes with asshole! Just you think about it, bubba buck!"

Angelica's intentions were thwarted by Bubba-Bob's rude intrusion. This might not be a morning for romance after all, might instead be a morning for murder. Angelica pushed back from her provocative position, sauntering along the bar to where Brogan still wandered at the entrance to his maze.

"I bet . . ." Bubba-Bob brought his flushed face up in front of Justo's. "Bet you could jump backwards through your asshole and land on a peso."

"Glad to take that bet." Justo pushed off the barstool and stood before Bubba-Bob. Both men appeared massive enough to support another five men standing atop each of their broad shoulders.

Bubba-Bob let loose with a grin. After chasing Brogan through his maze without making contact Bubba-Bob was in luck, he finally had a player. Oh how Bubba-Bob loved these moments of random chance, when he could butt his bulk against other men in test of physical time. Everything else in life was just so much fancy talk and cute fiberglass boats. "How much you wanna bet?"

Brogan spun on his barstool, up from the maze, banged Bubba-Bob on the shoulder with his fist to gain sudden attention for a line of truth which shined bright as the already wagered imaginary peso. "That's it! MK was the one tied, not Joy-Joy. MK was on a leash the whole time he was in Nam. Now he's down in Central America running with headless rats." Brogan looked quizzically from Bubba-Bob to Angelica to Justo, confused as a downed prizefighter emerging from a knockout fog. "Christ! Why couldn't I see it before? It's all so clear now. MK's got himself involved in the biggest tie-up game of his life."

Bubba-Bob did not hear a word of Brogan's revelation. He was waiting for Justo's proof of currency. Bubba-Bob didn't like cops, especially the one standing before him now, the one he had known all his life on the island. To others Justo was a tower of karate-killer toughness, a bad nigger with a Cuban accent who spouted cornball sayings. Bubba-Bob knew better. When he and Justo were teenagers they worked shrimp boats together. First time out, when the long line of drag trawls were hoisted aboard, dripping and stinking with a load of fetid dross only hidden pockets of the Gulf's bottom is capable of releasing, Justo ran to the gunwale and puked his guts overboard, the Conch shrimp-boat captain laughing in the putrid wind at the pukey boy: "Bettah go bhack to shore! Bhack to shore and be a bug-headah! Nevah gonna work nets wit dese mens! Ya gots a gurl's stomack. Bye-bye, Bugs!"

"*El pez por la boca muere.*" Sweet *anejo* gripped Justo's tongue. "The fish dies from an open mouth. You're a fisherman, you should know that."

Bubba-Bob's loose grin grew wider. This was a corny Justo saying he liked. Bubba-Bob was going to remember it, but he didn't see how it applied to him. The veins in his neck bulged, his hands clenched into fists, one went quickly into the air and crashed onto the bar, rattling glasses the length of the long countertop. "What's your fucking bet?"

The rattling glasses brought Brogan further out of his maze. "MK!" Brogan screamed at Bubba-Bob. "My brother's finally over his head!"

Bubba-Bob's fist came off the bar in fierce rebound, catching Brogan under the chin, spinning him off his stool and sprawling across the floor. "I don't give a diddily fuck about MK and his Nam bullshit!" Bubba-Bob spat at Brogan gazing up through an even more complicated maze. "MK doesn't scare me! Neither do cops!" Bubba-Bob turned back to Justo. "Cops on the fucking take same time as they rides their high horses!"

"*Algunos caen para que otros se levanten.*" Justo's words came as an afterthought, as if the exploding motion of his body required a concrete beginning. He followed instincts flowing through *anejo*-thickened blood, force from fists, knees and feet rearranging flesh and bone of another human's body. When a man becomes a weapon he surrenders to all consequence. The consequence was bleeding Bubba-Bob, thrashing on the floor next to Brogan, raising hands to ward off the weighty confusion of more blows.

"Bubba-Bob's not going to look the same after this." Angelica edged along the bar to Justo. "Should we call a cop?" She thought the cleverness of her remark might bring Justo to his senses before he pulverized what was left of Bubba-Bob. Maybe it was time to set the hook. "Why don't I sweep the drunks and deadbeats out? We'll go someplace where you can read in the bathtub with nobody yelling at you."

"Where?"

Set the hook and pull. "My place."

"Okay."

It was that easy. One last jerk on the line so the hook didn't rip from this hard-won prize. "What was it you said in Spanish before you laid Bubba-Bob out with all that karate stuff?"

"Some fall that others may rise."

Angelica's provocative pout swept up in a victorious smile. She had her catch in the boat, only thing left to do was take it home and fry it. "Honey, you're not through rising yet."

15

Ocho dreamed of conch fritters and slick oyster bellies in the backseat of Justo's car. Coming dawn pushed a swell of temperature before it, steam streamed heavenward from slick asphalt streets and steep slanted tin roofs of crowded houses, instigating a humid haze as Justo drove through damp heat ascending. The island wavered before him uncertain as an underwater vision, a glimpse of sun above glittered as if striking a vast watery surface, reminding of a far different universe. Rosella Rosella Rosella, *ojos que no ven, corazon que no siente*. Rosella, what you don't see won't break your heart. The *anejo* in Justo's veins filled him with a leaded weariness, he was too tired to concentrate. He forced his eyes open to the crack of sunlight breaking through morning mist. It seemed in these modern times everyone was too tired to concentrate, especially on the consistency of their lives. It was a time when even five-year marriages were a big deal, not like Justo's grandparents' time, when people married for life, for better or for worse. It was for their own good, kept them from making the same mistake over and over. Rosella Rosella Rosella. *Quien peces quiere, mojarse tiene.* He who wants to catch the fish must not mind a wetting. Yesterday Justo had set out to catch a fish in a sea of fishermen, now he was headed for Angelica's house, headed for a wetting.

Everything was confused with weariness. Who was the big fish? Who was the little fish? *Pez grande come al chico.* Big fish eats little fish. Angelica and Justo were two anglers in search of a sucker mouth. Maybe he was the sucker, but he had to follow his lead. The first thing he had noticed when he walked into the Wreck Room, even before noticing Angelica's shorts, was the day's daily witticism chalked on the blackboard behind the bar. Justo knew he could not ask Angelica who had authored the scrawled message. To ask Angelica would have made her the she-shark and him the bonita. Angelica had something Rosella did not, and she was not about to sell short. Justo had tried to sit quietly at the bar and order his *anejo*, not wanting Angelica to seize upon the expression he felt covered his face, not wanting her to inquire, "What's wrong? You look like you've seen a ghost." There was always the possibility Angelica authored the message. If so Justo was swimming with someone capable of putting a harpoon through his neck as well as his heart. No one was above suspicion. Bubba-Bob had a detour in mind for him, he wanted to let Bubba-Bob run his mouth off, talk himself out of what little common sense he had, give up what information he might hold. Bubba-Bob had pushed Justo along the detour of most resistance, forcing him to rise to the occasion. So now Bubba-Bob as a possible source of information was closed. Only Angelica's path of softest resistance was left open. It was Angelica's handwriting on the chalkboard behind the bar, Justo knew, had seen her written messages many times. The custom in the Wreck Room was for one of the customers to come up with the day's enigmatic quotation, then the bartender scrawled it in chalk across the blackboard to elicit further sagacious comments, or unleash a stream of derisive innuendo. A recent message inquired: HOW MANY HAITIANS DIE EVERY DAY TRYING TO SAIL TO AMERICA? The answer that made its way along the bar among the knowing during the long evening was simple: as many as can fit into a garbage can. The latest scrawled message was not so delicate as the one directing the Wreck Room habitués' attention to the lamentable shortage of garbage cans in Haiti. The message was straightforward, soliciting no enigmatic response, offering only a puzzled beginning:

HEY GREEN SAILOR!
FOR A GOOD TIME CALL 688 4352
—ZOBOP

A Green Sailor looks north to Cuban Martyrs. Justo still couldn't figure it. Zobop must have been in the Wreck Room last night. As Justo drove into ascending mist he tried to follow the trail of Zobop at the same time he pleaded for Rosella's forgiveness, begged protection of the Saints for what he was about to do. Justo had gone down on his knees and begged the Saints to save him before, save him from betraying Rosella. Never had he betrayed Rosella, had always adhered to his strict moral diet. Now he was headed for a wetting beneath Angelica's oceanic sheets, in search of the Zobop fish of fear. *Zobop*, sounded like a Memphis bebopper from the fifties. The only piece of shadow where Justo thought he glimpsed the shape of logic had to do with the toad in the cemetery. In South America those who believed in Macumba had a special way of dealing with a powerful rival who stood in their way, which was to write the name of the rival on a slip of paper and stuff it in the mouth of a black toad, then sew the toad's lips closed. So many Colombian Cowboys up in Miami believed in the effect this toad lip sewing had on their cocaine-running rivals it was rumored all the Florida toads had been used up and crates of fresh ones were airlifted in daily from Bogotá. Maybe Zobop had a powerful rival, maybe someone was cutting across Zobop's territory? But why would the toad have been placed on Abuelo's grave? No, this did not smack of a drug deal. Justo knew most all those players in town, none were called Zobop or used Macumba. Macumba was for South Americans, Key West was Cuban, it was a Santería town. What was happening was outside the accommodation as Justo knew it. Curses were often planted in obscure crevices of the cemetery during nocturnal services, but no one had ever offered a bufo toad with its mouth nailed shut. Certain squeamish elements of the island's citizenry discovered rat jaws, dog hearts and cat eyes when they arrived with dawn's light at the cemetery to pay their respects with bountiful bouquets of plastic flowers, but never was a bound goat with a slit throat discovered.

Justo was becoming convinced the answer rested in the cemetery; more than curses had been planted in its crevices, restless unearthed promises resided there too. He could not stop his mind from wandering off on the scent of yet one more plausibility, falling headlong down another path which might link the cemetery to something living rather than dead. Other love stories were buried in the cemetery besides Justo's parents and grandparents, one endured, its restless ending still haunted the town.

Justo grew up with the story of the Count and Acartonada, the female tubercular, a story rudely mythic, mocking any pretense the island city may have once had to a sane past. On the first friday of each month, while visiting the cemetery, Justo still felt he was treading upon the bones of Acartonada, buried not once, but three times, the last in secret, beneath a blacktopped avenue crisscrossing the city of the dead at the island's heart, condemned to restless peace in an unmarked grave. If love kills it can also give life. The frail Count was in his sixties when he arrived in Key West during the 1920s, his weakened European stiffness aided by a cane as he strolled city streets with the air of a displaced aristocrat, his bony feet sockless in battered tennis shoes, a monocle affixed to his left eye, worn as prominent badge proclaiming the fact he was Karl von Cosel, Dresden-born count, schooled not only in the infinities of astronomy, but also the finites of engineering and subtleties of metaphysics. A skinny man with goatish wisp of white beard and high bald forehead large enough to house two brains, the Count earned his way on the island operating the X-ray machine at the Marine Hospital. This arcane expertise brought the Count face to face with a fate he deemed worthy of immortality. Since the Count was master of the only ultraviolet X-ray machine between Havana and Miami he was called upon to examine a youthful Cuban, Acartonada. The crown of a carved tortoiseshell comb was set atop Acartonada's hair, kept brushed in black cascading waves over white shoulders bent from coughing fits. Deep within a hospital room darkened to the outside world this woman in her early twenties slipped a blouse from trembling shoulders, over breasts glimpsed by a man only once, a husband who disappeared after their wedding years before. In a room impenetrable as the blackest forest in Germany, pale Acartonada sat without knowledge she was enthroned on a bizarre altar constructed in the Count's brain, about to become a necrophiliac's bride eternal. Quick as a kiss the first ultraviolet flash sealed her fate to this balding European, his monocled eye pierced through inflamed tissues and bending bones to the hollow breath of her disease. The Count saw not a spirit atrophied, a woman scorned, or the skeletal core of a gypsy curse, he discerned a magnificent bloom of female flesh destined to be preserved. *El deseo hace hermoso lo feo*. Desire makes the drab beautiful.

Disease was draining the vital essence from the Count's Cuban flower, he plotted revenge on reality. What the Count conjured, as shades of ultraviolet light pierced his beauty's flesh, was an illumination to sear the heavens in its simplicity. The Count plotted nothing less than a getaway plane ride into eternity. His desire was unbridled, the clock and his heart went ticking, two time bombs racing one another for the soul of Acartonada. The Count opened his purse and purchased gifts for his newly beloved, he exposed the opposite of his Teutonic stiffness, solicitous charm. He called upon Acartonada at her parents' home, going down on bended knee before this vision he had privately bombarded with iridescent X-rays, begging for marriage. This bride once scorned was flattered by such intense, yet socially stifled, attention focused upon her by a man, even one so odd and old. What Acartonada had innocently exposed to the Count in the dark hospital room was a desire for health; her kindness toward him was a transparently clothed plea for physical wholeness, not a scream of lust to break the eardrums of the angels. The Count would have it otherwise, his solicitations growing more insistent. Acartonada refused to see him, closed the door forever on his dark room and its eerie luminescent light which made her skin glow the color of an iced blue corpse. She thought she was safe, unaware the clock ticked, the Count's heart plotted. When the hands of fate crossed the Count pounced.

It was Halloween, day of the dead, night of all saints, the end of another hurricane season marked by a festive parade down Duval Street. The parents of Acartonada, having helplessly watched her fade, covered her consumptive body in blankets, spiriting her to Duval Street in hopes the spectacle and fervor of this special night might raise her sunken spirits. It raised instead a hollow coughing from her narrow chest. In the universal panic common to distraught parents they cried out for help from any and all quarters. The Count appeared at their door with his ultraviolet X-ray machine. By the time the medical doctor arrived the daughter was dead. Acartonada was dead to all but the Count; for him the temporal engagement had ended, the spiritual wedding could now begin.

The Count prevailed upon the family to allow him the honor of erecting a baroque vault for their daughter which would be the envy of the saints. After the funeral the Count began a two-year vigil at the vault, until finally it was thought he had laid the memory of Acartonada to rest. A half decade slipped away before a teen-aged confidant of Acartonada's discovered the body had long since been freed from the wormy interior of its formidable sanctuary. Peering through the dusty back window of an abandoned slaughterhouse, whose every battered board and termite-riddled beam now formed the Count's shabby castle, the confidant spied the amber glass eyes of Acartonada staring from an ornate bed. The high, carved bedposts were draped by trailing webs of cheesecloth, forming a canopy over a half-sitting body clothed in formal bridal gown, the glint of a gold wedding band on one of the fingers. Expensive necklaces and bracelets adorned the neck and wrists of the person reconstructed of wire and wax, alone in the room with a pipe organ, an operating table and the dusty X-ray machine. Nailed above the door a sign declared LABORATORY.

At the Count's trial it became clear that years previous he had built the vault in order to enter it one day and lead his decomposing bride home. In the slaughterhouse bridal suite the Count played the pipe organ positioned next to the honeymoon bed so his beloved could hear perfectly. Each evening his fingers skipped across the keys, entertaining his sleeping bride with clouds of celestial notes from *Parsifal's* "Good Friday Spell." How close that Good Friday of true resurrection was only the Count knew. Before Acartonada's confidant brought down the curtain on the Count's domestic tranquillity he had been feverishly reconstructing the wood and tin carcass of an old World War I airplane. Soon the Count and his bride were to fly across the Atlantic to the fatherland, perhaps to winter in a Swiss sanitarium where Acartonada could heal her lungs. The trial judge concluded the eccentric foreigner, who had a way with mortuary wax and cosmetic applications, was simply mad. The Count was tarred and feathered with nothing more than the assignation of grave robber. Justo remembered as a boy joining the line of over three thousand people trudging past Acartonada's open casket in Lopez's Funeral Home. The Count's fragile, risen-from-the-dead bride was fully displayed to the town's curious. Abuelo had stood for the longest time peering into the casket, mumbling to Justo that there was, in the mad foreigner's devotion, something which touched all men who ever dreamed of enshrining their life's love in a shining, eternal moment. Maybe the Count's losing his mind over the girl allowed him to cheat reality. Perhaps madness alone could deliver man his eternal bride. Justo could still hear clearly the conversation after the funeral parlor parade of sightseers was over, in the back room of *la grocería*, Abuelo and the men talking of how soft and round Acartonada's breasts were, how her long black hair was still fixed proudly as a Spanish queen. "I would have been on her all the time too," one of the men laughed. All laughed. "That's the perfect kind of wife, one who never grows old, never asks you to buy her anything, and never talks back." What Justo did not know then as a young boy he knew now as a man. The Count's flights of fancy were not restricted only to freedom's joyride across the Atlantic. Discovered fitted between the fragile thighs of Acartonada's waxed and wired corpse was a smooth rubber tube, stuffed cottonballs at its bottom saturated with the spent frustration of the Count's mundane lust, the seed of desire at last taking root in the fertile hollow of memory.

Restless curses and plaintive promises were planted everywhere in the crevices of the cemetery. Driving through damp heat ascending into a brightening morning, Justo could not stop his thoughts from crossing at the cemetery, trying to connect with a love beyond the grave. A power unstoppable and sexual was implicit in the recent mutilations of the goat and toad. It was beyond Santería. In Santería there is no warning if one is the target of secret ritual, one just suddenly drops with a gall-bladder attack or an irrevocable pain through the heart. Maybe this was a voodoo deal after all. Justo would have to ask St. Cloud about Zobop. St. Cloud might know who or what Zobop was, if St. Cloud was sober enough to rub two syllables together. *Los niños y los locos dicen las verdades.* Children and drunks tell the truth. Lately it was hard to tell what the truth of St. Cloud was, bad enough when he was snooping around in the night after his estranged wife, now St. Cloud insisted someone wanted to harm him. No one was harming St. Cloud more than himself, struck dumb over a young girl. If St. Cloud did not watch out he would end his days like the Count, a *viejo verde*, an old man chasing young skirts. Something similar in St. Cloud's singular desire for Lila reminded Justo of the Count's fixation. The Count never did overcome Acartonada. After Acartonada's second burial the Count attempted to blow open the welded steel doors of the baroque vault. To keep the pitiful remains of Acartonada beyond the Count's earthly reach rumor was the family secretly reburied her a third time, in a metal casket deep beneath one of the cemetery's thick asphalt avenues. Nothing seemed to deter the Count, determined chaser of ghostly skirts; at his death another waxed likeness of his eternal bride was discovered in his shabby room. Some said the Count had the real Acartonada all the time, that what the family secretly buried was a fake, planted by the Count in the blown-open baroque vault. Justo believed no speculation, no matter how bizarre, could be discounted when it came to what a man will do to get a woman. St. Cloud was one to keep both eyes on, a grand loser, loses money, loses erections, loses wives. Justo did not think St. Cloud was in danger of losing his life, too much one of life's enchanted fools for that. Loser that he was, St. Cloud was central to helping Justo keep the Haitian kid from being snatched by Immigration and whisked to the Everglades detention camp in an abandoned missile base. Time was running out for Voltaire, Immigration had issued another detainer, trying to get their hands on him. Justo did not think he could convince the State Attorney's Office to cover him until he got a grand jury trial. At a grand jury trial Justo was convinced Voltaire would spring on involuntary manslaughter; for this he counted on St. Cloud's interpretive courtroom poetics. St. Cloud would have the grand jury mopping their eyes when they heard Voltaire's tale of terror. Time is what Justo needed, and in that time he needed to keep his eyes on St. Cloud, to save his pinch hitter for that fateful moment when he would step to center stage and knock the ball out of the grand jury hearing room. If it was too late for grand loser St. Cloud to save himself, at least he could resurrect the value of his existence by saving someone else.

Justo's job was to suspect everyone on the island of some sort of guilt or other. He did not figure St. Cloud to be a Green Sailor, Zobop, or Angel of Death, but one thing certain, St. Cloud was crazy as the Baron. For five years the Baron fed his bridal effigy of paraffin wax and piano wire a special diet of chemical solutions, praying for cellular rebirth of his sleeping beauty. For the ten years Justo knew St. Cloud the man always claimed he did not want any part of gaining forgiveness through forgetting. St. Cloud desired to keep the flicker of his failed history alive, a burning remembrance of mistakes past, conscience was his mother's milk. St. Cloud believed there was no rhyme without reason, no crime without passion. Justo knew St. Cloud was capable of killing for love, maybe already had, by killing his common sense in pursuit of Lila. Justo had watched St. Cloud become a *turrudo*, a cuckold, and one of his own making. But deep down what man wasn't a self-made *turrudo*, what man wasn't the fool of his own invention? No one knows what happens between another man and woman, no one can judge. To judge a fellow cuckold is to attempt to cuckold mother justice herself, and that, for Justo, was the final invitation to folly. Justo was on his way to join the fellowship of the cuckolds; he could not stop from judging himself.

Justo had instructed Angelica to go directly home from the Wreck Room and he would follow in his car so no one would observe them headed to her house. He knew he was in for a wetting. He pleaded with the Saints, and with the saintly image of sweet Rosella, to forgive him for what he was about to do. Justo was so overcome with his burden of assumed mortal sin before even arriving at Angelica's doorstep that he nearly missed the fast-moving apparition in the road ahead, its dark silhouette weaving sideways, erratic as a spooked manta ray. Justo backed his foot quickly off the gas pedal to slow the car as he jerked the steering wheel to one side, swerving from the man on a bicycle aimed straight for him. The man on the bicycle made no attempt to avoid Justo, the jagged tip of one handlebar scraping alongside the car as the bicycle rushed past. Justo caught a glimpse of Space Cadet's face above him, bland as a bleached pumpkin in the morning mist. Space Cadet's thick blade of braided gray hair trailed in a self-generated wind as he sped away in the high squeal of a bent bicycle wheel. Justo's sudden swerve to avoid a collision stalled the car's engine and threw Ocho off the backseat with a startled whimper; he turned to shout his displeasure out the open car window. Space Cadet had already disappeared into the blanket of rising heat.

"La cabeza blanca en canas, y los sesos por venir!" Justo slammed his fist onto the steering wheel. Gray-headed and still no brains! Damned druggie, probably powered by his own astral wind, spaced out and knocked up by punk mushrooms or bathtub designer drugs guiding him with bright lights from flying saucers only he could see. Justo started the car's engine and drove on. He could not suppress his rage and resentment at another of life's walking wounded begging to be run over by throwing himself in the path of the real world. Justo remembered when Space Cadet first appeared, toward the end of the Vietnam war, descending with other longhairs down the island chain like a plague of grasshoppers clinging to the last blades of wheat, hatched out of psychedelic-painted vans and converted school buses, bumping to a stop at the end of Highway U.S. 1. More than a few of the sporting local Conchs and sailors loved trying to knock sense enough into the bean-sprout-breath interlopers so they would turn tail and head out of paradise. Still they came, growing so numerous the local sports complained there were not enough beer bottles in town to bash brains back into these longhairs. Then a funny thing happened. Some of the Conchs went over to the longhairs because of their bare-breasted women in skimpy granny dresses with unshaven hair under their arms ripe as a damp scent of molasses. The local sports discovered the marijuana the longhairs had was a cheaper high than a case of beer, and it blew in on a never-ending Belize breeze and Jamaican wind. The strangest thing was the longhairs were not jealous of their bare-breasted women, encouraged them to be passed

around with the granola cookies, pot and Bob Dylan records. This was enough to make even the Nam-bound sailors take notice, many of them started going over the hill to nosh at the groovy trough of natural foods and unnatural acts. Acid, Speed, growling guitars and sugary sitars—seemed like the whole world was turning Hip, and the hot little island at the edge of the Gulf was winking a modern cool eye. A long time back that was, before Rosella was pregnant with Isabel. Now there were only the odd few longhairs left in town, like Space Cadet, wandering in a cultural combat zone, staggering slowly out of step, missing life's every other beat, the world long since passed by, most all the others having cut their hair down to a social regimental length a full decade past. Space Cadet was bent forever, like the wheel of his battered bike, sliding around town wearing his tight THE NEXT GENERATION T-shirt, convinced the planets were going to line up and bump each other out of the universe, as if God was a pool player about to sink the earth out of sight in the lefthand-side Black Hole pocket. If the Space Cadets of this world have their way, Justo banged the steering wheel again, there won't be a next generation.

The white glare of morning struck steep metal rooftops, behind shuttered windows sleepers stirred uneasily to clock radios heralding news of another day swelling with heat. Justo prayed the Saints were not asleep, but riding shotgun on his conscience. Coming from the far distance ahead at the end of the street was a creature scurrying quick as a messenger from hell. Was it the Saints answering his prayers with a sign of warning? The squat shiny form rolled closer, exposing its prosaic reality, nothing more than a flat-nosed truck with a bulbous metal tank attached to its back from which stubby nozzles extruded, fouling the air with a curtain of mosquito-killing insecticide. Justo pulled his car out of the way, cranked the windows up to block the spewing stench from the spray truck prowling for winged blood suckers embarked on sticking it to a rising population. Most people would rather live with an itch on their conscience than a bite on their ass. At this moment Justo felt he was no different. He waited until the raspy whine of the sprayer was far behind before pulling back into the street. Ocho was awake in the backseat, nuzzling his snout against Justo's shoulder, sniffing about for an errant conch fritter only a dog's luck might bring his way. Justo petted the searching snout. *Manea la cola el can, no por ti, sino por el pan.* The dog wags his tail, not for you, but for your bread. Man's life was not so different, Justo thought, a wag of the tail to the right person, or a check in the mail, a kind bark at night, or a warm body pulling into bed beside you, amounted to the same, so blessedly simple. Man is nothing but *el mismo perro con differente collar*. Same dog with a different collar. Makes no difference if the collar is carved of gold or woven with straw, man is a dog prancing on both hind twos, dragging his tail of telltale lust in the dust behind.

Something else ahead. More street action. What now? Justo took a deep breath, instinctively rubbed the gold wishbone chained around his neck. Could be the Saints were protecting him by throwing one obstacle after another in his path, preventing his cuckolding himself before the cock crowed an end to this early dawn. Renoir in his white suit stood in the middle of the street flailing his arms to the heavens, forcing Justo to stop. Renoir's fists banged so loudly on the car roof over Justo's head it was difficult to understand what he was screaming.

"Angelica's inside, said you'd be coming, got to help us!"

Justo's hand went to unhook the speakerphone of the police radio bolted beneath the car dashboard. "Somebody hurt?"

"Yes!" Renoir yanked the car door open. "Come with me, no ambulance. Angelica said you'd help, you'd understand." Renoir tried to grab Justo's shoulder and pull him from the car.

Justo pushed the grasping hands away and climbed out. "Where's Angelica?"

"Let's go!" Renoir spun quickly on his heels, running off on the sidewalk following a high wall painted the blushed color of a baby's bottom.

Justo ran after Renoir, through a wooden gate in the wall, along a gravel path beneath a choke of fat leaves sweeping down from trees crowded around shotgun cottages. Justo was being led into the hothouse atmosphere of one of the island's many gay guesthouse compounds. He had entered so quickly he did not know which compound he was in, many seemed interchangeable: Jasmine Arms, Plantation Oasis, Polly Parrot Perch. Although some were nothing more than tarted-up rusted hulks of dilapidated trailers and termite-riddled shacks supported on foundations of crumbling limestone, others were shockingly elegant, tucked behind towering walls hiding jeweled settings of planted exotica. There were a number of compounds that offered a discriminating clientele discreet diversions or, for the stag-hearted and not so discriminating, chancy nocturnal meetings with haughty male youths wrapped in an Apollonesque glow. Justo grew up learning more slang words in Cuban for homosexual than for any other possible predilection, physical action or emotional condition. This was an odd fact, one Justo often thought he should think about, but for some reason he rarely did, what one man did with another was of little interest to him. Justo remembered cousin Manuel, who had a furtive boyhood backyard bush affair with another boy. Manuel's Catholic conscience was haunted by such homophobic extremity he banged out twelve kids twenty years later to prove he preferred women. Justo based his distinctions concerning people on a simplistic sense of good and bad; good and bad could be split like a stone, one was pure or one was evil. Who did the going into somebody, and who did the coming out, made no difference to Justo, for him right and wrong had nothing to do with sex. It was only when a person had two bad sides that they got in Justo's way and would be knocked down never to rise again. In the early days, when Justo mixed more with the public and was less specialized, he did no more cop business in gay guesthouses than he did out in the motels lining the boulevard on the way into town. There had been one confusing moment for Justo in the early days, he was called by a panicked landlord to a shabby little house in a gay guesthouse compound, the doors nailed shut and the windows sealed with black tape. The tenants had not paid the rent for two months, the landlord was afraid to go in. Justo broke through the front door into the chill of air-conditioned darkness. He turned on the lights, exposing one large room sheeted in black plastic, a wide metal drain strategically set in the middle of the floor, a coiled garden hose in one corner. Justo never understood exactly what went on in the plastic room, whatever it was had nothing to do with two men loving each other, no more than incest has to do with fatherly love. Let the whole world bang hell out of each other was Justo's philosophy, as long as they didn't bang kids. Justo knew his ideas along these lines were primitive. He considered himself sophisticated in the way he charged life's ever-changing windmills, but on this issue he remained a product of learned Christian behavior.

Chasing Renoir on the crunchy gravel Justo's mind engaged in the strange clarity which accompanies the unexpected. He had noticed the trousers of Renoir's normally crisp white suit were soaked through from the knees down, streaks of sand clung to the dampness around the knees. "Hey!" Justo shouted to Renoir sprinting so far ahead on the winding path he was almost out of sight. "Not so fast!" The words inspired Renoir to race even farther ahead. Justo still had great power in his leg and arm muscles, but the breath of life was definitely growing shorter in his lungs. He was going gray and the gay rabbits were outrunning him, all he could hope for was enough oxygen in his brain to outsmart the rabbits. He lost sight of Renoir.

Justo's labored panting grew louder in his ears, he stumbled to the end of the white path, beyond the last cottage. The Atlantic spread before him, its inky chop edging out on hardened sand left behind a low tide. The crescent-shaped length of beach fronting the compound was empty, at its far tip the dark pilings of a pier marched into low water. From the long shadow of a piling the white suit of Renoir stood out, hands waving. Justo took a deep breath and sprinted around the crescent, strong salty air reviving his tired lungs. Renoir was not beneath the pier when Justo reached it; beyond the pilings, on a tangled bed of rotting seaweed marooned by the receding tide was a beached naked body. Angelica was bent over the body with both her hands spread on its clammy skin above the heart, bearing down with quick rhythmic bursts to pressure a sign of life from unmoving lips.

Justo became aware of his own labored breath again as he watched Angelica attempting to pump life into the prone body. "What happened?"

"Floyd had . . . an . . ." Renoir dropped to his knees on the sand next to Angelica, as if kneeling in anguished prayer. "Had . . . an . . . accident." Tears overwhelmed Renoir's eyes as he gazed up at Justo. "Floyd went out to the end of the pier, still dark. He dove off, forgetting the low tide. I don't know, maybe his neck is broken?"

"Keep pumping that heart," Justo encouraged.

Angelica did not look up, bent to her task, the muscles of her exposed upper arms straining to bring pressure to bear on the unresponsive organ beneath her fingertips.

Renoir gently cradled Floyd's head in his hands, brushing caked sand from the forehead, smoothing the damp hair. "Please don't, please don't," Renoir cried to the face with closed eyes.

"I need to know how long Floyd's been like this." Justo knelt in the sand, placed his thumbs at the corners of the body's eyes and pushed the stiff lids back, exposing two orbs of white, the irises rolled high, pointing to a brain which might be dead. "Keep pumping!" Justo shouted at Angelica. "Try it faster, thump-beat-beat-beat, faster, eighty beats a minute . . . that's it."

"Five, maybe ten minutes ago it happened." Renoir brushed more sand from Floyd's matted hair. "Pulled him from the water myself.

So early in the morning nobody was around, nobody but Space Cadet, who suddenly appeared on the pier. I told him to run over to Petronia Street and get Dr. Humphries, who knows Floyd. Humphries could get Floyd going again, but Space Cadet didn't come back, doctor didn't come. Floyd started coughing up water so I ran out to the street to use the pay phone when Angelica came by. Said she knew CPR and told me to wait for you, because you were right behind her."

"Why didn't you just call the emergency number?" Justo pushed the gray lips open, exposing a bloody tongue.

"We can take care of ourselves." Renoir's words were constrained, as if elucidating a difficult philosophy rather than issuing a simple statement. "We take care of each other."

"From the looks of it you sure have been doing a great job," Justo growled, leaning close to Floyd's flaccid lips. He ran a finger into Floyd's mouth, clearing a scum of sand, freeing the bloody tongue from a balled position at the entrance to the throat. Justo figured Floyd was gone, no breathing, no pulse, no vital signs at all. He had dealt with more than his share of stiffs who reached this stage, tried to pop life back into hundreds of dead drunks, drug O.D.'s, traffic fatalities, gasping heart attack victims and hopeless suicides. Not much to be done after a certain point. God alone knows that point, Justo told himself, placing his lips over the gray ones caked with sand and blood, pinching the cold nose off as he breathed four bursts of air into the cupped mouth filled with an odor of deep vomit, the odor that always reminded Justo of death's final scent. Justo judged himself somewhat less of a man for not being able to perform this life-giving task without feeling queasy. No matter how many times he gave mouth-to-mouth a foul bile rose up in his stomach, a stupid reaction when the high stakes of life were at issue. It was one thing to try to kiss life back into a woman who's been run down at a crosswalk, or a kid pulled from a backyard pool, another thing to be blowing into the lungs of a perfect stranger. Although Floyd was not a perfect stranger, more an imperfect acquaintance. Floyd was an over-the-hill muscles and mustache man, blew into Key West from the cold north many winters ago with a rich sugar daddy and a randy appetite which kept him prowling his youthful manhood away in the late-night gay discos. Floyd knew what certain northern men wanted when they slid south from their arctic confines. Though Floyd had long since gone bald he kept his muscles toned and pumped, his mustache and chest hair trimmed and dyed. Every day, after a night of fast music and faster action, Floyd could be found on one of the more obscure beaches in a bathing suit summed up by two shreds of cloth, one twisted rakishly around the waist, the other cinched tight between firmed hills of bare buttocks baked by the sun. Floyd was tanned blacker than Justo's African Aunt Oris was born, his skin gleamed with the artificiality of an enameled doll. Floyd's fanatical predilection to roast his buns round the daytime clock accounted for the nickname which chased him into the island's more catty crevices. A snicker and a wink were always passed along with the nickname, Fan-Tan. Fan-Tan, the most barbed of the feline tongues wagged, looked like an overexposed Oreo cookie, whatever in the world did Renoir see in that boy, honey? Don't you know Renoir deserves better than to pour all his hard money down that manhole? Renoir could hustle himself plenty of crisp muscles and mustache if he wasn't such a dear, so the cat tongues wagged. Fan-Tan was known as Floyd only to Renoir; no matter how the barbed tongues hissed, they could not pry Renoir's affection from Fan-Tan. Renoir was one of the few on the island secure in his bones with who he was. If Justo were pushed to the wall, even he would count on Renoir, a trustworthy man straight in his beliefs. On the matter of Fan-Tan, Renoir listened not to any ill-winded gossip, even though he knew Fan-Tan still slipped away in late winter afternoons to the sandy stretch before the seaside wall of West Martello Tower. The red brick tower stood as decaying vestige of a Union fortress once housing Civil War soldiers and prisoners. Now the citadel was home to the Key West Garden Club, within its crumbling walls a choke of trees dripped webbed blossoms of rare airborne orchids, beneath cannon portholes in the rounded parapet facing the Atlantic Ocean solitary men sometimes perched, peering from behind the glare of sunglasses across the sandy beach toward the wooden finger of a low-lying pier. In the declining afternoon sun the pier was often crowded with young men in brief bathing suits, their thoughts never drifting toward the schools of errant snook that roiled the waters beneath their dangling naked feet. Among insiders the pier was known as Dick Dock, among less tolerant outsiders, as Queer Pier. The pier daily spawned a well-known mating scene. Over the years Justo had seldom been summoned there to investigate big trouble, except for an occasional zealous sport fresh off the Miami shuttle plane who decided he liked to mug other men after fishing from them encounters of lust or explosions of guilt. The turf around the Civil War citadel was still a field of encounter for men from north and south, the threat of gunfire exchanged for the lark of spending anonymous sexual currency. Fan-Tan's random wanderings between the brick-walled tower and the peacock display of boys in bikinis on the pier was considered ill conduct only because it carried with it the public flaunting of his cheating on Renoir.

Justo was locked lip to lip in a dance of life and death with someone who, in Justo's schoolboy days, would have elicited sneers and jeers as a *cundango, pargo, amanerado, parquela, loca, mariquita, partido, pajaro,* or *pato*, a blatant excuse of a man to be beaten and bullied because of his desire for other men. Justo's lack of respect for Fan-Tan had nothing to do with the man's following the insatiable witch stick between his legs, relentlessly plumbing a flow of fresh encounters. It had to do with Fan-Tan's public cuckolding of Renoir, a subject Justo considered himself a recent authority on, one that rendered him a victim of his own contempt. Renoir was revered on the island as a white-suited pillar of society, he carried the sophisticated certainty of a man at peaceful odds with himself. Like Justo, Renoir's roots clung to the coral core of the island's history, he too believed in the accommodating system of weights and balances governing the island's daily doings. Beyond this belief Renoir perceived an existence on the island incapable of being understood solely in the lifetime of one human heart. What could be observed through the pinprick eye of Renoir's alert soul was that ghosts of pirates and wreckers had never vacated their island roost, still stalked the narrow streets, haunted bars, their tattoos glowing in time's dark vault. Renoir's finely tuned inner ear was forever cocked to hear distant swords and knives rattle, links of gold chain clank, ship planks groan. Deep in his piratical heart Renoir perceived Key West as an outlaw island of men, a Dodge City perched on the edge of the Gulf Stream, where men tolerated women the way sailors always tolerated them, in port, as diversions. Women are never at sea with men, never, that is the rule, the law inscribed in the bible of all ancient mariners, the one true lyric sung by every son of a sailor at sea, that a woman aboard ship will bring bad luck. For mariners, death is preferable to bad luck. Key West was an island at sea, an anchored ship of love pirates and dream wreckers, riding out tides of inescapable fate. If women were to mix with men, the devil lurking under the island rock would breathe a wind of doom to fill the sails of modern times with death and destruction. Renoir believed this, believed it as fervently as his father, Isaac, believed the opposite, seeking his salvation in the cradle of womanhood. Renoir was no simple supplicant at Apollo's white altar, he was a man among men who had forged a philosophy from the primal credo of the sea. Renoir lived and loved by that philosophy, flew the flag of his sexual politics at high mast, no matter how stormy the port.

"Floyd's alive!" Renoir shouted into Justo's ear. "Good God, Floyd's alive! Look, his chest is moving!"

Justo's kiss of life was being returned. A gurgle of breath escaped from Floyd's lungs into Justo's mouth. Angelica pumped the heart harder. Justo pulled away from Floyd's lips, pushed the flaccid eyelids open. Floyd's irises were startled with recognition of fear for what might have been.

"Give him a couple more hard pumps," Justo prompted Angelica. "Okay, that's it. You were great."

Angelica was able to look at Justo for the first time, her breathing heavy, exhausted. "We brought the mother back."

"*You* brought the mother back." Justo grinned as he stood, stretching a pain out at the back of his knees.

"God, Floyd!" Tears of relief flowed from Renoir onto the face cradled between his hands. "Oh God, honey, don't ever try that again." Renoir bent his face close to the quivering gray lips. "Never never again, please. I'll take care of you. I won't abandon you, promise . . . promise."

"I'm going to call an ambulance." Justo tried to reassure Renoir. "Floyd should be X-rayed, his spine might have been injured."

"No!" Renoir turned painful eyes up to Justo. "No hospitals. I can take care of him."

"That's not the point, he's—"

"Stay out of it!" The pain in Renoir's eyes turned coldly defiant.

"Look, it's the law. I wouldn't be doing my job if—"

"Your job's got nothing to do with it!" Renoir's voice exploded in a screaming ache. "What do you know about it? Nothing! I can take care of him! Don't think I can't!"

Justo reached a hand down to help Angelica up. "Guess we better leave." He felt a tightness in his chest. The emotion pouring from Renoir embarrassed him, it was as if he were witnessing an excruciating confession of love and cry for forgiveness. What was to forgive was not for Justo to know. What Justo did know was these two men should be left alone in this private moment of recaptured life. Justo slipped his arm around Angelica's waist as she stood. He did not care if anyone saw this gesture of affection in the full glare of a new morning. He walked slowly with Angelica around the crescent of beach. "Where'd you learn to pump heart like that? Had no idea you knew CPR."

"You work in a bar, you have to know it. Never can tell when some drunk is going to choke on his martini olive." Angelica leaned her body close to Justo; an intimacy had been shared between them this morning, far different from the one either originally had in mind. They were now bound together in a way stolen moments beneath sheets could never achieve. "Do you want to come home with me?"

Justo laughed nervously. "Somehow I don't feel very romantic." He rubbed his lips with the back of his hand.

"I didn't mean for what we had in mind before." Angelica looked at Justo with surprise. "I meant only for a cup of coffee or something. Feels weird. Just don't want to be alone, that's all."

Justo did not like himself for what he was about to do. He knew all through the early morning he was headed for a wetting, now it had taken place, he was not going to go home with Angelica. He tried to change the subject. "Feels weird to me too. How did you end up with those guys out there?"

"I was driving slow to see if you were still following, thought maybe you had tricked me and weren't coming. When I was passing the compound, there Renoir was, waving."

"Wonder why he didn't wake someone up in the guesthouse, or use their phone?"

"Panicked, I guess. Sometimes people do the opposite of what makes sense when they get in a tight situation." Angelica stopped and slipped from the protective grasp of Justo's arm around her waist. "Just like you."

"What do you mean?"

"Are you coming home with me or not?"

Justo was caught in his own trap. Angelica was right, he was going to choose the coward's exit. "Another time." He leaned and kissed her.

"Okay." Angelica laughed, reaching up to smooth his cheek with knowing fingers. "Another time."

Justo walked with her in silence along the beach, the sexual connection between them broken, replaced by something more substantial. In front of the high wall of the compound he watched Angelica drive away into the dying sunrise. His thoughts went across the island to Rosella rising from another night alone. He was indeed a very hungry man. He thought of his daughters shaking off troubled teenage dreams. He was a husband and father. He walked to the phone booth on the street corner and dialed the chalked number he memorized hours before in the Wreck Room. Justo had not wanted to do it this way, did not want Zobop to know he was on his trail of dead goats and cemetery poetry. The phone rang twelve times. Justo was about to hang up when he heard the click of reception followed by long silence. Suddenly Justo recognized the number he dialed. The rum-soaked syllables coursing through telephone wires were hesitant but unmistakable. Justo hung up. A Green Sailor looks north? The last voice on the island Justo expected to be on the other end of the line was that of St. Cloud.

16

SOMEWHERE along the way I lost the way and Lila became very fleshy, attractive to the bone, a seductive spice flowing in my veins." As his words slipped into late afternoon humidity St. Cloud kept an eye on the scorpion slithering down the yellow pine of the bedroom wall, its anchor-shaped tail poking nervously at the air. "She's more than a spice. I'm a hopeless junkie."

"Junkies are made, not born," Isaac wheezed. "Junkies mother their own monkeys and pack them around on their backs for the world's applause at self-destruction. You're no self-made junkie, you're a born fool, big difference." Isaac rolled his head on the pillow and joined St. Cloud's tracking of the scorpion's progress. "Anyway, the whole world loves a lover, and you're the second biggest fool for love alive after me. Don't understand your problem, other than it's been man's problem with woman since Eve sucked the worm out of the apple before offering it to Adam. No man has ever been handed more than an apple riddled with empty worm holes. You won't be the last to find out an apple a day won't keep the devil away. Peach nectar is not a bad tit to suck." A tiny gurgle riding a laugh came from Isaac's throat. "I'll be fucking angels soon." Isaac turned from the scorpion and winked. "What do you think of that? Feathered strumpets and golden trumpets for eternity, what a way to be dead."

"Think I've gone around the bend." St. Cloud spoke instinctively, without taking Isaac's offered exit of humor. St. Cloud was not going to quit at what he had come to say, at what he was trying to get at. He felt like a man trying to commit suicide, calling a friend in a fit

199

of crying drunkenness, pleading to talk, to be walked in friendship
back to reality.

"Just what *are* you trying to say?"

"Think somebody's trying to kill me."

"Haaahrumph!" Isaac snorted and turned back to the scorpion's
descent. "You deserve to be shot, damn fool, nothing but a pitiful
love bandit. None of us deserve to live, so what? You going to smash
this scorpion or let him bite us on the ass?"

"Let him bite us, we both don't have long to live anyway. I'm telling
you, Isaac, I might be killed. Just want you to know why, that's all.
Not that it's any big deal, just wanted you to know because I thought
you'd appreciate the reason. I'm sure it's got to do with my loving
Lila. Some kind of crazy Romeo and Juliet thing and I'm playing
both parts, but she's the deep off-stage shadow in the play. Something
hidden within Lila I can't get to, a danger there which doesn't want
to be unearthed. I'd kill for Lila. Justo says I already have, myself,
because I'm losing my mind like this, killing off my common sense.
Still got sense enough to know someone's out to off me. I'm not
talking the usual cocaine paranoia down here. I'm talking someone
desperate to get me."

"Tropical witchery is more like it, son. This girl's sucked the sense
out of your head and left you with balls for brains. Why in hell would
anyone want to kill you? Don't watch yourself the girl's going to do
the obvious, like they all do sooner or later, leave. Then you'll end
up pathetic as batty old Count Cosel, jerking off every night into a
pile of cottonballs. Young women in the tropics come and go, you
know that. They come and they go, but they don't grow. They just
go. Get ready for it. That's the real death you've got to face, the exit
of your Southern muse."

"Did I tell you earlier, I keep hearing strange music?"

"Hahrumph!" Isaac's bony chest heaved in a gasp of disparaging
air. "None of us deserve to live. Wonder we don't melt in our baths
as Picasso once said. Let me tell you about one of the dumb things I
did when I crossed the great forty-year-old divide. Took my easel out
of the studio, away from all the models, up to the mountains, got
myself prepared in the darkness, peered from behind the easel out
at the edge of the world, eager as a boy awaiting his first erection.
Was going to paint that sunrise quick as a snapshot, eternal as mc–
squared equals the banging dawn of creation, make a painting in the
new world between instinct and intellect, dismantle all color theories,

prove rainbows were only God pissing on earth. Was going to get that rainbow in a bottle, freeze it in time, pin it like a butterfly to the wall. Thought I could do that. Thought I'd learned enough at my advanced age to *un-teach* myself. There I was, poised on the moment. The canvas before me, brush in hand, wet palette of oils at my side. First light leaked from the heavens, birds broke song, sky cluttered a thousand colors in my eye. Awed and amazed I turned to stone. Broad daylight crawled over me, intense glare after color, empty canvas staring back at me." Isaac's words stopped, his bony chest swelling with another exasperating heave.

The scorpion was almost to the baseboard of the bedroom wall. "You didn't get it?"

"Course not, no fool can, or maybe only a fool can and I'm a failed fool. We know it's all abstraction, apparition. When you see a sunrise painting you are witnessing the pitiful subjectivity of the lousy artist fool enough to try and paint it. It's all illusory illumination, pure falsehood of light. The light's not important, it's the darkness preceding it, defines it, that place before there is life. That place defines this place." The scorpion touched the floor. "Do you get it, son?"

"Yeah. Now I know why you only paint women."

"*No!*" Isaac pushed his thin body higher on the stack of pillows. "That's not the point. The point is to try and paint your way out of the dark cave before creation, to constantly reinvent yourself. The point is, St. Cloud, if you want to go back to darkness I'm not going to try and stop you. Not going to hand out an intellectual argument as to why you shouldn't. Go ahead and travel back to darkness, smug as a wrong-way fetus, but don't moon around about getting killed over some Southern yam pie. You're too smart for self-pity and I'm too old for bullshit."

"Let me tell you about the strange music."

"Goddamn it, man, you haven't heard a word I said! I'm talking a painter's light, not radio romance."

"Music and light are connected." St. Cloud took Isaac's frail hand from the air and held it securely within his own, rubbing the blackened veins. "I appreciate what you're trying to tell me, and you are right, except I've got this strange music playing in my ears, a high-pitched squeal."

"Sounds like an island hawk."

"Yes, and until now I only heard it at night outside my bedroom window while I was in bed with Lila. I'd go outside and look around, but the bushes are too thick for me to make anything out. Hawks don't hunt late at night. This is something else, sounds almost like a tin whistle."

"Sounds more like you've got somebody lurking in the bushes who likes getting a look at your peach nectar as much as you do."

"It's been going on for some time. Sound is growing manic, unnatural."

"Maybe your peeping Tom whistles through his teeth while he watches you worship your Aphrodite. I might whistle too. Reminds me, where's Angelica? Where's Renoir? Supposed to be here, it's a wednesday. Maybe Renoir finally got the right idea watching Angelica posing for me across a year of wednesdays. Maybe they've run off together. I could die happy."

St. Cloud watched the scorpion slither to the floor, hairy tail twitching for action, then heading for the brass bed. "I phoned Angelica this morning. No answer. Another thing. Someone called me at dawn, then hung up."

"People get wrong numbers all the time, or maybe it was this Zobop guy. You told me you were going to have Angelica put your phone number on the Wreck Room chalkboard and sign Zobop's name to it to see what you could snag."

"Only action I've had on that one was two guys calling me for dates."

"Getting any more poems nailed to your front door with a chicken claw?"

"That's what I was going to tell you about earlier, it's what I meant about the music getting stranger." The scorpion slithered to the brass foot of the bed, bumped its head against the shiny metal three times before deciding to attempt the ascent. "This morning after the phone woke me up I heard the whistling outside again, very shrill. I stepped out to look around. Perched on the power pole above the cactus tree in my front yard was a hawk giving me a hard stare. It whistles and wheels off across the metal rooftops."

"Told you it was an island hawk."

"Thought for a minute it was a hawk all along, the two whistling sounds were so close. Turned to go back in and nearly tripped on a glass jar, the kind women used to can fruit in. The jar was on the top step where I couldn't miss it, very old and scratchy, filled with stuff."

"Filled with peach nectar." Isaac winked. "Keep rubbing my hand like that, feels good."

"Filled with rusty fishhooks, bent coins, twisted nails and another poem, its scribbling hard to make out, done with one of those felt-tip pens again."

"What's your friend Zobop got to say for himself now?"

"You remember what the poems nailed to my door said about a Green Sailor and the Cuban Martyrs?"

"Sure."

"This is even stranger. *Eight palms point the way to two thousand souls entrapped by barbed wire.*"

"That's it?"

"Signed, *Zobop.*"

Isaac turned his head on the pillow, the scorpion was eye level with him, wiggling its body on the ornate brass curve of the head stand. "You know," Isaac rolled his head back toward St. Cloud, the wrinkles of his face cracking into a smile, "you might have something more real than cocaine paranoia or alcohol guilt after all. Something going on, but I don't think it's any more than the usual hanky-panky what takes place on this island. Could be nothing more than a jealous Cuban who wants Lila and he's paid to have a Santería love hex put on you. I remember the old days here, I'm not talking of the Devil Dancers dressed in burlap with animal masks on who used to parade Duval Street. I mean the stuff going back beyond that, stuff that happened south of Duval, in what was called African Town. Your friend Justo knows, ought to ask him. There was a time when people in secret societies would kill anybody who revealed an evil truth. I'm not saying that's bad. In our society someone reveals the awful secret of how to make an atomic bomb in his basement and becomes a national celebrity. Seems to me you ought to get Justo's Aunt Oris to make up one of those lucky chicken wishbones like he wears. Never know, might work, saved Justo's ass more than once. There's a Conch woman lives across town by the old lighthouse, still throws a glass of water in the street every time a stranger strolls by her house, wants to wash away all those evil germs from nonbelievers, ward off bad spirits. There's a lake in front of that woman's rickety shack, even in middle of summer. People have a way of finding their own devils."

"Good idea to bring in some outside protection. I'll talk to Justo about getting a lucky bone." St. Cloud took Isaac's other hand and began a gentle rubbing between bone-thin joints. "Maybe I'll get Lila a lucky bone too."

"Can't hurt, might be somebody more lovesick over her than you, someone else who loves women too much, finds the perfect one and loves her to distraction. Distraction is the envy of evil. You're more distracted now than ever. Your hands are strong, I can feel, but they shake more than mine, not just from the booze either. I'm not saying you should give up drinking, nothing that severe, not worried about your swimming out of the hole of alcohol you've poured full in your life. What does worry me is you might not make it across the great forty-year-old divide with much of that fine mind left. I'm banking on you to make it. Don't let me down like Renoir, be a man, be a man for all men, to all women. It's important for men at my age to pick out a younger man and root for him, pass the torch. I don't want to see you hoodwinked by a Dixie charmer desperate to hook a husband who will keep her in credit cards and babies. Remember, women you fuck are the sum total of every man they've ever slept with. You don't have the slightest idea about where this one has been. As they say up where she's from, beneath every soft southern belle's nipple beats a heart of pure gristle. Be careful." The eyes in Isaac's shrunken face shone with the truth of worn chestnuts. "All of these moments we have here on earth are stolen, the trick is to never stop stealing, never stop with one woman, go on to the next. It's all about women in the end, all of them pretenders. That is the journey, to find the greatest pretender. As time runs you down one truth wears you out, the women get younger, the days get shorter."

The purple lids of Isaac's eyes weighted to a close, his hand slackened within St. Cloud's caressing grip. A fist of fear closed around St. Cloud's heart, perhaps Isaac was slipping away to the land of feathers and trumpets. St. Cloud looked up, his gaze escaping from the bedroom of the Bahamian mansion through high French windows, across the Atlantic's flat doldrums to the thin blue horizon which marked the last exit for everyone on the island. Maybe now Isaac was gliding out there, over clear water, through the illusive Green Flash, into false light, his body cut from space, pursuing the answer his lifelong chase of women across acres of stretched canvas thick with bright oil paints never yielded.

"Saw colors so beautiful, standing pricky as icing on a birthday cake. Maybe there is more than false light after all." Isaac winked. "Goddamn man, what are you whimpering about? I'm not going anyplace. Told you long ago, I'm going to die in the saddle." He smiled at the scorpion inches from his face, its slender stinger probing the unknown. "My little friend, time to take a ride. St. Cloud, you can toss him out now."

St. Cloud scooped the scorpion into his hand and hurled it through the open shutters. He turned back to Isaac. "Some day you're going to be stung. That will be the end of you, not doctors."

Isaac spluttered short yipping sounds which trailed away into a cackle. "I've lived with scorpions all my life. Nobody's ever been stung by one in grandfather Isaac's house, never will. Got to protect scorpions, don't, rats will overrun the place. Not a rat in the house. Rats or scorpions, one or the other, must choose."

"Think I've got both."

"You've got trouble, one has to go."

"Not up to me."

"No." Isaac turned his head toward a noise at the open doorway, glimpsing a shadow on the outer hallway wall. "It never is for people to decide. Rats and scorpions make their own decisions, don't know which it will be until the very end."

Renoir appeared in the doorway, thinner than the shadow he cast, paled to a ghostly silhouette in his white suit.

"What are you," Isaac called to the shadow-thin presence. "Rat or scorpion?"

Renoir ignored the question, moving quickly to the bed and taking his father's frail hand, feeling for the feeble pulse. "Have you taken your medicine?"

"Have I taken my medicine?" Isaac coughed himself almost breathless before answering. "God yes, but no thanks to you, you weren't here to give it. Where were you? The medicine I need now is a dose of Angelica's creamy thighs, have you ever noticed there are four distinctly different flesh tones between her knees and navel? She's not a blond at all. Where is she, the little cheat?"

"Probably spending the afternoon with her daughter, since she works nights."

"Tell me." Isaac sucked what little breath he had in and held it before exhaling his question. "Do you think Angelica is a rat or scorpion?"

"What are you talking about?"

"Got to be one or the other."

"It's not that simple, Father. There are other choices."

"There are no choices. You either love women or you don't."

Renoir released his father's hand. "Won't you ever let up on the heterosexual heroics, even now?"

St. Cloud feared Renoir was losing his ability to hold back his true feelings. Through the years Renoir had not so much succumbed to, as suffered, his father's constant emotional purges. There was an attitude about Renoir this afternoon of a man cornered, ready to strike back. Usually Renoir treated his father with a detached air of bemusement, observing the operatics from a safe distance of wit, often countering with his own brand of sexual bravado. St. Cloud was aware lately of a slow dissolve in Renoir's demeanor, not just the man's physical thinness going thinner, but a rope of some stark reality being pulled tight within, stretching to final breaking point.

"Guess I better be on my way," St. Cloud stammered.

"Sit down," Isaac patted the sheet beside him St. Cloud had just vacated.

St. Cloud sat awkwardly. He had always known Renoir was deeply hurt by his closeness to Isaac, the easy man-to-man rapport, the uncanny way in which both seemed to have the other's thoughts. In the past Renoir turned that hurt to advantage, fashioned it together with his father's mad musings into a personal definition of precisely what he himself did not want to be. In the dulled light Renoir's right eyebrow arched, taut as a bowstring ready to release an arrow of truth. "Really . . ." St. Cloud started to rise from the bed again, feeling like a target for whatever arrow might fly. "Got to run."

"Don't go." Isaac's frail hand tugged on St. Cloud's sleeve. "Have something I want to give you." Isaac turned to Renoir. "You should know, St. Cloud is caught between obsession and distraction. He's come to me because I'm a lifelong authority on matters arising from the pursuit of women. Someone's put a love hex on St. Cloud and he can't stay drunk enough to avoid it. What do you think of that?"

Renoir's arched eyebrow went higher.

"What would you say if I told you someone was out to kill our St. Cloud?"

"I'd say," Renoir eyed St. Cloud through his threatening arch, "that the women of this world would heave a collective sigh of relief."

"Someone named Zobop wants to throw St. Cloud into a voodoo soup. How do you like that?"

Renoir's arched eyebrow flattened, his pencil-thin mustache drew thinner across his lip. "What was it you just said?"

"I said Zobop—"

"Somebody named Zobop spray-painted a yellow X across my door this morning. Sprayed it tall as a man."

St. Cloud had the illumination he always feared, a familiar nightmare stepped from intoxicated dreams and beckoned. There really was a Zobop leaving his calling card all over town. "Was there . . . was there any poetry written? Small pieces of paper maybe, with writing?"

"No."

Isaac pushed higher on his pillows. "Then how do you know Zobop slashed the X?"

"A signature was under the X. *Zobop.*"

Isaac's skinny chest expelled an exasperated gasp. "Just what we need in this town, a voodoo graffiti artist. One thing I can't stand is bad public art. St. Cloud, open that drawer." Isaac pointed a bony finger at the nightstand next to his bed, its top cluttered with bottles of medication.

St. Cloud cracked the drawer open, exposing more bottles, stacked twelve deep, elixirs to get a man up, down, sideways gone, or off the planet.

Isaac laughed. "Keep these pretty babies as my private stash, case some rascal doctor ever decides to cut me off. Pull the drawer all the way open."

St. Cloud slid the drawer slowly; at the back was the blunt handle of a revolver.

Isaac wheezed. "Take it out."

St. Cloud removed the revolver and slid the drawer closed.

"Been keeping that revolver for years. If a jealous husband ever showed up, I'd be ready. A sporting man can never be too careful, but it's no use where I'm going." Isaac raised his hand and clutched the front of St. Cloud's sweat-stained shirt, pulling him closer. "Might need it where you're headed."

"No." St. Cloud shook his head. "Made a pact with myself years ago while I was in the antiwar movement, no guns."

"Just what do you think?" Isaac's words were nearly breathless, rasping with urgency. "You think Zobop's interested in some pacifist pact you made with your starry-eyed college-boy self? Take the weapon. When you get that lousy voodoo graffiti artist in your sights, tell yourself you are plugging him for me, if that will appease your lingering nonviolent conscience."

"Don't want it."

"I do." Renoir grabbed the gun from St. Cloud's hand, slipping it beneath his white suitcoat and behind a thin alligator belt.

Isaac turned to Renoir. "The hell you say. You don't know how to use it, never wanted to handle one before. What do you think you're going to do with it?"

Renoir rose, an enigmatic smile creased his lips, expressing a cross between contempt and concern. "Homosexual heroics, Dad. You and St. Cloud go back to discussing locker-room politics." His shadow disappeared through the doorway.

"Son of a bitch." Isaac's brown eyes shone once more bright as worn chestnuts. "We must stay alive for this, St. Cloud. My son's got some of the old man's wood in his pecker after all."

17

S T. CLOUD was a rat. Until now he thought himself a scorpion. Lila was the scorpion, the choice had been made. Rats had gnawed through the core of his rum-soaked soul and nested. He was a less than cunning rodent who could not control his desire for the inevitable numbing scorpion sting. A grand confusion clawed into his normal emptiness, what he had lost with Evelyn he felt he could renew with Lila. He had baited a trap with the meat of nostalgia for the man he no longer was, the trap was about to slam shut. The nausea that shook him awake each morning after a late night of drinking launched him into another day of feigning that he was a human being. Physical wretchedness had become a welcome tonic, spiritual debauchery was the dulled diversion he craved, plucked the wings from his wobbly flight, settled him down to grounded reality. Someone meant him great harm. Zobop was the least of his problems now. Someone meant to harm him wholly. He suspected that someone might be himself.

I myself am not myself was a consoling sentiment St. Cloud had stolen years before from a dead poet. He believed this sentiment demarcated a jumping-off point to the infinities of his own existence. The poet who penned the thought walked away from his life one day into California's high mountains never to return, an early soldier of faith missing in action. St. Cloud only now realized the poet walked into his life, not away from it. Perhaps his own flight from California to Florida, from youthful ideals to a fountain of hopes, was his way in, not out. St. Cloud composed himself with the fidgety anticipation of a man standing at the gates of his own disappearance. Beckoning beyond the gates was the disturbed vision of Lila, indistinguishable between love and desire. Lila was an ache of confusion, a bruise on his soul, spreading inevitably as a warm wind steals south each winter to escape trees hung with frozen oranges. Heat from Lila's lips burned through St. Cloud's skin, melting the rational ice of his mind. As his passion deepened, the petals of Lila's true purpose yielded final discovery, she was more than he imagined. Lila brought St. Cloud to the awareness he was far less the man than he took himself to be. There was serious damage in his eyes when he faced himself in the mirror, it could no longer be hidden. Worse, Lila's clear eyes gazing up into his reflected perfectly his inescapable predicament. Even when Lila's body moved beneath him, then was pinned by the muscled scissors of his bare legs, they both stopped, stilled in the moment, aware his damaged image played off the sea-green surface of her eyes, aware that beneath the bright marine surface Lila was drifting swiftly elsewhere, into a murky universe where St. Cloud followed awkwardly, a lost fool shadowing a foreign spirit, riding the tide of surprise to its final beach. Alcohol had pickled St. Cloud's bruised Piscean soul, his bones were fluid, fish scales covered his flesh, what he needed most was resilience. When he bubbled with a gasp back to the surface of the present after a breath-held diving pursuit of Lila's fleeing spirit, certain knowledge awaited him. Lila loved someone else. The deep off-stage shadow in the play was emerging.

Strange music pierced the windowpane above St. Cloud's bed, beaded sweat skimmed the edge of his body, falling like rain onto Lila beneath him. He was maddened with heat, Lila was improbably cool, her body dry, except for a slick of dampness holding him effortlessly between her legs. The strange music broke through the humming blood in St. Cloud's eardrums. He could not bear to face the marine clarity of Lila's eyes reflecting his image as she lay beneath him so cool. He would rather face the music than face that image; he turned to the strange music. Lila's fingers rose along both sides of his neck to intertwine, fingers guiding a tightening fleshy net. She pulled him down again, scent of magnolia flowing into his mouth. St. Cloud melted, sure as a cube of sugar in a hot glass of water. Strange music chimed in his ears, he was compelled to take up pursuit of Lila, only in such a moment did she leave a murky passage for him to steal through, penetrate her innermost thoughts, break into her submerged past. She allowed herself to cry and confide, until she came back to her beginning, and took him there too.

How young Lila was then, Miss Lila Sue-Lynn Defore, not much different from most other Southern girls next door, except a certain sullen beauty unmistakable from the start, which had males from nine to ninety crowding around, thick as moths swarming about a drive-in movie screen on a muggy June night. It was not that Lila was not smart, she just never had a chance. Like many of her sisters of that time, her cultural endeavors extended not much further than a twist of the radio knob to tune in citified country crooners from Atlanta slogging through their predictable lyrics with the professional plunk of house painters rolling on interior latex. Lila's beauty exacted a certain toll on the world, brought everything around up short, in her presence the usual dwindled to the inconsequential. The antiquity of Lila's beauty emerged not from hot Georgia clay, but from a time before men and women existed, a glimmer in a distant universal sky of what perfection could be if molded of flesh and blood. All of this existed beyond Lila's awareness, to herself she was simply the expected naked body reflected in the mirror. Lila took no more note of her image than a dog casually catching its reflection in a rain puddle. The manner in which men treated Lila she assumed was how they treated every other female, with jealousy and persistence, their crude insistence foreshadowing future guilt. Lila had brothers, she had sisters, they treated her as nothing more uncommon than a house sparrow, having seen her form and flower. Men came to the house for all the sisters from early on, such was not unusual, but something did occur which was. When Lila reached eighteen men stopped coming around, even the boys she knew from high school no longer fumbled on the phone for dates. Lila had become intimidating. A grace gathered round her beauty, forging a magnetic field of protection which put off the young and unwise. After a time this magnetic field inverted its own law of protection, coming to attract first the soundly stupid, then the profoundly dangerous.

Roger "At the Ready" Johnson was soundly stupid. The stupidest thing Roger ever did was marry Lila. Roger liked to brag before he was killed that he was the cleverest boy in the marijuana patch. Hadn't he snared himself the catch of the county? And all Roger had to do to win this trophy was accept an invitation to dinner. Roger had not been invited to Lila's family home by Lila, but by Lila's mother, Margaret-Lynn. At forty-eight, with a trick or three up her sleeveless dresses, which showed off a shape to keep up with the fast curves of her best-looking daughters, Margaret-Lynn was not so much concerned her last unmarried daughter would sit home alone another friday night, as she was frantic her third husband, the one she married when Lila was a little girl, was after their last big fight not going to come back to her, ever. Margaret-Lynn thought Roger might appreciate one of Lila's special kind of home-cooked meals, then maybe a glass of California wine, then maybe a few of Roger's special marijuana smokes, for Roger was always at the ready, biggest marijuana grower in the county, thirty-four years old with a mean laugh, twelve muddied four-wheel-drive vehicles, no bank account, and enough cash to buy himself a small country, which was not about to happen since Roger never journeyed beyond the large but isolated county he was born in, except to go to war. One thing sure, Roger knew the county's every back road and person, lawful or not. Roger was available and farm-face attractive, most of all he was wealthy in the ways of those locals who knew how to bid up the high side of a crop easily grown and in rising demand. Roger was also always ready to knock his women around, or walk up to a man and bite his ear off if he suspected he'd been soured on a deal. Roger had an eye for women well mapped out by other men, and a large belly for home-cooked meals, a man of simple tastes with a demanding appetite.

Margaret-Lynn was uneasy about whether Lila's cooking would altogether agree with Roger, for her youngest daughter's cooking was, well, not usual, some even went so far as to call it odd. Margaret-Lynn plotted her evening with Roger carefully, it wasn't her fault if her sweet youngest was eager to hide herself behind an apron in the kitchen. If Lila was bent on spending her days whipping up her odd fare, then it was the least a good mother could do to provide an appreciative male audience to woof it all down. Roger was good about it that first night he was invited over, though his goodness may have oozed from two joints he smoked in the cab of his high-wheeled pickup speeding on his way to Margaret-Lynn's house. That night Roger ate seven helpings of Grasshopper Mousse, country gentleman enough at the end to burp with appreciation and raise his glass of California wine in congratulations to the chef. Lila, not used to anyone saying anything about her cooking, since the whole family had grown accustomed to the unusual nightly fare, raised her own glass of wine and invited Roger, with all the genteel conviction of her Southern hospitality, "Y'all come back, heah?"

Late into the night after Lila's first culinary triumph Roger whirled Margaret-Lynn around the crowded dance floor at the Ace in the Hole Bar and Lounge, then spun her along twisting roads in his pick-

up and came to a hard stop before his forty-foot luxury trailer in
the woods. He hauled Margaret-Lynn down from the high-wheeled
cab and carried her past his barking pack of bloodhounds right into
the trailer's bedroom. With no words Roger cranked up the blare
of a country crooner on his expensive Japanese stereo, pulled
Margaret-Lynn's sleeveless dress off in one deft rip and caressed her,
never less than roughly, in prelude to physically thrusting his thanks
into her for earlier having allowed him to dine in the presence of
such a miraculously beautiful chef. In the morning, in the trailer's
fancy kitchen aglitter with built-in appliances, Roger ever at the ready
beat Margaret-Lynn to a black-and-blue pulp because she burned his
scrambled eggs. "How could the mother of such a miraculously
beautiful chef fuck up scrambled eggs," Roger screamed at a cowering
Margaret-Lynn on the kitchen floor. He tossed the rubbery mass of
eggs to the snarling bloodhounds, pushed crying Margaret-Lynn into
the high cab of the pick-up and took out across his fields of marijuana
growing proud as Iowa corn beneath the shimmering protective green
canopy of tall hardwood trees. When Roger shoved whimpering
Margaret-Lynn from the pick-up in front of the little house she called
home, Lila was not there, but Roger took up Lila's invitation from
the night before just the same. Driving away Roger shouted to
Margaret-Lynn he'd be back the next friday for a home-cooked
evening.

Lila never had a real Daddy. She had a Daddy, but to her he wasn't
real, since she never laid eyes on him after age five, by then there
was a stepdaddy who called her darlin and patted her on the head
for wearing such a prettyful dress. Maybe that is why Lila was attracted
to all the wrong things in Roger. Some people said it was the reason
she married him. When Roger came back for dinner the second friday
he brought the California wine, ten bottles. Margaret-Lynn said
nothing about anything, it was as if she had written a bad check and
now the cops were at the door demanding payment. But it was not
police at the door, it was Roger, talking loudly about his okra crop
with repeated knowing winks, so everyone understood it was marijuana
he was talking about, not okra. Roger crowed about how he had
invested wise and could keep his bloodhounds in squirrel hearts and
gator tails, and his own ass high and dry above the deep Georgia
winter mud when he rode over to the Ace in the Hole in a four-
wheel-drive machine. None of this mattered much to Lila, for as
unimpressed as she was with her own beauty, she was even less

interested in things that could be bought and sold. Lila had her standards, her life was not cramped, no more than any female American teenager's life is cramped who has television and the freedom of choice to turn its channels. One day, two years before Roger, when Lila was emotionally wrung out from all the country crooners crying on the radio, she had spun the afternoon TV dial in search of soap-operatic relief and come upon a new program direct from Atlanta, and she was hooked. Lila was fourteen then, when she walked in public she turned her shoulders in on herself to hide her full breasts. She always spoke softly, for no matter how inconsequential her conversations were, they broadcast quick as telegraphic messages to any male within a forty-mile radius. The day she found "Suzy's Southern Style Cooking Show" on television was not any different from any other day in Lila's life, yet it would in its way butter her future, slip her into a world she never suspected existed. She would spend the next two years of her life cooking just to realize how hungry she really was.

Suzy made Lila what she was, though Suzy remained less than what Lila became. Suzy appealed to the hallowed hominy-grit reality of Southern homilies, aiming her television show into torpid afternoons of housewives and brides-to-be seeking to spice up predictable home lives with retooled recipes for all things Southern, from chicken to chitlin. The afternoon Lila stumbled onto Suzy, Suzy was administering the final flourishes to Bayou Crawdaddy Jambalaya, but there was something about the way Suzy set about her task, a way in which her smooth white hands never seemed to touch the foods she prepared. Suzy's honey-colored hair swirled up in a coil above her forehead, where never a bead of sweat nor the slightest frowned wrinkle appeared. Suzy glided about the grandiose pillared TV studio set cool as Scarlett O'Hara preparing to single-handedly entertain an appreciative regiment of wounded Confederate soldiers. Suzy flirted and flittered, chattering away in intimate drawling syllables which conjured from thin air visions of Dixie Fried Catfish and Alabama Soda Cracker Shortbread. Suzy was having a party. Suzy never talked down to her food, it was as if someone else were preparing it and she was delighted to have been invited over to discover it. Suzy never mussed nor fussed, popping from the oven Tennessee Hush Puppies deftly as rabbits slipped from a magician's hat. Suzy ran a swell sorority of culinary gals. She never let them forget they were all in on it together, in on the secret of how simple it was to slay men at the dinner table. Yes

Ma'am, simple as Shoo-Fly Pie. If you did not know you were in Okra Gumbo country then you had no God-given Southern rights to be eyeballing Suzy's show at all, for it was certain you could not tell Florida Squid Casserole from Texas Tomatoes Stuffed with Succotash.

Suzy brought Lila along slow and easy, for Lila had caught the first part of the twelfth rerun of Suzy's twenty-part show. It was simple enough for Lila in the beginning to tackle the Ham Slice with Cranberries; from there she graduated straight up the ladder to the true purpose of Suzy's show, pride in Southern sisterhood. Until Suzy, Lila never thought much about anything other than the ordinary passing of the days. It took someone on television, who could not see Lila, to talk to her like she was a regular person. Lila listened. For some people, monks on a lonely mountaintop throw light into the dark canyons of life. For Lila, the sound of Suzy's spoon in a bowl whipping up a Natchez Rutabaga Surprise rang clear as a calling bell in the wilderness. Lila loved to cook, she just needed someone to cook for.

Roger dined on Suzy's Southern fare, prepared by Lila, for twenty-two fridays in a row, and popped one hundred bottles of California wine before he ever popped the question. It never occurred to Lila to get married, any more than before Suzy it ever occurred to learn how to well-grease an eight-inch baking pan when making Louisiana Walnut Fingers, but once encouraged in that direction Lila was not about to let the potential recipe for life's happiness slip through her fingers. Margaret-Lynn held her peace when Roger popped the question, figuring that maybe she got beat up because she was not the young and beautiful one who canned Red Pepper Jam, besides, there was a certain pride Margaret-Lynn had in her youngest when she tucked an apron around her waist, displaying her wisdom ways about a tidy kitchen. Margaret-Lynn cried at the thought of her youngest being married away, partially because she knew there would be no more Griddlecakes With Buttermilk Gravy dinners, but mostly because she could still see those bloodhounds snarling around Roger's trailer. Even so, in a county where most girls marry boys who go off into the service and take their new wives to foreign northern cities, Margaret-Lynn was glad Lila would be close, unlike her other daughters who divorced and then had to travel a goodly ways back home. At least Lila would not have such a long car ride when she wanted to return.

What Lila brought out in Roger was not his best, for Roger was not filled with a best or a less than best. Roger was filled with Roger, which was a steady way of life which had been going on in the county from moonshine bootleggers to Bible-thumping preachers to marijuana farmers. All that really changed over the generations was the brand of truck a man drove, or the breed of dog he fed his table scraps to every night. For some reason Roger's breed of bloodhounds never growled at Lila, he ventured the reason was they liked her Blueberry Ice Box Pie. Things went well for Roger and Lila in the trailer that first winter, straight through spring and summer, into fall when Suzy's television show went off the air. The problem was not that Suzy's show was canceled, the problem was what it was replaced by.

"Cooking French with Carl" was what Roger figured ruined his marriage at such an early stage, so he took to leaving the trailer early in the day for the Ace in the Hole until late at night, rather than hang around and see what that fruit Frog was turning his wife into. "Cooking French with Carl" was unlike anything Lila had ever seen. At first Lila resented the fact that Suzy's Southern sisterhood of lofty scents and basic aromas had been snagged from the heart of weekday afternoons. Carl anticipated Lila's misguided loyalty, he did not plead or beg for her attention, did not placate nor attempt to enjoin her in any new conspiracy. What Carl did was what Suzy did not. Where Suzy developed her intrepid troops through working the vein of vainglorious Southern smugness amongst the pillared antebellum splendor of her phony TV kitchen, Carl dared and challenged his nubile culinary novitiates to be something they never thought of being, open-minded. Open-mindedness to Carl was Continental cuisine, and on *the* Continent there was only one religion, French food. Carl made food, but he preached an implicit attitude of life. He wore a suit and striped tie on the TV set of his stainless steel kitchen, and he was not only ready, but insisted on, taking Lila places she had never dreamed of going. Carl used the stove and its blue-flaming gas burners as a magic carpet. He invited his "ladies" to blast off from the torpor of their Southern afternoons and join him, not as lover or sister, rather as coexplorers of realms both magical and historical. At the conclusion of each journey served up by Carl, one could sit down and eat dreams.

It started going bad for Roger with the *Sauté de Lapin Vin Blanc*. Roger liked it, but what he did not like was what it was called. Roger figured food was food, up until now he had been a good sport. He figured Lila learned stuff from Suzy that as a man he was not cut out for, sisterhood of the cooking Confederacy stuff, handed down from generation to generation to television station. Roger was an uncomplicated meatloaf-and-yams man who slurped his way through Lila's fancy Southern fare mainly because he wanted to devour Lila, whose body he had lusted after ever since the first night she gave herself over to him in the trailer as bloodhounds outside howled for more Blueberry Ice Box Pie. Roger could not believe something so perfect as Lila's body could exist outside the colorful centerfold pages of the magazines that cluttered his trailer before Lila threw them all out. What did Roger care if she threw them out? Nothing, he had the real thing. Now Carl the Frog was trying to steal the real thing in broad daylight of the television's afternoon glare. Roger wanted to drive to Atlanta and blow the Frog's pink guts all over the stainless steel kitchen, but he knew the Frog was too clever for that, the Frog had prerecorded his afternoon stunts. As Roger drank his beery brew and scowled his way through long afternoons down at the Ace, he burped in remembrance of whatever trick Lila had adorned his plate with the night before. Roger came to hate *Noisettes de Porc aux Pruneaux*, he especially despised *Rognons en Casserole*. The Frog food was fuzzing up Roger's capacity to do business as usual, the bloodhounds didn't bark anymore, his last marijuana crop got the leafy mold and smoked up acrid. He thought about where he had gone wrong, where he had softened. His mistake was he let Lila get away with any damn thing she wanted. He should have taught her early, should have slapped her gorgeous ass up red, then no TV Frog would have messed with her mind and jerked his chain.

While Lila whiled away her afternoons with Carl, patting pork chops dry with paper towels and arranging layers of leeks with a spatula into a buttered baking dish, she never dreamed Roger was unhappy with her, for Roger was always raw around the edges, scowled at the rough men who worked his fields at night, snarled at his bloodhounds when they did not challenge intruders, and glowered at any man in the Ace who so much as glanced at her over his can of beer. Roger was normally ill-mooded, his business was none of her business, her business was to be a faithful wife and keep the artichokes boiling. It came as no surprise when one night Roger drove up in the pick-up and slammed to a stop in front of the trailer, stomped past the silent bloodhounds, sat at the kitchen table and demanded to be served. Lila was not quite ready for him, he was early for dinner, but she was happy to have him there. She had spent one hour with Carl that afternoon learning all about *Boeuf à la Mode en Gelée*, a pot roast of beef in aspic dish requiring fancy footwork, combining a lineup of beef stock, gelatin, peppercorns, Madeira, seeded tomatoes, chopped parsley and garlic. It was a showboat concoction, one of Carl's favorites, loaded with history as to how it was served to French royalty seated for grand picnic luncheons on the vast lawns of Versailles. Lila presented her triumph to Roger.

"Goddamnit, don't want no more fuckin Frog food!" Roger sent the grand slab of perfectly done beef just past Lila's head, it thundered against the trailer's aluminum wall, showering an aspic rain. "Fuckin fed up," Roger screamed above howling bloodhounds set off by the thunderous crash. "Fed up and pissed off! Why can't you make fuckin American burger food!"

Lila never had a chance to answer the question. Roger grabbed her by the hair and whirled her around, slamming her against the aluminum wall into the quivering aspic slime. His clenched fist rose, ready to drive home the full meaning of his disappointment with his new wife's daily menu, when a crazy thought jumped in his mind, freezing his fist in midair. The serene beauty of Lila's face dazzled him, it appeared to be cut from the densest piece of white marble. His crazy thought was, if he struck Lila he would be striking an unbreakable statue of stone with a fist of flesh and bone that would surely break. Roger dropped his fist and his crazy thought went away. "Get your coat!" He snarled his command with the same tone of brute arrogance he used when giving orders to truckers before they roared away from his fields with their baled loads in early fall. "We're goin dancin at the Ace!"

Like her mama, Margaret-Lynn, Lila loved to dance. Dancing was the one thing Lila loved to do more than cook, it was what she had before she found Suzy in the afternoon. Lila was a natural dancer, self-taught, a graceful breeze of a being on the roughest of dance floors. The night of the quivering aspic Lila sat silently in the pick-up as Roger roared along the back roads in a fury to hit the Ace. She felt a new sense rising within, not fear, but a feeling she had suddenly been put in touch with something important, strange excitement. The excitement was not aroused by Roger wanting to pulp her like an overripe tomato, but by Carl. Lila understood now what Carl meant earlier that afternoon, when he confided with a wink across the aspic frothing to a rise in a large copper pan over a stiff blue flame, "*I didn't learn to cook because I like to eat.*" Lila was discovering just what the true nature of her suppressed hunger was. Roger's quick turn to violence freed in her a pure daring newly born, for until now Lila never questioned her role in her own life. She was not going to stay with Roger; the surprise in herself was tonight she was determined to do something about it. When the flashing red glow of the neon arrow pointing from its roadside perch to the entrance of the Ace came into view around a snaking turn on the dark highway Lila knew what she was going to do.

Roger had one final act to play to exhibit to an uncaring world his wrath over the emasculating fact a sneaky prerecorded Frog had stolen his wife's affections and filled her mind with unfit thoughts. The act was to drag Lila onto the Ace dance floor and dance living hell out of her. Usually, when Roger danced with Lila, the men along the crowded bar were silent with covetous jealousy, and the women bottled their catty irritation with comments about how Lila never wore any nail polish, lipstick or underthings, but tonight there was more whooping and hollering than normal at a new band just fired from a big motel up on the Interstate at the outskirts to Atlanta. The boys in the band were young and mean and still pissed at the motel manager, who had fired them for encouraging their fifteen-year-old groupies to gather around the motel swimming pool in the early a.m. and slip their colorful panties off to pee into chlorine-clear water as truckers roared by on the Interstate with appreciative horn blasts. The boys in the band up on the platform were playing music from the sixties, and the ladies and gentlemen at the bar could get behind that, to the tune of reordering each other tequila blasters and rum busters. When Roger dragged his wife out onto the dance floor and threw her around to a chaotic beat so sinister even the boys in the band could not follow, the crowd grew appreciative and restless with anticipation. Either Roger's old lady was going to slap him in the face or run off with another man, it was clear, and people were taking bets on which was going to happen when.

What rubbed Roger raw, chafed away at him in even a worse way than Lila's philandering with the cooking Frog, was how she danced. It was not that Lila was a better dancer than he was, because Roger was never certain a man should be out in public shaking his ass anyway, so he did not figure he had to be very good at it. What worked at Roger was how Lila drifted away from him the moment they hit a dance floor. She never looked at him while they danced.

He was always forced to gyrate around into unseemly compromised positions simply to steal a look into his own wife's eyes. His gyrating was never of any use, Lila never noticed he was there. It made no difference what music was being played, Lila made her own, gliding away on it rhythmically into the deepening groove of a trance. It was then Roger could feel her cheating on him. He knew she was dancing with someone unseen in a far-off place. On the dance floor a spell was cast over his wife, falling thick as a blanket of fog between them. Roger never discussed this cheating with Lila, but it was always there, separating them, damp and impenetrable. Tonight Roger was determined she would have to notice him, if for no other reason than simply to plead for mercy.

Dancing stirred in Lila an intense feeling of escape, to her couples existed to split and spin from one another, into a place of uninhibited movement. Lila was as unaware of Roger's hatred of how she danced as she was of how she ignored him after they began dancing, for then he simply ceased to be, and she soared. But on this night of the quivering aspic Roger was holding her down. In the swirl of the crowd, and the ratty race of bad guitar licks screeching from the boys in the band, Lila felt her arms bruised from Roger's rough pawing. She struggled to find a familiar escape hatch of rhythm to sail off through. Roger's clumsy feet stomping on hers kept her earthbound. Each time she tried to escape his overreaching grasp he came bumping crudely into her, trying to nail the cast of her gaze with a mean glare. Lila was not soaring, she was for the first time in her life pinned to the moment on the dance floor.

It was never Lila's way to encourage the urgings of men toward her, a calculated shyness was her shield to fend off life's mounting tide of admiring males. What Lila never did was make loose eye contact with a man, but on this night, as aspic slid down an aluminum wall in a marijuana field filled with howling bloodhounds, her eyes swept the length of the bar, tangled with the only pair of male eyes not seeking her above smirking lips. Like everyone else at the bar, the man sat with his stool turned to face the dance floor, watching the spectacle of a husband trying publicly to stomp his wife, except this man was not leaning forward with leering anticipation, his back was pressed straight against the long counter. Lila felt his intentions coming at her heart like a knife, a pain uncoiled from him across the dance floor and coupled with her new sense of reckless being.

"I'm sick of it, Roger!" Lila shouted into the music, surprised at her own words, surprised they stopped Roger cold. She stood at the center of the dance floor, out of breath and alone. Something had finally gone right within her, an awakening which brought her up short. Without hesitating she walked over to the man whose pain was calling her. For the first time in her life Lila thought she could help someone, she never felt that strong before.

The man accepted Lila as if he had been patiently awaiting her all his life, he simply swirled around on his stool and ordered her what she always drank. Lila pressed in next to him and raised the glass he offered to her lips. Her body was hot and flushed, the man was strangely cool, yet she sensed her power over him. She did not need a key to unlock the steel door he kept forcibly closed between him and the outside world. What made him unapproachable to others made him vulnerable to her. Lila brought no history with her, having left her old life on the dance floor, that is why he had no lock to keep her out. Lila existed as an immortal moment, her awareness did not transcend the immediacy of her being, nor trouble itself with distinctions of distant times. As a Southerner her consciousness was flattened between the Civil War and Vietnam, those two conflicts crossed over in her mind and fused into a single notion of vague valor, for this reason she could not possibly understand who this man was, where he had been, and so approached him without fear. She could and did feel the pain rise from him, whether the pain's source originated in the fields of Gettysburg or the jungles of Vietnam meant less than nothing to Lila, and everything to the man she found herself next to.

What Lila did not know Roger did. Roger hated the man at the bar more than the way his wife cheated on him with a ghost while she danced. The man at the bar was not special simply because he had been in Vietnam, every bubba-buck in the county between the ages of thirty-five and fifty had been in Nam. The man at the bar was special because he had no allegiances. Because the man had no trust, he had no fear. The man lived easily as a python with an undigested rat in his belly. He did not sweat and he never got drunk, worse, he did not live anywhere in the county, appearing time to time from nowhere, hiring men to work for him. Mostly the men he hired were out-of-work shrimpers who drifted far inland looking for flatland work, mostly they were black and desperate. The man figured sooner or later these men were going to sicken and tire of being forever dealt a hand of four jokers, and finally would go out and take what nobody let them earn legal, which would land them in the pen. This was their lives, what they could not pay for in money they would pay for in time behind bars, such was the only measure of commerce they could count on. The man offered these men what they had not counted on. He offered them fifty thousand dollars to run boatloads of cocaine up through the Yucatán Strait. A certain percentage of them would be caught, they would do time in Mexican jails, that time would be paid for by the man, up to ten thousand dollars a month, until such time the man bribed the Mexican officials to let his employees go. The black shrimpers looked at the job as an insurance policy, one way or another they were going to do hard time in this lifetime, why not get paid for it? If they made it through the Strait without getting busted there was a cash bonus. So when this man showed up in the backwater towns along the Gulf between Mobile and Tampa, he was greeted as a Santa Claus in jungle fatigues, a one-man social security agency. Everyone said with a wink the man's occupation was selling maritime insurance. To some the man sold an alternate path through an unfair world, not to Roger. Roger had been in Nam and cut off a fair number of Gook ears himself, he recognized the man's sour swagger, a swagger most left behind in Nam, as well as the crazy gleam in their eyes. This man paraded his swagger and flaunted his gleam. Roger knew the gleam was not that of a killer looking for prey, it was the prey looking for a bullet. The swagger was not in the walk, it was the manner in which the body swayed between the magnetic pull of two poles.

Roger was a farmer and proud of it, a grower of good times and quality weed. Roger hated cocaine smugglers and figured sooner or later they were going to burn everybody's life down, or drown the world in white powder cut from Indian veins. Roger resented it when the man came into the county and every deadbeat sucked up to him to make a fast haul on a slow boat out of Colombia. Roger hated the little gold monkey skull the man wore around his neck on a thick gold chain. He hated the little white business cards the man handed out which read INTERAMERICAS MARITIME INSURANCE ADJUSTERS LTD., PANAMA CITY, PANAMA.

What attracted Lila was a silent scream rushing from the man she alone could hear. Lila knew indirectly only what she overheard about the man when Roger growled and blustered to his truckers that, mark his words, the cocaine sharpies were going to make the drug trade worse before it got better. Not that Roger did not want marijuana to stay illegal, he did. Roger wanted what he called "a fool's measure of fair profit." If corn was illegal Roger would grow it to get his fool's measure, but he did not want outsiders coming into the county jacking around the labor market with big money made on foreign-grown goods. The cocaine sharpies were doling out so much money it was getting impossible to find a bubba-buck to truck a marijuana load up the Interstate anymore for less than twenty times union wages. Cocaine was ruining the trade. Roger swore more than once if the man so much as looked in his direction he would feed the guy's balls to his bloodhounds. But until tonight the man never looked in Roger's direction, he talked only to those he somehow knew wanted to talk to him. The man had no friends, no connections with people outside business at hand, always traveled alone. Sometimes Roger saw the man speeding by in a fancy rent-a-car on an isolated back road, off to lay a pile of cash on the old lady of one of his bubba-bucks salted away in a Mexican can. Roger took all this in, bided his time, he was after all a man of crops and weather reports.

The boys in the band serenaded Roger, alone and befuddled in the middle of the dance floor, staggering beneath the spinning disco globe while his wife accepted the drink offered her by the man at the bar. It never entered Roger's mind any woman of his would walk away from him in a public place, make a clown out of an honest farming man. It happened, now there was only one honorable way out. Roger would deal with the man later. In a second he covered the distance between himself and Lila at the bar, grabbed her by the shoulders, spun what was his around and dragged it onto the dance floor. The boys in the band whooped with rebel yells and broke into their best honky-tonk tale of sorrow sung on the back of loopin guitar wails. Roger began his frantic stomping, he shouted at a totally silent and still Lila. "What's wrong with *you*, babe!"

Lila turned her back on him and walked out the swinging doors, across the gravel parking lot to the phone booth beneath the flashing neon arrow. Her fingers trembled but her mind was made up. She dialed the number, when she heard the familiar voice she pleaded, "Mama, I'm down at the Ace. Can y'all pick me up?" Lila heard only the first part of Margaret-Lynn's voice coming back through the line static; "What's wrong, hon? Has Rog—"

Roger's hand wedged the booth door open and tore the phone from Lila with such force its steel connector cable ripped from the wall. "Haul your ass into the pick-up!"

"I'm not going to!"

Roger pulled Lila from the booth as easily as he tossed heavy bales of marijuana up onto his trucks. "Goddamn bitches are all the same!" He snarled his revelation into the night. Lila stumbled beneath his grasp, small stones pricking her knees, trickles of blood tracing her legs.

"Roger, listen to me. I've decided—"

"What'd you say?" Roger stopped.

"Decided I want to live a—"

"Shut up! Not talking to you! Want to know what *he* said?"

From her crouched position Lila lifted her head. Across the gravel lot glowing red from the overhead sign was the man from the bar, framed in the doorway of the Ace.

The question from the man across the gravel came again, a flat midwestern voice. "Thought your wife might appreciate one more dance before you take her home."

"Sheeee-yit!" Roger's fingers opened in a quick muscular spasm and Lila was loose. "Just what I fuckin figured I heard!" Roger's words were not directed toward the man, nor toward Lila, his words roared in disbelief up to the flashing arrow. He calculated most men he met in his lifetime were born dumb, standing before him now was the dumbest of all come to collect his prize, and he was going to give it to him. Without another word Roger marched across crunching gravel to the pick-up, yanked the door open, reached up behind the backseat and unhooked the rifle from its window rack. Son of a bitch if some men don't have balls for brains, Roger hissed under his breath, for the life of him he couldn't figure such stupidity. He threw the safety off above the rifle's trigger and wheeled around, bringing the man up in the cross-hair sight. This was one dumb bunny Roger was going to gut-blast off the playing field.

The scream Lila thought she alone could hear from the man at the bar earlier she now heard from herself. The man's hand flashed, too late did she realize he had a gun. The crack of a bullet tore through Lila's scream into Roger's chest, wobbling his knees as he stumbled forward, the rifle still raised. Roger's eyes rolled upward toward the red arrow, something badly broken within him, something which would never be fixed.

Lila was afraid to move. Maybe the man with the flat voice was going to shoot her next. Nobody was coming out of the bar to help her. She knew they wouldn't. This was the way things were settled in the county. No one was going to get between anyone else's trouble.

Everybody had to make a living one way or another. Lila's instinct was to run to her dying husband. It was not much of an instinct. Roger's attempt to stamp something down in her had the effect of bringing something new up. Her voice was shaky but she spoke her mind. "Do y'all like French cookin?"

MK smiled, his foreign midwestern voice oddly soothing to Lila's Southern ears. "Long time ago in Saigon, had a Catholic girlfriend, all she ever cooked was French. Can you do *Coquilles Saint-Jacques*?"

18

EALITY'S submerged shadow took shape slowly for St. Cloud. Survival forced him to seek a new pollen to open the petals of Lila's true purpose. He turned his passion into the deeper intention of trust, trust became the pollen. St. Cloud crawled, self-effaced himself, committed acts of ruthless shame, all to gain Lila's trust. He had gone so far as to help her buy the pug puppy. During moments of confessional trust, as Lila's lips pressed against his ear in fearful whispers and conjured her intimate past, St. Cloud knew his callow plotting had succeeded. He did everything to gain Lila's person, swim with her soul, marry her flesh, sought against all odds the feverish flowering of her lithe body as it loosened to spin around his until he felt cocooned in a glistening moment, pooled in silk, then the silken pool would mirror, shatter, allowing disjointed shards from Lila's past to cut into her immediate desire. There was a fusion of ferocious intentions as their naked bodies pursued an inner distance across the expanse of white sheet beneath the dusty window above his bed. Ultimately Lila prevailed, coming through St. Cloud with the force of desperation, trying to satisfy hidden need, satiate enormous longing. It was then St. Cloud realized his competition for Lila's soul was more than a ghost.

St. Cloud had reeled a treasure up from Lila's submerged past, but the full weight of the bounty's apparent truth was slow in coming. Callow cajoler riding the tide of surprise to its final beach, his cunning had to be forever on the move, winning Lila over patiently one moment to the next. Lila had begun for him as untried female perfection, an exquisite statue he was intimidated by for fear its integrity would disintegrate if he tried to break down its parts. As the cracks in the statue revealed themselves, opened to expose veins of complication, the thunder of his ignorance deafened him. How wrong he had been from the outset, his crooked crawl of drunken pursuit of Lila, and the net of idealism he cast over her, paled against the brutal truth of her young life. Everyone warned him, even Evelyn, who tolerated his masquerades of romantic pain as she would a brother's, rather than a former husband's. Evelyn warned he was infatuated with an idea of his own poetic conjuring, had dealt into a rigged game where the joker was the dealer. Lila was far from the cool unruffled surface St. Cloud first imagined. He was no more than a worm floating at the bottom of a female sea, a blinded male whose pursuit of female perfection was driven by fleshy greed and unwieldy desire to bottle outright the sex of youth.

There were places Lila led St. Cloud he was not prepared to go. Months before, when she drifted alone during late nights from bar to bar along Duval Street, he was willing to accept whatever destination caught her fancy. Watching one night from a hidden vantage point in the jostling bar crowd, as she danced her way through a long line of suitors with the queer smile on her face fixed far away as if keeping step with an invisible partner, he made the discovery there was one constant to her desire to dance beyond the periphery of emotional attachment. The constant was Brogan. The mescal worm could have been messing with St. Cloud's brain, or rum was floating away what was left of his common sense, but it took him some time to figure Brogan's being in one or another of the dance hall bars Lila passed through was beyond coincidence. Lila was meeting Brogan clandestinely in the most public of places, a unique coupling of purposes. But what was the purpose of each? Brogan was not without his own style of attraction, despite his jaded past the desperate twinkle of a treasure searcher sparkled in his eye. St. Cloud figured Brogan too old for Lila; though Brogan was his own age, St. Cloud deduced he was the younger of the two, for he had killed off any hope of catching up to his youthful ideals, his abandonment of conscience entitled him to suck from a personally styled fountain of youth.

No tricks were required for Lila to meet Brogan in any number of back-door situations far from the prying eyes of a bar crowd. Lila could easily have gone to Brogan's house. What eased its way into the swamp of St. Cloud's inebriation was a notion simple in the extreme. Lila did not want to be seen going to Brogan's house. She never once brought his name up, never greeted him on the street. Lila spoke with Brogan only when she danced with him. Brogan was the only one she spoke with while dancing, that was the oddity. St. Cloud noticed, for he alone was trailing Lila on her late night sojourns, watching randy sideshow suitors hoot their lust, grovel for her attention, then run for another shot of bottled courage. What rose clearly from this confusion was Lila did not want to be associated with Brogan in any way other than what appeared socially casual. The reason for this was for St. Cloud to fathom.

The confessional bits and pieces of Lila's childhood and marriage to Roger came together and ended in the parking lot of the Ace in the Hole, where her new life began, and what brought her to Key West started. She never mentioned where she had gone with MK, for how long. Her history with MK eluded St. Cloud, until he made the connection with Brogan. St. Cloud had walked the wobbly plank of trust to get this far with Lila; he knew if he asked her a question, any question, about her past, the trust would be broken. She had to come to him on her own, her telling emerged from a new need. He had asked Evelyn what she knew of Lila, she knew less than he did. He admired Evelyn's targeting of people, in their early college days together at Berkeley she could, after five minutes in a room full of antiwar organizers, pick from the intent, moppy-haired radicals the five most likely to be FBI plants. Evelyn told him Lila's gorgeous flesh masked a hand grenade ready to explode. Perhaps the explosion had already begun with his infatuation, had destroyed his sense of reason. With reason or not, St. Cloud believed the duel for Lila was between himself and MK.

While watching Brogan and Lila dancing St. Cloud recalled the forewarning thrown out by Bubba-Bob in a distant and all but otherwise forgotten drunken night at the Wreck Room. "Be careful with MK, or you'll end up like Karl Dean at the bottom of the sea with sharks sucking your brains out." St. Cloud did not understand Bubba's meaning at the time. Bubba-Bob owed him a favor, maybe the warning was the favor. Karl Dean had been MK's boy, one of the best cigarette-boat runners MK had, he could maneuver a load of marijuana at cut-throat speeds through moonless nights across back-water flats better than any boat jockey from Key Largo to Key West. MK started Karl off when he was sixteen. Karl had already dropped out of high school for fast money off-loading marijuana bales from shrimp boats when MK took notice and totaled up the future for him, which came out to a zero sum. As a local boy fond of shortcuts Karl had one of two choices, move up in the trade or pump gas for the rest of his life while waiting for his mama to die so he could sell her house to a rich northerner. Karl was impatient, he did not want to wait for his mama to die; besides, his mama had just remarried. Karl was a flashy kid who fought with the other off-loaders on the shrimp boats, that's when MK noticed his quick hands. MK's instincts told him Karl could run a boat into tight spots where a man with a brain wouldn't. What appealed to MK was the fact Karl's brain was far slower than his body's reflexes; by the time Karl's brain told him not to do something his body had already reacted, like racing a loaded cigarette boat across a low-tide cut of coral even a fast-moving tarpon on the run from a fishing boat would not risk cutting his belly on. Working for MK Karl made enough money to buy him and his mama big houses on Big Pine Key where a man had room to stretch his stuff along the zigzag of dynamited canals far from the back alleys and claustrophobic lanes of Key West. Karl was happy until cocaine replaced marijuana as the high profit item sealed in the thirty-foot hull of his cigarette boat on late night runs. Things were getting riskier and more profitable, not as they used to be in the laid-back days of marijuana; the boys on the off-loading mother ships were no longer good ol' shrimpers, but fast Spanish-talking guys with excitable eyes and bulging guns tucked beneath their belts. Karl wanted his piece of the bigger pie. Since his brain was not smart enough to tell him to work for someone who would pay him more money, he started grumbling that MK let his people do with less than their just rewards. Karl's talk got so bad people walked a wide path around him. People were not afraid of Karl, they were afraid of what MK was going to do to him, they did not want to be around when he did it. It got so that Karl, who was a top gun on the off-shore power boat race circuit, was having trouble finding sponsors to put him up for a race. Karl needed sponsors, he couldn't sponsor himself. Where was he going to tell the IRS he got the money to race the whole season through in boats whose maintenance costs were more than the average man made in a year? He couldn't say he got it from selling his mama's house in Key West for a half million, he already did that to smoke-screen the houses he built on Big Pine Key. People knew Karl was in trouble when he couldn't get a sponsor for the offshore championship in Key West last fall. When Karl did get a sponsor at the last moment people thought, well, maybe MK wasn't so tough after all, maybe he had been gone from the island too long, running everything from Central America, maybe the Colombians with excitable eyes from Miami were moving on MK's paradise franchise. In the past no one broke from MK. Karl Dean broke. Maybe MK wasn't strong enough to teach Karl Dean a lesson. It had become a test. Karl Dean's cocky ways, and the fact he got a sponsor to race in the championships at the last moment, might mean MK was no longer part of the local accommodation. These were thoughts people had when Karl Dean pulled ahead last fall in the championship race. These were thoughts people no longer had when they watched the reruns of Karl Dean and his boat exploding into a rain of fiberglass and flesh. Karl's copilot, who ended up with him as shark bait, had a family in Sombrero Key, word was the family received international money orders from a Panama bank every month. MK took care of his own. People understood the lesson taught last fall. MK could make people grand with money, or quickly dead from revenge. When the Coast Guard inquired into the explosion of Karl Dean's boat they concluded the force of the blast was far greater than any which could have been generated by fifty gallons of jet-fuel held in the three on-board tanks, a blast of such magnitude had to have come from another source. The Coast Guard never ruled out the probability of plastic explosives, but there was not enough debris left floating on the water to make a definitive conclusion. People who knew MK had already drawn a conclusion.

Brogan was Lila's connection to MK, brother to brother. MK was not the only high roller in Key West, there were many others, high up and low down, on both sides of the law, who wanted MK put out of business, or the business put to MK. That was the reason Lila never went to Brogan's house. How innocent for Lila to be seen dancing one dance with Brogan, never more, then sending him packing like any other struggling suitor. If the wrong person knew Lila's connection to MK she could be used against him, her life bartered for vengeance in a sinister game not of her making. St. Cloud understood the ghost he was dueling was MK, but someone else may have made the connection too, Zobop. The high whistle St. Cloud heard outside his bedroom window could be a death tune, the scribbles of poetry nailed to his door could be a beast toying with its prey. Bubba-Bob's warning could be ringing true, to get involved with MK meant mayhem, if so St. Cloud could count his remaining days on one hand. Perhaps Bubba-Bob blundered onto the connection that Lila was MK's young peach, kept precious and hidden away in the backwater confines of Key West. Bubba-Bob was too clever a fisherman to declare publicly he had made such a discovery, he did not want to end up on the wrong end of the food chain, but he would tip off a friend he owed a favor about troubled waters ahead.

St. Cloud ceased being a bull rocking in a woman's sea, seeking the gyroscope's center of gravity to right the way; the grand confusion clawing into his normal emptiness left his less-than-steady hands shaking with anticipated dread. I myself am not myself, as the man said. A sideways slither is often the quickest way home. There was another bull now, standing between himself and MK, a bull of contention that existed long before Lila came between them. Justo was the one to define the bull for St. Cloud, often repeating his Abuelo's tale of *al alimón*, the blood dare, a duet of death fought by two matadors in distant Spanish times. Few witnessed *al alimón*, but it was sworn to have happened, the gypsy poets still sang its sad glory, to fight *al alimón* was less than bravery and more of blood belief, for the bull was fought by two matadors at once, armed with one sword and no cape, no lance-bearing horsemen to prick and harass the adversary. The matadors took turns meeting each charge of the bull by using the other man's body as a distracting swirl of cape; the alternating unarmed man was at great peril, using his body as a feigned thrust or protective shield. The man with the sword played his risk to the finest; if he did not judge correctly where he himself would have placed the human cape, he would drive the sword through flesh of the other man. No words passed between the two matadors, a false move by either meant death, their blood instinct facing the attacker must flow in unison, harmonious purpose preceded all thought. These two were beyond brothers, dueling in hopes of achieving blind faith; to escape being trampled their faith became at the moment of truth pure revelation. The enemy was not the bull, it was whatever might stand between these two, preventing them from becoming one mind, heart and hand with common purpose. If something stood between them their defeated blood would commingle in the dry sand of the arena.

Things were no longer so confused for St. Cloud, the burning hoop of completion smoldered before him, he understood the nature of the bull. The full-blown mystery opera of MK was revealed and St. Cloud was part of it, the odd circle after a generation passed had closed. The bull between St. Cloud and MK was Vietnam, the war of their youth bonded them to a brotherhood of outsiders, unless they could fight the bull *al alimón* they were condemned to die in the arms of each other's memories, their defeated blood commingling in the dry sand of a distant past, forgotten by a world long since moved on to fresh pain.

St. Cloud felt the rope of self-betrayal binding him to MK tighten with painful urgency; because of Lila he had to devise a way to cut through knots hardened by a generation of hopelessness. Lila could be the way out, St. Cloud had no misgivings about the origination of his fanatical desire for her. If he could convince Lila his offering of trust was the beginning of love, then he had started undoing the ties that bind. If MK was keeping Lila in Key West for the same reason, holding out a last hope, planning to return, then he would kill anyone who attempted escape on his magic carpet.

St. Cloud was determined not to let Lila down as he had Evelyn. He had started so young with Evelyn, but a man cannot marry his conscience. There was a purity of purpose in Evelyn from those early college days of protest which she still carried forward. Evelyn was ever graceful, slipping from beneath the weight of youthful illusions as easily as a snake sheds the skins of its seasons. He remembered when they met in 1966 during an antiwar march, pushing through the college town streets crowded with sign carriers, "HELL NO WE WON'T GO" screamers, and sound trucks blasting political accusations. St. Cloud sensed a sensuous purpose about Evelyn being jostled in the crowd, the crush of strident protesters accentuated her girlish body. He felt she was out of step with the indignant rhythm propelling marchers around them; his own outrage at bombs raining from B-52s on remote villages eight thousand miles distant was surmounted by an embarrassing desire for this thin girl at his side. He thought she could see his naked intent, that he was exposed for what he was; he tried to disguise his lust, wrapping an arm around her shoulders as if to protect her from the shoving crowd. What he sought was the sexual source of her commitment. He held her like a cripple clinging to a crutch. Slung around his neck was a pair of binoculars which gave him an idea. He suggested they get away from the crowd's determined militant air, things were getting messy, bottles were flying, glass was breaking, there was trouble ahead, a sure trap, he had been down these streets before, he knew. He also knew a way to the rooftop of the college bookstore, where they could survey the sweep of the entire protest with the binoculars, and his yearning for Evelyn could be spent, far above the heady atmosphere of idealistic histrionics.

They drifted to the back of the chanting crowd, along streets left deserted in the wake of the passing protest, then cut across alleys, ascending a rickety fire-escape ladder up a three-story brick wall and onto the bookstore rooftop. The scene below was not what St. Cloud expected. The familiar grid of city streets was laid out beneath them, the usual police barricades placed at busy intersections to force the march along an orderly course, but beyond the front line of the march, in the only direction the crowd could move between barricaded side streets, were helmeted police waiting with riot clubs. Through his binoculars St. Cloud focused on rooftops above the street where the march was about to come to a surprising end; the rooftops were lined with sandbags, manned by young uniformed National Guardsmen with mounted machine guns aimed down at the street. "Rats in a maze!" St. Cloud shouted into the din of loudspeakers and sirens swelling up from below. He turned away in disgust, a disgust aimed at himself. What a stupid way to try to end a war. Where the crowd was he did not want to be. He was going to stay one step ahead of the game, keep one foot out of the maze, ready to run from what he saw as an exercise in mass impotence. His flight from the madness of war would be his life, he would kill his life off in silent protest, turn his back on his future potential. As he peered through the binoculars on that long-ago day of his first date with Evelyn he could still hear her saying, "You're wrong. They aren't rats, you are the rat for running from it. You'll see, this will end it, but not for you." Evelyn's words still rang in his memory, with them he recalled the sound of the helicopters clattering above them on the bookstore rooftop, clouds of tear gas from the choppers' steel bellies floating into streets below, and he could no longer see, gravel pricking into his knees as he fell, his eyes throbbing as if pierced by a rain of cactus needles, a fire raging in his chest, a fire the eruption of vomit spewing from his mouth could never put out.

The differences were there from the beginning. Evelyn carried her ideals with her, St. Cloud was on the run from his. A man can't marry his conscience, but St. Cloud had been fool enough to try. He wasn't certain if he married Evelyn because he loved her, or because the shared idealism of their youth proved a stronger passion than the urgent sexual desire that originally brought them together. What Evelyn said about him from the first was true, the root of his restlessness could not be torn from him. He was part of the generation conceived under the cloud of Hiroshima and came of age during the

time of Vietnam, one of Uncle Sammy's marked babies. A strange
stain of guilt covered him, an implacable atomic dust gnawed at his
essence. Evelyn refused to allow the shadow of the cloud to keep her
shivering in the dark crevice of despair, she understood no one could
outrun the cloud, it is in the heart, forever. But the heart harbors
other things, the balances and weights of truth and survival, the
knowingness of when to shed the afterbirth of former selves. Evelyn's
sense of survival was stronger than St. Cloud's, she knew her strength
pulled him head over heels for her, but nothing remains the same,
nothing is forever, she taught him that. Maybe she hadn't. Maybe St.
Cloud would never learn, continue to fall in love with abstractions to
avoid the true lessons of the heart. Evelyn was lost to him as they
journeyed from those early college days of commitment, lost because
he could not find himself.

The unshakable guilt of Vietnam became St. Cloud's mistress,
swelling to disproportionate balance between himself and Evelyn.
Even in long moments of passion, Evelyn knew she shared St. Cloud
with something else, that he owed his allegiance to his assumed
collapse of bravado. She sensed he harbored his sexual energy, as if
it were a sin to spend his essence on anything more intimate than his
desperate sense of loss. What had been good between them in the
beginning went quickly bad. Evelyn could trace it to that first day on
the bookstore roof as the rain of tear gas clouded overhead; it was
their collective beginning and St. Cloud's personal end, for he was
powerless to shift the predictable course of the antiwar march below
in the streets, let alone derail the roaring train of history called the
Vietnam war, destined to derail in a crash of disorienting despair. It
was on the bookstore roof where St. Cloud surrendered his youthful
ideals. Watching the diminutive protestors in the maze of streets
below marching toward inevitable failure, he saw clearly that his way
was to become a warrior of the shadows, to trade his life for all-out
war on war, declare war against his own country, become a human
bomb, an incendiary physical device, an instrument of destructive
force equal to the destructive force operative in the steaming jungles
eight thousand miles away. To stop the war St. Cloud would have to
sacrifice himself, no quarter could be given, no reserve sought, by
necessity he must become the ultimate weapon, destroy the infra-
structure of his own society. Whenever bombs rained from bays of
B-52s eight thousand miles away he would provide equal explosions
in his homeland. Power lines, bridges, dams, roads, all would be

blown. The country would tremble beneath a violent finger of disaster pointed by one of its own. The bones of those who spoke broken promises would be broken, no prisoners would be taken. Release was to become a terrorist, a fierce wind of retribution culminating in one's own fiery reprisal. Release was the extinction of madness by madness.

Evelyn alone understood St. Cloud's innermost failure; he was incapable of crossing the line, could not pass the point of no return, could not justify what it would take to win. Even if St. Cloud could stomach it, even if to splatter the blood and bone of his own countrymen across a map of justified reprisal was imaginable, it remained in the end beyond his doing. It was not that he was a coward, it was simply he was not a killer. That is why he was against the war from its origination. He could not become a killer, even for a cause he deemed far greater than the mediocrity of his own existence. Evelyn understood the suffering of St. Cloud's soul. To what reality he finally emerged was not important; what was important was that he escape the Black Cloud, understand at last he was capable of change, accountable only to himself. Evelyn had discovered this truth within herself before she discovered St. Cloud, for it was not St. Cloud who discovered her in the mayhem of that long-ago antiwar march, it was she who was seeking him in her dusty sandals and thin dress, stalking the male wounded, sniffing for the scent of fear she knew so well. Though she was only twenty at the time she had traced in a few short years a lifetime of despair and guilt over the war eight thousand miles away, which was driving an endless stake through the heart of her generation. As she watched the stake being driven ever deeper it became horrifying to her that so many were unaware of its lethal presence, as if the stake had driven out the capacity for remorse, leaving a large part of the generation face down in a brain-dead field of apathy. This fact above all others drove Evelyn to desperate extremes, left her with the unmistaken calling that she alone must assume the agonizing guilt denied others. Antiwar marches and public screams of protestation were no longer enough for Evelyn. She felt compelled to pursue fateful acts. In the eternity of the few years before she met St. Cloud in the crowded streets of a college town, she had danced naked on a bar top in a roadside strip joint near the sprawl of a California airbase constructed in the midst of onion fields unfolding to the horizon. Evelyn's teen-aged body gyrated nightly to the thunderous roar of Vietnam-bound transport planes overhead, which dwarfed the metallic incantations of guitars from loudspeakers surrounding her. Smoky air swirled about her sweat-slickened turns on the bar as eighteen-year-old boys followed her every move. The hair of the eighteen-year-olds was cut recruit bristle short, their creased battle fatigues creaking with untried embarrassment as their upturned faces sought a reflection of redemption in the shine of Evelyn's stiletto-heeled shoes stamping out the wailing guitar beat on the bar top. The muscles of Evelyn's calves tightened within nylon stockings gartered by a lace noose cinched about her waist. Her fingers traveled an outline of breasts, up to shoulders thrust back as she arched, arms outstretched behind, a curved bridge beneath the overhead spin of a mirrored globe flinging light across faces excited by a stripped-down oiled body begging to be held as affectionately and with such wanton consequence as a recruit fondles his first rifle. After each of Evelyn's nightly go-go performances she would lead a recruit into the cubicle recess of a motel room next to the strip joint, take a bland sweating face between her two cool hands and gaze into eyes with hope carved from them with her sure purpose, like a fortune-teller melting the marrow of a new believer's bones. All the while the roar of transport planes shook the already trembling motel bed. Planes landed and departed on runways reaching to the horizon of open California farmland. White flowering fields of onions sur-rounded the activity of men on the runways, whose machines had no relation to the tilling of the earth. Beyond the runways, past the camouflaged hulks of barracks and galvanized metal warehouses of munitions waiting to be loaded, were grand piles of harvested onions, mountains of vegetables exuding a pungent odor of earth salt to sail the wind, powerful enough to bring tears to men's eyes as jet engines rent the air, as steel bellies of planes yawned open to offer bodies in green rubber bags inside stacks of shiny aluminum caskets, as long lines of recruits in green uniforms stood ready to march into the yawning bellies. The eye-tearing salt scent of onions traveled for miles, down the highway, past crowded go-go bars and topless-bottomless strip joints, through the whine of the sucking motel air-conditioner into Evelyn's flared nostrils as her mouth moved on a sweat bland face, her hips rising from the shaking bed to meet the thrusting weight of a shuddering body, at that moment her lips flowered with their true purpose, her heated words released into an unsuspecting ear: "*Don't go. Just turn your back on it and walk away. Hell no, don't go.*"

Evelyn could not stop a war, but she could start a man's conscience.

Some of the bland-faced recruits walked away from her bed, away from the airfield, drifted down the highway, distancing themselves from a killer identity before it was too late, abandoning their own names and families, slipping into neutral countries, or disappearing into the cracks of a burgeoning underground. Some marched to a new drummer of inspirational purpose, others were forever condemned to uncertainty, letting their hair grow long and their memories short, starting new lives, forgetting old hurts. In one way or another, those who walked away from Evelyn's bed with conspiratorial words ringing in their ears severed forever the tenuous thread that connected them to the mighty notion at play on the glistening tarmacs of the airfield of men leaving a country at peace to make war in another country. This severing happened not in a flash of illuminating cowardice or elevated consciousness, but in an unpredictable moment when a young girl surrounded by the air-conditioned wind of sweet onions whispered, *Don't go*. Some didn't. Evelyn never knew, Evelyn never counted.

Evelyn carried her message from the onion fields into the big cities with college campuses not yet awakened to the consequences of a stake being driven through the heart of the least suspecting. She looked the predictable type on a college campus. She looked neither for nor against anything, espoused no political cant and outwardly breached no social contract expected of someone her age. She quietly worked the fields of academe. At night, in her bed, her success was her swift surprise, her whispered avowed purpose. Naked college boys were into her before gauging the true depth of her intention. The boys rose speechless from rumpled sheets, tried to pay her or kiss her, but knew from the expression in her eyes there was only one earthly payment expected of them. Evelyn was there for *them*, presenting in passion's irrational moment the only rational way to pay the bill. She never knew if they did, never knew which way they drifted when the draft notice came in the mail. She didn't have the heart to look back, there were more colleges, all across the country, she didn't have much time, and when she felt she was losing the battle, she headed back to the airbase in the onion fields, to the bar top surrounded now by even more bland faces, not hundreds, but thousands: black, brown, white, red. It was in her heart her job to strip bare and mount the bar top, on the off chance a bland face would see reflected his road to redemption in the shine of her stiletto shoes. Long after the music stopped none of the bland faces, not those choosing to travel the thread from a country at peace to a country at war, nor those who drifted away to an inevitable uneasy peace with themselves, knew what happened to the all-American–looking girl who danced naked on a bar top in a neon-lit strip joint at the edge of onion fields. She became to them as much a dream as their own youth had become. They could not know she grew an independent life in her from those endless sweaty nights. Although the growth deviated from her avowed purpose, Evelyn let the forming human buried deep in her belly be.

Perhaps it was the season of killing Evelyn was in the midst of? Whatever it was, Evelyn could not destroy something in the center of her to keep others alive, to do so would give the lie to the who and why of what she had become. She too drifted off down the highway, but it would have to be a different way now. She chose a large city along the San Francisco Bay, where troop trains passed through. She lay down with others before the trains carrying cheering and jeering recruits leaning from open windows with fists of stiff-fingered Victory signs raised. She did this until she grew too obviously pregnant to be pulled from iron tracks by nervous troopers, led handcuffed to the siren wail of a waiting police van. Necessity dictated a settled existence, but not a still life. The coastal city she retreated to was thick with fog and young men hiding behind long hair and beards, men who one way or another had cut the thread between war and peace, created a limbo of exotic dope, chanted the lyrics of a brash new music making its own circular history, from this they prayed a new life would mushroom, for this new life they needed children not attached to the old thread. Evelyn lay among many of these men, although she had a new life of her own within, she had not sought them out for that purpose, but they quickly understood their hunger for her. The bearded men envied and stroked her as she watched for the one among them most desperate for the gruel of her avowed purpose. Finally she found one who had already been to the war eight thousand miles away, then climbed back from the end of the thread to his place of inevitable uneasy peace. His face was no longer bland, only uneasy. He had skipped being a man, had jumped from boy over man to become a killer, only nineteen. Initially he followed the thread from peace to war because his father had been a soldier in another war and was proud he too had a son to offer. The son knew little about war, only that his father needed his offering, so off he went eight thousand miles to prove the thread remained unbroken. Quick with his hands and possessed of fierce eyesight, he became a hog driver of a Chinook chopper. He learned in the air quickly, to feint and fake, zig and zag, jockeying that bitch hog through rain of hot onto any piece of smoking defoliated jungle real estate Charley had put a down payment on that day. He lived to be radioed in on top of the heat, he ate the rush of wind coming through open chopper doors, cursed his way through incoming zing, suck and slam of shrap hellbent on opening his hog like a can of worms, he waved and spit at the little yellow gods pumping blue-green tracers up from below trying to bust his metal bubble, bust his ass back down to klick zero. On he soared, to a cool pie-in-the-sky 2,500 feet and higher, straining rotor blades whining a song of freedom above the moans of blood-splattered wounded grunts slumped all around him. When he dropped toward the ground he stuck mean and low over sloggy rice paddies so close he could reach out and stick a phosphorus grenade up a water buffalo's ass, instant barbecue bovine for Charley and friends. Later, at night, he would bask in air-conditioned splendor, the jungle's mosquito hum in his ears, ice in his veins, vodka in his glass, opium in his pipe: *Migh migh migh said the spider to the fly* on the radio. Daddy would be proud. Son had proved it, saved the day, the mighty thread remained unbroken. A flyboy's dreams took flight, after all, he sought no wider war.

He sought no wider war, but soon enough little gold clouds began to pursue him, surrounding his earthbound body in damp dawn revelations. The little gold clouds came at first sporadically, so no one noticed. Then the clouds appeared more frequently, then predictably, until every morning he was awash in little clouds becoming a big cloud spreading on the bedsheet. No longer a daring flyboy, he had become a sailor adrift. He awoke to the acrid smell beneath him, and realized the barracks of snoring flyboys in bunks lined on either side of his had lost confidence in him. He was given an honorable discharge for a less than honorable situation. Uncle Sam cannot have his steel-nerved pilots running around in the jungle wrapped in diapers. He questioned himself into three parts. Was he pissing from fear of combat? Fear of death? Fear of retribution from his father? Three parts with one possible answer rising above all others. Was he a coward? He had gone from a boy to a killer to a full-grown baby wetting the bed. The army psychiatrists assured him of his bravery. Perfectly normal what had happened, happened all the time to the toughest in such stressful situations, when he returned stateside the problem would dry up in two or three weeks, he'd see. He didn't see, he panicked. A year went by and always the gold cloud was there in the morning. Nothing could stop it, not blocking out what he had done in the hog eight thousand miles away, not going on a week-long water fast. Even when he stopped eating it made no difference, he continued to piss the essence of his life away, piss himself down the drain. This played havoc with his mind, but it was secondary to a new problem, which was immediate and devastating. The problem never occurred in the jungle, but it did stateside in the city. He began to frequent bars in search of women, and because he loved alcohol, the numbing effect it had on his fingers, until all feeling fled and he had to work his brain hard to conjure what sensation of feeling in his extremities was once like. He kept up this alcoholic intake until the numbness took over his brain, and he forgot whatever he was thinking about, dead to the conscious world, exit of the benumbed. Around this time he became quite charming to women at the bar. He had no idea what he was actually saying, but whatever it was women were amused by it, by his reckless emptiness. The women took him home, but since he was without feeling in his extremities they had to support him, wedge their bodies under his limp arm, forming a female crutch, which would eventually give way, spilling him across a strange bed. After a while he would feel something, not actually feel something, but think something, then whatever it was disappeared and dawn broke with a great gush of a golden cloud, and he awoke to a woman screaming beneath him, struggling to free herself from more than just the excess of the previous night's antics.

The golden cloud stalked him everywhere. He would be standing on a street corner waiting for a bus when unexpectedly the cloud would break with a rush, an embarrassing rampant run descending the length of his leg, he would feel his pants, pat them down, but always they were dry. He would be waiting at a market checkout counter, struggling to hold the cloud back, but could sense its slow seeping, an implacable revealing leak, when he hefted his heavy bag of groceries he would steal a glance at his zippered crotch, all dry. The golden cloud was driving him to manic distraction, pursued him right into his dreams. All night long he swam in a yellow sea with no shore in sight. After awakening from near drowning, the bed sheet was always dry. Only at dawn, when he fell into deep sleep, exhausted from outsmarting the cloud, would a soggy reality finally overtake him. In despair he gave up women. He took to doing drugs, deducing their psychedelic and hallucinatory capabilities would dry out his impure thoughts, fry his brain, rendering him light as the magic feather which allowed Dumbo the elephant transcendent flight, high over rice paddies and circus tents, above bamboo hootches and steel skyscrapers, above all clouds. He grew his hair long and hid behind a beard. His once fierce eyes took on a distant watery look, two bottomless wells. This damp despair attracted like a dowser a pregnant woman he found himself stroking one night after he poured on the charms in a local bar. The woman was possessed with an invisible magnetism, a water witch of the soul plumbing his depths. He loved the round hill of her belly. When he burrowed his head between her spread legs he remembered anew what it was like to be with a woman. He lay an ear to her swelled stomach and listened to the far-off water sounds of another swimming being, floating in dark and foreign fluid, waiting like him to be born on a wave. The woman seemed to know everything about him he himself was afraid to tell. When she awoke with him that first morning, adrift inside an acrid golden cloud, she reached out and stroked his head like a newborn. *You shouldn't have gone*, she purred. *I'll stay until you stop this*. She never told him what he had done eight thousand miles away was wrong, she never spoke of the jungle. Finally the golden cloud passed from his life, into its empty space flooded unspeakable dread, an all-engulfing fear of retribution. What his father thought of his cowardly exit from the field of valor was the least of his problems now. He took to pumping needles into his veins, filled with any new and fiery narcotic hitting the streets, trying to mainline his unutterable sense of guilt, anesthetize his soul. *Poor baby*, Evelyn purred, and hers was born dead. Evelyn took the needles from the veins of a hog driver flying high on a magic feather, then plunged them into her own flesh. How much can one give to stop a war, knowing there will be others?

St. Cloud had not surprisingly stumbled upon Evelyn in the antiwar crowd on that long-ago day of their first meeting. Evelyn discovered him. Staggering from the wreckage of a young life grown old, she was not the vulnerable creature he thought her to be. It was she who saw within him another saint to save. She turned a new corner, away from the psychedelic trip wires of drugs, which St. Cloud despised as self-serving distractions from the fight to stop the war. He became her fresh target. She decided the last to be saved were the antiwar soldiers, for one day they would be left with not only a lost war on their conscience, but a lost cause as well. A ferocity of separately held beliefs fused St. Cloud and Evelyn together. They fell immediately into step. Before St. Cloud could turn back he was into Evelyn's vocation. She strummed his strings, built his ego, pledged to stick by him through thin and thinner. With passing years she plumbed her hidden agenda. In moments of ecstasy she would bury her nose in the damp hair beneath his arm, her nostrils filling wide with naked scent, a consuming female at an inexhaustible salt lick of male vulnerability. Ultimately her female nurturing transcended his mundane politics. Rock-bottom reality could not be avoided. She herself was the salt of the earth. It was to women she finally turned when she turned from St. Cloud. She spun inward toward sensuality of friendship, slipping from burden of youthful illusions, gracefully as a snake sheds the season's skins. While her purpose bloomed red as a rose in the hothouse of Key West, St. Cloud slid deeper into his slot of guilt. The more she stretched toward illuminating sunlight, the further into the shadows he dissolved, finally disappearing into a crack of acquiescence, no longer a player, reduced to a mere observer. It was not that Evelyn was attracted to her own kind in a sudden coup d'état of the heart. It was simply that on an eventual night a pair of hands held her exposed feet and stroked them as if they were the silkened dough of newly formed loaves of bread. The hands were female and grew warmer with sliding friction, raising from Evelyn a heat of expectation. Knowing thumbs and kneading fingers released from her fleshy soles an indescribable ache. It was not tenderness nor sisterly directness which turned Evelyn pliant. She yielded to tearful initiation of healing touch, a sincerity of common cause. For the first time she was detached from a past filled with despair, from a future urging destruction. She was jubilant. She felt as naked and fulfilled as Jesus on the cross.

Evelyn had at last made a pact of peace with herself, even though this led her away from St. Cloud. Every new life begins new problems. She still followed former sorrows and opened herself to St. Cloud when he came to her under cover of the Black Cloud's shadow of guilt. But each time he came into her she was in reality sending him off. He was on his own now. The closer he came to personal destruction the closer he came to enlightenment. Evelyn kissed the thought of him good-bye. In her heart Evelyn bid St. Cloud farewell, and a fond farewell to all the Black Cloud boys. So long, happy trails, good luck. Godspeed.

19

O YOU HEAR my strange music? Now you know my secret. I cannot begin to tell you all the things I am. Do not rest easy, for I am not who you think me to be. Have you been holding my hand in yours? Do we see eye through eye? Can you hear with earless ears what you could not hear with ears? Do you trust me to right the way? Remember what that poacher in the Everglades said, the man with the anchor tattooed on his arm, the one who boasted he slaughtered ten thousand alligators in the mangrove swamps? You don't remember, don't know the history of your world, can't recall what happens day to day in your own life. The tattooed poacher who killed ten thousand of an animal specie inhabiting earth before the joke of man was an embryonic pea brain stuffed in an ape's skull, bragged, "If you don't talk, you don't get caught much." I don't talk at all. The purity of my actions speaks from memory, for I am the Great Corrector, and correct I will, my will be done with a vengeance. If someone steps beyond the circle there will be recrimination, the Dancing Devil to pay. My will will be done on earth as it is in hell, everything must flow back within the circle. What more can you expect from a world without hope, people too fooled by false gods to despair? You say people have a way of finding their own devils. I say, what is a devil but another false god? If you can be fooled into despair, then you can be tricked into redemption, for what is the chick, but the child of the egg? Look me in the eyes and tell me you don't despair. You can't. You would rather run over the last Florida panther in cars going nowhere, rather feast your fast-food palate on the last egret egg, anything but to look me in the eyes. Behold. I am the Green

Sailor. I am the Cuban Martyrs. I am the malaria-infected laborer of Flagler's Overseas Railroad. I am all these things, dead and buried in the island cemetery with its eight tall palms pointing the way to its entrance gates. I am all mysteries waiting incarnation. I am your teacher. *Ya ye, moin nan sang he! Yah, yeh, I am in the blood, hey!* And I tell you a screaming deluge is coming out of Africa greater than any howling hurricane. Look in my eyes. Do you see the yellow circles? Do you see the bull falling with the knife blade in his neck? You better get down on your knees, pray you see the bull falling to his knees in the yellow center. A healthy man cannot make a sick man well, but a sick man can make a healthy man ill. I feel your hand trying to pull away. You don't like what I bring you. You find distasteful how the teacher treats the sick pupil. Well you aren't going anyplace, because there is no longer a place to go. You can flee the tiny circle of this island, but that will only lead to larger circles with more bulls falling to their knees. No, you aren't going anyplace, because the final circle becomes the smallest, it is the circle within you, ignorance is the target of self-destruction. You carry the seeds of your demise within. All I have to do is wait and watch, then turn my back on your deafening cries as you plead for mercy, plead for a reborn body, for a fresh soul. You beg on bloodied knees for me to correct the uncorrectable, perform the miracle of all mysteries. Let me stick this piece of advice on your pleading tongue, prick up your ears before I take them to make another drum. If you are a good student who bodes ill, not a queasy, lockjawed follower of false singing prophets spilling their incessant swill on radio airwaves, then maybe I can be of assistance. If all the senses haven't been squeezed from you by your idle talk, idle sex, tasteless food, families without fathers, fathers without mothers, mothers without children, children without a past, future without people, water without purity, unexploded bombs stuffed with the best offense is the best defense, stuffed with the fire of ultimate extinction, then maybe you have finally come to the right place. Ah, that is better, your hand relaxes in mine. Don't cry, wipe that tear from your eye. You have no right to weep, tears are the milk of vanity. The last panther in the Florida Everglades does not cry. The last panther hunts to live.

Time was when people could be happy as pet pigs following a butcher with a stick or a house painter with a mustache. Time was when people would willingly trot after any Moses waving a sacred staff, eat bananas from the tree of life Adam planted in Eden, drink paint thinner from a silver chalice, and feel content, stuffed, enlightened, most of all saved. Time was when an alligator tooth, three bat wings and a rat fur could buy protection against evil wind brewing. No *ouanga* is strong enough to stop what's coming now. Time was when the Virgin of Miracles miraculously appeared atop a palm tree to heal the future and forgive the past. The Virgin has fled, swift as a white dove winging into setting sun. Listen to me if you want your babies born with less than two heads, your beans boiled, your cassavas cultivated, your coffee brewed, your dead to walk from their graves and the living to walk on water. Listen to me above the water's roar, for I am not a beggar on horseback, a pious politician riding a goat, a prattling priest with a toad for a tongue. I am purity, a snake crawling, a hymn in the sky, a lullaby in the mouth of a babe, a blade falling across a bull's neck. You can light candles for me along the riverbanks, but you will not see me. You can eat red meat, red mango root, red beans, drink red rum, red wine, red bull blood, but this will not feed me. Life does not sustain me, light does not illuminate me, fire does not burn me, time does not define me. I take your sweaty face between my hands, hands soft as newborn turtles, I hold your fate within silken fingers, I kiss your lying mouth, lick lizards from your lips, suck hummingbirds from your heart. Do not bite the tongue that feeds you. You are my pup, you are my pup. Your head upon my lap, your hand upon my private parts, I am your funny guillotine.

I have had it ALL. Your mind-bent drugs cooked up by middle-class mugs, your bogus religions invented by thugs in sharkskin suits, your senseless wars and sleepwalking peace, your coming attractions of pieces of ass that never come. I am not some zonked-out critter with bullet holes for eyes and a bucket of beans for brains. I am a trinity of magicians, master of night forests, lord of night earth, king of bright cemeteries. I am sovereign in all these realms. I stoop to touch your troubled body, unbandage your damaged eyes, my hands upon your aching feet, my fingernails cutting through wax in your ears. Feel my lips move on your skin, the heat of my breath on the fur of your belly, your thighs yielding. I am phallic purpose rising, antibiotic treason spreading, purple corpse spinning. Read the map of my lips as I suck where no bee dare trespass.

> *i Love*
> *you Love*
> *he Loves*

she Loves
they Love
all Die.

Ah! You are beginning to understand, beginning to see in darkness. You are divining your own Yankee Devil Dandy, tasting the salad of contradictions, embracing the science of all my Mysteries. *L'Amour.* My child, it is that simple. Love will kill us all.

Sperm is being misspent, the fruit of the womb shrivels in bitterness. "But what can I do?" you feverishly ask. "I did not create this world," you moan. Did it ever occur to you I *did* create this world. Creation begets destruction. Even your man Einstein knew the world begins with a bang and ends with a whimper. Is that your sobbing I hear again, your song of impotence, tears as futile as unhatched turtle eggs being snared by sea gulls and torn to pieces in the sun? Get a grip on yourself to save yourself. No Guru's diet can cure you, no soap-opera star can live it for you, no rock and roll pied piper can lead you, no television preacher can absolve you, there is no splendor in a rat's ass. You cannot hide any longer behind skirts of ignorance. You are guilty and must pay off your sin in wages of retribution. You have cast impurities upon the waters. I guard the crossroads of the great flood gates, control the deluge, correct the imbalance, destroy to create. Come close. Tell me, which came first, the maggot or the fly?

Oh, I almost forgot. Are you coming to my birthday party? Many people are. I hold it every year in the cemetery, the morning after All Saints' Eve, that's Halloween to you. It is a party for Loas of Darkness, underworld lords reborn into bodies of the living, into the fresh souls of cast-out disbelievers. There will be three new graves this year, empty and deep, and I will fill them. I will send Horsemen from beneath the oceans to go riding to bring me three souls tainted and tarnished, souls that feed poison to the Saints, drip death in the water. Then I will sink the three into the underworld for all to mock, send them running through hell and beyond in gasoline jackets. They cannot escape the purity of the circle. I will cleanse them and purify them with fire. What is left will be virgin. What is left will be fit for a Loa to slip into on the bright morning of my birthday party, when sun in sky glows righteous red over the Green Sailor, over Cuban Martyrs, over wings of an Avenging Angel. The three graves will be covered by dirt, the documents of destruction within weighted with triangular mounds of stones, the former occupants sent to hell on the back of an earless goat. Only then will the Loas be released in fresh souls, free to walk among the living, free to select whom they shall save when the deluge comes. The Loas and Saints are watching always, but you do not know them to see them, for when they possess your head they inherit your future, you cease to be. Too late now, you are indoctrinated.

If the world is going to hell in a basket, then I've got the basket. When the flood comes my raft rides high. Some people call me a gangster, a hex doctor, a charlatan without portfolio, a sorcerer with no rhyming religion, no singing spirituals, no happy herbs, no grinding magic stones. Don't you listen to their spider tongues, I've got the vaccine. I've got the cure, I need only the jawbone of a dog to make things right. Auto-Zobop, my Tiger-Car, you can't miss me in it. I drive by night, my lights beaming a blue streak to right the way. Some people call me a gangster, don't you heed their serpent fangs. I am a mob, a howling pack, a force that can turn in a heartbeat a man into a beast to be led to slaughter. My Ghost-Car is not to be eluded. I am here to tell you as water screams in my brain and blood bumps in my veins, while hairless swine slip on distant muddy mountain slopes and green monkeys chatter with laughter in jungles, that it is too late for you. The eternal X cannot be eluded, it will be branded on all disbelievers. Those who step outside the perfect circle will be brought to heel, delivered to swift judgment in this world, everlasting damnation in the next.

I see you quiver. After all, you came here seeking my comfort, my cold mind, my hot forehead, my steel hide, above all on high seeking absolution with your teary eyes pleading. Don't try to kiss my hand. Get up off your knees. Begging will not secure an honest measure of protection from me. You cannot hail me as your new Loa, salute me as if I were your Drill Sergeant. You cannot trot along in my righteous path, hot as a bitch hound in heat hoping for a hard bone. You cannot bow and scrape to me, for I am not vanity, I am purity. I am not power, I am reality, guardian of earthly and heavenly gates, Master at the Crossroads of all fates, Keeper of all Fallacies, the answer to your unspoken prayers. Do not mistake me for the Messiah. The day you go down on your knees it will not be in obeisance to a false prophet, it will be to accept the blade of the sword across the back of your neck. I will cut you open like a paper envelope, announce to the world the contents of the dead document within. The same way the brains of a sacrificial goat are beaten from its head, with swift hammer blows between its horns, before the knife is drawn across its throat and its dripping life-giving blood is tasted by all those within the circle, in such a manner shall you also receive salvation. I hear you plead ignorance, protesting you did not know there was a perfect circle of absolution, claiming you were born unaware of purity, born bent by corruption of profit without effort and exploitation of Nature without recrimination. Degradation and despoliation are left in your path as you slouch from your Babylon of modernity, slink off in your space capsule, rocketing away from your history of plunder, implanting in a pure universe pods of decay. Well, let me tell you, you ain't gonna make it this time, you ain't gonna get away with it. Zobop is here to be a stop to it, end it, amen. So sit down, shut up, pay attention. Prick up your earless ears and get an education short and to the point. When it is over you will know why I am not who you think me to be.

It is wrong to try to cheat death. Do you remember 1906, when the army of laborers building Flagler's Overseas Railroad relied on crude barometers, which were nothing more than water-filled glass jars with weeds on the bottom? No, you remember nothing. When the weeds in those jars began to float toward the top it signaled air pressure was dropping and a vengeful wind from Africa was on the rise. On an October night of 1906 the weeds floated right to the top of the jars, but it was already too late, winds were storming over a hundred miles per hour, snapping steel cables anchoring the houseboat barracks of Flagler's army. The Eye of the Hurricane was bearing down without pity, sharks were rising in the twenty foot tidal surge. Many of the screaming men swilled vials of laudanum from first-aid kits, minds going adrift as waves smashed into houseboats. A Gray Ghost appeared from the Eye of the Hurricane, it flung boats, machines and men southward into the churning Gulf of Mexico. In a puff the Gray Ghost reduced Flagler's grandiose army to fish bait. Why do I tell you this, you ask? Is it because of my distaste for Flagler, a corrupt old Capitalist in a straw bowler hat who sacrificed the lives of hundreds of work-a-day blokes in the construction of his get-rich-at-any-price scheme, to make of the Florida Keys nothing more than a concrete and iron railroad spur to South America, an elaborate dock of dreams where a cardinal Capitalist could pile ever higher his plunder from the planet, his crude barrels of crude oil, his sagging sacks of gold? No, that is not why I tell you this. That is history you should know, the simplicity of greed itself. I tell you this because my brain is waterlogged and the weeds are rising fast. Do not be so blind as to think there is a prescription for exemption you can swill like laudanum before the howling wind of retribution arrives. Do not think there is a route of escape across land or water. Do not try to cheat death. Do not forget, four hundred years before Flagler began construction of his pornographic greed scheme, the Spaniards named many of these martyred Keys *matar hombre*, kill man. *Matar hombre*, that is what I aim to do.

Come back here! I told you there is no escape. Don't be foolish, it is almost over for us all, soon the finish. You have no more routes of escape than the sailor boys in the boiler room of the USS *Maine* had, when the ship shook in the night with a steel twisting blast, sinking to the bottom of Havana Harbor a near century ago. No escape over water or land. One hundred years before that blast in Havana Harbor Englishmen and their hired jackals pursued Caloosa Indians the length of the Keys, then stripped their meager possessions, stripped their red skins, fired musketballs through their hearts, the Union Jack flapping over their sun-bleached skulls. The Caloosa had no more escape routes than José Martí's ragtag brigade of liberation martyrs had, when they launched from these shores a crusade to free Cuba from Spain. Martí, who dreamed of a free nation of islands, stretching from Cuba to Key West, up to the peninsular tip of Florida. Martí the poet patriot, whose compatriots blew Judas kisses to their Iberian overlords, while others rolled out a blood red carpet of revolutionary fervor extending into the twenty first century. Martí, whose fiery speeches of justice, freedom and democracy raised hard currency to outfit an army, whose poetry inspired troops into battle. No escape for Martí, caged by Colonial captors, betrayed by a web of assassins, sold out by his own for no more than the cost of a loaf of bread. I hear you say, of what interest to me are the bashed skulls of forgotten Indians, the blasted bones of sailors on watch in distant harbors, the choked cry of freedom in the murderous hothouse of Latin American politics, of immigrant railroad laborers eaten by sharks and alligators, bitten by rattlesnakes and malarial mosquitoes, crushed beneath trestle bridges and swept to sea by hurricanes? What does it have to do with my life, you shout! Relax, I'm coming to that.

Life is only for foxes and turkeys, have you ever noticed? Reality is that right around this smogged-up, ozone-burnt, battered globe there are men waking up every morning with their fingers twitching uncontrollably, men who have to either masturbate or strangle some-body. It's the same the world over, city-wide and country-narrow. It's a fox-eating, turkey-shooting gallery out there. If you had a brain to give it all half a thought, it would make the hair stand up on the end of your dick, curdle the milk in your maternal breast. The end of the world is a necessity, necessity is a mother, brother. What I'm preaching here is the *Adios Twentieth Century Cha-Cha*. Some dance, some don't, some won't. Hear my words, spread my advice, dance my tune, listen to my strange music. If I make imperfect sense of an imperfect world, then I am right. You are without history, a baleful follower to inevitable slaughter, whereas I am born of memory. When the atomic dust falls on the last parade of your heroic antics I alone will know the escape route. If it is true that hope is the last thing to die in a man, then I say fear is the first thing to live, fear of your fellow man. Are you getting the picture? Do you see the weeds rising?

Beware the silence created by noise of your radio airwave pursuits of teenaged angst and lust. Will you never grow up? While you fiddle with the amplification of electronic instruments to give volume to your collective voice the end is falling all around, predictable as volcanic ash. Without me as guide there isn't a natural chance to escape the coral rubble of this island, yet you still refuse the obvious. You wouldn't see the lightning bolt until it blasted the nose off your face. That's right, now you're learning, I'm here to guide you. I've been around for 175 million years, just like the sea turtles. Do you still have my turtle hand in yours? I am the survivor who refuses to succumb to your polluted seas, your poisoned rivers, your lakes of industrial pus, your streams of toxic piss. I am power and purity, not some great blue heron stumbling spindly-legged through a black mangrove swamp with a gut full of radioactive mud worms eating at my vitals. Righteousness gnaws at me, nibbles the edges of my soul, bites my toes, propels me into the night where a new kingdom must be carved out if a new day is to dawn blood red. You say you can't understand any of this, that it's mumbo-jumbo jibberish having nothing to do with the likes of you. Well that's just what will be the death of you, because I know your casket size. There is no escape without me, others have tried, I will tell you the story of one. Maybe you've learned enough of my language by now to understand my stories are not what you think them to be, but first let me ask you something. Have you ever noticed how people are like fireflies? People lose color as they grow older, burn out, fade. Ever notice that? Of course you have. Good, because if you stick with me you will have eternal life, *glow*. My bright fire is on the water, purity is just around the corner.

My heart is a bomb ticking, like the bomb which blasted the Green Sailors to fish bait in Havana Harbor. I am sly as a mouse. No one can outrun me, no one can outrun their own history, black or white. Do you remember that tall, dark brooding man who returned home to the island after the First World War? Of course you don't. Elanya was his name, highly decorated he was, a trunkful of medals for valor above and beyond the call, but he was ignored like all the rest returning from a battlefield of distant and noxious trenches, from a war shrouded in gaseous vagaries. Men like Elanya were not like the boys returning three wars later from the mud suck of Southeast Asia, moaning into their beer that they were not exalted for the blood they let. Would you pin a medal on a carpenter hired to hammer a nail? Would you pin a medal on a lion tamer who sticks his head in the lion's mouth? No. Then why pin a medal on a soldier hired to fire a bullet through the heart of another soldier? It's a job, if you're drafted to it, do it. If you don't want to do it, it's your job to get out of it. So grow up, drink your beer and shut up. Elanya knew that, all he wanted on his return was to be left alone. He didn't bleat and moan for a hero's parade or a gallant statue to be erected in the local park to honor his killing. Nobody cared about the bullet scars in Elanya's hide, and he didn't show them off. They only cared when Elanya took up with a woman from across Duval Street on the dark side of town. They jailed him for the lewd indecency of loving a woman of different color. Wasn't any need to give Elanya a trial, a lynch mob broke into the county jail, roped him hand and foot, trussed him like a turkey, dragged him screaming down the mile of dirt road leading to Martello Tower, the red brick fortress next to the sea where soldiers once manned cannons to blast their invading brothers in a war called Civil. On the very last electric power pole in front of the Civil War citadel Elanya was hung by the neck, welcome home, hero. Turkeys and foxes. The foxes knew all along Elanya was from the island of Elanya in the Lesser Antilles, an island where matters of color played no role in affairs of the heart. In Key West Elanya had passed himself off as white, at most as a mulatto, nevertheless, always on the pale side of black, and the good citizens believed him, after all, he was a veteran. What the foxes hung that day was the idea of a white man who loved a black woman. What they killed was not a black loving a black, but a man loving a woman. Run nigger run. I am the victim and the victimizer. That is why I tell you these things, to teach you of mistakes past, so you will eventually become smarter than an insect, have a memory, build a history. Remember, a fly or a wasp does not know who its father is, very little separates you from their world, if anything.

So there, I have told one of my promised stories and have but few left. Don't become cocky with this new knowledge, there is a difference between heard and learned. Don't think because you are a being that you are necessarily a human, such would be fatal. We are about fatality here, reality of survival. If some have to die so ideas of others may flourish, so be it. So it be in the beginning as in the end. Do you see the green monkey grinning in Africa, high in the tree? The green monkey has a secret he shares with me and withholds from you. What you see is a playful primate, a creature of childish proportions. When one grows weak, cannot keep swinging through leafy jungle canopy, loses its grip and plummets to earth, the others fall upon it with a screeching chatter, tearing the fallen's furry limbs, pounding the fallen with a fury of fists. Death is not an exotic exit. Death is a door hammered shut. The so-called beings of human are not so suave as the green monkey. The beings of human suckle their sick, coddle their ill, such will be the death of the living. Green monkey blood is loose among you, and you are not monkey clever enough to stamp it out. I am forced to go forth in search of purity, cleansing the circle. My blade of righteousness is aimed at those among you with green monkey blood pumping in their veins. They will not escape, the eternal X cannot be eluded. I intend to finish with my purpose. I am a wasp buzz in the ear of reason, whispering your mother's name, exposing your father's bastard treason. I am a little blaze, growing. I am a big *bamboche*, a grand party of deliverance. I am the little world called upon to save the Big World. Green Sailors, green monkeys, all blown to microchip bits. You can be saved if you know your history, if you understand I am not a simple aberration, a fabulous apparition, a dead document sealed in a bottle, floating in a dream pool garden. I am inevitable intolerance, and don't forget it, as you have forgotten all else. It is my job to make the intolerable tolerable. I am indomitable as the current of the Gulf Stream coursing with 75 million tons of water each second, a force greater than all the earth's rivers combined. Do you hear the roar of water over my head, do you see the weeds floating to the top of the jar, do you see the circle closing, do you understand now you are standing within it, without eyes to see, without ears to hear? All God's creatures got to make a living, and I am your guide. A lit candle burns atop my skull, there is only one last step to take, one final act remains to complete. No, it is not an Act of Contrition, it is an act of retribution. The bull is cleansed and perfumed before its beastly bulk is butchered heavenward. Shuuush! Hushabye my baby. Stop crying, we are almost there.

Don't worry chilrens, Mammy's at the wheel of reason, Zobop's at the wheel of the Ghost-Car. They say Zobop is a mob of sorcerers, magical gangsters who transform their victims into goats and toads before slaughtering them. They say Zobop has been given a burning charm from the Loas, for Zobop cleanses the earth of the foul and failed, leading them to the slaughterhouse to the march of a drumbeat. They say Zobop has intercourse with evil spirits, suckles from a fountain of fresh terrors. They say Zobop goes about the night in a Tiger-Car, an Auto-Zobop which careens through the heavens, along dark country roads, beaming blinding blue from bright headlights. They say Zobop feeds salt to zombies, which wakes and shakes them to acts of free will. They say Zobop kidnaps children. Lies! Zobop does not disturb the dead. Zobop inhabits the dead. Zobop kidnaps no one. Zobop did not kidnap you. Zobop just likes to take people for a little ride in his Ghost-Car, up the street of illusions, down the avenue of dreams, around the curve of illumination, over the cliff of doom.

You-bop
He-bop
She-bop
They-bop
We-bop
To-Zobop

Bop till you drop. You think I'm kidding? Just wait. I drive by night. Do you see my clever soul? A newborn New World monkey at the wheel of misfortune. Here we go. Hang on!

You don't like it, do you? If I am everything you are not, then you are everything I am. You want to run, you want to close your ears, to close out treason of misfired reason, but you can't. You are still with me because you are me. Look here, my darling suckling pig, my tireless turtle hatchling, the feast is in the wood. You don't know what I'm talking about? For three hundred years you don't know what I've been talking about. Three hundred years ago the great fleets of Castilian plunderers were cut to ribbons on coral off the Florida Straits, sunk to sea bottom, weighted by bullion and precious stones. For three hundred years this cargo attracted men like those who went down with the ships, men who didn't make their own fortunes, spent lifetimes scratching the earth's crevices in search of treasures bought by sweat of others. Men who mined the currency of cultural droppings which had fallen into cracks of history, or sunk to bottom of timeless ocean. Scattered around this island, in any direction you choose to sail, are treasures on the ocean floor still untouched. The wood of sunken galleons once transporting fabulous treasures now nurtures implacable shipworms. Shipworms feast upon a banquet of seasoned timber while surrounded by worthless dull gleam of gold and emeralds. Do you finally see the value of what I offer? Your treasure has no currency in the natural world. Heed my world if you do not want to end up a dead document. The feast is everywhere around and you turn a blind side to it, ignorant to turtle hatchlings moving toward false light of shopping centers, panthers coming up from the Everglades to cross deathtrap highways going nowhere. So I am forced to action. I start my engine. I roar to life after life. The Ghost-Car is on the prowl tonight. Zobop the Great Corrector is loose. He is not who you think him to be. He is a feast in the wood, a blue streak in the heavens, water on the brain.

Water and wind, wind and water, they bore all plant life to this island in the beginning. Water and wind brought life, water and wind will take it away. I place my lips to the *lambi*, the sacred shell of the conch. My breath blows a message which opens the heavens, parts the pearly gates, calls upon the wind to sail ships across water to a magic spot, where those who survive dwell in perpetual mystery. I summon wind to raise the sea over this island, drown the disbelievers for one and all. I condemn tainted souls to a fate worse than life on this putrefied globe. Nothing shall be left except voices over still water, no more roaring cascade in my brain, calm prevails as waves smooth themselves overhead. The chattering screams of green monkeys heralding the deluge is finally silenced. In the east, sun rises in an Avenging Angel's outstretched hand, graves yawn open around her as mounted Horsemen storm from beneath the sea, thunder ashore on raging tide of dead documents. I feed the sea, sow the waves, reap the tide, ride the current, time is on my side. I dance the time of my history while God is out to lunch and worms feast on wood. I right the way. I write the way. I write. I am witness. I am testimony. I am writing right, the right exit. Dead documents float ever swiftly to ocean surface. Furious weeds rise in a jar. The yellow circle closes. The steel cage clatters down around us all. Look at me, straight at me. Peer into my face. Escape awaits through my eyes. The only escape route is through the Eye of the Hurricane. I am the Hurricane. Get out while you can. Are you with me? Yes! Let's go then! We are storm riders! We are in orbit! At last! Know my language! *A-OK! A* through *ZZZZZZ-Be-Bop Ah Lu-La! ZEROBOP!*

We see Eye through I now. You knew you were me all along, didn't you?

BOOK THREE

MADONNA **O**N **T**HE **R**EEF

20

CAYO HUESO ES EL PAIS DE SIGUARAYA. Key West is the land where anything goes. On this evening of All Saints' Justo didn't know if things were going to the Gods or to the Devils. One thing certain, things were already going their usual loco. Justo touched the gold bone at his neck as he made his way toward music blaring from crowded Duval Street ahead. All Saints' Eve always spooked him, spooked him as a kid, spooked him more now. Made no difference if All Saints' Eve was also called Halloween. On this island Halloween wasn't a night which brought out gay children costumed for treats. Instead it released the child within adults. It was an excuse for masked nocturnal antics, dancing in the streets, ceaseless prowling through raucous bars and discos in search of illicit treats. A night spent hidden behind the costume of an ape, a Bozo clown or an impeached president, one could don the ego of another, the droll become garish. Accountants miraculously transformed into barstool Romeos, bank clerks slinky as short-skirted Lolitas, randy divorcees slippery as oil-slick Valentinos, and nervous Navy housewives purring hot as fresh whiskered cats in black leotards. *La vida es un tango.* Life is a ball.

The ghosts of All Saints' Eve, and the goblins of Halloween, had lately given way to an official Mardi Gras–style frolic, a high time of civic-minded madness, renamed by the city, Fantasy Fest. Beneath the costumed sheets of Fantasy Fest's ribald revelry was a not-so-disguised plan designed to lure ever more northern tourists into the jaws of the island's insatiable hunger for fast bucks and quick turnover. The warily wise native Conchs slammed their shutters, waiting for the brassy overflow of masked tricksters to blow away in a whirlwind

259

of hangovers, empty wallets and guilty consciences. Fantasy Fest
obliterated a once serious date on the calendar, the end of hurricane
threat, another furious season survived, not that there still weren't
tropical storms off the coast of Africa capable of cooking up a two-
hundred-mile-an-hour surprise. The Conchs knew the main danger
was past, even though the official hurricane season didn't end for
another month. Conchs understood the nature of their weather, with
each sweltering dog day, from beginning of August right through
end of sweaty October, gathering storms grew more frequent and
belligerent. A beefy squall could turn overnight into a swirl of
devastating windy skirts, sweeping the island's inhabitants into the sea
beneath a twenty-foot wall of water. Justo could live without Fantasy
Fest, it had become less of one thing, a corruption of many. No longer
a simple kids' holiday or a religious celebration for the devoutly
superstitious, not even the official end of hurricane season. Because
it was not what it pretended to be many people mightily aspired to
make it into a real excuse for riotous behavior. *Cada uno tiene su modo
de matar pulgas.* Everyone has his own way of killing fleas.

Fantasy Fest was not a cop's favorite holiday. Justo was normally
at home that night, surrounded by close *compadres* drinking *compuesto*
and playing dominoes in his living room as tangled scents of squid,
chicken and shrimp drifted from the kitchen, where gossipy chatter
of Rosella and the women added spice to a boiling stewpot of Paella
Valenciana. While masked revelers danced to a worrisome beat in
distant streets Justo smugly thought, as he watched an opponent's
bridge of dominoes about to fall, *puerco con frio, y hombres con vino,
hacen gran ruido.* Cold pigs and drunken men make a lot of noise. But
this Halloween Justo was not spending a tranquil night at home. He
was in the midst of drunken men, drunken pigs, drunken lions, Little
Bo-Peeps, Attila the Huns and Andrew Jacksons, a howling mob of
counterfeit inebriates. He was in a *sofo con*, an embarrassing fix,
hoofing it without the authority of a *perseguidora*, a police car. Why?
Because, *eres como Canuto, mientras mas viejo mas bruto.* The older you
get the dumber you are. His elaborate scheme to keep control of
Voltaire's destiny had collapsed. Not only had the Coast Guard sent
in a squad of lawyers to argue the city of Key West had no jurisdiction
over what transpired on Voltaire's boat while on the high seas, the
grand jury refused to hear the case on a battery of technical points,
not the least of which was a lack of evidence to find Voltaire accountable
for anything other than nearly starving to death, much less man-

slaughter. To make matters worse, while Justo investigated the drug murder of a Massachusetts felon on the lam, cut off in his prime by a blast from a sawed-off shotgun behind the All-You-Can-Eat fried chicken diner out on the boulevard, two Federal Marshals from Miami showed at the jail in an unmarked van with blacked-out windows to haul Voltaire to the Everglades detention camp. *Mal día.* On top of this a Southerner recently recruited by the police department, a six-foot-five genius who thought Don Cervantes Saavedra was the name of any Cuban refugee running for mayor or caught doping grey-hounds before a big Quinella, had complained up the chain of command that Justo kept a dog in his car while on duty. The blister-faced recruit maintained Justo's behavior violated regulations, a threat to dignity the force worked hard to maintain in face of a sullen and apathetic public. Justo knew, from reliable information of scammers working the seamier side streets off Duval, the Southerner was a heavy-handed skimmer of narcotics seized in daily busts. This white man in blue did not like Justo's skin hue, distrusted the way Justo chose to turn a blind eye to smaller infractions in order to bag bigger game. Complaints about Ocho, coupled with the honor Justo brought the department in the case of Voltaire, compelled his superiors to make him a small present. Despite seniority he was busted back to a street beat during the baddest week of the year, the week of Fantasy Fest. Justo was allowed no comfortable loose *guayabera* shirt to walk the streets in, instead he had to stuff himself into an iron-creased suit of regulation rayon blues he hadn't worn in years. A too small visored police cap perched atop his head; revolver, riot stick and handcuffs swung at his hips as he patrolled his beat with a static squeal coming from the two-way radio crammed in his back pocket. *Mal día*, what a bad day. What a bad situation. *Quien al cielo escupe, en la cara le cae.* He who spits toward heaven has the spittle fall back in his face.

Lately heaven seemed to be raining displeasure on Justo. He blamed himself for Voltaire's fate. True, no good deed goes unpunished. He knew he shouldn't have tried such a crazy stunt to keep Voltaire bottled up in the judicial system so he wouldn't be grabbed by the Feds and sent back into the jaws of the shark. But anything was worth a try, and with St. Cloud working in the same direction he thought, well, now it saddened him what he thought that long-ago day when the Coasties towed the refugee boat into Mallory Dock. He had thought wrong. *Se la dejaron en la mano.* He was left holding the bag. Still, he had one card to play before the game was over. He was determined to take the last gamble to get Voltaire back. To make the gamble work he needed St. Cloud again. Somewhere in the gang of celebrants crowding the streets on this Halloween night of fantasy festivities he was bound to run across St. Cloud. St. Cloud was not one to miss a party, especially where the promise of free rum was loose in the air.

WHAT'S 1 MILE LONG?

FLOATS AND GLOWS?

MAKES MUSIC?

IS TOTALLY CRAZED?

The question chalked on the blackboard behind the Wreck Room bar counter did not pose much of a challenge to the customers shouting for another drink. The answer was the Grand Costume Parade, making its noisy way down the one-mile length of Duval Street past the Wreck Room windows. Justo attempted to catch Angelica's eye as she pacified fruit-hatted Carmen Mirandas, hoop-skirted Dolly Madisons, and intergalactic travelers sporting tinfoil antennae. Even the boisterous Bubba-Bob had exchanged his captain's cap for a broad-brimmed cowboy hat. Things were definitely not as they should be. In the slot behind the bar where Angelica normally worked alone, five bartenders scurried with trays of foaming drinks. Justo couldn't shout his question to Angelica, if she had seen St. Cloud. The noise inside the room was louder than the loudspeakers booming Japanese rock and roll from a truck rolling by outside. A thirty-foot glitter-scaled Godzilla reared from the truck's flatbed, a vomit of foil-wrapped chocolate kisses erupting from the beast's mouth onto grateful revelers lining the street.

"You want to go to Hollywood?"

Justo turned to find the voice directed at him in the crowded room.

It was a raspy voice. Its owner wore red tights and purple high-heeled shoes, a pink rabbit stole was slung over skinny cocoa-colored shoulders, a blond wig with a dazzling rhinestone tiara topped the whole affair. Green lipstick around the voice's mouth puckered in a large, "O, oh, ohh! You come with me, honey, and you come to Hollywood."

Justo stared into the voice's smooth face, its eyes covered by a black Lone Ranger mask. He didn't know if he was being hustled by man or woman, though he had a strong suspicion. The creature raised a bony hand, its painted fingernails digging into Justo's elbow.

"C'mon sugar, let's fly to where I can make you a star." The voice darted from a tongue close to Justo's ear.

Justo was in the trap a good cop should never be in, caught off guard. A queer embarrassment flushed his face ruddy purple. He couldn't decide whether to book the creature pawing him, or laugh off the proposition.

"Don't be shy, honey. I'll be gentle as Lassie. Maybe you don't trust me to make you a star? Maybe you don't trust women? Let me tell you something about women."

The green lips were heating to their subject. Justo felt the hot air from them on his cheek as he turned to catch Angelica's attention again. Maybe if he ignored the clutching creature it would slither back under its barstool. No such luck.

The green lips loosened with philosophical fervor. "Women know nothing of truth. Lies lies lies. Quack quack quack. Say whatever they want to suit themselves. Know what people say? A lie is a man's last resort and a woman's first aid. Have you ever noticed how a bad woman always gets a good man? Which are you, honey, a bad woman or a good man?"

"A *bad* cop."

"I knew you weren't a cop right off. Watched you come in. Stiff and stuffy in your butch blue suit, trying not to be noticed. Says to myself, this black boy is so uncomfortable. He should be masquerading as the Tin Man, or maybe delicious Dorothy herself."

It was worse than Justo first imagined. Green lips figured him for an impostor, a shoe clerk or a lawyer decked out as one of Key West's finest. That was the trouble with Fantasy Fest, nobody was who they were supposed to be. Green lips had a point. Justo probably could command more respect dressed as the Tin Man on a night like this. "Look," he growled even more menacingly. "I am a real cop. Don't push it."

"No such thing as a real cop," green lips snickered. "Only traffic cops and crooked cops."

"Listen—!" Justo grabbed the rabbit stole draped around skinny shoulders and twisted it into a knot beneath green lips' chin. At times like this his Cuban Spanish came instinctively faster than his English. *"Agila! Vete a la puñeta!"*

"Does that mean we are engaged?"

"Beat it! Go to the devil!"

"Don't want to go to the devil." The pucker of green lips dissolved into a pout, painted fingernails digging deeper into Justo's elbow. "Just want to go to Hollywood with you. Want to make you a matinee idol."

Justo didn't have time for this. From the corner of his eye he saw the white cowboy hat of Bubba-Bob bobbing above crowded heads, moving toward the door. He stiffened an index finger and brought it up in a swift poke into the hollow beneath green lips' Adam's apple. A surprised gasp whooshed from green lips, the skinny body teetering backwards on spiked heels.

The cowboy hat of Bubba-Bob disappeared out the door. Justo bulled after it through the menagerie of bizarre beasts and femmes fatales of both sexes, pushing his way into the even greater crush of Duval Street. He had a hunch by following Bubba-Bob he might find St. Cloud. There were few men not island-born Bubba-Bob deemed worthy of sharing drink with. St. Cloud was definitely at the top of that list. Bubba-Bob owed St. Cloud a large and life-saving favor. It was St. Cloud's glib tongue that saved Bubba-Bob from a cruel end worse than Karl Dean's. Even though St. Cloud's saving of Bubba-Bob's skin happened several years back, it was still talked about from bar to bar as if it happened yesterday, making St. Cloud a local hero in some quarters. Justo knew the truth of the matter. St. Cloud had walked into the wrong bar at the right time. It was more than St. Cloud's rum-loosened tongue that rescued Bubba-Bob from what was menacingly aimed at him. What was aimed at him were three *Marimberos* fresh from Bogotá. These weren't just any three Colombian cocaine cowboys, they were on the trickle-down payroll of MK. They had been with MK since the early days of flying small planeloads of marijuana, up to the present time of running cargo ships of cocaine into Florida more frequently than ferries across the English Channel. Over the years the *Marimberos* enforced MK's standard rule of trade: delivery plus two weeks to pay for the shipment. It was delivery plus two which brought the *Marimberos* to Key West in a rented Cadillac with blacked-out windows. They came to teach a lesson to a commercial lobster boat captain who had the bad manners not to pay for his load of cocaine passed from an MK mother ship. The Captain swore the Coast Guard busted his boat twenty miles out from Cuba, but the uniformed men who made the bust were put-up guys hired by the Captain, it was a straight rip-off. MK knew things were loosening around the edges, screws had to be tightened. He was forced to run a school of show and tell, his *Marimberos* constantly called upon to hold classes. Last Christmas they had been in Tampa, delivering a textbook lesson on the ABC's of inter-American commercial ethics to a drug lawyer working both sides of the line. The lawyer's name was Woof-Woof, a handle applied because he could woof down a half kilo of coke faster than an anteater hoses up a jar of honey, and because his bayside estate was guarded by two vicious pit bullterriers. Woof-Woof entertained guests by commanding the pit bulls to attack the smooth trunk of a royal palm soaring from the divingboard end of his swimming pool. Released from chained leashes, the ax-shaped heads of the pit bulls would strike the trunk with razor teeth, their bodies rising higher with each ferocious bite, like mutant monkeys from hell ascending Eden's last tree. The bowwows were no problem for the *Marimberos* when they arrived at the locked gates of Woof-Woof's estate Christmas Eve, because MK knew everything about Woof-Woof. Woof-Woof was not unlike many lawyers MK put through law school with money laundered cleaner than a convent girl's underwear. When the *Marimberos* tied Woof-Woof up in his living room they told him he had been naughty, but they were going to feed him well. They sat him on the shiny red tricycle he planned to give his nephew for Christmas, from there he could watch as they unwrapped his presents beneath the decorated pine tree. They chained the carnivorous canines to the chrome metal legs of a suede sofa, and helped themselves to Woof-Woof's buckets of champagne, cocaine and Quaaludes. So many presents to open, so little time until the hour of the virgin birth. The presents did not bring out the Christmas spirit in the *Marimberos*. They fought over a diamond pinky ring, silk neckties which could be worn to a marriage or a funeral, and a gold bracelet engraved with WOOFIE MY SAVIOR, LOVE KIT KAT. The boxes of Swiss chocolates and Florida fruitcakes the *Marimberos'* shared with their bound host, shoveling bonbons and glazed figs into his mouth until his cheeks bulged and saliva dripped from his lips onto a fattened belly. The famished pit bulls snarled, but received not so much as a sugared plum. What revived the *Marimberos* festive spirit was playing back recorded messages on Woof-Woof's telephone answering machine. Aside from business and family ring-ups many young women were attempting to solicit the favor of a return call. One solicitor purred in a velvet voice which drove the *Marimberos* to manic distraction as they dipped their beaks into finger-thick lines of cocaine. *"Woofie honey, you there? This is Meow-Meow. Five in the morning and just got in from Coconut Grove. Famished for your you know what. My tongue is furry and white. Meow-me-yow. Where is Woofie when Kit Kat needs her special thing?"* The *Marimberos* howled, the starving pit bulls growled. Everyone knew where Kit Kat's special thing was, stuffed full of Christmas goodies and bound naked to a kid's bike. The *Marimberos* were rocking with the yuletide spirit, they gobbled handfuls of Quaaludes and set about decorating Woof-Woof. They wound electrical tape around his head and over his mouth, then draped the attached links of kosher hot dogs over his shoulders and across his fattened belly. The two drooling brutes chained to the sofa eyed the fleshy decoration just beyond their straining reach with proprietary interest. Woof-Woof had yet to say a word, assuming the *Marimberos* were sent simply to scare him, but with ten pounds of hot dogs clothing him he decided it was time to cut a deal, he knew where all the bodies were buried, he was indispensable to MK. He tried to shout his terms. The sounds coming from his taped mouth were like hollow gasps from a rabbit clubbed back of its head. At sunup the phone started ringing again. The *Marimberos* played back the voice of a small boy wanting to know if Santa was bringing him a red bike, another voice whispered in a whiskey-throated purr that it was fresh from the shower and desperate for Woofie's special thing. The *Marimberos* shouted at Woof-Woof. They were confused. They couldn't comprehend why a man with a license to steal, a prosperous American drug attorney, would chisel a lousy hundred grand by skimming money he was supposed to move through safe banks in Mexico so MK's imprisoned black shrimpers could return to business. Why would such an educated man with a mansion on Tampa Bay, a yacht tied out front and Kitty Kat girlfriends, go up against the accommodation? Was it true the Feds were about to nail him with twenty-two conspiracy counts and he had already flipped to them? The *Marimberos* were full of questions as they continued to deck Woof-Woof out like a butcher's Christmas tree. They demanded answers, but all they got were muffled blubs from Woof-Woof's taped mouth and ever more urgent calls from meowing Kit Kat. The pit bulls were lunging at the scent of a meal in the air. Did Woof-Woof know pit bulls ate all of their prey after they killed it, bones and all? "I want my special thing," Kit Kat pleaded. "God bless ye merry gentlemen," the *Marimberos* toasted each other with champagne and released the voracious animals. As the pit bulls tore into the flesh of their overdue present the *Marimberos* slipped off to the airport, were back in Bogotá by late Christmas day. Not unlike the Three Kings of the Orient nearly two thousand years earlier, theirs was simply to bear witness to a fait accompli. It was for others to puzzle the truth of mysteries, divine or mundane.

When the *Marimberos* stepped from the Cadillac in Key West they had in mind for the lobster boat Captain a lesson similar to the one taught in Tampa, but no two lessons are alike, especially since the *Marimberos* fingered the wrong man. They found the Captain's trailer among hundreds rowed in a dusty field behind the dog track, its humped living quarters surrounded by stacks of dilapidated wooden lobster traps. Over the locked front door was a KILL CASTRO bumper-sticker. The *Marimberos* kicked down the door. Nothing inside moved except a circling goldfish in a glass bowl atop a groaning refrigerator. The *Marimberos* figured the Captain was at sea, pulling up a day's worth of traps. They decided to wait out the sun's slow descent over Key West in the darkest bar they could find. That night, when the greyhounds chased the metal rabbit around the track, they would return to the trailer and teach their lesson.

Angelica took the *Marimberos* for the usual high-spending cowboys down from Miami after having scammed a success, with nothing more on their minds as they settled onto stools in the Wreck Room than to burn off stacks of hundred-dollar bills. She served them expensive tumblers of French cognac. Beneath dark brows they had the smoldering look of Latin sex in their eyes which Angelica so approved of. The oldest, about twenty-five, spoke perfect English. She liked the fact he didn't wear a tight Hawaiian shirt opened to his guts with heavy gold chains swinging from his neck. He wore an Italian suit with a soft silk tie, a diamond pinky ring glittered on one finger, around his wrist was a gold bracelet engraved with WOOFIE MY SAVIOR, LOVE KIT KAT. She asked Woofie if he played guitar, because he kept drumming his manicured fingernails on the bar. His name wasn't Woofie, he said, it was Hectore. He boasted of having studied at college in New Jersey, engineering. He was no Indian who worked his way out of the jungle grinding coca leaves to paste in stone bowls, wearing a two-thousand-dollar watch even though he didn't know how to tell time. He was of the educated elite, an integral part of the industry which provided more than half his country's hard currency. He was, if not the best and the brightest, the meanest and most adaptable. Angelica would take him home in a wink, except she was working and had to close up the bar alone. She could tell from the

halos in the pupils of Hectore's brown eyes he was luded and coked
to the gills, he'd be flying to the moon without a pilot by the time she
called the night's last call. When Hectore's runny-nosed cohorts
disappeared for a twelfth trip to the bathroom in half as many hours,
he inquired politely if Angelica had any Cuban cigars. Before she
could answer, Bubba-Bob, perched on the stool next to Hectore,
offered free and voluminous advice. "Don't serve Commie drags here.
Want that Commie shit, why don't you swim the ninety miles and
light up in the Workers' Paradise." The spin of Hectore's eyes didn't
seem to register the insult, but at the far end of the bar St. Cloud
heard Bubba-Bob's thick syllables slipping through a rummy sea. St.
Cloud attempted to screw himself straight on the slippery barstool, it
had passed the hour when most die-hard whiskey sulkers and gin
gulpers staggered off into the precipitous night. He raised his glass
to make a toast, surprised to discover Angelica, Bubba-Bob, and a
dark guy drumming his fingernails against the mahogany bar top,
were the only ones left in the smoky room. "God pity the sailors on
a night like this," St. Cloud blurted. "What is that supposed to mean?"
Bubba-Bob demanded. St. Cloud kept his glass of rum aloft, a shaky
amber beacon shining out to all on land and sea navigating the
precipitous night, "Someone says he's swimming to Cuba for a cigar,
God be with him!" "That's the dumbest thing I ever heard," Bubba-
Bob slammed his fist onto the bar. "Angelica, bring this piece of squid
bait another rum." Angelica grimaced, "You already bought him the
last thirteen." Bubba-Bob hunched his thick shoulders, "Somebody's
got to pour sense into him, might as well be this bubba." Hectore
stopped drumming his nails against the bar top; the lobster boat
Captain he was looking for was called Bubba Jonesby. St. Cloud raised
his refilled glass to Bubba-Bob, "Here's to the greatest shark killer in
the Keys." He glanced down at Bubba-Bob's thick white socks, then
winked at Angelica. "Here's to the island's best-dressed Captain, with
or without his white socks on." Bubba-Bob shoved his glass to Angelica,
"Fill it up, and give the Commie a shot too." Hectore's mind was
flying around the room, for the past six hours he had been standing
next to the man he had come to teach a lesson. Life is always playing
jokes. Hectore smiled at Bubba-Bob, "I too hate the Commie mu-
chachos. What I meant was I want a cigar made by Cubans here. This
used to be a famous place for Vueletas." "Not anymore, bubba,"
Bubba-Bob's big hand slapped Hectore's padded silk shoulder.
"Cuban-made cigars around here have gone the way of pink flamingos

and twelve-year-old virgins." Hectore raised the glass of rum Angelica poured to thin lips curving into a smile. His eyes roamed over Bubba-Bob as he sipped. He had his man; ugly red face, fish-stained pants, a Captain's cap cocked over bristling hair with the stenciled message: THE BUBBA BUCKS HERE. Hectore thanked Bubba-Bob for the drink and inquired what his last name was. "Don't have last names in this town," Bubba-Bob's callused fingers squeezed Hectore's silk shoulder. "We're all bubbas here. Ain't polite to ask a man his last name or what his line of work might be. Know what I mean?" Hectore's cocaine-propelled brain understood perfectly, he was glad he had Quaalude parachutes trailing his zinging thoughts, so many options to play, quick lessons to be taught. His mouth was dry and his shoulder twitched beneath Bubba-Bob's grip. His wide-eyed gaze skidded along the back wall to the door of the bathroom where his pals were. He slipped a hand under his jacket, feeling for his switchblade knife as he cocked a foot beneath Bubba-Bob's barstool. Twenty-four ideas jumped between his ears, he grabbed the last one, kicking the barstool from beneath Bubba-Bob. The two *Marimberos* rushed from the bathroom, rubbing runny noses and waving revolvers as Bubba-Bob crashed to the floor. Hectore dug a knee into Bubba-Bob's chest, holding him down, the switchblade flashing in his hand. St. Cloud turned slowly on his stool at the far end of the bar, so this is how the world ends, he mused, watching the two *Marimberos* lock the front door and rip the phone from the wall. Hectore pressed the switchblade against Bubba-Bob's throat. "What's your last name?" "Bubba-Bob." "The rest of it, you white fuck," the blade drew blood. "Sweeny," Bubba-Bob croaked. "Robert Anthony Sweeny." "Don't boo-shit me," Hectore hissed. "Why would he do that?" St. Cloud asked in perfect if slurred Spanish, swiveling his stool to face Hectore. "Bubba-Bob lies, you cut his balls. Doesn't lie, off comes his head. He knows you're going to slice him up, least he can die by his right name." The two *Marimberos* moved toward St. Cloud, Hectore waved them back. He needed time, an ocean of options leapt in his head, bright ideas swift as fish in a barrel, he grabbed a fish, it flew from his mouth toward St. Cloud in a big laugh followed by darting words. "Maybe instead of cutting the bubba's head off I will take your eggs." The *Marimberos* turned to see if Angelica was sharing Hectore's illuminating humor, he always had such right ideas, like the pit bulls dining on kosher lawyer in Tampa, or the frog sewn into the mouth of a banker's wife in Panama City. From Angelica's position behind the bar she saw no humor in the situation. One of the *Marimberos* fixed her with a conspiratorial leer, she backed toward the cash register, cracking a defensive smile. Hectore stood up from Bubba-Bob's flattened body, starting toward St. Cloud. St. Cloud raised his hands, "Okay, I see you won't be satisfied till you get what you want. Angelica, give the man a real Cuban smoke." Angelica wiped her sweaty palms on her white shorts, "A Cuban smoke? Ah . . . oh sure. A Cuban smoke." She moved slowly, so the *Marimbero* leering at her wouldn't think she was planning a fast move. She reached behind the cash register and slid out a wooden cigar box. The *Marimbero* grabbed the box from her hands and flipped its lid open. "That box of cellophaned puppies is the true item," St. Cloud advised. "Purebred Cuban Vueletas, smoothest tobaccos ever rolled between human hands." The two *Marimberos* lit up, smiling with satisfaction, offering the box to Hectore. Hectore hesitated, the knife swinging at his side, silver fish jumping in his head. So many options, eggs to cut, heads to roll, cigars to smoke, a blond woman to unwrap. The leering *Marimbero* leaned across the bar and shoved a lighted cigar into Hectore's mouth. A cloud of blue smoke rose as Hectore attempted to collect the silver flashes jumping in his head. He decided to exercise his sense of fair play. "Roll me a dollar bill," he ordered Angelica. Angelica rang the cash register open, rolled a bill and handed it over. "Alonzo, draw a line down the bar to the drunk, the *borracho*." The leering *Marimbero* next to Angelica looked the length of the bar to St. Cloud sipping his rum and grunted, "It's too far, and he's too drunk, it's a waste." "Alonzo!" The *Marimbero* sullenly dug a glass vial of cocaine from his pants, unscrewed a plastic cap and drew a snow-white line along the shiny mahogany counter. Hectore sauntered to St. Cloud, the knife in one hand, the rolled bill in the other, his words sliding from the corner of his mouth around the cigar. "Which of these do you want, *borracho*?" St. Cloud weighed the two choices, "Not polite to turn down a buck." Hectore winked, handing over the dollar, "Your bubba bucks here, no?" St. Cloud eyed the trail of cocaine stretching to him along the bar, "If I bump that whole line I'll be bucking from here till Fourth of July. Why don't you just cut my balls off and have done with it?" Hectore slapped St. Cloud on the back, "That would be too easy. If you can't suck the whole line, *then* I take your eggs." St. Cloud slipped unsteadily off his stool, shoved one end of the rolled bill high into a nostril and bent over the line, set to snowplow through five feet of 100 percent Colombian pure and certain he wouldn't live to tell the tale. "Don't keep us waiting," Hectore's voice coaxed with a laugh. "We have a job to do." When it came to cocaine St. Cloud wasn't a big tail wagger, he could take it or leave it. In a town where it was always around he preferred to leave it, not that he was high-horsed or defied prevailing fashion. He considered himself the upholder of a more genteel tradition, the conversational drunk. Although he made little conversation outside the dialogue existing in his pickled brain, he craved the way alcohol rattled loose syllables, then clanged them together like well greased sabers, creating sentences that slipped off one another with strikingly misguided purpose. As a word man of lofty alcoholic standards what he disliked most about cocaine was the cheap trick it played on human animals, who, after riding a bumpy line or two, thought they had something important to say. Time after time St. Cloud had been subjected to the late night torture rack of these animals jumped up on marching powder with nowhere to go, convinced their simplest guttural burp heralded an avalanche of syntactical inspiration to be seized upon by all and held up for lucid dissection. When these nervous animals finally produced entire sentences, no matter how boldly inane the content, they assumed their utterances had split hidden knowledge from the stone of wisdom. Such behavior was enough to make a drunken word man puke. St. Cloud was rabidly against legalizing cocaine, not because it was evil novocaine for the brain, a far more insidious threat prevailed. He dreaded being condemned to a coke-snorting generation with nothing to say but refusing to shut up. "We are waiting, *borracho*, time to blow out the candles." Hectore's words caused St. Cloud to hunch closer to the line. What the hell, he thought, he could use a little predawn pick-me-up. In one heroic inhalation he soared up the line, the searing cut of coke driving like an icepick up his nose, behind his eyes, through his brain, banging into his cranium, leaving him dazed with numbness as he came up for breath, his startled eyes focusing on Hectore's knife coming down toward him in bright light, its sharp tip stopping before his forehead. Hectore's voice came through the bright light, "Maybe that bump will loosen your tongue. What is the name of your Captain friend lying on the floor pretending he is an unborn chicken?" St. Cloud's tongue wasn't loosened, it was thick with numbness from the base to the tip. "Rubba-Bub Beaney, allweady tud yu," St. Cloud mumbled, trying to get his numb tongue to work. The knifepoint pushed into his forehead, opening the way for a drop of blood to roll down along the side of his burning nose. Hectore pulled the blade back from St. Cloud's skin, he liked this *borracho*, he was not afraid to die, there were not many jokers such as this left in the deck, most were like the Captain cowering on the floor. Hectore decided this *borracho* was not a man who stayed drunk because he was a coward, he was something different, a man who stayed drunk because he was brave. This was one of the fast ideas swimming in Hectore's brain, he thought it so brilliant he allowed himself the luxury of taking a deep drag from the smoldering Vueleta, blowing a pungent cloud of smoke into St. Cloud's face. "Are you not lying to me, *compadre*? Isn't the name of your Captain friend Bubba Jonesby?" "No, he's not lying!" Angelica shouted. She now understood clearly what was happening, the *Marimberos* were MK's men come to teach a lesson to Bubba Jonesby for violating the accommodation. She wished Brogan was in the bar to straighten the cowboys out, but he was in the Caribbean chasing the rumor of another three-hundred-year-old wrecked galleon. "Check the wallet in Bubba-Bob's pocket. You'll see you've got the wrong guy." Hectore smiled through the swirl of blue smoke surrounding him, "Don't have to check no wallets. I've got *my* bubba." St. Cloud freed the thought on the tip of his numb tongue, "Angelica's telling the truth, he's not your bubba." The words emerged in perfect Spanish. Whenever St. Cloud snorted too much coke he began thinking and speaking in Spanish, his mind laced with Latin sounds. The alchemy of alcohol and cocaine rendering him fidgety as a cat with a melting bone stuck in its throat. The bone was Pablo Neruda's poetry, slashing passages of it escaped St. Cloud, as if from the lips of another man in another time, trumpeting the mawkish and maudlin, the sublimely humble and less than redeemable, a bravado of loose language rolling dangerous as whiskey barrels on the precipitous deck of a storm-tossed ship rounding Tierra del Fuego, blown forever off course in a sea of no rules, boastful waves crashing overhead, promising to sink from sight sordid prayers of hope, while the poet's voice struggles from parched pages, sly verse winging duck-swift on waxed wind, above cargoes of lies capable of crushing syllables from oranges, seeds from tongues. God pity the wizened cocaine sirens howling on a night like this:

"Balboa, you brought death and claws everywhere into the sweet land of Central America, and among those hunting dogs your dog was your soul. Mother of stone, sperm of condor, high reef of human dawn, of the many men who I am, they disappear among my clothes. In films

full of wind and bullets I goggle at the cowboys, I even admire the horses, but when I call for a hero, out comes my lazy self. I want everything to have a handle, everything to be cup or tool, letting birds loose, undoing images, burying lamps. It would be delightful to scare a notary with a cut lily, or to kill a nun with a smack on the ear. The moral of my ode is this, beauty is twice beauty, and what is good is doubly good. The evenings of the woman chaser and the nights of the husbands come together like two bedsheets and bury me. The monkeys braid a sexual thread that goes on and on along the shores of dawn. I speak of things that exist. God deliver me from inventing things when I am singing!"

Hectore was stunned at the blast of language from St. Cloud. Of all the flashing fish churning the addled water of Hectore's cocaine-dazed brain, the most improbable had jumped tonight. The last thing he expected to hear uttered in a Key West bar was the monumental refrains of Pablo Neruda, whose poetry in Latin America was committed to heart, along with such dates as when Simón Bolívar freed Colombia from the Spaniards, by schoolboys, right-wing judges and Communist priests. "A miracle," Hectore proclaimed, jamming a Cuban cigar between St. Cloud's lips and lighting it. He stared into the dilated eyes of this stoned Norteamericano, who didn't look Spanish but roared epic poetry in a pure Castilian tongue, a miracle improbable as a dog singing an opera in the sweetest Italian voice heard since Michelangelo was paid for his St. Peter's paint job. Hectore was in a swoon, this poetic Caruso next to him was stoned out of his mind into the mind of another. He ordered Alonzo to chop new snow-white lines on the bar top to celebrate the miracle. Angelica dispensed more cigars and popped a bottle of cognac. She didn't understand a word of the Spanish that rolled from St. Cloud's lips, but knew something sensational was happening. Hectore declared the Caruso next to him was nothing short of a saint, only a saint could make such heavenly sounds. The newly sainted St. Cloud told Hectore that he already was a saint, his name was St. Cloud. The saint told Hectore he was making a horrible mistake, that the big man lying on the floor quiet as a billiard ball was really named Bubba-Bob. Everyone in Key West was called bubba, Hectore had the wrong bubba, his bubba lived out by the dog track. If that weren't true, Hectore was welcome to cut off the eggs between the new saint's legs, all dozen of them. Hectore was confused, the more cognac he drank the dizzier he became. He believed he had witnessed a miracle, but he was running out of ideas faster than he was running out of cocaine. When light of a new day appeared through cracks in the Wreck Room shutters, Hectore confided that he loved St. Cloud. He whispered that he wanted to believe what the saint said about Bubba-Bob, for he did not want to teach a lesson to the wrong man, but how could he believe what the saint told him was true, not some trick fish chumming up the swirling waters of both their stoned brains? Hectore demanded from the saint only the truth, then the real miracle happened. St. Cloud looked up to the wall clock behind the bar. It was five minutes to five. He declared that Hectore would hear the real voice of Neruda before the cocks crowed. "Impossible," Hectore shouted. The whole world knew Neruda died a broken man after Chile's last freely elected president was shot to death in his palace while still in pajamas. St. Cloud coolly inquired, if Hectore heard Neruda's voice, would he free Bubba-Bob, would he have faith? Hectore knew this was nothing more than the blessed madness of a crazy saint, but what did he have to lose? If the saint was right, a miracle, if not, chopped eggs all around. St. Cloud instructed Angelica to set the dial of the bar radio to a specific station. Nothing came from the channel except raspy static, piercing the dense smoke of the room. Alonzo pressed his hands to his ears, screaming Hectore was a fool playing a madman's game. Hectore's confusion turned to agitation, he raised his knife, the blade facing St. Cloud, "No fucking tricks!" The hands of the wall clock pointed exactly to five o'clock, through radio static a blast of martial music charged into the room. A fervent roll of drums preceded the husky surge of an army chorus, voices rising in rhythmic unison, praising in song the virtues of glorious revolution. Hectore's back stiffened. The army chorus gave way to a children's choir, the Cuban national anthem winging into the bar on the airwaves of Cuba's most powerful radio station. Ninety miles away the anthem roused farmers to work, rallied bureaucrats, motivated lovers and liars, awakened babies, welcomed home cheating husbands and lost fishermen. As the lilting lyrics faded the sonorous intonations of Pablo Neruda's voice boomed across the Florida Straits, his breath birthing a poetic Southern Hemisphere of clouded volcanic peaks, raging rivers, deserts of copper and jungles of gold. Hectore dropped his knife, his face glowed from alcohol and drug abuse, his eyes brimmed with tears. He had witnessed a true miracle, was in the presence of a verified saint. Outside in emerging dawn the cocks of

Key West crowed. A bet was a bet. Hectore wept, throwing his arms around St. Cloud. Lives were saved.

FOLLOWING the white cowboy hat through the crowd of costumed people jamming Duval Street, Justo laughed about the life-saving favor Bubba-Bob owed St. Cloud. Most amusing was the fact such a salt of the sea, with a captain's knowledge of tides and stars, who knew the trickiest currents along the reef and the deepest secrets of bottom fish, remained oblivious to other rules of nature, ignorant to energies abstract and unseeable, this learned wayfarer, who disdained all pursuits beyond those yielding a livelihood from brute will and strong hands, holding himself erect as the standard bearer in the brotherhood of hourly wage earners, had zero comprehension of men who made poetry, much less ever heard of the Chilean poet whose words St. Cloud conjured from static air that long-ago night when he found himself in the right bar at the wrong time. Not all considered St. Cloud a local hero, some said he just pulled a wild gamble with the *Marimberos*, which inadvertently saved Bubba-Bob's life. Justo knew better, he knew St. Cloud stumbled home each night from the Wreck Room at early dawn, was the kind of man to listen in illumination of alcoholic stupor as Radio Havana signed on the air with rousing revolutionary fervor and recorded verse of South America's twentieth century Shakespeare. If St. Cloud hadn't been on top of his game Bubba-Bob would have ended as Hectore promised, with his asshole chained to a palm tree. When Hectore left the Wreck Room the fateful morning of Bubba-Bob's first poetry lesson he threatened that if St. Cloud was playing false and Bubba Jonesby was not to be found at his trailer by the dog track, then not even Neruda, risen from the dead and walking across water ninety miles from Cuba to Key West, could prevent St. Cloud's eggs from being smashed to powder as his body beat it to hell. Justo knew Hectore never came back, the *Marimberos* were not to be seen again, nor was Bubba Jonesby, for the following stone-crab season a crab trap was hoisted up while hungry sea gulls swirled overhead, within the dripping marine slime covering the wooden slats was the largest stone crab ever seen, its orange pincers slashing out a foot from its hubcap-sized body. Inside the slats with the feisty monster were mangled bones and the bare white orb of a human skull. The forensic experts in Miami could not match an identity to the strange bony crab bait, but the gut of the giant crustacean yielded a jewel of information, a high-school graduation ring. The ring bore the insignia of Key West High, its gold sides stamped with the same graduation date as Justo's. Raised initials carved in the center of the gnawed metal band were barely discernible: *BJ*.

"Hurricane be comin! This parade be wrong! Ol Mister Finito's goin blow a hole through this island!"

Justo was startled by the words shouted at him from behind on the crowded street, a hand came down on his shoulder. He pulled away from an insistent grasp, turning quickly around into the toothless grin of Bonefish.

"Know how I be knowin Finito comin?" Bonefish ran a bony finger alongside his sun-scarred nose and tapped its bright red tip. "With this hooter is how I knows. Can smell Mister Finito before he gits out of Africa's, when he's nothin more than a baby squall. Can smells him comin cross warm waters. These peoples here paradin in streets don't know Mister Finito like I knows him, don't know he's out there lurkin. Finito don't take no holiday on Halloween, he be up to somethin. These paradin peoples be drunk and wrong, they be dead wrong. This tired old fish know what he know."

Justo was losing sight of Bubba-Bob's cowboy hat floating off in the crowd as Bonefish shouted his doomsday pitch above brassy blasts from a Bahamian band of black men strutting past in rows of snappy white uniforms.

"Hey, you need an aircondishner? I got two!"

Justo did not answer, leaving Bonefish behind as he pushed into the crowd.

"Know what else I gots sides the aircondishner?" Bonefish dug his hands into his bulging jacket pockets, "Got me some alligator pears!" He held aloft two gnarly green globes of fruit. "These avocados be savin you! After Mister Finito roars through gator pears be all they is. C'mon back, bubba. Finito be stormin tonight. You gonna die out there with no meat."

A wedge of human-size dancing pumpkins blocked Justo's path. He was afraid he was going to lose complete sight of Bubba-Bob's bobbing cowboy hat. He knocked down two dancing pumpkins refusing to move aside, making only ten yards before being stopped again. A middle-aged woman in a Wonder Woman costume stood before him, waving a foot-long stick with a jagged tin star nailed to its tip.

"You a real cop or what," the masked Wonder Woman demanded, pointing the sharp star into Justo's face.

"Real," Justo grabbed the star stick. "Out of my way."

"Sure you're not one of those butch bimbos? Town's full of disco drag queens and butch bimbos. Impossible to tell who's cruising who. Told my husband not to bring me here. This place is a drag compared to New Orleans Mardi Gras, a fat dud."

"Go back to New Orleans then, and move aside."

Wonder Woman stepped defiantly forward, spreading a bed-sheet cape from outstretched arms, exposing a shapely body encased in skintight red, white and blue star-spangled outfit. "My husband's President Lincoln, see him over there talking to a palm tree? He's the one with the phony gray beard and black top hat? He might be six foot three, but he doesn't have Abe's foot-long magic twanger between his legs. I mean he's got nothing. Just like this town, a real fat dud. Understand?"

"No, and I don't care." If this middle-aged cutie did not have sense to back off he was afraid of what he might do. Over the top of her spread cape he saw Bubba-Bob's white cowboy hat cross Duval Street in front of nine marching men dressed as saw blades, waving a banner: MIAMI CHAINSAW BAND.

"If you're a real cop, do me a big favor." Wonder Woman's lips formed a wry smile beneath her masked eyes. "Call me a cab. Flew in here two days ago and I can fly out the same way." She turned her wry smile toward Abraham Lincoln and a youthful man, naked except for a brief Tarzan thong slung around his waist, a spiked crown of palm fronds wreathed around his head. "Abe can stay here and marry that date palm he's been chatting up for the last hour. If Abe thinks I'm going to put up with that anymore, he's crazy. This is one Wonder Woman who won't sit around waiting for an emancipation proclamation of the sexes, not when there are jet planes she won't. Hey, what's that? You really *are* a cop!" Wonder Woman's words were interrupted by static squeal of the two-way radio hooked to Justo's belt, a dispatcher's voice announcing a breaking and entering five blocks south, an officer on the scene requesting immediate back-up.

Justo knew it was nearly impossible to move a patrol car through the costumed crowd of revelers, which meant he was the closest cop to give assistance. He also knew who the officer calling for backup five blocks away was. He took off running.

Wonder Woman whooped with excitement, waving the star stick over her head, as if she had been transformed into the Good Witch of the West, bestowing her blessing on a confused Dorothy racing toward Oz.

Justo headed away from the crowd, sprinting down a back alley, emerging onto Whitehead Street. In the distance rose the silhouette of the lighthouse built after the 1840 hurricane, its brick bulk towering above cigarmakers' shacks. The brilliant lantern eye of the lighthouse had been dark for a generation, no longer guiding ships. The lighthouse guided Justo, he turned the corner before it, stopping at the sound of a burglar alarm ringing from within a wooden shack weathered silver by a hundred summers. Faintly discernible letters on a battered tin sign above the shack's front entrance had not changed since Justo was a boy: A. GARCIA & SONS * BUCHES * BOLLOS * CUBAN SANDWICHES. It was still Justo's favorite *buche* shop. Pacing beneath the sign was one of Key West's finest, the redneck rookie whose complaints had led to Justo's walking a beat this Halloween night. One of the rookie's hands fidgeted nervously on the handle of a holstered .38, the other hand grasping a flashlight, its sweeping beam landing with a blinding flash in Justo's face.

"What took you so goddamn long?" the rookie drawled in a guttural growl. "I put the call in twenty minutes ago."

"Kill the light!"

The beam flicked off.

Justo stepped forward. "What's the deal?"

"Break-in," Rod hissed. "No sign of forced entry here, must have broke a back window. Still inside because there's a wall of cactus behind the store, a monkey couldn't get over it. Have to come out this way." He yanked his gun from its holster. "I'll slip around, cut the electricity to the alarm, then flush em out."

"No," Justo pulled his own gun. "We'll go in together in case there's a surprise. They make a break and we lose em, tough, better to play it safe."

"Chickenshit way to do it, but you got seniority." Rod scurried off into darkness along the side of the shack.

Justo waited until the electricity was cut and the alarm died. Muffled parade sounds floated from the far distance. He noticed the houses surrounding the shack were dark behind closed shutters. He crouched low, carefully making his way along the wall of the shack. He heard

Rod smash the lock of the back door and stomp inside without waiting. From the other side of the iron-grated window where Justo stood Rod's flashlight flared with brightness, exposing Justo in perfect target outline. He dropped quickly to the ground, crawling on his stomach, the barrel of his revolver pointing the way as he slipped through the back doorway. Rod's flashlight beam found him, sweeping over his body.

"Turn the damn light off," Justo whispered.

The beam flicked off, Rod slid up next to Justo. "Just wanted to make sure it was you."

"Who did you expect? That's the second time you've jacklighted me like a deer."

"Shhhh," Rod's hand touched Justo's shoulder. "There it is again, hear it?"

Justo heard nothing, at forty his hearing was not what it once was, too many guns had gone off next to his head. Sometimes he couldn't hear Rosella, whispering something special into his ear. The last thing he wanted was for the Southern blister breathing heavily into his face to find out he was hard of hearing. "Sure I hear it."

"Somebody up front by the *buche* steamer. Thought I heard em when I came in, put the light up there but couldn't see nobody."

"Maybe hiding behind the counter."

"Let's rush em."

"Hold on. Could be a kid or something, let's find out."

"Might be armed. Can't afford to take chances," Rod's breath puffed in Justo's face.

"We take the chance. If they were going to open up they would have done it when you barged in the door."

"I say don't wait for more backup, rush em now."

"Dammit no." Justo had trouble keeping his angry voice down. There were many ways he had imagined himself dying, but being shot in a Cuban sandwich shop on Halloween night was not one of them. "I said wait."

"I'm not going to lie here on my gut forever. Who knows if we'll get backup on a night like this?"

"Okay, you slide over against the wall so we both don't get nailed when I shout our ID."

"That's more like it." Rod nudged Justo's ribs with the barrel tip of his revolver, then slid away.

Justo waited until his uneasy breathing steadied, then blurted, "Key West Police! Throw out your weapons and stand with your hands up. You will not be hurt!"

All was quiet at the other end of the dark aisle. In the stillness Justo's heavy breathing came back, blood thumping in his eardrums. He decided to sit tight, time was on his side, time is the ally of the pursuer. A shuffling sound came from behind the counter at the front of the shop, it was the last thing Justo heard before five shots fired from Rod's gun, thundering together in deafening clap.

Rod's flashlight clicked on, its beam piercing the dark aisle, illuminating a wooden counter splintered by bullet holes. The beam climbed to the top of the counter, exposing the chrome-handled gleam of an ancient *buche* machine. Shelved above the steamer were cans of condensed milk, two of them blown open, the wall behind splattered white. The light clicked off.

"Justo?" Rod's husky whisper came through darkness from the far side of the room. "You think I got em?"

"Why the Christ did you *shoot*?"

"Heard em making a move on us."

"Told you to wait it out." Justo flicked on his flashlight, shooting the beam up the aisle.

Rod's light came back on, its beam crossing Justo's. "Looks like I got em, huh? But there ain't no blood anywhere, just milk."

Justo stood cautiously, keeping the light beam and his .38 aimed at the counter. "Go see what you bagged. I'll cover."

The shadow of Rod's bulk rose from across the room, he stalked up the aisle, Justo's light beam stabbing into his back.

Justo mumbled impatiently beneath his breath. Rod was embarked on another ignorant move, placing himself in the line of fire in the event someone came up shooting from behind the counter.

Rod stopped and peered over the bullet-riddled counter, holding his gun at the ready. "Well, kiss my ass good-bye!"

"What is it?" Justo moved quickly up the aisle. Maybe Rod had shot a kid attempting to steal the cigar box of money old Garcia kept hidden. Justo pushed Rod aside and leaned over the counter, shining his flashlight down. In a puddle of milk dripping from exploded cans above was the largest Cuban Death's Head bug Justo ever laid eyes on, big as a rat, its antennae trembling with confusion. Iridescent eyes gleamed from the insect's hoary head, beneath its twelve legs scuddling through creamy ooze was a wire lead, one end connected to an alarm bell on the wall, the other attached to a cigar box stuffed with money under the counter. The bug had tripped the alarm wire on its way to raiding a bag of sugar near the cigar box. "Congratulations," Justo shined his flashlight into Rod's perplexed face. "You almost blew away a prize-winning bug."

"Don't patronize me, porch monkey." Rod waved his gun. "It's a mistake anyone could have made." He aimed the gun down and fired, blasting a fist-size hole in the floor, obliterating the bug.

Through ear-splitting reverberation triggered by the gunshot Justo shouted, "What did you call me?"

"You heard it," Rod screamed in Justo's face.

Justo was aware of how close Rod's big body was to his, how they were both the same size, black and white versions glaring at one another. He felt the muscles in his right arm twitch, preparing to slam his flashlight's metal butt into Rod's sun-blistered face. He hesitated. He sensed a painful hole opening in his stomach, a hole like the one created by the bullet just fired through the floor. Overwhelming rage welled up from the hole, he knew he was going to kill Rod. He had to outthink himself before it was too late. He spun around and walked down the dark aisle, out the door, away from raging instinct, not stopping until he reached the lighthouse. He stood trembling beneath the tower which no longer guided misguided mariners, but still lorded it over streets of modest shotgun houses, the neighborhood where Aunt Oris lived and chickens pecked in backyards planted with tropical fruit trees, a place marked on early Key West maps as Africa Town. A place still called Nigger Town, Black Town, Tan Town, or home, depending on the color of one's skin. A place where for generations there were churches, schools and movie theaters *for Coloreds only*, a far cry from the distant world a few blocks away across Duval Street. As a boy Justo journeyed to Aunt Oris' shack from the other side of Duval, where he lived, because his people were considered Cuban, not Colored. In those days the ice-cream man still called to children in the street before Aunt Oris' shack, men gathered up at the corner grocery store, and women watched over all from porches behind picket fences. It was a time when the lighthouse lantern still burned, its bright beacon passing over all on the island equally, but not passing over equals. The steady light glossed over obvious separations, vicious hates, and institutionalized fear. Now even that light was darkened to nothing, but reality was illuminated for Justo. He wanted to hurl Rod's white carcass into dark sea, but there are times when a man must choose his own life above others, save himself from himself. At such times a man must look within for guiding light, steer his ship from harm's way. Justo forced himself to walk toward the babble of distant Duval. The shadow of fear was filling with evil and there was a long way to go before the witching hour struck. He had to find St. Cloud before the light went out for everyone.

21

EVERYONE is selling false goods, guilt is the currency of fools, Evelyn reminded St. Cloud of this many times. He was mystified as to why he should be thinking of this as he stood in a crowd cheering the brassy blast of a passing Bahamian band, even the blood buzz of rum in his veins couldn't blot the thought. His mind was the mainspring of a clock undone, he was out of sorts, a cuckoo in a cockroach body, a scorpion in a burning palm tree. Even Bubba-Bob had not recognized him earlier, but that may have been because this was the first time he had come down from his barstool to join the Duval Street frolic on Halloween night. Usually St. Cloud let the party come to him. Tonight he donned an appropriate disguise, dealt himself in with the hordes of masked merrymakers surging through city streets. Bubba-Bob may also have not recognized him because his arm was around Scarlett O'Hara. The ruffled top of Scarlett's scooped dress revealed curvacious breasts uplifted by a corsetted waist. She was a five-alarm item stopping every male in her path, but the flutter of her lashes above cool green eyes dispatched foolhardy drunks and misguided adventurers back into the costumed crowd. Bubba-Bob had not paused to bray macho compliments only because he was on the singleminded prowl for St. Cloud. It never occurred to Bubba-Bob, passing by in his white cowboy hat, that Rhett Butler, with his arm cinched around Scarlett's waist, was St. Cloud. Like nearly everyone else in town Bubba-Bob had never seen St. Cloud wearing anything other than rumpled pants, ratty seersucker sports jacket, and a sweat-stained sailing cap. Bubba-Bob had passed Rhett and Scarlett by without so much as a knowing wink or outraged hoot, but

Bonefish stopped dead in his tracks. Bonefish deduced here was a real Southern gentleman and his lady, who must have dire need of an air-conditioner in their antebellum mansion. He had air-conditioners to spare, was willing to oblige the needy, even if they already were rich.

"El Finito be on his way," Bonefish hopped from one foot to the other with great urgency before Rhett and Scarlett. "Be here by midnight," he turned his bent nose heavenward, nostrils twitching at night sky. "You feels the weather creepin up your backs? Oppressive weather. Weather what's hot and calculatin. Wants to explode in your face. Wants to be done with you. Maybe you need an extra air-condishner? How bout a brand-new toaster still in the box? Got me electric blankets and car tires too. You be havin these things cause this tired ol fish be too smart to outrun Mister Finito. You try drive off this island cross the bridges, Mister Finito he go chase you. He go chase you, an he go get you."

Lila nudged St. Cloud, she wanted him to make Bonefish go away, his rantings frightened her, his bone-sharp body pushing too close.

Bonefish dug into bulging jacket pockets and pulled out glistening green avocados, holding them to the sky in outstretched arms. "Take these gator pears," Bonefish's mouth opened in a sly smile. "You need meat to survive."

Lila nudged St. Cloud harder, but realized he was not concerned with Bonefish's raving, was even amused by it. She wanted to walk away, but the press of the crowd prevented her. Too many strange things had been happening to her and St. Cloud lately. Things she knew not the design of seemed to be closing in.

"I'll take one of those pears." St. Cloud placed the open palm of his hand before Bonefish in order to receive the blessing of fruit.

"Take two!" Bonefish thrust both avocados at St. Cloud, startled someone finally heeded his warning about oncoming disaster. "Those gator pears be savin you." He backed into the crowd, pointing a finger at the sky. "Smell the air. Always before Finito comin the air be filled with the stink of dead turtles."

St. Cloud shoved the fruit into frayed pockets of the long-tailed tuxedo jacket he wore. Like a proper Southern gentleman, he sipped his libation from a flask, a not so small canteen sloshing with rum. "Hey, come back here!" He called to Bonefish, whose thin body was being buffeted in the opposite direction by the current of the crowd.

"I could use that air-conditioner. Never had one, just sweat it out every year. Come on back!"

"No time! Smell the turtles. Save yourselves." Bonefish disappeared behind a wall of secretaries from Miami dressed in pink pig outfits, fighting their way closer to the muscular black men of the Bahamian band strutting their musical stuff up Duval Street.

St. Cloud looked to the night sky. He couldn't smell anything. All he saw were overhanging balconies weighted with merrymakers hurling water balloons, firecrackers and confetti bombs. He sensed no hint of boisterous weather lurking offshore. The usual murky humidity prevailed, fuzzing the outlines of near and far images, decomposing distinctions, in a rush to replace old rot with fresh-born. No dead turtles were spinning from the sky, only costumed inebriates stirred the pot of mayhem from above. St. Cloud smiled, Bonefish was probably the only one on the island not trying to peddle false goods. Bonefish wasn't trying to sell anything, he was trying to give it all away. He was dead right about one thing, sooner or later the Mister Finito he talked about was going to come blowing hard out of Africa to take the island back down to its lowest common organic currency, reinstate a natural order. No more Fantasy Fests then, just conchs cooing in sea moss, manatees mooing in mangroves, flamingos flaming through cloudless sky above an island wiped clean of all commerce other than whiptail lizards dividing delicious fire ants with flocks of chirpy palm warblers. Such sights St. Cloud hoped to see, but when the end came no one would survive to tell the tale of what happened after the two-hundred-mile-an-hour west-moving mass of rising hot air hit town. No one except maybe Bonefish could survive that, and he certainly would have no use for people then, no guilt would burden him. A simple string of pearl perfect islands would be left, stretching from the Dry Tortugas to Miami's Key Biscayne, naked as the day Ponce de León sighted them in spring of 1513, afloat in timelessness, exactly where St. Cloud wanted to be, on a newborn land with Lila. It takes a fool to love like a fool. After the hurricane St. Cloud could slip from beneath the rock of self-contempt, swim to surface illumination where Lila beckoned. Temptation was on the rise, St. Cloud was prepared to cash in his fool's gold, set aside despairing over his failed past in order to risk defeat anew. He was dueling against the omnipresent shadow of MK for Lila, but the main adversary was Lila herself. She had the instinct of youth to remain free, this instinct was his most formidable foe. To accomplish his own salvation he had to destroy Lila's independence. Her unsullied female wholeness he now risked despoiling. Within the sea-green depths of her eyes the true stakes of the game were reflected. The battle was to secure her trust in order to dominate her soul. Lila was not about to surrender without fighting off all comers, her instinct to remain free was a tenacious rope which might prove impossible for any man to cut. No matter how complicated and unjustified St. Cloud's pursuit of Lila became, he was compelled to continue until they were bound forever, or severed forever. Like any intelligent man engaged in combat against beguiling female weaponry wielded with intuitive force, he understood he was the lesser of the two warriors, but he was determined to prevail, and was not above employing any low-down trick to accomplish his exalted male purpose. He eagerly exploited every opportunity which highlighted his weakness, demonstrating he was the least strong of the two of them, throwing himself upon the threshold of self-pity, debasing himself in order to win over his opponent's maternal instinct for nurturing the weaker of the species. When this obvious trick failed to suffice he marched off in search of an arcane arsenal which she would never suspect, called in spooks, spirits and saints of both black and white magic, which is why he allowed Justo some months earlier to present him to his Aunt Oris.

Justo had not taken St. Cloud to meet Aunt Oris because he thought the man was simply confused with desperate desire for a younger woman, he took St. Cloud because he thought Aunt Oris might save his life. There were many things that occurred on the island best left unexplained, these were the things Aunt Oris understood, she worked both sides of the spiritual street, calling upon deities from two cultures. In her nearly century-old body, with its twig thin bones and small skull pulled tight with dark luminescent skin, there resided a presence transcending merely human endeavors. Aunt Oris possessed a prescient practicality of survival, embracing religiosity unencumbered by formal teachings, inspired by pragmatism in a world not ruled by doctrine, but dominated by sheer force of individual will. The net of Aunt Oris cast far and wide, gathering in young and old across the island, yet her powers remained unspoken to outsiders, were never referred to directly by insiders. To conjoin Aunt Oris' beliefs with one's own desire for healing and protection offered a powerful bonding unto itself. Hers was power not predicated solely on obeisance and ceremony, rather it was rooted in that most simplistic of all faiths, faith in oneself, then faith to step outside oneself.

Aunt Oris was blind, but even if she could see it would make no difference that St. Cloud was white, she recognized no color. She saw not into people, but through things. She did not need to be told of toads in the cemetery with mouths nailed shut, of hanging goats in the bat tower with ears slashed off, nor be informed of a connecting line of bizarre poetry which inexplicably ran through her great-nephew Justo and the outsider he brought to her house. She needed no reminder that the shadow of fear was rapidly filling, that Justo sensed deep in his soul something far more sinister than Colombian cowboys loose in the streets, preparing to strike. Justo need not explain he wanted St. Cloud kept alive because he was more than a close *compañero*, he was a touched soul, with the gift of tongues. That gift, if directed, could touch others. Justo still intended it to touch Voltaire. He had not sent prior word of his visit to Aunt Oris. She always knew Justo was going to appear, and lit perfumed candles at her bedroom altar to Santa Barbara days before he arrived. She was more than a blood relation, she was his spiritual Godmother, protector in this life and guide into the next world, the one who placed Saints in his path to guide the way. If he betrayed the Saints she would be aware of it. He had to prove his faith continually, only the faithful could battle spirits from beyond. With the Saints on his side Justo could fight Zobop, but for St. Cloud to survive he must prove his faith. Zobop was not one thing, but many, a magical gangster who changed victims into beasts before slaughtering them. This Justo learned from Aunt Oris; her eyes, which could not see the present, still saw the past. She spoke to Justo and St. Cloud of a time in the old land, before even Slavers came, in villages where people feared to venture from safety of mudded huts, because beyond in dark bush was Zobop, who was not to be denied. "And what about this?" Justo asked Aunt Oris, rising from a chair in her kitchen where he had been listening, placing between the polished whites of her palms the old glass jar filled with rusted fishhooks, bent coins and twisted nails, which had been mysteriously left on St. Cloud's doorstep. He sat back down and winked reassuringly at St. Cloud, who had no idea what was going on. The kitchen was cluttered with bundled herbs and dried flowers of every scent and color, faded photographs of black Saints torn from faith-healing magazines papered the walls. On top of the refrigerator a bronzed cross writhing with a plastic crucified Christ was illuminated by flickering red votive candles. The blade of a severely sharpened machete gleamed in one corner. Curious youngsters peered through an open window at St. Cloud, behind them muscular men stood watch over the old woman who lived in the little shack longer than anyone remembered, who spent freely from her treasure trove of generous spirit, a woman they would lay down their lives for. Chickens in the yard cackled as a white fan-tail pigeon landed in a jacaranda tree blooming purple. Aunt Oris shook the jar Justo had handed her, listening intently to the rattle of hooks, coins and nails within. She raised the jar to her ear, bending to its rounded cool shape, as if divining the roar of the sea within a conch shell. Her white hair fell across her face, covering the jar. Her knees came up beneath the simple cotton of her dress as she pushed back in a cane rocker and hummed, not sounding a tune or hymn, but a distant, private incantation, building momentum. The creaking rocker swept her near weightless being to and fro across the plank board floor. Over the heads of curious children at the window the white fan-tail pigeon appeared in a flurry of outstretched wings, catching a precarious perch on Aunt Oris' shoulder. The sudden apparition surprised St. Cloud, he'd seen his share of park pigeons swoop and drop their splatter of white poop on many a statue, but he had never seen a wild pigeon land on a person's shoulder. Quickly as the fan-tail achieved its balanced purpose, it lifted from Aunt Oris' shoulder, fluttering around the room, a trapped spirit in dim sunlight, finally finding the open window and winging away over the heads of the incredulous children, who jumped back at the sudden voice coming from Aunt Oris. Shouted words drowned out the loudly creaking rocker, words reverberating with the nervous intensity of a young bride testifying to eternal fidelity before a church full of strangers. "Aint seen no bad as dis since we wer'n de times of Mistah Roozvelt. Durin de Big Wind, de times of de Big Breath of O comes blowin o'er dis islind. Lordee laud, de peoples deyblowin way'n yonder inta de ocin's graves. Go'n comin agin, yah yah, comin agin. It wer'n de year de Flaglir fella's rayroad done blow'n down, an de sponges, dey all die in de ocin's bed. An my husbin cry'n cause all de fishins in de ocins be dy'n too. I sez husbin, hushin now honie, be mo bettah by'n bye, ya'll sees. Jes pray to de O. O makin show yo gits de pay." Aunt Oris stopped rocking, holding the old jar in quivering hands, her molten gray eyes going through Justo across from her, her forehead folded in wrinkles of concern, her voice swiftly changing to that of a terrified small girl calling down a narrow alley at phantom shapes moving violently in darkness. "Oh Mistah Filor sly as de mouse, but he doan be what dey thinkin he be. Ya'll lookin in dis here bottle from de sea. Ya'll thinkin yo see Jay-sis in dis here glass prisin. Ya'll thinkin dese nails be from de Jay-sis cross, dat dese hooks from Saint Petrie's boat in de sea of Gal-o-lee, n dese coins be from Jewel-yes Seizure's purse. NO. Ya'll bin thinkin wrong. Dis jar no sign Jay-sis a comin. Dis here be Filor's work, he be a bufo toad talkin through sewed up lips. Filor's like de crab, what is mo bettah den de man, cause crab doan need no helpin hand makin his palace in de sand. Dis here be no *Guede Ni Bo*, ain't no Jay-sis descendin. Dis be *Ti Puce lan d' L'eau*, a lil flea in water. Dis be hissin an kissin *Danbhalah* his many selfs. Y'all bewares he doan gits no drum to makes a Big Wind a'comin. Serpent man *Danbhalah* gots no ears. God takes em long agos, stretched em on de temple drums so only Priests can talk to *Danbhalah*. Sometimes *Danbhalah* go in disguises, lookin to makin a false drum to fool de peoples he is a Great Papa drum talkin from de temples. *Danbhalah* takin de ears from de goat to makes his false sound ring true, mislead peoples from de righteous crossroads." Aunt Oris' frail body collapsed in the rocker. Sunlight through the window above the children's silhouetted heads was almost gone, the candles atop the refrigerator flickered down, throwing shadows across the walls of sainted black faces. Aunt Oris' eyes did not close. She sat in almost complete stillness, her shallow breathing barely perceptible, as if in deep yet wide-eyed sleep, dreaming an upright dream while sunlight melted. Murmurs from the muscular men in the yard grew lower, then stopped. A clouded sense of foreboding gathered in the small shack. Justo lit a beeswax candle in a coconut shell atop a high bureau of drawers. A moaning came from Aunt Oris. Her body heaved in a shudder, anxious words sputtering anew from her lips, catching Justo up with a start. "Oh migh divine Horseman! Doan let dem trap yo! Run migh man! Pray to de Great Papa before de boat sink!" The words hurled at Justo as Aunt Oris bolted to the edge of her rocker, trembling hands reaching out in darkness, running over Justo's face as tears flowed down her own. "Oh migh sweet blood, migh soul, migh mighty Horseman!" The words rasped in near breathless sobs. "Doan yo let Zobop cut his yellow X on yo chest! Doan be fool to step into Zobop's yellow circle!" Aunt Oris slumped, her sobs quieting as worried murmurs from muscular men in the yard started again. Justo sat back down next to

St. Cloud. Aunt Oris' cotton dress appeared to be a simple shroud draped on the fragile outline of her body, her lower legs seemed invisible, her shoes empty of feet. A detached voice emerged from her with disconcerting strength, unwavering, its intentions directed straight at St. Cloud. "Yo be bad luck! A hex man! Born wit de name *Saint*. Only Saints be *Saints*, born wit out sins. Saints sins later, when dey doubts de holy truths. Yo gots to believe to be de Saint. Uproot doubts. I see doubts follow yo like clouds of rain. I sees arrows in yo heart from Queen Erzulie, Mistress of Water. Yo gots deep water in yo brain. Erzulie is drowning yo in her swamp of kisses. The Queen be laughin at yo, cause yo no Saint. Her kisses be wet but her hearts be dry. Cause yo doubt, Erzulie go drown yo. Zobop's go'n put his yellow X on yo, less yo wake up. Yo got to believe. Here yo go, boy!" Aunt Oris' hands dipped into the folds of her cotton dress. St. Cloud could not see what she was doing. The motion of her hands finally came up in dim light, flinging an object at him. It struck his cheek and fell to the floor. "Yo put'n de magic on," Aunt Oris' voice urged. "Keep de magic round yo neck so Zobop can't git it in his noose." St. Cloud felt on the floor for the object. His fingers traced over a wishbone on a braided string necklace, dried pieces of fowl meat still clung to the bone. "Dat magic keep yo safe, be good as Justo's chicken bone, only doan be gold. Justo believe, he touch gold, den de loa gods feel him callin. Yo must touch bone to believe. Even den loa Saints may no feel yo callin." St. Cloud looped the wishbone charm around his neck in darkness. After a while he heard the creaking of Aunt Oris' rocker again. She cooed in a pigeon contented voice. "Dat mo bettah. Now yo doan doubts so much. Believes what I tells yo bout de Queen. Yo no gits Erzulie like a regular Saint. Gots to feed her specials. Not wit prayers 'n candles. Not wit monies 'n male perfumes. She is sea, pearl of de ocins. De pearl of fish be its eye. Pearl of turtle be its foot. Pearl of octopus be her belly. Gots to feed de Queen differents if yo wants journey to *Zi let En Bas De L'Ea*, de islind way down yondah under de sea. Gots to go down dere where de souls wid no eyes livin. Gots to go dere if yo is de Saint."

Aunt Oris instructed St. Cloud on matters of cunning and survival which surprised even Justo, who brought him to her seeking protection against an evil operating by ancient rules and perverted ritual. St. Cloud did not leave Aunt Oris a true believer, but with a recipe to entrap his personal Erzulie in the most improbable manner imaginable. He was determined to unlock the door into Lila's good graces,

insinuate himself by any means into her youthful heart. Aunt Oris
did not give him the key to Lila's door, she gave him the key to a sea
of green banana chutney and sweet yam meringue. When a woman
asks a man if he loves her, she is not expecting an answer, she is
seeking reassurance. When a man cooks for a woman, he is not
providing a meal for her belly, he is denuding the soul of his male
mystery. If there is one thing common to most women it is, given
time to discover, they will always choose a man of substance over
mystery. A clever man divests himself of mystery, knowing that when
it comes to matters of cohabiting with the opposite sex, the predictable
bread of daily sustenance prevails over a salad of promised tomorrows.
Thus St. Cloud's new credo, his secret weapon in the duel for Lila.
It was not a mere cook he became, nor a chef of exemplary culinary
audacity, on that score Lila herself was not to be undone; instead he
stirred up a storm of possessive passion, utilizing herb extracts and
root powders to win his cause. Verbena oil was employed to lure his
love, rosemary to encourage devotion once love was lured to bed, a
smattering of ground coral powder to ensure time with love in bed
was harmonious and sustained, passion flower, so love leavened
passionately, mustard seed to elicit beautiful children, black snake
root to make love's heart soft, basil to keep her body supple, orange
blossoms so love's secrets would be left beneath her bed pillow each
morning. These elements were tossed into the nightly parade of dishes
St. Cloud prepared for Lila, an exotic, ever changing fare with origins
in the Caribbean and West Indies, all the way back to Africa, straight
from Aunt Oris' lips to St. Cloud's ears. He haunted the local Cuban
botànica shops for hard to procure substances of both natural and
suspicious origins. He presented himself each morning at the open
stalls of the two greengrocers on the island, stalking between mounds
of tangerines, tangelos and tamarinds. Afternoons he haunted the
charter boat anchorage, in hopes some unsuspecting angler from the
Midwest had reeled from the depths an ugly fish rife with prickly
scales and ripe with gluey eggs, which could be panfried in guinea
cornmeal and jellied shark fins, the odoriferous result free to swim
into Lila's soul. When they dined in his small house at the end of
Catholic Lane next to the cemetery, a charm lamp always burned
between them. The lamp was a half coconut shell filled with crystallized
maple syrup and blackstrap molasses; beneath the goo was a black
magnet, above it was stuck a lone beeswax candle, just like the one
glowing atop the bureau of drawers through the long night when

Aunt Oris tutored St. Cloud on the ways and wiles of Erzulie, instructing how a mere mortal man could protect himself when setting sail across the Queen's perilous sea.

Lila didn't know what accounted for St. Cloud's sudden domestic turn and storm of delectable delights. He cooked all day in the kitchen of a tiny house which felt like the interior of an oversize cigar box, its century-old cypress wood walls veined with termite channels, reeking of damp earth and stewing vegetables. Something about St. Cloud's newly acquired mantle of unabashed lunacy worked away on her. His antics seemed even more playful than those of her eager pug puppy, which chased its stubby tail round and round in St. Cloud's kitchen as he tossed God knows what into steaming black kettles atop the stove. Lila asked why jasmine-scented candles burned in every corner of his hot humidor of a house? He laughed, saying it was because he put a love hex on her, if she didn't watch out he would put one on her dog too. She inquired why he never removed the chicken wishbone necklace around his neck? The tips of the brittle bone were broken off, the charm resembled nothing more than a calcified stump, yet he even wore it in the shower. He answered deadpan, that if he took off the charm his fairy Godmother would fly away. She asked why he kept a split moonstone under his bed? He explained it was because a snake cannot be caught with perfume alone. Gradually Lila began to realize how far St. Cloud had traveled to take her away from herself. That was what intrigued her, his willingness to give himself over to something bigger than what he knew. Such was his strangeness. She asked him a question which never before occurred to her, a question she never put to any man. As soon as she asked, she didn't know why she had.

Lila asked St. Cloud if he loved her. He was silent and turned to the kitchen screen door leading into his garden planted with Senegalese calabash, Mexican jicama, Bermuda onions, and Jamaican honeysuckle vines slithering up the trunk of a papaya tree. A chameleon clung to the outer surface of the door, claws anchored in the screen, tail swishing across wire mesh. A red bubble of flesh pulsed in the lizard's throat as its green body bobbed to a slow heartbeat. "I'll give you a piece of my heart," Lila heard herself say to no one in particular in the steamy kitchen. "It's not your heart I want, it's your soul," St. Cloud answered, stirring a bowl of cold strawberry soup with a wooden spoon. "I want all the way into you, to what you're hiding from yourself. I want to dive down and get it." This was the strangeness Lila felt confused by, "Why me?" St. Cloud sipped a taste of cold strawberry from the wooden ladle, "Because I know what your soul is going to look like." "What?" "The quiet surface of the mangrove flats on a bright afternoon. Through the quiet your soul will come bursting, the spinning arc of a silver tarpon flashing in pure oxygen, twisting free from the depths. I want that silver flash." Lila moved toward the offered wooden spoon and sucked fruit soup, with strawberry seeds on her lips she challenged him, "All you want is to catch and devour me." St. Cloud put his arms around her, pulling her body to him, a heavy breath of strawberries on both their lips. "No, I'm not after that tarpon to fry it and eat it. I want to stroke its silver body with my tongue, feel its wet purpose." The chameleon released itself from wire mesh, leaping over backwards into the garden after a flitting bug. The pug puppy whined at Lila's bare feet, it wanted whatever she was eating. St. Cloud held tight to Lila's supple waist, if she was going to come crashing up through the bright surface he wanted to be with her. She moaned softly, not with desire nor frustration, "You're so strange." The puppy moaned with greedy hunger. A muffled thump of drums drifted into the kitchen on hot wind from the cemetery a block away, announcing the funeral procession of a prosperous black citizen from the far side of Duval Street. St. Cloud placed a hand beneath Lila's chin, turning her face to his, "Come . . . up out . . . of yourself, to where I am. You won't be sorry. Trust . . . me." Lila's eyes gleamed jade green, leopard eyes moving over melting iceflow, no footprints left behind on dazzling crystals, only animal magnetism pulling with irresistible force. "My my," St. Cloud sighed. "Green light." The strawberry blossoming of lips touched the tip of his heart. "Are you there? Come closer." She undressed, giving full decoration to who she was, each garment discarded revealing a design of flesh made manifest, a silver shadow moving across a tight white sheet, a silken invention of such purity the velocity of its intention assumed uncontrollable force. His hands traveled her naked back, fingers spreading across a cool moon. Still, he did not have her. He had yet to make her trust, bring up an ice-breaking laugh from her depths, settle her at final ease. His lips went to her ear, whispering a Creole poem he hoped would turn passion's tide, about a man grown fat from female worship, a man who couldn't get enough, kept coming back for more:

"Black bird of my heart, whose breasts are oranges,
more savory than eggplant stuffed with crab,
you please my taste better than tripe
in the pepper pot;
Dumpling in peas and aromatic tea
are not more hot.
You are corned beef in my heart's
customhouse;
The meal is syrup in my throat;
The grouse smoking on the platter,
stuffed with rice.
Crisper than sweet potatoes,
browner than fish fries,
My hunger follows you
whose buttocks are so rich
in food!"

Lila was completely silent. St. Cloud thought once again he had gone too far, around the curve of no return, broken the mood in a gamble for something grander. The strange music, like a high whistle from a wheeling hawk, which he often heard as he rolled across the white sheet with Lila, came through the dusty windowpane above his bed. He held his breath, the strange whistling stopped. From the distant cemetery a different music sounded, over the heads of cement cherubs and marble-winged angels an uplifting blast of trumpets encouraged the mournful drums beating a man's last time. Lila turned, her breasts brushing St. Cloud's chest, words from her lips coming full in his mouth. "You are . . . so . . . strange." Her words whirled away in a closed space of tongues striking fire. St. Cloud knew then he had her soul. It was too late to celebrate, Lila had stolen his entire sense of self. At dawn he wandered into the little backyard garden, sat among rowed cabbages, beneath the papaya tree with the honeysuckle vining up its trunk. He removed his torn T-shirt, exposing neck, chest and arms covered with round bluing bruises from the night before, when Lila's softest kisses left the imprint of bullet holes on his skin. As morning sun sailed overhead, climbing to ever more brilliant heights, St. Cloud made a discovery. He was a marked victim of wounds visible only to himself. He pushed from the cabbages, unsteady on quaking legs, cocked a hand over his eyes to shield himself from the burning orb in the heavens, which only now revealed its true shape, a ship with sheeted sails fullblown in a clouded wind. The victim of invisible wounds saluted the Queen passing overhead. Sail on sailor in sea of Erzulie.

22

S T. CLOUD had alligator pears in his pockets. He had the stump of Aunt Oris' wishbone securely anchored on the string around his neck. He had the beautiful Southern belle of the devil's bewitching ball standing at his out-of-date tuxedoed side. He had everything, ready to take on whatever might come at him from the crushing crowd of Duval Street. He was better prepared than a Boy Scout dropped into a foreign forest. He had avocado meat to eat if Bonefish's Mister Finito slipped into town on a tailspinning wind. Although the air remained still, empty of turtle rot, was perfumed with breath of night-blooming jasmine, he stood guard, his canteen filled with *clarin*. If a hex came wanging down Duval with his name written on it, he was ready. Rum and Aunt Oris' wishbone charm fortified his more than normal queasy nature; if forced to choose quickly between the two, he wouldn't hesitate first to drain the canteen of its secretive syrupy power. Not that he was a disbeliever in Aunt Oris' signposts pointing to salvation in this world, and everlasting grace in the next, the problem was many of the revelations which came from her that night of their first encounter could have originated from an idle town gossip, as well as from an active spiritualist. Aunt Oris was blind and couldn't read, but someone may have informed her about the local newspaper article reporting the discovery of a mutilated goat in the Sugarloaf bat tower. Few people knew of the yellow X painted on Renoir's door, but many saw the X on the jailhouse wall after Voltaire was whisked north to the Everglades camp. Someone may have informed Aunt Oris about such mysterious events. It also wasn't certain her knowledge of Zobop was prescient. St. Cloud himself had caused Zobop's name to be chalked on the Wreck Room message board, hoping to expose the cryptic scribbler's identity. Aunt Oris' awareness of Zobop's cemetery poem about Filor's sly old mouse may have come from Justo. Since Aunt Oris was destined to be buried in the family plot, Justo may have felt compelled to call in some white magic to defend the sacred ground against otherworldly desecraters. St. Cloud was not a total disbeliever in Aunt Oris' mystical powers because she was right about the most important thing. What she told him about the pain in his heart was true, and he had followed her cure of an aphrodisiacal menu to the hilt, wangling his way to happiness through prescribed potions and edible concoctions. If he had not gone to Aunt Oris there would be no way in tricky Erzulie's great watery universe that Rhett Butler would be standing with his arm around Scarlett O'Hara on this Halloween night, marveling at masked men dressed in black tights and top hats, marching behind a truckload of Carmen Mirandas cavorting to rhumba music. Piercing the Latin beat blasting from the truck was a singular sound, like the squeal of a high-wheeling hawk. St. Cloud knew the sound well, it was the sound he had been hearing through his bedroom window whenever he was with Lila. The sound came from the marching men in jaunty black top hats, all were blowing tin whistles clenched in their teeth, creating an earsplitting chorus which scraped at the night sky. The whistle blowers passed, leaving one behind, who swung a white cane aloft, pointing to words painted on a cardboard sign he held: VOODOO SPACE INVADERS FROM FORT LAUDERDALE. The man's head jerked rapidly from side to side, his face powdered pasty white; through eyeholes cut into his mask bloodshot eyes glared. St. Cloud felt a sharp stab in his back.

"Hey bubba! That your skinny ass inside that tuxedo? What you supposed to be, circus barker or Confederate pimp?"

St. Cloud turned, Bubba-Bob loomed over him, grinning beneath the cowboy hat. "Christ!" St. Cloud screamed above a spirited high-school band costumed as tail-swagging crocodiles hot on the heels of Voodoo Space Invaders. "You scared hell out of me, jabbing your finger in my back like that!"

"It's Hell-O-Weanie bubba!" Bubba-Bob laughed, slapping St. Cloud on his padded tuxedo shoulder. "Treat or be tricked!"

"I'll treat!" St. Cloud handed Bubba-Bob his canteen of rum. "It's pure Haitian, knock your hat off."

Bubba-Bob raised the canteen and sucked like a nursing calf, rum running from both sides of his mouth. "Some treat," he burped, backhanding his wet lips. "Why, Miss Scarlett!" He swept his cowboy hat off and bowed. "Ah am most sorry ah didn't notice your lovely Southern self earlier." He winked, "but I musta passed by yore cute lil ass thousand times fore figurin who all you and this Reb gigolo really was."

Lila raised the secondhand fan she was carrying, fluttering it before her plastic Vivian Leigh face mask. Her voice slipped from behind the mask, muffled and mock Southern sweet. "Suh, a true gentleman nevah would admit to not recognizin the finest part of a Confederate daughtah's anatomy, no mattah how many times he passed it by."

St. Cloud took the canteen back, chuckling behind his plastic Clark Gable face. "You're losing your feel, Bubba."

"Losing my feel! If I so much as touched Lila's little finger, you would blow me and my charter boat straight to hell with one of those firebombs you learned to make in college. You'd probably make sure I had a load of schoolteachers from Miami on board just for good measure."

"True." St. Cloud took a swift slug of rum. "But I'd let the schoolteachers off first."

"Look at that!" Lila pointed to the most enormous float in the parade, being towed by a high-wheeled pickup and headed straight for them.

"Damn if it ain't *King Kong*!" Bubba-Bob stepped into the street, as if he were going to challenge the thirty-five-foot-high gorilla dressed in a hula skirt of palm fronds and undulating mechanically to loud Hawaiian music. Cradled in the towering beast's hairy arms was the nearly naked blond body of Angelica, squirming to tropical rhythm and screaming she was being kidnapped to the hooting crowd. A sign planted in thousands of flowers surrounding Kong's giant bouncing feet advertised: DRINK AT THE WRECK ROOM AND SINK FROM SIGHT!

"Whoooie! Hi-ya, honey!" Angelica called from her hairy aerie to Bubba-Bob. She snaked a bare leg from her dancing partner's insistent arm, the red-painted nails of her foot pointing at Bubba-Bob. "C'mon and join me! Baby won't bite!"

Bubba-Bob waved his cowboy hat. He turned to Lila with a mouth-splitting smile. "Ain't she a homewrecker!" He grabbed the canteen from St. Cloud. "Let me wet the whistle, this night's getting hot!" He belted a mouthful of rum and wrapped a brotherly arm around St. Cloud's padded shoulders. "Ya know, I owe you. Get what I mean, *owe?* Just give Bubba-Bob the word if there's anything or anyone hassling you, point their jelly ass in my direction. I'll snip their balls and run em up the flagpole." He took a philosophical swig of rum, then offered the canteen to St. Cloud by slamming it into his tuxedoed chest. "Tell ol Bubba here if you getting any shit. I'm serious as triple bypass surgery. They mess with St. Cloud, then they messing with the big Bubba." He pulled his cheek out with a thick thumb and let it whack back against his teeth with a loud slap. "They might as well kiss the baby's ass good-bye, cause that's the last crack of light they'll ever see."

St. Cloud finished what little rum Bubba-Bob left at the canteen bottom. "There is someone whose balls you could prune. If I could only find him. Nobody can find him."

"What's that coming?" Bubba-Bob looked over St. Cloud's shoulder. King Kong and his blonde had vanished up the street, replaced by the tenth high-school band of the night, costumed like a nightmare Mexican dinner and blowing a stormy version of "Seventy-six Trombones." "Whose balls did you want pruned? Couldn't hear you. Damn trombones! Hey, these high-school girls get cuter every year! Hot hot hot! Look at that enchilada over there. The one next to the red bikini dressed as a bottle of taco sauce. Light my *carne!*"

St. Cloud's eyes caught something strange moving through the crowd. He didn't know exactly what it was, but he could sense it. He saw it through the rows of bare-kneed marching schoolgirls, moving on the other side of the street, darting around a fat man costumed as Humpty-Dumpty who was vomiting in the gutter. Behind the fat man's egg-shaped bulk St. Cloud thought he saw a white and black blur disappear into the crowd. Maybe he hadn't seen anything at all. Maybe the rum and masked mayhem of the noisy night were wearing him raw. He slipped his arm around Lila's waist. She laughed, fluttering her fan at his plastic movie-star face. Her hand came up beneath the tails of his tuxedo, rubbing the knotted muscles in the small of his back, kneading the tension from him, unraveling his paranoia. He closed his eyes, concentrating on the strength of her fingers. He thought about the recipe for rhubarb-chinaberry pie Aunt Oris gave him. He wanted to go home and bake a pie with the potency to draw a woman to a man. Aunt Oris promised her pie had more power to attract a woman than if St. Cloud were to wear a dead hummingbird around his neck. Dead hummingbirds did have their advantages, often they were the only magic capable of luring the black bird of a woman's heart into the cage of love. The big problem with a dead hummingbird came about if the suitor wore it on a day deemed incorrect by the calendar of Saints and Loas. If the suitor made such a mistake he stood a better chance of being struck by lightning than he did of striking his unsuspecting object of desire with cupid's arrow. Aunt Oris warned St. Cloud about young men found along deserted pathways on Caribbean islands each spring, their bodies ripped open by lightning, dead hummingbirds tied about their necks. St. Cloud thought a rhubarb-chinaberry pie was a safer bet than a dead hummingbird. He did not want to walk around like a rum-soaked lightning rod defying Loas he had yet to identify, especially since he felt, for once in his life, he was on the right track with a woman. He wasn't quite walking on the smooth side of the street, as Justo would say, but headed in that general direction. Above the calming sensation of Lila's touch he felt a severe jab in his back, directly under his right shoulder. He thought Bubba-Bob was poking him again, then realized Bubba-Bob had moved to the other side of Lila, cheering on the hot enchiladas and sassy tacos. St. Cloud turned around and faced a skeleton trying to poke him again in the back; it was the white and black blur he thought he saw disappear across the street behind Humpty-Dumpty. The skeleton was a sinister apparition, covered by a black rubbery skin painted with realistic luminescent bones.

"Great getup!" Bubba-Bob swung around and complimented the skeleton. "Shit bubba, I'd like to use your rubber-covered ass as bait-lure for marlin. Bet if I trolled with you I'd hook up in no time a world-class fish."

The skeleton raised a silver knife.

"That sucker looks real." Bubba-Bob reached up to touch the gleaming blade.

The skeleton jerked the blade back, raising it high in the air, beyond Bubba-Bob's long reach.

"Hey! Who are you?" Bubba-Bob stepped toward the skeleton. "Brogan? Is that you dressed in this weird shit? That's something you would do!"

The knife slashed down, aimed at St. Cloud.

Bubba-Bob grabbed the bony wrist wielding the blade, trying to break its momentum. The skeleton's wrist slipped from his grasp, the knife continuing its downward thrust, barely missing its intended target, slicing along the side of St. Cloud's tuxedo, stabbing the bulge of avocados in his coat pocket. Bubba-Bob banged his hulk into St.

Cloud, slamming him to the ground before the sharp blade had time to rise and strike again. The costumed crowd shoved and screamed. Bubba-Bob's fist swung up, his broad knuckles aimed at the skeleton's skull face. The silver blade flashed, cutting the air out of Bubba-Bob's body as it plunged deep into his chest.

From his position behind a hysterical hoop-skirted Little Bo-Peep, Justo saw Bubba-Bob go down. The skeleton's knife flashed again. Justo pulled his gun and fired in the air. The crowd dropped to the ground, leaving the skeleton standing alone, its knife poised above St. Cloud. The skull face snapped around, searching for the gunshot source. Justo aimed his revolver; it was a dangerous shot, if he missed the skeleton he might hit St. Cloud. In the second it took to decide to pull the trigger the skeleton leapt over St. Cloud, disappearing behind flower-encrusted wings of a Space-Shuttle float.

Justo pushed screamers aside, bulling past the spacecraft. He saw a white and black blur cut across the intersection, headed in the direction of Whitehead Street and the old lighthouse. He played a hunch. If the skeleton thought he would radio ahead to have the lighthouse end of Whitehead blocked, then the skeleton would turn in the opposite direction, toward the abandoned Naval Base, where it could lose itself among deserted buildings sprawled between the brightly lit activity of downtown and the Atlantic Ocean's vast darkness. Justo did not radio ahead. If his hunch was right, there wasn't time. He turned into a narrow lane which crossed over to Whitehead. If he was fast enough he could cut the skeleton off as it doubled back, headed for safety of the Naval Base. When he huffed his way onto Whitehead Street he saw his hunch was right. The skeleton was racing along the sidewalk, straight for him. Justo dropped into a firing position, his gun aimed at the rush of luminescent bones. If he could take the creature without killing it, he would. If it didn't stop, he was going to blast it. He had no idea what was inside the black rubber suit, maybe bullets couldn't stop it. His finger went to the trigger. The skeleton seemed to read his mind. It spun and sprinted across the street, hit with a smashing clang massive locked gates leading into the Naval Base. Before Justo could get off a shot the skeleton leapt onto the gate's iron grates, pulled itself hand over hand to the top and dropped to the other side on all fours. It darted away down a deserted avenue cast in deep darkness beneath the overhead spread of giant banyan trees.

Justo ran to the gates. He was getting too old and slow for this.

Maybe this night was meant to teach him his time of trying to keep peace in the jungle of the streets, with or without a patrol car, was over. He felt like a creaky gorilla, grunting and groaning his way up the iron grates, kneecaps banging painfully, the skin of his chin scraping. The arrow-tipped spikes at the gate top tore through his uniform, he hung in precarious balance fourteen feet above the street. With a supreme effort he hefted his weight over the spikes and dropped to the other side, landing with a force that knocked the wind from him. He lay sprawled on the ground, his holstered gun jammed sharply under his hipbone. He forced himself to a wobbling stance, his uniform ripped and bloodied. Every part of him hurt, but every part seemed to work. He had successfully scaled the locked Presidential Gates leading to Harry Truman's Little White House.

Justo decided not to radio for backup to hunt the skeleton through the military ghost town. To find this particular white and black needle in the haystack it would take one man, not fifty. The skeleton did not need to be pursued as much as it needed to be outsmarted. To attract an elusive needle a strong magnet was needed. Justo figured he was the magnet. He rubbed the gold wishbone at his neck, slipped the revolver from its holster and hobbled forward. Ahead in darkness he heard another sound, high-pitched, like a screeching hawk, but oddly melodious and humanly insistent, a strange sort of music he never heard before. He moved from the potholed center of the once grand avenue leading to the Little White House, hopped up onto the cracked sidewalk, following the row of overgrown banyans. He thought the music was coming from the gutted military post office in deep shadow across an expanse of parched lawn. He continued cautiously, from one banyan to the next. The music stopped. He leaned against the trunk of a banyan, holding his breath until the music started again. The music changed position, coming from farther up the avenue, where the monolithic Navy foundry loomed in moonlight. The music seemed to originate from inside the foundry's steel doors, which stood open to a cavernous red-brick space. Justo crossed the avenue to the corner of the building, pressed his back against the wall as he edged toward the steel doors, when he reached them the strange music stopped. He didn't hesitate, slipping quickly inside. He switched on his flashlight, offering himself as a target, his drawn revolver ready to fire upon the slightest movement. His eyes began to adjust to what seemed sheer blackness, slowly shapes emerged, becoming identifiable objects. A rustling of wings came from high above, joined by piercing squeaks. Bats swirled in the peaked ceiling, soaring on rushes of hot air escaping through roof vents. Even in daylight it was difficult to take in the complexity of the cavernous foundry, its vaulted brick support pillars marching off at right angles to deserted offices, supply and boiler rooms, and beyond to the main gallery, where hammers and wrenches were once wielded by muscular men bending white-hot steel over brick-pit fires, creating shapes to replace mechanisms that powered dynamos of ships and submarines. Overhead, chain pulleys draped from timbered rafters, capable of swinging half-ton engines into the air with the ease of lifting a baby from its bath. Suspended from one of the chains was an anvil, its steel nose becoming visible as its mass swooped through air on groaning chain, smashing into the wall next to Justo's head with an explosion of brick and mortar. Blinding mortar dust stung his eyes, he fell to his knees, trying to sense where the next attack would come from. The strange music started again, screeching like a tin whistle, coming from all corners of the foundry before moving outside, heading up the avenue toward the Little White House.

Justo felt his way in darkness from the foundry, stumbling up the avenue, stopping beneath towering date palms. He rubbed his stinging eyes. Before him the tin roof of the Little White House sloped sharply from two stories above, the front door was boarded over, a steel grate covering the window next to it pried off. Justo climbed through the opening, stepping into foul darkness. The house had been abandoned for years, but its dilapidated state and the glory of former residents attracted a stream of vagabonds and derelicts who managed to break in, regardless of patriotic efforts exerted by local civic-minded officials. Over the years hundreds had spent a day out of the rain, an afternoon out of hot sun, a night getting drunk, or a moment shooting up, in the gutted domain of a dead president's vacation digs. The once pristine quarters were rife with shriveling turds, dried vomit and an overwhelming acrid scent of urine. Mildewed mattresses, beer cans and liquor bottles littered the termite-riddled floor of the living room, where sunburned reporters from around the world once crowded for press briefings beneath cooling blades of ceiling fans as secret service men went silently about their business. Justo accidently kicked one of the beer cans beneath his feet. The sound of strange music he was following stopped. He cautiously stepped forward, feeling an odd squish underfoot. The putrid stink of a rotting rat wafted into his nostrils. The strange music started again. It came from upstairs. He followed the music up a steep staircase, the mahogany banister beneath his hand splintered and grimy. At the top of the landing the music became more insistent, emanating from a bedroom where President Truman once slept, haunted by dreams of rumbling battle and rumored peace. When Justo took a creaking step toward the closed bedroom door the music stopped, he pressed against the wall, counting ten before swinging around and kicking the door open. The room reeked of death, he suspected a trick. He swept the flashlight beam over an object hanging from blades of a ceiling fan. It was Marilyn's Andy, the oyster-shucking scammer, naked and roped by the feet, ears slashed and throat slit. Across the wall behind was a giant yellow X, a note nailed to its center:

> *FIVE DOLLAHS WAS DEY FINE!*
> *FILOR'S SLY AS DE MOUSE!*
> *FILOR GONE GIT YOU!*
> *RUN NIGGER RUN!*

Justo heard the whistled pitch of strange music. He peered through broken windowpanes into night. A white and black blur flitted beneath palms, vanishing into the crevice of a shadow. He had not seen anyone run so fast since three months before, when Renoir led him on a breathless chase to the Atlantic's shore.

23

IT'S NOT that when you're younger you have a bigger sexual appetite, it's when you're older you've just suffered through too many mediocre meals. So many little men with big ideas about women, even I know when to throw in my hat."

"You've got all the time in the world, honey. Don't you worry." Angelica shifted her weight from one foot to the other, wiping a tear from the corner of her eye as she laughed. "You've got me, model, muse and nurse. Who could ask for anything more? You're just being selfish and cranky."

"I am selfish. The selfishness of growing old is to do all the listening while others do all the talking. My problem is I just didn't listen enough when I had the chance."

"Because you're a painter. Painters listen with their eyes. You saw plenty."

"I've made a mess of it. Like all artists, I was lonely and absurd, then I got the poison, *praise*. I had too much attention. Success is the end of everything, the beginning of nothing. You know, one rat can birth a hundred other rats in a year, but can't create a dove or a lion, just more rats. I know many painters like that. I kept trying to give birth to a new me with each painting. What people don't know is the works of mine hanging in the world's museums are more of the same, dead rats in gilded frames, dead rats with million-dollar price tags."

"Don't do this to yourself," Angelica could not stop her tears. She stood at the foot of the big brass bed, fully clothed in a light summer dress; she even wore shoes. "Don't quit."

"Didn't say I quit. I'm sketching you in my mind right now, even though you're not nude. Flesh is only so much clay, it's whose hands it's in that counts."

Angelica gave a brave laugh. "Keep feeling me in your mind, I'm much safer there."

"That's not all I'm doing in my mind."

"Good. Keep it up!" Angelica forced an air of teasing merriment into her voice. "How do you know I'm not nude? You can't see further than the nightstand next to your bed."

"An . . . An . . . Angelica, what do you take me for, an old man who goes out to the dog track once a month to bet his Social Security check?" A renewed sense of challenge gleamed in Isaac's eyes. "I could paint you as a briefcase full of dirty socks and Vienna sausages and it would still walk off the canvas as a voluptuous nude. Painters and prizefighters have to get up off the canvas before the final count."

"Good, then no more talk about rats."

"Rats have legs too, a job to do."

"They might have legs, but they don't have my ass."

"Noooo." Isaac laughed painfully, a hollow wheeze pushing from his bony chest. He sucked in his breath to form new words. "They don't have your light either, that light is the one corner left in heaven I haven't been able to paint my way out of. I'll tell you something I've never told anyone. I didn't have sex with my models before painting them. But look at me now." The breath of his words seemed to be dying away, fading back to a whisper. "I'm like distracted old Walt Whitman, who lived right up to the end for the act of creation, lice prowling through his thinned white hair, searching his scalp for a noonday suck, while beneath his thick skull were dreams of birchwood horizons and hard New England Back Bay boys. I think the poets get up off the canvas best, better than heavyweight fighters even. You know, Justo came by here last week, told me a story about that poet he loves so much, that Gargonzola guy. Well, it seems old Gurglezona got dotty as Whitman at the end, kept asking everybody what time it was, then would go to the window and complain he couldn't see any landscape, just a giant blue spot. That's where I'm headed now, beyond the landscape of flesh, beyond the wild blue yonder. I want to get the color right for once, got to be the right light. Do you know how many blues there are?"

Angelica sat quietly at the foot of Isaac's bed, staring at the floor as her body shuddered.

"The length of forever, in human terms, is the shadow of a lifetime.

All life creates light, all light creates shadows. Must define shadows if you are to get it right. I couldn't get the shadows right, now it's too late. Ah, but then, even failure isn't forever. Isn't that right, St. Cloud?"

"I've been working on it." St. Cloud squeezed Isaac's frail hand grasping his. Seated in a chair next to the bed, St. Cloud gazed through the windows, across a darkening sea to a thin blue line on the horizon. The longer he stared at the wavering line the more it seemed to contract into a simple blue spot.

A hollow coughing laughter spurted from Isaac's lips. "There's hope for you yet, St. Cloud. Just might succeed where I failed. I've been a fraud all my life. Don't want to be a fraud in death too, like that midget buried in the island cemetery who insisted they box him up in a full-size casket. No dark child's crib for him, he was going to be carried out on the shoulders of pallbearers like a regular man. Didn't fool anyone but himself. Once they are in the ground everybody is the same size to the worms."

Isaac seemed to be floating atop the white-sheeted mattress, suspended in undisturbed stillness. St. Cloud and Angelica had been by his side since early morning as he ebbed and flowed, coming back again and again from long hours of silence, jerking awake with startled wonder. The stacked bottles of pills on his bedside table were undisturbed. His desire was not to be drugged when he was dragged from this world, he wanted to see if death had a face, what color that face was. He did not want to be tricked at such a late date. He felt reassured with Angelica standing at the foot of his bed, an angel anchoring him to the heaven of lust he pursued on earth.

Sobbing filled the room from the foot of the brass bed where Angelica sat. Isaac's purple eyelids slowly opened. He forced a wink in Angelica's direction. "Darling angel, I'm not dead yet."

"Dammit, Isaac." Angelica pushed herself up and came to him, laying a hand on his forehead. "Don't be such an old son-of-a-bitch and keep scaring me like that."

"Me and Renoir," another whisper escaped Isaac's thin lips. "We grew up together."

"He loves you." Angelica traced her fingers lightly on Isaac's perspiring forehead.

"You promised not to phone him."

"I won't. He's always so thoughtful. I'll bet he walks through that door any minute."

"In many ways I don't blame him, but in many ways I don't feel guilty."

"It's not about guilt. You know what it's about."

Isaac said nothing, his eyelids beginning to sink again.

Angelica wanted to keep Isaac alert. "What about you, St. Cloud? Seen Renoir?"

"Not since before Fantasy Fest."

"Fantasy Fest?" Isaac's eyelids stopped their downward slide, his head turning toward St. Cloud. "Any news about Bubba-Bob?"

St. Cloud lost his focus on the thin blue horizon through the French windows, sky was closing over sea, salty breeze slipped into the bedroom, heavy with humidity. He felt pressure in his head, a storm in the making, a rain to dissolve dog days of summer which had lingered past their oppressive prime into fall. "Bubba-Bob's going to be all right. Said to tell you he knows what a marlin feels like when it's pole-gaffed."

"He's tough as a marlin."

"Like you, too ornery to die."

Isaac's chest heaved with a choking cough, he cleared his throat to get his whisper of a voice back. "You still got that lucky bone Justo's aunt gave you?"

"It's around my neck."

Isaac blinked his cataract-clouded eyes in St. Cloud's direction. "There can never be too much magic on this island. Oris keeping you busy spooning love hex soup to the Dixie Peach?"

"Lila's moved in with me. Guess she likes my pie crusts."

A laugh squeezed from Isaac's throat. "Now you're in trouble. Once a woman moves in, no amount of voodoo can move her out. Even Oris can't help you with that."

"Lila's different. Think I've got a chance at something, probably my last chance."

"You don't know it, but your last chance walked out the door with Evelyn. There was one worth fighting for."

"I fought."

"Yourself, still are."

"Hey . . ." Angelica laughed. "What about me? Maybe I should fight over Evelyn too. You guys make it sound so good."

"You're not fighting for anyone, you're mine." Isaac's fluttering eyelid stopped halfway in an attempted wink.

Angelica looked at St. Cloud, encouraging him to keep Isaac alert.

"Did Justo nail that skeleton yet?" She nodded vigorously for St. Cloud to speak up. "What's *new* with the skeleton?"

Isaac's faint breath echoed Angelica as he began to slip away. "What's new with the skeleton?"

St. Cloud stroked the blackened veins on the back of Isaac's hand. "Justo says with this voodoo and Santería stuff, you never know if one person is involved, or a mob. Justo plays his cards close."

"Cards close," Isaac exhaled.

"Justo does think he figured out the Zobop poem."

"Zobop poem," Isaac barely breathed.

"The *two thousand souls entrapped by barbed wire*, that's the cemetery with its high fence. *Eight palms point the way*, those are the palms on Passover Lane flanking the cemetery entrance. *A Green Sailor looks north to Cuban Martyrs, where the tree of life grows from their heads*, refers to the sailor statue in the plot where battleship *Maine*'s crew is buried. The sailor's right hand is cocked in salute northward, where José Martí's liberators who died invading Cuba are entombed. Opposite the Cubans is an enormous breadfruit tree. Seems simple once you know, but who could have known? Justo says a toad helped him figure it out."

"Toad figured it," Isaac whispered.

"What Justo hasn't puzzled is the *Angel of Death smiles upon all*. Hundreds of angel statues are scattered across the cemetery, small plastic ones, large marble ones. Everywhere you look angels are hovering over graves or looking over their wings in preparation for celestial takeoff. Which one is the Angel of Death? Aren't they all?"

"Aren't they all?"

"Somehow this Zobop has everything tied into the cemetery, even the yellow X. An X in the Little White House bedroom where Marilyn's Andy was killed, one on the jail wall when Voltaire was released, another on Renoir's front door. Then there's the first X, the one Justo found on his grandfather's grave. All roads seem to cross at the cemetery."

"All roads crossed."

"You once mentioned there were guys on this island in secret societies ready to kill anyone revealing an evil truth. Aunt Oris says you're right. In some of those societies a new member had his chest shaved and marked with a yellow X, was forced to kneel within a circle of yellow chalked in dirt. He drank the blood of a goat whose throat had been slashed, while others called upon Nanga, Big Evil, to kill the initiate if he betrayed the brotherhood outside the circle."

"Brotherhood?"

"That's what Aunt Oris calls it. Last time they paraded around dressed as devils in top hats and tooting whistles was in the twenties. The ceremonial killings ended way before then. Sure, chickens and goats are still sacrificed, cats and dogs too, even dove hearts and shark eyes turn up at the feet of the Hurricane Virgin in the grotto of the Catholic church. Nearly any living thing you can think of has been strung up and wrung out to amend or avenge some purpose on this island over the years, to set things right, beat back evil, bring up the good. There are still *botànicas* in town hawking faceless cotton dolls, magic needles to stick them with, Evil Eye potion spray in a can to paint them with and bat blood mixed with Holy Water to anoint them with. Half the cocaine smugglers in town buy protection from a Santería godfather or godmother, wouldn't dream of running a scam without feeding the Saints on prayers and thousand-dollar donations. People who buy into that can't buy out. Some are more religious than the Pope, others are simply afraid, more spooked than a rat in a shithouse."

"Spooked."

"Everybody's spooked one way or another and tries to do something about it, light a candle, have a shot of alcohol, say a prayer, smoke a joint, go on vacation, sacrifice a pet cat, turn on the television, any damn thing. Not sure what I'm talking about. Maybe this Zobop doesn't make any sense. Maybe that's the real thing, no sense to be made anymore."

"Sense?" The breath of Isaac's word barely made it beyond his trembling lips. "In my . . . day . . . people didn't ask so many questions. In my day people didn't need . . . so many answers. I need a blue spot."

In the failing light of the bedroom the shriveled skin of Isaac's bald head against the pillow made him appear like a freshly unwrapped Egyptian mummy, a weathered boy-king, gazing at a world filled with treasures no longer of value. The rasp of his breathing heaved his thin chest. Through French windows evening over water darkened to night, distant horizon exposed by lightning fingers pointing toward Cuba. Booming thunder marched in from the ocean, shaking Isaac's Bahamian mansion to its coral-rock foundation.

Angelica stared at Isaac in flashing lightning, a half curve of smile on her lips, as if she knew all along the value of a muse was only justified if it led to enlightened finality.

Rain fell on Isaac's mansion, blowing through the bedroom windows, dampness stalking wooden floor, inching toward the boy-king afloat on his brass throne, his purple eyelids fluttering, lips trembling a release of words. "Angelica . . . tell me . . . what do you see outside . . . its color?"

Angelica jolted, she thought Isaac had died. Her face turned to rain streaking through the windows. "Silver."

"Silver?"

"Vivid silver, fluorescent, like the color used on cheap velvet paintings, superficial but sincere."

"Cheap painting. Superficial . . . but sincere."

Wind shifted outside, pulling the slant of rain, water no longer driving into the room, falling straight to earth.

St. Cloud felt no movement from Isaac's hand cradled within his own. He forced himself to speak. "Want to hear again what happened when I went north to give Voltaire money to pay off those Haitian jackals?"

"Want to . . . hear. Can't . . . believe it."

There was a slight pulse in Isaac's limp wrist as St. Cloud began his story.

24

VOLTAIRE lost his security. When Immigration got him away from Justo it was only a matter of time until he was shipped back to Haiti. If he survived the Tontons he still needed to come up with two thousand bucks to pay off the smugglers. Doom all the way around. Voltaire was headed to the slaughterhouse same as his Uncle Romulus, going to be chopped like a pig. My idea was to get twenty-five hundred bucks. Five hundred to bribe the Tontons, rest he owed smugglers. If he was a goose who could produce that kind of money, in a country where a *paysan* makes less than two hundred bucks a year, I reasoned the Tontons wouldn't kill him, figuring on more gold to come their way. Problem was, I didn't have twenty-five hundred, didn't have anything, but Justo came up with a thousand. The rest I borrowed from Evelyn. She was happy to part with it, even quoted that old saw, 'If there's a man you never want to see again, lend him money.' She said if I paid the money back it meant I'd changed my act and was working at something steady. If I didn't, at least Voltaire got the money for another chance. Either way, Evelyn considered it a no-lose deal, even loaned me her van to make the drive. So I drove north to the detention camp in an old missile base on the edge of the Everglades, not far from the outskirts of Miami. Behind high fences hundreds of Haitians milled before concrete barracks formerly housing missiles. The guards searched me like I was point man of a breakout team; I flashed a phony letter stating I was on official business. Making it in was easy, hard part was getting to see Voltaire. No visitation rights allowed the Haitians, they have fewer rights than hard-core cons. Inside the administration building, originally the base command

312

bunker, my ID was checked. I was led down a corridor into an office crowded by desks, a rattling air-conditioner blew a stale breeze around a woman behind piles of papers. 'Mrs. Mulrooney,' she pumped my hand briskly, 'have a seat. We don't get many Key West visitors, you're the first. Mostly we get reporters, especially since last week.' I didn't want to appear ignorant, but I didn't know what happened the week before. 'Yes, last week,' I winked. 'That's part of why I made the drive up.' 'Good thing you didn't come any earlier. We weren't letting anybody in for a while, not even the press pool. It was that bad.' 'Just how bad?' 'Bad enough.' Mrs. Mulrooney turned her nose up at my sweat-stained cap, as if trying to determine which had most likely been around the world more times, the crinkled canvas cap or my sun-lined face. 'Just who is it you are here to see, Mr. Sitclod?' 'St. Cloud. I explained at the front desk, here to see Voltaire Tincourette.' 'You are aware, no visitation rights allowed detainees while in custody of Immigration and Naturalization Service?' 'I'm aware, but since INS is under the Justice Department, thought you might sympathize with my situation. There were charges brought against Tincourette when he entered the country illegally in Key West. His charges were dismissed.' 'So why are you here?' 'I was Tincourette's court-appointed translator. There are still a few questions we would like clarified concerning matters pertaining to what transpired on the vessel which transported him to this country. Everyone on board the boat except Tincourette arrived dead.' 'What's so unusual about that? Illegal Haitians come ashore with nearly every tide in South Florida.' Mrs. Mulrooney lowered her arched eyebrow. 'We had thirty thousand come ashore last year, another ten thousand intercepted at sea. Thirty percent of the refugee boats making the six-hundred-mile run sink. We'd be doing everyone a big favor by stopping those boats from ever leaving. It's a political situation unfortunately, not a humanitarian one.' 'Better the shark's bite than the dictator's kiss.' 'That's easy for you to say.' 'Not what I say, it's what *they* say.' Mrs. Mulrooney's eyebrow arched again. 'Don't tell me you've come all this way to speak up for the poor Haitians?' 'I don't speak for anyone. I speak a passable Creole, that's all. You know the Haitian expression, *youn ti chape*?' 'I'm not a linguist, Mr. St. Cloud. I'm an administrator.' 'It means "little escapee." Voltaire told me it's what they call a child in Haiti, because half of them are dead of disease before age five.' Mrs. Mulrooney picked a pencil up from her desk and pressed its rubber tip against her cheek. 'We are overworked and understaffed here, our armed guards aren't soldiers, they are rent-a-cops. We are detaining people who enter this country illegally. This facility isn't just for Haitians, it was used during the Mariel boatlift from Cuba, a hundred and forty Cuban *boteros* an hour were being brought here. The Cubans are gone now. INS does not say who is a political refugee and who is not. INS upholds the law as it is interpreted.' 'Even though it's interpreted differently for different people?' 'We have fourteen hundred Haitians here, more in camps further north. It's a difficult situation for all, yet they keep coming.' Mrs. Mulrooney was plainly exhausted, overwhelmed by an inexorable tide going right over her head. *'Très triste.'* I shook my own head. 'What does that mean?' She looked at me warily. 'It means very sad. May I see Voltaire now?' 'Yes, it is all too sad.' She pushed the point of her pencil harder against her cheek. 'There was a breakout last week.' In that moment I realized why she was being so equivocal. 'Voltaire's escaped, is that what you're saying? I can't see him because he's gone? Gone and nobody knows where he is?' Mrs. Mulrooney laid her pencil on the desk and quickly stood. 'Come with me.' I followed out into the long corridor, she walked ahead with an air of uncommunicative resolve, finally we were outside, passing rows of tents crowded with Haitians. The tents were pitched on concrete pads where missiles once poised. Behind the tents men leaned expectantly against a ten-foot steel mesh fence separating them from women's and children's quarters. Some touched fingers with wives on the opposite side, clinging to the steel barrier. Only disjointed whispers were audible in thick heat slowing motions, giving the men an appearance of moving and talking underwater, maneuvering through a vague dream. They were trapped in the land of the free with no specified time of imprisonment to be meted out before liberty was to be gained, detained in caged limbo while law moved invisibly toward conclusion, the expression in their faces balanced between dejection and resignation. A few huddled around portable radios, waiting word from a Miami station that came through in their own Creole, word that would offer hope of motion with purpose. Mrs. Mulrooney stopped before the open door of a cinder-block barracks, she turned, admonishing me not to linger. I followed into a sweltering room rowed with hundreds of cots. Sunlight sliced from barred windows across a large blackboard chalked with TIME-DAY-MONTH. ARE YOU A STUDENT? WORKER? SINGLE? MARRIED? HAITIAN? SICK? HOW SICK? I caught up with Mrs. Mulrooney striding among the cots, acknowledging with an officious wave the sea of male faces turned toward her. She stopped before a gaunt man slumped at the edge of his cot, gnarled hands supporting his head as he studied the floor. He raised his eyes, his forehead furrowed in deep lines, a stubble of mustache beneath his nose spotted gray. He looked fifty, I think he was thirty, he said nothing. 'This is Hippolyte.' Mrs. Mulrooney tapped the man's shoulder as if he were a sleepwalker. 'He speaks no English and I speak no Creole. We only have a few people on staff who even speak French. Perhaps you can persuade Hippolyte to tell you what happened to your friend.' On the cot next to Hippolyte two men playing dominoes interrupted their game, eyes searching me, fearful another outsider had come to inflict hardship. Mrs. Mulrooney sensed my hesitation. 'Ask Hippolyte about the breakout.' In the most disarming manner possible I made my inquiry. Hippolyte listened solemnly, uttering only, *'Très triste.'* He found the floor more interesting than my questions. The men on the next cot resumed their domino game. From the far end of the room sudden squeals and wild applause exploded, a television game show had been turned on. A circle of silent men were observing television people, not understanding their words, nor the significance of flashing numbers and loud buzzers, prompting the television people into uncontrollable fits of crying and kissing. Into the vast room the television master of ceremonies' voice rose above all else: *Is the third couple going to chance the optimum card or bet the hidden agenda?* I knelt next to Hippolyte, switching my questioning from French to a conspiratorial Creole. 'I am a friend of Voltaire Tincourette. I have journeyed here to visit with my friend, to make a gift.' Hippolyte's gaze came up from the floor, slowly taking me in, focusing on the white man who spoke Creole with a foreign accent, the stranger who had the tongue of his people, but not the heart, and definitely not the skin. His gaze caught on Aunt Oris' Lucky Bone dangling from the braided string necklace around my neck, then moved from the bone to my eyes. His words came with subdued deference: 'Ask this policewoman why it is they have captured us and try to make of us women?' I translated to Mrs. Mulrooney. 'Tell Hippolyte that's nonsense.' Mrs. Mulrooney smiled reassuringly. 'We are not putting female sex hormones into detainees' food to make them grow breasts. This is foolish rumor started by troublemakers in Miami's Little Haiti. Tell him not to believe everything he hears on the radio. We are not trying to make men docile. Tell him to eat, it is safe American food. He is wasting away to nothing.' I repeated Mrs. Mulrooney's sentiment to Hippolyte. He confided he himself had seen breasts sprouting on men in camp, heard their voices going higher every day, this started before the breakout, the police people were trying to make of Haitian men she-goats in a pen, what was their crime, they wanted to work honest, risked their lives for that, they were not thieves, not drug men, not assassins, back in Haiti everyone spoke of Miami as the place of honest work, where a man could earn security, now it was clear, white goats were different from black goats, he was a believer in *Bon Dieu*, Jesus Christ, but why did camp police hand out English Bibles, no Haitians he knew read English, every day he was given poisoned food, made to stand outside in the heat, given more poisoned food, came back in the barracks, slept the day away, every day a death, many people tried to commit suicide, all they wanted was *viktoua net, complete victory*, they were not trying to invade the United States, just victory to work honest, for that they were treated worse than dogs, turned into frightened she-goats. Hippolyte stopped talking, as if realizing he confided too much to the wrong person. I bent closer, searching out his downcast eyes. 'I cannot be a friend to everyone in this camp, but I was a friend to Voltaire. I came here to help him, please help me do that.' The furrows in Hippolyte's forehead deepened, he bit his lower lip, holding back a slip of the tongue. I tried another tack. 'Did you own land in Haiti?' His head snapped up, defiant pain in his eyes. 'Do you take me for a tramp, I am no vagabond, I had some small lands in Haiti, I had my security, I even had a garden-wife to watch over my corn and yam grow, but there came more and more no rain, I had to go to Dominican Republic and cut in cane fields, when I come back Tontons have squatted my security, they say they are the man now, they take my garden-wife and say if I don't go away they will take my life too, I left for Port-au-Prince, where *paysans* with no security live in streets, they told me in Miami is courage, is work, so I go, I still have sugarcane monies from Dominican, I go first on night boat with many *paysans* to the Bahamas, then I bribe for trip from there on smaller boat to Miami, a fishing boat, I am forced to stay below with other *paysans* in fishing boat hold, everyone sick from fumes, smugglers won't let us come up for air, they say American Coast Guard is all around looking for us, we have to shut up, then the engine stops, a smuggler comes below and shouts about a big Coast Guard ship steaming toward us, everybody should give him their monies, watches, any values, because we can jump overboard with life preservers, Coast Guard won't see us on dark sea, they will chase lights of fishing boat, but will find no illegal *paysans*, then fishing boat will come back to pick us up and we will be free, but *paysans* shouted why should they give up their values before jumping, smuggler said because seas were rough, no way to keep values dry and safe while in water waiting for fishing boat to come back, some did not believe smuggler and shouted so, he screamed there was no time, Coast Guard was steaming, if *paysans* needed proof, hurry up to deck and see for themselves, we did, across chopping waves was blinking light and blast of loud horn, *paysans* handed over their values and jumped overboard with life preservers around their necks, fishing boat swung around, churned away, sound of its engine gone before *paysans* realized blinking light was not moving, blasts from its horn coming no closer, it was a light buoy marking a shipping channel, almost none of *paysans* could swim, they were hardscrabble farmers helpless to currents, many cried and prayed, begged great loas for mercy, but we were already drifting from light buoy, not long before sound of horn could not be heard across water, some of us tried to raft our preservers together, maybe by dawn we would see shore, know which direction to head for, since I was a canecutter I had powerful arms to pull with, I grabbed a woman by hair and pulled her with me, as water grew colder she grew limper, until I realized I was towing a dead person, I let her slip from me, then sharks came, screams of others not clinging to our raft of preservers came to me in darkness, one screamer was small girl, I remembered she had been wearing a red frock bought by her mother in Bahamas so she would look pretty when she got to Miami, I swam toward her, red frosting was on churning water in moonlight, I shouted for everyone to be calm, no splashing, no kicking, nothing to draw sharks, I was surprised when sharks did not return right away, I expected my body to be cut, slightest nudge against my legs made me shudder, I laughed at thought sharks would have better meal than I ever had, by morning I saw glitter of Miami Beach mansions, soon real Coast Guard roared toward us and here I am, where I found Voltaire, but not until the breakout, I didn't know him before, he too had come across water, like everyone else was afraid.' Hippolyte's gaze slipped away, across rows of cots with men sprawled atop them like floating bodies. His gaze steadied on the back wall, its hard surface painted with colorful density of jungle, palms towering in a cool world, howler monkeys swinging through vines, red-winged parrots flying, chartreuse butterflies above a lagoon, a white panther at water's edge, its eyes not agitated by predatory purpose, but open and questioning, large human eyes. 'Voltaire,' Hippolyte intoned, 'he was not a strong canecutter like me, did not know of him until we went over the fence, had not risen that morning with head full of escape, early afternoon was waiting my turn at outdoor privy, for days was rumored carloads of sympathizers coming from Miami to make world aware we were being given woman drugs, poisoned food was growing us thin with exhaustion, as I opened privy door I heard car horns on far side of administration building, protesters banging at gates, bottles and stones crashing, gunshots, smoke and gas burned my eyes, vomit spewed from my mouth, ran to back fence, joined a scramble of climbing men, barbed wire tore my hands, I dropped to saw grass on other side, behind me a ragged boy, blood soaked his torn clothes, we ran, that night in tall grass he told me he lost his security, Tontons had sent Zobops after his uncle in Haiti, chopped his uncle with axes like a pig, he said Zobops chased him across water, shooting flying fish at him, so he prayed Papa Agwé for redemption, and Horsemen came from beneath sea during night when stars fell around his boat sailing from Haiti, Horsemen placed a *ouanga* around his neck, anointed his forehead with holy ashes from a *richaud*, whispered in his ear freedom was close, not to be a mischiefmaker, to swim into forgetfulness, deny memory, these things Voltaire spoke as wind strummed saw-grass sea surrounding us, all night world was lit by lightning, thunder in yonder, hot rain spitting, mud steaming, fish flying in memory forgetting, security was coming, Papa Agwé would save us, I believed what he believed, there was no other belief, he was my sweet lamb, we slept, awakening to a world of dense smoke from fires started by lightning, we wept, we were lost, hard ground of high grass gave way to swamp, we were knee deep in our struggle toward freedom, overhead whine of airplanes, I did not know if they were searching us or making war on distant fires, gray day bled into gray night, black sun became black moon, Voltaire was babbling, splattered with ash and blood, he passed out, freedom was close, we could not stop, I slipped my arm around him, he weighed less than a flying fish, I carried him forward, only once did his eyes open, he mumbled to Papa Agwé, mud sucked our feet, stink of rotting plants in our noses, buzz of mosquitoes in our ears, flesh swollen from bites, we traveled the here to there, smoke turned brilliant red with dawn, a new day cleared, in distance giants marched on horizon, an army of Saints, I was no longer afraid, I was not a vagabond from the sea, but proud *paysan*, people would offer me assistance, giants grew taller, coming closer I saw they weren't Saints marching to a new world, but power poles charred by fires still puffing smoke beneath them, the poles lined a canal, pointing direction sun was rising, blackened earth was hot beneath our feet as we followed poles strung with humming wires, water sluiced swiftly in canal below, singing a clean sound, Voltaire awoke, water always leads to something good, what it led to was a bridge of cars passing overhead, before us water disappeared into a steel mouth of pipe, we stumbled up a rise onto hard black field of cars parked between painted white lines, ahead glittered a glass palace surrounded by flowering trees and waterfalls, this is where canal water must have disappeared to, we were thirsty and dirty, we wanted to drink and bathe, we followed crowds of people inside the palace, where heat was sucked from day and breeze blew, we saw no animals but heard sweet chorus of invisible birds, Voltaire hobbled forward on muddy feet, beneath him slippery floor reflected treasures from mountains of clothes, jewels, and television sets, I shouted for him to come back, I did not know if I was in his dream or he was in mine, maybe we had both been shot climbing the camp fence, we had gone to hell in fiery Everglades, but Voltaire's prayers to Papa Agwé gained us escape and we were in heaven. If I was alive I did not know how long it had been since I last ate or slept, two days or two weeks, I chased Voltaire through treasures, he stopped beneath a sign:

BASKET-O-FRUITS-N-GIFTS

Baskets of heaped fruit beckoned, Voltaire rocked his head to music of invisible birds, his fingers gliding over golden oranges, ruby apples, emerald pears, perfection not seen in our insect-riddled land of shriveled trees, food fit for feast of Saints, he peeled plastic skin from a ruby apple, raising fruit to lips as angry words he could not understand screamed from a woman stalking toward him, he was like a sleepwalker shaken awake, he extended the apple to the woman, she stopped, as if the apple was a bomb capable of destroying glass palaces, behind us was shouting, I turned, a uniformed black police shoved through a crowd, Voltaire smiled and stumbled toward him, offering the basket of fruit, they were going to collide, I shouted for Voltaire to stop, he did not hear me in his dream, a gun flashed from black police, terror in Voltaire's eyes, Tontons had found him, fruit jewels scattered as he ran across slippery mirage, black police went after him, I chased on blistered feet, Voltaire was quick as rabbit, he ran out onto a busy highway, dodging speeding cars, horns honking, black police shouting, he streaked beneath an overhang of traffic lights, not seeing a truck hit him, hurling him onto hood of a car swerving in squeal of brakes, slamming him to pavement, across a yellow X large as a man, when I got to him blood rushed from his lips, I cradled him in my arms and prayed Saints wake us from good dream turned nightmare, white letters were beneath yellow X, I did not know their meaning, but memory has a picture:

LEFT HAND TURN ONLY

Oh my sweet lamb.' "

25

THINK he's gone. Do you hear me?"

St. Cloud tried to sort his thoughts, to push past the vision of Voltaire lying dead in front of a shopping mall at the edge of the Everglades, a place where the march of modernization overtook the millennial crawl of sea surrendering new land. The vision refused to recede, Voltaire on a yellow X, spinning counterclockwise, suspended between two worlds. Angelica appeared before him. It had stopped raining, dawn illuminated the thin blue horizon.

"You've been talking all night." Angelica's fingertips touched St. Cloud's cheek. "Didn't want to stop you, it's what Isaac wanted."

St. Cloud's thoughts were muddled. The frail hand he held within his own was lifeless.

"Tried to call Renoir again, still no answer."

"Answer?" St. Cloud looked up into Angelica's face. No tears were in her eyes, just a clear gaze of blue. Maybe this was the last thing Isaac saw, stripped of all landscape, his giant blue spot, pursued to the end. St. Cloud did not want to let Isaac's hand go, as long as he clung to it the connection between them remained. His mind drifted back to the story he had been telling, there was more to it, a strange ending. He recalled the silence after Hippolyte finished the breakout tale. As Hippolyte stared at the floor his own eyes went to the jungle painted across the back wall, the white panther peering back at him. Thunder rumbled across surrounding Everglades, slowly Hippolyte's words made their way from scarred lips: "I used to be a strong man with security, a man who could cut cane twelve hours a day, sometimes if a man loses the swing of his machete from tiredness as he slices cane, and the blade strikes him in the heat of the moment, his pumped-up blood will jump from the wound in minutes, he will die in the fields, I have cut myself twice, cuts deeper than a boar's bite, then bound my cut from cloth of my torn pants, walked ten miles home over mountains and across streams, I was so strong, look at me now, wasting away because of no work in camp, without his security a man is nothing, his body quits if not used as loas deemed, I weigh no more than one of Voltaire's flying fish." Hippolyte's words stopped, as if his breath was even too much of a burden to bear. St. Cloud bent before him again, reached into his pocket and withdrew the envelope containing twenty hundred-dollar bills. He pushed the envelope into Hippolyte's gnarled hands, claiming it was a gift from Voltaire, who wrote St. Cloud he wanted his friend Hippolyte to have it. Hippolyte turned the sealed envelope in his hands, pondering its contents, he had not asked for gifts, furrows in his forehead deepened, maybe this was a trick, after all, St. Cloud only *said* he was Voltaire's friend. There were many things in this new world Hippolyte did not know, mysteries beyond belief. One thing was not a mystery, he knew Voltaire was a *paysan* like him, unschooled. Voltaire could not write. "I did not come to Florida for sunshine," Hippolyte whispered hoarsely. "Neither did I," St. Cloud whispered back. Hippolyte rose from his cot, crouched before a footlocker and opened its metal door with a small key. He slid the envelope inside and gathered something swiftly from the back shelf into his fist. He sat on the cot holding his fist before St. Cloud's face. "Voltaire died without security, not without spirit, I took this from around his neck as loas called him home, if you are his friend it should be with you." Hippolyte's fist opened to reveal the pigskin ball of a *ouanga* wound with goathair, bloodstained and mud-soiled. St. Cloud did not touch it, it was the only security Voltaire had in this world. "Take it," Hippolyte urged. "Some things are meant to be, maybe you are not so white after all."

Hippolyte's words echoed in St. Cloud's mind as he clung to Isaac's hand. Some things are meant to be simply because they exist, that does not make them easier to understand. He thought of what he learned after leaving Hippolyte, returning to Mrs. Mulrooney's office with its air-conditioned breeze, while back in the vast room men on cots sweated out another day. He was sweating too, listening to Mrs. Mulrooney tell him Voltaire would have died even if he had not been killed on the highway. She said Haitian activists caused such a stink about rumors of female hormones in detainees' food that doctors made an examination. They found some men had yaws, a flesh-rotting disease the United Nations claims has been wiped out. They found something else, a lingering pneumonia which wastes a person away. The pneumonia is linked to a virus in Africa, started by green monkeys or something, nobody knows for certain, so new it doesn't have a name. Immigrant Haitians have the highest chance of developing it, except for homosexuals. The doctors had no idea how many men in camp were homosexuals, they knew to a man how many were recent arrivals from Haiti. They asked permission to run tests on blood from Voltaire's body. He had the green monkey virus, they figured Hippolyte had it too.

Angelica's voice floated through to St. Cloud. "Why don't you go home and get some sleep, honey. You've been up all night."

St. Cloud squeezed Isaac's hand, he couldn't bear to let go. Angelica seemed far away, dawn spreading purple behind her through the window. "You've been up all night too."

"For me it's easy, I'm a bartender. Isaac could trust me to stay awake for him. Let's call his doctor and leave before the press gets here, Isaac would never want his friends to witness that."

"Yes . . . you're right. If we can't get ahold of Renoir we'll have to let the doctor know."

"Go on. I'll make the call."

"Sure you don't want me to stay while you do that?"

"Go."

It was time. St. Cloud reached deep into his pants pocket and withdrew Voltaire's *ouanga*, placed it within Isaac's hand. He folded stiff fingers over the pigskin pouch, then laid the hand atop Isaac's still heart. He did not need the *ouanga*, he had Aunt Oris' lucky bone. Wherever he was headed he considered himself bulletproof. He pushed up from the chair.

The curtains framing Angelica at the window lifted in the wind, white rising wings at her shoulders, poised for flight. *Go* formed on her lips. Isaac was a luckier man than most.

St. Cloud descended into the cavernous foyer, feeling his way through sheet-shrouded furniture. He emerged onto the dilapidated veranda, pushed through the Spanish laurel's curtain of hanging roots. Whitehead Street opened before him, its pavement stopping

where the cement finger of the southernmost point monument rose
at the Atlantic's edge. Stiff wind swung from south to northwest, sure
sign the jaws of dog days were finally loosening their grip. The
churning ocean was not its usual transparent blue, but opaque indigo.
The storm that passed during night left isolated clouds on the horizon,
beneath them spun spidery waterspouts, ghosts waltzing toward Cuba's
rattling sugarcane fields and papaya girls flirting with mango eyes.
St. Cloud did not heed tropical temptations beyond waterspouts. He
headed in the opposite direction, across island toward home, where
Lila waited.

Narrow streets were filled with chorus of frogs croaking from damp
gardens as evaporating rain steamed off tin roofs, lizards leapt from
sidewalk cracks while rats rustled in palm fronds, on Catholic Lane
Lila was sleeping. St. Cloud entered the house quietly, not wanting
to awaken her. A note he tacked on the bedroom door was still there:
*You are the corned beef in my heart's customhouse, my hunger follows you, no
wonder crude.* He smiled; beneath his note Lila had written: *Your beef
is corny but your wonder is not crude!* He pushed the door open. Lila lay
asleep, ceiling-fan blades stirring a breeze over her curved nakedness.
What he needed to soothe his nerves was not a shot of alcohol, but
to drink in the vision illuminated on the bed by dawn light. Strange
music came quickly to mind. He thought he imagined it. Quickly as
it came it went. Maybe what he heard was the fan's electric thrum.
He was afraid he might be dreaming, same way Voltaire thought he
was dreaming the glass palace. He touched the lucky bone at his neck.
A screeching sound jolted him, sounding like a hawk's call or a blowing
whistle. Lila opened her eyes, shadowy movement flitted across the
window behind her. "Stay where you are," St. Cloud whispered. He
walked quickly through the house, stepping out the back door into
the garden, pushing through banana leaves. The strange music
stopped. Across rowed vegetables a papaya tree rose, halfway up its
trunk was Lila's pug, a spike driven through its skull, its throat slashed.
He saw the naked shape of Lila through the bedroom window, one
hand covering her mouth. A jar glinted from blood-spattered cabbages
beneath the papaya. He opened the jar and withdrew crumpled paper
scrawled with purple ink:

OL FILOR'S SLY AS DE MOUS! HAH!
AMONG 2000 TRAPPED SOULS THE ANGEL OF DEATH AWAITS

HOLDS IN HER HAND RISING SUN OF YOUR FATE
DON'T BE LATE FOR YOUR BIRTHDAY PARTY!

St. Cloud let the bloody jar slip from his fingers and tossed the note into cabbages. What Justo said about everything leading to the cemetery was true. He started walking, crushing tomatoes and turnips beneath his feet. He heard Lila screaming for him not to go. He ran from the garden.

THE GATES to the cemetery were open, someone had smashed the chained lock. St. Cloud hesitated, catching his breath, a line of eight palms guarded the entrance, their frond skirts rattling overhead. In the city of the dead the first thing to greet him was a sailor statue perched atop a granite pedestal amidst tombstones marking casualties of battleship *Maine*. The copper sailor had weathered a sea-green, as if an underwater vision dreamed above ground by those buried below, one hand held an oar, the other frozen in northward salute toward home. Someone had painted the sailor's eyes yellow, blinding his vigil for ready rescue. St. Cloud looked in the direction the sailor could no longer see, across a skyline of tombstones and tin-roof mausoleums ensnared by overgrown vines. The metal clasp of a rope dangling from a flagpole clanged in the wind, tapping an inscrutable message. The wind also brought a hollow banging from the far side of a concrete hump housing generational graves. St. Cloud crept to the large tomb and pressed his back against its concrete wall, sliding to the corner, startling a greyhound with its snout caught in a vase of plastic flowers it was trying to drink from. The greyhound slammed the vase against the tomb, struggling to dislodge the improbable muzzle. The vase slipped free, scattering plastic flowers. "Ocho," St. Cloud called after the disappearing dog. "Where's Justo?" Only moaning wind came back in answer. If Ocho was around it meant Justo was close. There was no movement in the streets. St. Cloud headed in the direction of the sailor's blinded gaze, toward the monument to Cuban Martyrs. Strange music began, its sharp sound leading to an obelisk fingering skyward above a forest of marble headstones. From the obelisk tip a hawk eyed St. Cloud as if he were a blundering mouse. The hawk's beak opened, squealing pithy disdain as it took flight over stone angels weighted forever to earth. Strange music whistled through the air. Tombs and graves St. Cloud hurriedly passed were a blur, anyone could be hiding among the dead. A LOS

MARTIRES DE CUBA arched before him in metal letters, he edged past a granite pillar etched with dates of century-old Cuban battles. Where he thought the strange music came from, there was a glass case harboring a fleshlike root, a plaque announcing: *Tronco de Tamarindo bajo cuya sombra conspiraban, los patriotas Cubanos.* The root was from the tamarind tree beneath which the patriots plotted to liberate Cuba. From his vantage point among buried freedom fighters St. Cloud had an unobstructed view to the sailor staring with yellow eyes. *A Green Sailor looks to Cuban Martyrs, where the tree of life grows from their heads.* He spun around, back through the gateway to the martyrs was the spread of a breadfruit tree; its massive roots had toppled a line of gravestones like dominoes. Among fallen headstones were three freshly dug graves. St. Cloud peered into one of the deep holes, at bottom a bufo toad hopped in angry loops, attempting escape up slippery walls. "Justo," St. Cloud whispered. Only Justo knew the meaning of the Zobop poem. He turned from the graves, searching for Justo, a sign of revelation. *The Angel of Death awaits, holds in her hand rising sun of your fate, don't be late.* Don't be late? Rising from the cemetery's east, above Jews buried from sight behind a high fence scrolled with B'NAI ZION, was the sun. St. Cloud ran toward the ascending globe. *Don't be late.* Ahead loomed an angel, feathered wings arched, cascade of hair falling across shoulders, an outstretched hand offering a bouquet of lilies to a grave lost from sight in weeds. Strange music floated along cemetery streets, converging on the angel bathed in blood-red light. Against the sky a woman's-tongue tree rattled a racket of seedpods in the wind. From behind the tree a form astride a bicycle appeared, its black rubber skin painted with luminescent bones of a human skeleton, top hat clamped on its head, eyes blacked out by sunglasses, screeching whistle between teeth.

"St. Cloud!"

Justo was running from the Cuban Martyrs, gun waving in air, his shouted words lost in wind and tin-whistling.

The skeleton's legs pumped the bicycle furiously, a knife flashing in his hand. St. Cloud bent his arm to block the blade's thrust. Whistling was shattered by gunshots striking the skeleton's rubber chest. The bicycle's momentum carried the skeleton onward, knife still poised. Two more shots fired. The skeleton pitched over rusted handlebars, crashing the bicycle to the ground.

Beneath arched wings of the angel was Renoir, his revolver aimed above St. Cloud's shoulder. Rising sun behind the angel showered brilliance around Renoir, he disappeared into light.

Justo knelt before the skeleton sprawled across the wrecked bicycle, pulling the rubber head mask off with a loud elastic snap. The unseeing eyes of Space Cadet rolled white, the released rope of his braided hair unraveling to the ground.

"*A santo de que?*" Justo looked up at St. Cloud.

In the name of what?

26

Adios Twentieth Century Cha-Cha. Such was the message. No matter which end of the telescope Justo looked at it from, there wasn't a round world of sense to be made of it all. Such were the facts of the round and flat worlds, as for the other world's, nether and upper, they were not for him to trifle with. Even if it were possible to salt the tongue of a bufo toad with the speech of spooks and saints, it couldn't say much with a nail driven through its lips. Space Cadet knew that, Justo knew a thing or two more. The thing that kept him going from sunup to sundown was what he leaned upon in Vietnam, then cashed in when he came back from war; to make a good act of contrition, offer back evil to the source from which it originated. Justo made a good act of contrition after Vietnam, still had his mental health. What he learned in his own defeat of comprehending war was simple truth, a man who believes in contrition will always win out over a man who believes in destruction. Space Cadet believed in purification by destruction, didn't understand evil exists in the name of many things, good rests uneasily among them, such was the accommodation.

Justo had been driving the streets of Key West for two days in search of Renoir. The bag of conch fritters on his car seat was empty, just as his head was empty of ideas about where to find Renoir. He had turned the island on its ear, pressed the button of every scammer for information, rampaged every gay bar and disco, flipped every trick who owed him a favor. What he got were looks of fury, as if he were Pontius Pilate asking apostles to squeal where Jesus hid after slipping his guarded crypt. Half the State of Florida was looking for

Renoir. No one thought he would stay in Key West after the shooting. From what Justo discovered at Renoir's house, there was no question his prey would not stray.

Justo's gut was on fire from a bellyful of fritters and time was stacking up against him. The search for Renoir had to end at four o'clock or there would be the devil to pay, worse, there would be Rosella to answer to. Today was Isabel's *Quince*, three hundred people invited, the women's ballgowns ironed to a sheen, the men's tuxedos rented, twenty pigs roasting, the band warming up. Justo was spending a fortune, his belly burned hotter. If he wasn't at the hotel by four o'clock, smiling wide as a banquet pig with a red apple in its mouth, Rosella would have his hide and the devil his due.

Ocho leaned over the car seat, his tongue slurping Justo's cheek. The animal devoured a bag of fritters for lunch and whined for more. Justo pinched the dog's ear, warning it to get its vice under control or it would be back on the track chasing a metal bunny for a living. The image of the bunny inspired him, he slammed the brakes and wheeled the car around, heading toward the Wreck Room.

CRAZIES 0

GAYS 1

BETTER LUCK NEXT TIME!

The chalked message on the blackboard left no doubt as to which side of the cemetery shooting at least one of the Wreck Room regulars was on. The boisterous noontime crowd pushed at the long bar. The stool next to Handsomemost Jimmy was empty, left open for customers to whisper comforting commerce into his ear before striding purposefully to the bathroom. Justo slipped onto the stool. Handsomemost did not turn to see who his new customer was, continuing to sip his Scotch, his gold rings clanking against cold glass.

"Whose side you on?" Justo's voice rose into the crowd's roar, calling to Angelica as she splashed beer into mugs. He wanted to arrest her for indecent exposure, but this was no time for sport.

Angelica spun on high heels, the mugs foaming in her hands. "I'm on the side of the true and virtuous. Your side, sugar. The side of common law for uncommon people."

"I be see'n a three-sided asshole once," Handsomemost slurred into his Scotch. "But ain't never seen no straight cop."

Justo leaned toward Handsomemost. "That's because cops don't have assholes."

"Why you be foolin with me? Done told you where Space Cadet be livin. Not for me, you all never findin what hole that cat crawled from. That cat never had no mammy's titty milk to suck. That cat sucked acid all his life. Dude was evil, nimble evil. Nimble evil be evilist of all, cause you don't know where it's at till it too late."

"True enough."

"Dog-balls true. So don't be foolin with me, cause I tipped you where ol nimble evil done lived, if you call all that crazy shit livin."

"Didn't come to pin a good citizen's medal on you for helping out on that."

Handsomemost swiveled slowly, his eyes cloudy within fleshy slits. "We gots no more business. Ought to leave, but you won't. You're like an itch lookin for a scratch."

Justo nodded at Angelica. "Mind if I have one of those beers? I'm steaming in this coat."

Angelica pushed a mug to him. "Never seen you in a tuxedo before. I like that color on you, baby blue, matches your eyes."

"My eyes are brown." Justo lifted the mug, not taking his brown eyes off the cryptic smile poised on Angelica's lips.

"Can't a fishin man get served?" Bubba-Bob slipped up behind Justo.

"How'd you get out of the hospital?" Angelica leaned across the bar, kissing Bubba-Bob's cheek. "Thought they were keeping you another week."

"Can't keep a fishin man down. Walked out. They got me wrapped tighter than a ballyhoo on a marlin hook. Got drugs in me a Miami greyhound would envy. Can't feel no pain, perfect time to look for trouble."

"How about my place after work?"

"Thank God my balls aren't wrapped in tape too!"

"How bout you?" Angelica turned to Justo. "Want to get lucky?"

"Want to get another beer."

"You got it." Angelica refilled his mug. "Never seen you drink on duty before."

"See this Palm Beach pimp coat, you think I'd wear this on duty?"

"Oh yeah, forgot, today's Isabel's big day. Just a few hours away, isn't it?"

"Justo always be on duty," Handsomemost mumbled. "Always got de itch."

Justo looked at the message scrawled on the blackboard: CRAZIES o, GAYS 1. "You know where Renoir is, don't you?"

"Rabbit gets trouble, gets hisself a hole."

"You told me about Space Cadet's hole."

"You owed me for not popping that run-out dog of yours."

"You might need another favor."

Handsomemost snarled in his Scotch, "Done need no favors, got all I needs. Ladies I gives favors. Mens I gives shit."

"Even MK?"

Handsomemost turned his cloudy eyes to Justo. "Watch your tongue."

"Thought you didn't need no favors?"

"Listen," Handsomemost hissed, "what shit you be carrying?"

"MK's coming back."

"You be tryin to jack off my ego?"

"Don't believe me. Just willing to do a favor, guess you don't need it."

Handsomemost stared into his Scotch, silent as a drowned man.

"Here's to Crazies, that they might even the score!" Bubba-Bob raised his mug. "You can piss, you can moan, but you can't kill all the Crazies. God bless their looney tunes!"

"To Crazies," chorused many in the crowd.

"Fuck you," voted others.

"I gots my numbers covered." Handsomemost pressed his thin lips together. "But MK ridin back into town, gots to be no good for some."

"Where's Renoir?"

"You ain't spittin acid in my eye? MK's headed back?"

"Heard MK's coming to get his girl."

"Girl? I knows everythings, never hearda no chick."

"Lila."

"That little redneck skirt St. Cloud's been chasin?"

"She's a lot more skirt than you think."

"Wheeewh. MK had a bitch hidden in the woodpile all the time."

"Coming back for her, and other things."

"Other things?" Handsomemost stood, running hands over silk black clothes to smooth creases. "Time to rock and roll." He tapped the toes of his alligator loafers. "How'd you get word anyway?"

"Brogan, he accommodated."

"Thanks for the chit and the chat."

"Hey! Where you going? You owe me."

"Try Dick Dock."

"Already did, first place I looked."

"Up behind there, in the old fort where they got that garden. Try the orchids."

"Certain?"

Handsomemost poked a bony finger into the ruffled front of Justo's shirt. "Certain as your granny used to wash dishes for white folks." He backed away, his bony finger still pointing. "I don't owes no favors. You owes me."

Someday, Justo promised, he was going to blow the mustard off that strutting hot dog. Someday when there would no longer be anyone to accommodate, even halfway. What he told Handsomemost about MK was only half true. Handsomemost was so smart, he could figure which half to believe.

Angelica poured Justo a beer. "If it's true about MK coming, St. Cloud better catch the first rocket out of town."

"Lila's left. Saw her headed over Cow Key Bridge in her convertible about six this morning."

"How do you know she's not coming back?"

"I can tell by the look on a woman's face if she's driving off this rock for the last time."

"Look into my face." Angelica rested her chin in her hands, inches from Justo. "What do you see?"

Justo studied the blond closeness, sweet breath brushing his skin, his face flushed. "I see pleasure and pain, a homewrecker in search of a home, a woman too honest to take *I do* for an answer."

"You see too much, honey." Angelica's lips came closer, her hand touching his cheek. "Go home to your warm Cuban bread. Go home, family man."

Bubba-Bob slammed his fist on the bar. "Goddamnit! A fishin man can't get a drink because the bartender's hustling the heat!"

"Only trying to bribe him with my good looks and high-school education. No money changed hands."

Bubba-Bob slid onto the stool vacated by Handsomemost, his hand locking on Justo's shoulder. "Let me buy you an *anejo*, hear your little girl's getting married today."

"Not married." Angelica opened a bottle of *anejo*. "It's sort of a debutante's ball. Fabulous gowns and a big feast."

"Sounds goddamn expensive." Bubba-Bob squeezed Justo's shoulder. "How much money you make as a cop? Maybe you want to go king-fishin with ol Bubba, pull some extra bucks into the boat."

"I'll take that *anejo*."

Angelica poured the rum with a sly wink. "Today's worse than a wedding. Give your daughter away and get nothing back."

Justo raised his glass in farewell salute to Angelica, she still remained the wildest flower in his life. *"No hay rosas sin espinas!"*

There are no roses without thorns.

THERE WERE no roses inside the Civil War fort, no shackled Confederate soldiers, no fat cattle to feed Union troops. Towering brick walls constructed to withstand pounding of cannonballs fired from offshore ships now protected the local garden club's offering of southern flora. Palm-lined pathways led to a lattice-covered grotto choked with vivid growth of orchids. Within the grotto's overhead tumble of filtered light Renoir was not to be found. Justo opened a door onto a footpath winding beneath fragrant magnolias to a fence at the Atlantic's edge. A solitary figure in a rumpled white suit gazed through the fence's chained links.

Renoir knew Justo was coming. He did not attempt to run. Behind black-lensed glasses his attention remained fixed on youthful males in sleek swimsuits reclining along the arc of a wooden pier. Older men, fully clothed, moved cautiously among the youths. Renoir's words were flat as the sea beyond. "That's where I first met him. Suppose it would be better if I could say he wasn't like the others. Fact is he was just like the others. That's what attracted me from the beginning. Funny, those things, attractions, yearnings which can't be denied."

In blue heat beating on his blue coat Justo was sweltering. He had been in such a hurry he forgot to leave the coat in the car. Something prevented him from taking it off. He felt he had to keep it on in front of Renoir, like a badge.

"Out on the pier is where I met him. Wasn't his beauty attracted me. Most people couldn't see past his beauty, beyond tanned muscles he was always flexing. It was his vitality got me. So many people in life are dead to their visceral selves, tell themselves how life should be before they live it, what rules will dominate, what rules will repel inexplicable attraction. They never play another game. My father was like that. Isaac set out to become famous, fame became his cage. Only room for one in the cage of fame, everyone else is locked out. I was locked out. But *my* man was a wild creature, couldn't be housebroken, refused to be caged. No rules of attraction or domination for him, no rules period. You don't know what it was like to wake up at the crack of dawn with that urgency. Like sun coming up, everything possible, life on the rise."

Justo cleared his throat, sweat poured from his body, the blue coat soaked through. "Guess we all live by the notion there is something bigger than we are, something to bet one's life on."

Renoir wheeled around. "What would you know about it?"

"You're right. What can someone like me possibly understand?"

"Nothing is what. You want the truth? Truth is, the singularity of your hetero friendships chills me to the bone." Renoir turned the glare of his sunglasses back to oil-slicked bodies on the pier. "My man came down here to cheat on me. I came here to cheat on him too, but I couldn't free myself to be with anyone else. Wonder if I'll ever love someone so much again? To want to cheat on him to hurt him, continually test what we have. You see, it has nothing to do with preference, everything to do with desire. But you don't see, do you? Don't see."

Heat and *anejo* were unraveling Justo's senses, what happened two days before seemed so distant, when he had smashed through the front door of Renoir's house after the cemetery shooting. Inside the bedroom he felt himself winding back through time, as if he were the person stumbling upon Count von Cosel's beloved bride. The eyes staring from the bed mirrored a backward journey beyond burdensome physicality, toward peace never offered the living. When the ambulance arrived the body was smoothed into a stretcher, borne from sheltering shadows of Renoir's home into a sun of disquieting intensity. "You did your best." Justo heard his own voice coming back to him. "Cared for him until the end. There's nothing bigger."

"How long will it all hold?" Renoir leaned heavily against the fence, his white suit darkly smudged from sleeping on the ground. "I wanted him comforted. Is that asking too much? Couldn't bear his being with strangers."

"I hate to be the one to tell you, he's in the hospital. It isn't as good, but he's getting the right kind of attention, I made certain. Don't blame yourself, you did everything."

"Everything? I couldn't go back to the house, you had it watched. When he needed me most I failed. It was all I could do to stop Zobop, I knew who he was after next. Couldn't go to my father the night he was dying, because of a yellow rock thrown through my window with a note around it: *The Angel of Death awaits, your fate rises with sun in cemetery.*"

"I got the same rock-thrown summons."

"I found the biggest angel in the cemetery and waited behind it."

"Smarter than I was, so many angels. Should have figured it though, the biggest angel is atop the grave people believe von Cosel's bride was secretly buried in. For all I knew, when St. Cloud came running into the cemetery, he could have been Zobop, I almost shot him. I stayed low, something had to pop, everything had been too well planned."

"Planned?"

"Maybe that's not the right word. Madmen don't plan things so much as they hatch plots. You were right about fearing for Floyd's life. He was part of a connection, running through you, to St. Cloud, to me, to Voltaire. All connected in a chain of events going back to when I took that *ouanga* from Voltaire on the refugee boat. Space Cadet was in the crowd on the dock, saw me take the *ouanga*, also saw you on the beach that morning I gave Floyd mouth-to-mouth. I hadn't realized Floyd tried to drown himself that morning. Didn't make the connection until I discovered Floyd's illness. Space Cadet made his connections long ago, thought he knew where all the secrets were buried."

"What about Marilyn's Andy?"

"In the wrong place at the right time, up to nothing more than scamming at Sugarloaf when he came upon Space Cadet sacrificing a goat in the bat tower. Deal is, only the initiated can witness a sacrifice, for the unclean to do so is to ordain their own sacrificial end. In the beginning I thought we were up against a new cult. It was worse, the madness of one person who thought he was many. Takes only one person to shoot a President, kiss the cheek of Christ. No bottom to what humans will stoop to, no end to what they'll place their faith in. Space Cadet was a full-tilt Space Graduate, all the way to top of the class as Zobop. Everything he imagined was real, because he acted upon it. *Lo que de noche se hace, de día aparece.* That which is done by night can be seen by day."

"He's gone now, it's over."

"All evil springs from the same source, stamp it out here, pops up there. I found where he lived, under the Seven Mile Bridge, inside the tunnel carrying telephone and water lines. Crawled on my belly through the dark to where he last holed up, traffic thundering overhead, waterpipe hissing in my ears, everything slick with mildew. Found a box of newspaper clippings and journals dating back to the sixties. The journals were all marked *Tiger Car Manual,* except the most recent, *Adios Twentieth Century.* Space Cadet wasn't one of the walking wounded, he had on track shoes, speeding toward destruction, a generational time bomb. He was trying to bullshit the gods, believed the severed ears of Satan were drumskins beating out his destiny, telling him what to do. No drums in the tunnel, only journals to explain what he was hearing, the clippings to tell us what he was twisting, like the ones about that infection started by green monkeys which St. Cloud said Voltaire had. If I hadn't read the clippings I wouldn't have realized what Floyd was suffering. Space Cadet was convinced the earth would rot from its core if he didn't protect the purity of water, which roared over his head through the pipe in the tunnel. He made connections, not so random selections. Those who threatened purity had to be sacrificed. Everything followed ceremony. Sun rising over the cemetery after All Saints' Eve was the anointed time for *Bamboches Guede Mysteres,* big party for the Mysteries, when the dead arise and mount cleansed bodies, ride fresh souls. Space Cadet bent all rules, also bent his back digging our graves in the cemetery, ready and waiting."

Justo pulled a handkerchief from his coat, mopping sweat from his brow. He looked beyond the curved pier to the Casa Marina Hotel, he was going to be late for his daughter's *Quince.* Cars from far away as Tampa were filling the hotel parking lot. He took another swipe at his sweaty forehead.

"Way I see it, Space Cadet knew too little about too much. Important thing is it's finished, you stopped it."

The handsome lines of Renoir's face were drawn down in the high sun to a wash of weariness. Pelicans landed on pier pilings, spreading wet wings to sea's reflected heat. "Used to come here every day after school at the end of World War Two, when the hotel was taken over by the Navy for officers' quarters. All those gentlemen in white."

"There's an all-points bulletin out for you."

"Crisp uniforms, sun couldn't uncrease them."

"Why don't you hand over the gun so we can ease this show on the road."

"Gun?" Renoir faced Justo. "I traded it to Handsomemost, so he would keep people from telling you where I was. It's probably in Puerto Rico by now."

"If I make the arrest I've got to read you your Mirandas, cuff you up and haul you in. Don't want to do that. Just go peaceful, turn yourself in voluntary. We'll have a shot at springing you on self-defense."

"Now that I don't have Floyd there's no place to go home to." Renoir removed his sunglasses, squinting in strong light. "Tell me, did you ever come down here after school?"

"Surrender voluntary. Simple as that. Maybe I can spring you to see Floyd."

"Won't be time for that." Renoir slipped his glasses back on.

"You'd be surprised what I can arrange."

"That's something no one can arrange."

Justo knew he was definitely late for the *Quince*. The band had begun in the hotel ballroom, music floated out the high-arched doors, across white chairs on lawn rolling to sea's edge, guests were glancing at watches, wondering where he was. He tried to think of his daughter in her formal gown, radiant, a beginning. He placed a hand on Renoir's shoulder. "You know, an enemy is made for life, but a friend can be lost in a moment. I don't want to lose you."

Renoir did not turn his gaze from the pier, looking straight as he spoke in trembling voice. "I want to thank you for saving Floyd that morning on the beach."

"I wouldn't hesitate to do it again."

"This illness Floyd has, more revelations are coming out. They say it can be passed by blood contact. I remember how badly Floyd's mouth was bleeding that morning when I pulled him from the water. Thought he would bleed to death, then you kissed him back to life." Renoir pressed his hands against the fence, fingers lacing through chain mesh in a tightening grip. "It's true, a friend can be lost in a moment. Watch yourself, Justo, watch very closely. I worry about you."

"I pray for you."

"You still don't understand."

$\mathbf{27}$

ANY DAY that begins with a nightmare is a day that will turn upright. In St. Cloud's nightmare he was sitting ringside among a sweating mob watching a tattooed baby contest. Each squirming contestant was held by its tiny feet in ring center by a proud mama, then turned slowly to ohhs and ahhs from an appreciative crowd. From the soles of their feet to the crowns of their hairless heads, the babies' bodies were elaborated with tattoos depicting everything from tropical birds to battleships sunk in forgotten wars. The last contestants were twins, boy and girl, held high by a daddy instead of a mommy. Daddy's own skin was camouflaged with a million needle pricks of tattoo ink. No matter where the overhead spotlight struck daddy's corpulent body, every inch of his hide told a story. Daddy swung squalling twins by twin heels, twirling them to a blur, then stopping short, stripping diapers to expose on dimpled buttocks a spreading tattooed bloom of prize-winning roses. Daddy smacked the blooming buttocks, stoking them fire-engine red. The more twins wailed the more daddy spanked. The crowd grew unruly and booed. The more the crowd booed the more daddy paddled. The plump posteriors became too hot to handle. Daddy plunked babies into buckets of cold water to cool their angry roses. The crowd rose in unison: *Fix fix, we demand money back!* The cry woke up St. Cloud. Lila was not next to him. The fan whirring over his bed sounded like the uproar from a distant crowd. Sun streaming through the window was ablaze with late morning fury above his bed. In the kitchen, taped to a jar of papaya preserves he had made himself, was a note: *I go where I want to go. There are no knots. Love y'all.* A knock came from the front door

as St. Cloud read the note for the fifth time. He opened the door. A fat man bearing striking resemblance to daddy of twins handed over a letter. Fat man demanded St. Cloud sign a paper declaring he had received the letter, then wheeled off on a bicycle up the lane. St. Cloud ripped open the envelope. After all these years his divorce from Evelyn was finally finalized. In one morning St. Cloud's wife and girlfriend were out of his life forever. Life was a fixed event. By the time he stumbled outside with his nightmare hangover and double dose of reality, he was half-cocked and fully loaded, insultingly late for the *Quince* of Justo's daughter. If there was a crooked way to walk a straight line St. Cloud still hoped he could find the zigzag path.

THE PARKING LOT of the seaside hotel was crowded with cars from everywhere in Florida. Bellhops guarding the lobby entrance insisted St. Cloud present his invitation to the private party under way. This was not what St. Cloud needed, in his half-cocked position he was only a hair-trigger pull from detonating. Didn't the uniformed inquisitors preventing his entry realize Henry Flagler's hotel at the end of the ocean-going railroad was designed to receive dignified persons? A spitting rage would erupt from Uncle Henry if he learned esteemed guests were detained at the portals to paradise promised.

"I know you!" A bellhop pointed a gloved hand at St. Cloud. "You go out with Lila Defore." He nodded to the others. "It's okay, let him through."

St. Cloud screwed himself erect, proceeding into a lobby of mahogany walls soaring to blades of ceiling fans stirring rarefied air.

"Lila sure is a honey, and what a dancer," the bellhop called after St. Cloud.

The muscles of St. Cloud's body tightened, he spun around. "What do you mean, I go out with Lila? Do we go out for pizza, to the dog track, to church, to a Miami motel? What cheap shot do you think you're shooting, she's a *good dancer?*"

"Back off, man." The bellhop raised gloved hands. "Why so excited? Didn't mean anything, just a figure of speech."

"Watch your speech."

From the distance a band sizzled a sassy Cuban tune. St. Cloud followed the music, stepping onto a broad portico accommodating the flow of Justo and Rosella's families. The blackened bodies of pigs on silver platters were being shuttled by grunting waiters through the crowd. St. Cloud felt he had crashed a wedding party of strangers,

his manner of dress violating the *esprit de corps* among richly appointed troops joking in Spanish. The drift of music came again, he snapped his fingers to its surging rhythm. If only he had brought Lila, then he wouldn't be so out of place. A woman called his name.

St. Cloud was always surprised to see Rosella. He thought of her as a giant pillar supporting Justo, in reality she was short and plump. This afternoon the lines around her mouth molded into a broad smile. She reached up on tiptoes and kissed his cheek.

"What are you doing all alone? You must get some Cuban food." Rosella slipped a hand around his waist.

St. Cloud tried to think of a way to buy time, make any excuse as to why he had cold feet, felt naked without Lila at his side.

"You like the band?"

"Great band."

"Justo found them. Come, let me fix you some *Tocino del Cielo*, Bacon from Heaven."

St. Cloud smacked his lips. "Does it go with burnt pigs from hell the waiters are dishing up?"

"You're always kidding." Rosella laughed. "I never know when to take you seriously. There's something else I have which might tempt you."

"Cuban girls?"

"You only want to look at them. They are different from other girls."

"They sure are, they have Cuban fathers at home."

"Didn't mean *that*. Quit teasing and come along." Rosella tipped up on her toes again, whispering confidentially. "*Compuesto*. Abuelo's secret recipe."

"Love it, but I quit drinking for Lila. You remember my girlfriend? I brought her to your house for dinner."

"How could I forget. Isabel thought she was the most beautiful girl in the world. Where is she?"

"Maybe if I had a *compuesto* I could answer that question."

"Don't be so serious. Today is a joyous occasion, we want you with us."

Rosella led St. Cloud from the shadows of the portico to the loud music of the ballroom, where Justo twirled Isabel to the conclusion of a dance, her white taffeta dress clouding around her, a rhinestone crown sparkling atop coiled black hair.

Justo glad-handed a path through the congratulating crowd, stop-

ping before an ice swan supporting a bowl of *compuesto* on its back. He spun Isabel before St. Cloud. "Isn't she a gorgeous fifteen? And the dress, Rosella made it herself. Even if you had the money, couldn't buy a dress like this."

"Beautiful wife, beautiful daughter." St. Cloud pumped Justo's hand as he admired Rosella's handiwork on Isabel's slender body. The African and Latin blood racing through Isabel's veins conspired to create a creature of unnerving queenly poise. She stretched a gloved hand toward him.

Justo pulled cigars from his tuxedo. "How about a hand-rolled Cuban, no machine-made crap." He puffed the cigars to life, handing one to St. Cloud. A smile widened across his face, he held Isabel close. "*El sol sale para todos.* The sun comes out for all."

"Come on, Dad." Isabel rolled her brown eyes. "Don't do your corny Spanish stuff."

"Corny! St. Cloud, give me a *compuesto.*"

St. Cloud clanged glasses with Justo. "To sun rising for all." He couldn't take his eyes off Isabel, he wondered who the lucky boy would be. He poured another *compuesto.*

"Got to watch Abuelo's secret blend," Justo warned. "The anisette in it will slip up when least expected. You'll think you can walk on water. Thought you gave up drinking for Lila?"

"She left. I don't know what went wrong."

"Didn't she warn you?"

"We were getting along fine."

"I don't mean about that."

"What then?"

"MK . . . he's headed here."

"Brogan." St. Cloud gulped his *compuesto.* "Must have told her MK was coming."

"Figured you knew."

"I knew it had to happen, but not so soon."

"Maybe not soon enough. You know, I've always tried to treat a woman well, ask Rosella." Justo looked around. "Hey, where's my wife? Anyway, if you can't seduce a woman with kindness she isn't worth keeping, especially the young ones. Younger women are a foolproof way of making men fools, because the older you get, the younger they get. You'll end up like a greyhound on the track chasing a bunny forever out of reach."

"The younger they get," St. Cloud mumbled, trying to steady his

shaking hand as he poured another *compuesto*. "Sounds good to me."

"Dad." Isabel poked Justo's arm. "This is really boring. I want to dance."

"Boring? You think it's boring, men dying of broken hearts? You're right, it is! Go on and dance, honey."

Isabel kissed Justo's cheek and started to leave.

"Wait." St. Cloud set his empty glass next to the melting swan. "I'd like to dance with you."

A violent cough came up from Justo's chest, cigar smoke fuming from his nostrils.

Isabel patted him on the back. "Okay, Dad, it's not like I'm a bride or something."

Justo struggled to regain his breath, spluttering his words. "Isabel's too old for you, St. Cloud. She just turned *fifteen*."

Isabel stroked Justo's arm. "Don't worry about St. Cloud, he's so ancient." She turned her eyes on St. Cloud. "Kind of cute though, in a weird way."

"Look over there." Justo pointed his cigar into the crowd. "It's your cousin Alonzo from Key Largo. You don't see him except at Christmas. He's asked you to dance three times already. Take him up on it. I've got something to talk over with St. Cloud."

"Why not?" Isabel smiled, gliding off.

"You and me, St. Cloud, I don't know." Justo puffed his cigar, trying not to choke as Isabel asked her surprised cousin to dance.

"Don't know what about us?"

"We're the end of something, least *I* might be the end." Justo's eyes went to his dancing daughter, his shining star of Cuba. "Aunt Oris says it takes a black bean in the yellow rice to spice things up. Could be I'm the last black bean in the pot."

"What are you trying to tell me?"

"Used to be simple around here. A man sat on his porch with a good cigar and honest rum, waiting for a cool breeze to blow up his *guayabera* shirt."

Rosella appeared before Justo. "You're not going to escape without our dancing."

Justo slipped an arm around Rosella's plump waist. "*Niña*, I will dance with you until I die."

St. Cloud watched them whirl away. They had become a rare item among modern-day lovers, between them existed passion without

perversion. Maybe that's what Justo had been trying to explain with his talk of being the last black bean.

"Hey man!" The bellhop who appreciated Lila's dancing tapped St. Cloud on the shoulder. "Telephone call."

"Who could know I'm here?"

"Beats me. Take it in the lobby bar."

St. Cloud hurried to the quiet of the lobby bar, a white-jacketed bartender handed him a telephone.

"Sorry not to be there with y'all." The words coming through the telephone line were slow as a summer day in Georgia. "Tell Rosella and Isabel congratulations."

"Where are you?"

"Got to go."

"I'll come and get you."

"Just wanted to say I'm leaving and all."

"How far away are you?"

"My Mustang acted up. The garage sent a boy to Miami for a carburetor. Not easy to find."

"That car's older than you are."

"You're strange."

"Lila?"

The phone went dead.

"Lila!"

Somehow there had to be a way, an answer puzzled. There were no clues in her voice, but there was a sound in the background, airplanes. St. Cloud handed the phone to the bartender. "What's the next commercial airport up the Keys?"

"Marathon, bout an hour up."

St. Cloud ran back to the ballroom, pushing his way into the crowd. "Justo! I've got to use your car."

Justo kept dancing, Rosella's cheek resting on his shoulder. "What for?"

"Lila. I can get her back."

"Can't let you use it."

"Why not?"

"For official business only."

"That's bull!"

"I know." Justo quickened his dancing to match the band's sizzle. "You've had too many *compuestos*."

"What kind of friend is that?"

"The kind wants you to stay alive. Told you, those *compuestos* will have you thinking you can walk on water. You're crazy as it is. She won't come back."

"You're wrong!"

St. Cloud ran from the ballroom, pushing bellhops aside as he rushed out the hotel entrance. Maybe Evelyn would let him use her Kiss My Linda truck. Maybe? He kept running. Coming toward him was the driving force of an answered prayer, a divine wind of fortuity.

"Say-hey bubba, where you be off to in such a hurry?" Bonefish pulled his rusted station wagon to the curb and leaned his grizzled face out the window. "Not so fast. You want my waffle iron? You gonna love my waffle iron."

"No! I want your car."

"How bout a nice toaster? Takes four slices at a time. You could use that."

"Your car, Bonefish. You've been trying to give everything away, you won't need it anymore."

"Huh?"

"Finito's coming, like you been saying all along. There's no time."

Bonefish threw the car door open, jumping free of the automobile as if it was about to burst into flames. He grabbed St. Cloud's shoulders, his eyes burning with redemptive fervor. "I told you, bubba! I told everyone but they wouldn't listen. You be the first to see the truth."

"I can see it!" St. Cloud slammed the station wagon door behind him. "No time to talk." He squealed away from the curb on a tread of burning rubber, Bonefish running after him.

"Don't let Mister Finito catch you on the Seven Mile Bridge. He catch you on that bridge, you gonna die like a rat!"

ST. CLOUD sped across bridges jumping from one Key to the next, but he remained on the zigzag path he traveled since the day he walked into the bird shop and encountered Lila. He was on a final joyride aimed toward crackup or blowup. He slammed on the car brakes, skidding off blacktop to a stop. Across the highway was a familiar sign on a rusted roof: TROPICAL MAMA'S BAR-B-Q PIT. He played a hunch, turning the car onto a coral side road, toward the trailer-camp terrorist who brutalized his family. He stopped before the shiny hump of a trailer. Ed sat in the open doorway picking his teeth with a broken wire from the organ in his living room. Alice was staked to a pipe between Ed's feet, she lunged on her chain, her canines chopping air before St. Cloud.

Ed grinned. "Knew you'd be back. People get a taste of my pugs, always return for another bundle of joy."

"Call off the Doberman!" St. Cloud shouted above the beast's lunging roar. "I need a dog."

Ed jerked Alice's chain, strangling her to a whine. He winked at St. Cloud. "You've come to the right outpost." He disappeared inside the trailer.

Not a sign of wife and kids anywhere. Just as St. Cloud suspected, Ed was a monster.

Ed popped through the trailer door with an armload of flat-faced puppies. He strolled to the station wagon, proud as a papa in a maternity ward. "Take your pick of the litter."

"The litter? How could your bitch have another litter since we were last here?"

Ed continued his earnest ear-to-ear grin. "Pugs fall from the sky like coconuts. All a fella has to do is scoop em up."

"I don't have time to investigate miracle births." St. Cloud opened his wallet, thinking if Justo hadn't hustled that last court interpreting job he wouldn't be counting out four hundred and fifty bucks.

"Five hundred."

"Five hundred? We paid four fifty."

"Cost of living increases." Ed shoved a yelping pup into St. Cloud's arms.

"First time I heard of coconuts having a cost of living increase." St. Cloud handed over another fifty.

"Prices going up everywhere." Ed pocketed the money. "Check the frozen food section next time you're in the supermarket. Just ask that pretty young wife of yours about that. Costs lots to raise five boys in this day and age."

"Yeah sure!" St. Cloud backed away from Ed's squirming brood and lunging black mascot.

A Mercedes limousine rolled up, blocking St. Cloud's station wagon. The driver was an attractive woman with a silk scarf knotted around her neck. Five boys bounced on leather seats around her. The smallest boy waved. St. Cloud recognized him from when he and Lila bought the first pug.

"Hi, honey," the woman called to Ed. "Have you fed the puppies? You promised not to start without us."

St. Cloud couldn't get away fast enough. Something was seriously wrong. Why would Ed's wife have a new Mercedes when they lived in a dilapidated trailer with five kids and Ed sold dogs for a living? Ed's world was out of whack, unless he was a drug scammer, and his wife working as a nurse was an act. *Pugs fall from the sky like coconuts.* St. Cloud was going to tell Lila about what he saw, she wouldn't believe it. He was even more convinced Ed was a wife and kid beater. He took solace in the fact that some day the law of averages was going to reach out and collar Ed, bring the scammer to heel, even way down here.

Late afternoon sun slipped toward final meltdown into mangroves as St. Cloud sped north to Marathon, counting mile-marker signposts flicking by on the side of the highway, each sign registering one more mile traveled from Key West, mile zero. In another age the length of the Keys was spotted with stone mounds thirty miles apart, the distance between mounds what an Indian could cover by canoe and overlanding during a day. Now stone mounds were replaced by tin signs emblazoned with white numerals. St. Cloud passed forty signs in as many minutes, past Ramrod Key, Big Pine Key, crossing over looming Seven Mile Bridge, above swift current of Moser Channel, separating Lower Keys from Upper Keys. He was getting close, hurling through Pigeon Key, dropping down to Knight Key at mile marker 47, into Marathon, where the roadside clogged with high-speed commerce; gas stations, neon-circled fast-food joints and convenience stores. Among it all was what he was looking for, a jutting strip of airplane runway. An auto mechanic's shop commanded the corner of a side road leading to the airport. St. Cloud stopped before the shop's open garage door; inside, raised on a greasy lift, was an old Mustang convertible.

St. Cloud kept his motor running. "Excuse me," he shouted to a man in coveralls hammering a bent tire rim. "Could you tell me where the owner of that Mustang is?"

The mechanic stopped his banging. He rubbed the hammer head against his oily cheek as he sauntered to the station wagon, looking down at St. Cloud suspiciously. "You her father or what?"

"Sure am."

"She don't look old enough to drive. Tell your little girl it's ready. Gonna be ninety-five bucks. She got a credit card?"

"She's good for it. Where is she?"

The mechanic pointed the hammer at a cinder-block building

squatting behind faded canvas awnings in a weedy lot. Neon letters blinked on the rooftop: SAIL AWAY MOTEL. "Over there, round back by the water."

St. Cloud parked the station wagon and walked across the weedy lot with the pug tucked under his arm. A wood ramp led behind the motel, ending before an expanse of gravel staked with plastic flamingos. The pink flock leaned at dangerous angles on steel feet, painted eyes staring to ocean's edge, where Lila watched laughing teenagers fishing from a pier, waves murmuring at her bare feet. St. Cloud feared going farther. Perhaps Lila was an illusion, like the Madonna on the reef, her siren's calling song wooing sailors to sea bottom. A cold current of dread flowed through his heart. Lila's body merged with water, cold current flowing around her submerged nakedness, bearing with it a surge of turtle hatchlings, beaked mouths clacking as they finned through her parted legs, brushing thighs, seeking breasts, nudging nipples, urging sustenance. Blue current bled milky white, the siren's song wailing. Lila floated toward him, salty perfume on lips, slithery seaweed entangling his bull weight, plummeting him to Erzulie's green depths.

"Y'all found me." Lila's voice surfaced on murmuring tide. "Knew y'all would come." She reached out and stroked the head of the squirming puppy.

"I know all about MK."

"It's not MK." Lila pulled him closer. "I left because of y'all."

"I don't understand."

"MK sent me to Key West to wait, but he never came. Month after month I got postcards from different Latin American places, all said the same thing: *Not this trip*. My life became uncomplicated, no longer a husband, not even MK. He knew it was impossible to escape himself, so he let me go. Then y'all came along, insistent, like MK, same knots on the inside. Y'all were looking for commitment. If I stayed it would be walking away from myself."

The intrigue St. Cloud constructed to win Lila collapsed. He had taken a calculated risk and lost. Against other men he could compete, he could not compete against willful spirit, youth will not accept proximity of vulnerability. He did not know if he trusted himself enough to set them both free. He had only one way to find out. He kissed her.

In the solar system of Lila's experience St. Cloud was a foreign planet spinning to motives beyond comprehension. She was caught in a polar slide toward an emotional opposite. When the male arc of his body rose, a coiled response unraveled from her, the probe of its progress tipped by her tongue, beyond passionate yielding to chance understanding. Lila broke free.

"I have to go." She smoothed her skirt. "Started this morning and I'm only at mile marker fifty."

St. Cloud held out the puppy. "Would you like him?"

"After what happened to the first one? Can't have another." She walked off across the expanse of gravel.

St. Cloud followed her to the mechanic's garage, waiting as she backed the convertible out.

The mechanic swiped his sweaty forehead with an oily rag. "Some good-looking daughter you got. I were you, wouldn't let her be driving with the top down. Lots of guys will be after her."

The convertible stopped. "Wait a minute." Lila climbed out, rushing to St. Cloud. "On second thought I'll take him." She snatched the wriggling puppy from his arms and ran back to the car, the dog licking her cheeks as she drove onto the busy highway. She looked back. "We'll find each other again, promise!"

The mechanic slapped the rag against his palm. "Find each other again? Funny thing for a guy's daughter to say."

St. Cloud stood at the edge of the highway, watching the southern light of his life headed north. He decided not to set immediate course down the Keys to mile zero. He walked around behind Sail Away Motel, strolled through the leaning flock of flamingos to murmuring tideline. Music swelled from his ache, a zingy beat of papaya passion and mango persuasion, waterspouts danced across ocean's horizon, beyond the last American wave, where storm warriors rode bareback on howling wind, where rain from New Spain spattered giants in forests and pygmies in cities, where Christopher Columbus hit his home run into the flat outfield of the Caribbean, where despots conspired to throw out the first hand grenade of the next warring season, where young men grew old waiting for the telephone to ring, where the last battle a man fights is with himself, where the beat of the Twentieth Century Cha-Cha has to be faced, yonder yonder yonder, where light on sea flashes blue, green, then surrenders her gift.

"Where do you think you're going?"

The question did not come from the sea. It came from land.

"Answer me! Where do you think you're headed? I followed you from the *Quince*. Knew there was something off, more than Lila. Told you that *compuesto* would have you thinking you can walk on water."

St. Cloud turned toward the black face on shore. "The New World."

"Perfect! I heard on the squawker coming here, five refugees on a raft of truck tire inner tubes floated over. Don't know how the sharks missed them. Coast Guard bringing them in. Going to need your forked tongue in court, always be a need for a translator in Babylon."

Justo stretched his hand across water.

"Lila promised. She's coming back."

"*Cristo volvera tambien.*" Justo pulled St. Cloud to firm ground.

Christ is coming back too.

Thomas Sanchez spent his youth in northern California, where he began his first novel, *Rabbit Boss*, on a cattle ranch at the age of 21. One year later, he received a master's degree from San Francisco State University. *Rabbit Boss*, a hundred-year saga of a California-Nevada Indian tribe, was completed when Sanchez was 27. After publishing a second novel, *Zootsuit Murders*, in the late 1970s, he was awarded a Guggenheim Fellowship for his third novel, which became *Mile Zero*, written during the 1980s on the island of Key West. Sanchez divides his time between California and Florida.

A NOTE ON THE TYPE

This book was set in a digitized version of a type face called Baskerville. The face is a facsimile reproduction of types cast from molds made for John Baskerville (1706–1775) from his designs. The punches for the revived Linotype Baskerville were cut under the supervision of the English printer George W. Jones. John Baskerville's original face was one of the forerunners of the type style known to printers as "modern face"—a "modern" of the period A.D. 1800.

Composed by PennSet Inc.
Bloomsburg, PA

Printed and bound by The Haddon Craftsmen, Inc.,
Scranton, Pennsylvania

Designed by Iris Weinstein